Fark in the Time of Covid
The 2020 Fark Fiction Anthology

Good Evening.

Or perhaps Good Morning, if you happen to be reading this in the morning. I could say Good Night, if it's after dark where you are, but that sounds kind of strange. I suppose if you happen to be a time traveler, you could simply travel through history to find a suitable evening or morning to make this preface make sense, but in that case, what are you doing in 2020 at all? This year sucks. Go to some time that's fun, like the roaring twenties, or that brief period in 2403 where fashionable people wear pumpkins on their feet in place of shoes and the sidewalk pasta machines dispense spaghetti-on-a-stick for only a few million Earth Dollars.

2020 has not been a kind year, for a number of reasons. Many of us have spent parts of the year in various lockdowns or quarantines due to the Covid-19 pandemic. This has had an indelible effect on many of us, and in some ways, this is reflected in the fiction you are about to read. I find it fascinating that this year our submissions contained a staggering number of science fiction entries, which one might say mirrors the science fiction reality we find ourselves in.

But—you might counter—we are not here for fact, we are here for fiction, and what you hold in your hands is the best fiction that the brilliant minds of the community at Fark have created. Tales of fantasy, science fiction, mystery, humor, and horror lie in these pages. Or, screens I guess, if you're reading this on a computer or tablet or something. Either way, read on!

Fark.com, the online social community from which all of our submitters have been drawn, is variously known as one of the oldest and most successful online communities still active, one of the 100 largest English-speaking websites on the net, a wretched hive of scum and villainy, the birthplace of Florida Man, and so on. As it is a community based almost entirely on the written word, Fark tends to attract and keep some of the masters of the craft, and in your hands you hold the collected best fiction this community could produce. Some of these stories may move you. Some of them may frighten you. If at least one of them doesn't make you laugh and look around nervously, then I'll be surprised.

In keeping with the organization and layout of Fark.com, with its stories broken down into tabs—the Main Tab, the Sports Tab, the Business Tab, and so on—this anthology has been broken up into tabs by genre.

We begin with the Fantasy Tab.

—BB

Table of Contents

The Fantasy Tab
Spring Heeled Jacqueline   9
The Golden Oscillator   23
The Prey   35
Diogenes the Talking Dog Meets
      the Necromancer from the Fourth Dimension   41
This Town   79

The Science Fiction Tab
The Resurrections of Amy Yakimora   101
First Contact at the Second Hole   131
The Ultimate Monster   135
The Numbers Man   151
Janissars   167
Warped Drive   193
The Machine   209

The Humor Tab
Tag 'Em   219
It's Only Vampire   227
Florida Vacation   235
Basement Apartment—All the Med Cons   249

The Mystery Tab
White Line Fever   257
The Terrible Burden of Love   261
Hargis   265
Murder, and a Multitude of Other Sins   277

The Horror Tab
Run for Your Life	293
The Spirit of the Mountain	307
Vox Odio	319
A Skirmish Outside Beaufort	325
Meat. The Parents	335
My Two Dads	341
Nightrunner	347
The Triumph of the Claw	351
Acknowledgments	373
Copyright Acknowledgments	375

The Fantasy Tab

Spring-Heeled Jaqueline
Jason Allard

Jaq clung to the shadows as one of the duke's guards passed by the garden gate. He marched past, feet crunching along the gravel walk, oblivious to all but the small circle of light cast by his lantern. A dozen more paces, and he was out of sight beyond a large hedge.

Skipping over the path, Jaqueline crossed the manor's broad lawn. The short cropped grass offered no cover, nor concealment under the light of the full moon. She reached the waist-high wall separating the veranda from the greensward.

A few lights glowed in the servants' quarters, but the rest of the house stood dark and silent. The duke's bedroom lay on the third floor.

Natural athleticism and enchanted boots brought her to a second-floor balcony in a single bound. A second leap placed her crouching on the sill of an open window. Jaq spied the duke asleep in his grand feather bed.

She stepped down onto the wooden floor, polish gleaming in the moonlight. Seven steps to the edge of the bed. Jaq drew her father's sword, Cat Gutter. She leaned closer, readying herself to strike. Thibaud Montpessier, Duke of Aumale was the last survivor of the cabal which had defrauded and murdered her father. Another moment and her father would be avenged.

Something was wrong.

The duke's nose was small and up-turned, not a hawk-like beak. The wooly caterpillars over his eyes were now as neatly manicured as the lawn. He smelled faintly of *eau de toilette* rather than brandy and cloves. A long, dark wig sat on the stand atop the dressing table, yet a fan of sable ringlets covered the quilted pillow.

The not-duke trembled under the covers.

Jaqueline pulled back slowly. Her eyes cast about the room. The wardrobe door flew open. Jaq threw up her arm, shielding her eyes from the sudden blinding light of an unshuttered lantern.

"I have you now, villain!" the duke bellowed. A pistol fired. The cloak's protective charms caught the bullet with a flash of purple fire.

The bedroom doors yawned wide and Jaq saw the shadowy forms of men-at-arms stampede towards her, armed with swords and carbines and spontoons.

Jaq sprinted and leapt through the window. Her cloak billowed out behind her like the wings of an enormous bat. She landed as gently as if she had merely hopped from a stool. Shouts and shots followed her as she ran for the edge of the manor's grounds, but neither gave her pause.

She reached the bordering wall, guards all but nipping at her heels. She vaulted over the brick barrier and disappeared into the slumbering city beyond.

"Did you hear? The Assassin tried to kill Duke Montpessier last night."

Jaqueline glanced at the small knot of other students readying for fencing class. High-born ladies all. Like her, they wore stiff jackets with high collars and fighting trousers reinforced with leather to protect against the blunt practice blades. Jaq adjusted the straps of her metal mask. Dueling scars were a mark of distinction for a man, but never a lady.

"I wonder when the Scarlet Chevalier will stop him," Annette said. Her father was a southern marquis with several successful vineyards.

"Why would they fight each other?" asked Cosette, a cousin to the young queen, the king's second wife. "I wager they're in league. The Chevalier only protects peasants after all, and the Assassin only kills nobles."

"The Chevalier protects the helpless," Charlotte said

quietly. The least of the trio, she was the seventh daughter of an impoverished baron from the northwest coast. "At least, that's what all the stories say." Jaq once again thanked God her name didn't end with "-tte".

"That's just silly." Cosette put her fists on her hips. "I've never heard of him rescuing a noble from robbers."

Charlotte pulled on her own mask. "I doubt he would consider someone with an armed escort to be helpless." Her voice was distorted and strange coming from behind the pierced tin plate. Jaq followed them out to the sparring floor.

The Academy of Saint Antonious had been built and had operated for over a century with the sacred mission of educating young noble women. A woman who graduated from the Academy could have her pick of powerful suitors. Most of the reigning queens across the continent had passed through these halls.

Almost all of the courses—mathematics, languages, astronomy, dancing, theology, medicine, rhetoric, and more—were taught by learned nuns from across the continent. Only the fencing and marksmanship classes were taught by a man.

Señor de la Vega attracted a lot of attention from the students. Not only was he the only man inside the campus walls, but he was tall, dark, and handsome, with a well-trimmed moustache and warm eyes flanked by laugh lines. Only his limp and the numerous pale scars on his arms and face detracted from his beauty.

He handed out practice weapons as each girl passed through the door. Short and light, the blade was only a round steel rod with a bulb at the tip, rather than a sharp point. The hilts sported clamshell guards and a knuckle-bow, all of brass, and a wire-wrapped grip.

Señor de la Vega paired the girls off. Once again, he saw fit to set Jaq against Cosette. This afternoon they were to practice lunges and parries. A simple, back and forth exercise.

After a few passes, Cosette added a riposte to her parry, flicking the tip of her sword against Jaq's mask. Tink. Tink. Tink.

"You move like an old sow," Cosette said. She put her hand over her mask's breathing holes, as if to stifle a laugh. "You need to be faster and more aggressive if you want to beat me."

Jaq moved back to *en garde*. Cosette skipped forward,

pushing off with her back foot. Rather than deflect the thrusting blade with her own, Jaq slipped to the side, letting it pass. Cosette stumbled closer. Jaq punched her between the eye slits with her sword's knuckle-bow, throwing her hips into the strike.

Cosette fell, unmoving. The nosepiece of her mask was dented. A thin trickle of blood snaked out from under it. Jaq glanced around at the rest of her class, all stopped and starring. She prodded Cosette in the chest with the tip of her blade. "I win."

Anette dropped to her knees and ripped her friend's mask off. The blood dribbling from Cosette's nostrils stood vivid crimson against her pale skin. Anette tapped the girl's cheeks.

"You broke her nose," she said.

"I am here to teach you to fence to improve your poise and grace," *Señor* de la Vega said, fists on his hips. "We are not here to practice tavern brawling." He paused and watched Annette trying to rouse her friend. "What do you have to say in your defense, Miss Savoy?"

"Savoy is my stepfather's name. Mine is Siegert."

"I'm glad we cleared that up. And about this?"

"I decided not to aim for her throat."

The blademaster threw up his hands. "You might've killed her then."

Jaq pulled off her mask. She watched Cosette's eyelids flutter as Annette's ministrations began to revive her. She shrugged. "And nothing of value would've been lost."

Señor de la Vega moved faster than Jaq expected. She heard the resounding pop of his palm meeting her cheek a heartbeat before the pain flared from her face.

"Report to Mother Superior for punishment," he said, looming over her. He stepped back and pointed to Annette and Charlotte. "You two, take Miss Boivin to the infirmary." He turned on his heel. "The rest of you, get back to work. I haven't heard the bell for Nones, so you are still mine."

Jaqueline lay on her side, trying to focus on reading a treatise on the nature of God as written by a mad hermit almost two centuries ago. The gnawing knot in her empty belly didn't help her concentration. The archaic language did nothing to aid her comprehension. Worse still was the burning pain still smoldering in her rump. Mother Superior could've taught *Señor* de la Vega's class using a switch.

A soft knock at the door. Jaq closed her book, and then slowly rose to her feet. She shuffled across the small room, gritting her teeth with each step. The door opened with a dull thunk from the latch and a brief squeak from the bottom hinge.

Had Jaqueline been expecting anyone, it would not have been one of the "Ettes". Yet, Charlotte stood there in the dark hallway, a cloth-covered tray in her hands.

"I brought you some dinner," she said. "I know you're supposed to be on bread and water, and I thought you might like something more." She studied Jaq's face. "I didn't spit in it or anything."

Jaqueline stepped back and opened the door fully. Charlotte swept in. She set the tray down on the room's table, pushing a small pile of books out of the way. She whisked away the cloth, revealing a small loaf of crusty, dark bread and a generous bowl full of a thick stew of beans and beef. A second bowl held a small pudding studded with bits of almond.

Jaq stared at the sudden bounty. It appeared to be a veritable feast compared to the fist-sized hunk of bread she would have for breakfast and again for luncheon. "Why?"

Charlotte clasped her hands, wringing the cloth between them. She shifted from one foot to the other. "Cosette's awful to me, though it's nothing compared to how she is to you. When you knocked her down, I wanted to cheer. I just wish I could've worked up the courage to do it myself." She pulled out the lone chair from under the table. "You've got to be hungry. Sit. Eat. Please."

Jaq looked at the chair. Its wooden seat had been polished by the backsides of generations of young women. Her own throbbed. "I think I'll stay standing."

"Oh." Charlotte pushed the chair back. She looked at Jaqueline's feet. "So, it's not just going to bed without supper, is it?"

"Twenty-five strokes a day for the next ten days, not counting Sunday. At least Mother Superior waits until after classes to

13

administer them. There's a chance I'll be able to sit down by morning." Jaq picked up the bread. Her belly rumbled. "I hope."

"I'm sorry."

"Don't be. It was worth it."

Charlotte laughed. It was surprisingly pretty when it wasn't in response to one of Cosette's comments.

"In that case, I'm sorry I couldn't smuggle you anything better to drink than the water you already have." She smiled, then looked away. "I should go and let you eat in peace. I'll see what I can do until you're allowed to return to dinner."

"You can stay. If you like." Jaqueline wasn't sure why she'd said it. "I was just studying. Trying to understand what Eusebius was saying." She took a bite of the bread. It was still warm in the middle.

"It's good that you don't understand. If you did, you'd be as crazy as he was. There was a spring in his cave, but he preferred to store his own urine in jars and drink it instead."

Outside, the heavy bell in the chapel steeple began to ring. Three peals. Curfew. At any moment, some of the nuns would begin patrolling the dormitory halls, looking for lights under the doors.

"*Merde*," Charlotte swore. "I need to go."

Jaq opened the door, easing the bottom hinge almost to the squeaking point. "Thank you, but don't get yourself into trouble on my account trying to bring me more tomorrow. I earned my punishment."

Charlotte squeezed through the opening. "The Scarlet Chevalier seeks to right injustices wherever he finds them. I should try to do the same."

She gave a Jaq a quick smile, and then disappeared into the hallway as silently as she had arrived.

Jaqueline returned to the tableside. She sat gingerly on the bed, finding the mattress to be a tolerable, if not comfortable, seat. She blew out the candle and feasted by the moonlight filtering in through her high, narrow window.

Over the next few days, Charlotte did her best to keep Jaq

fed. Once it was nothing more than another heel of the hard bread the nuns gave her, with a small pat of apple butter. Another night, she managed half a roast chicken and a small pitcher of diluted wine. In classes, she hardly spoke to the Ettes, and no longer laughed when Cosette made a joke at another's expense.

For her part, Cosette redoubled her efforts to make Jaq's life miserable. Sitting near her in class, sharing treats and delicacies with the other students. Snide comments. Obstacles shoved into her path. She'd even enlisted the aid of students outside of her coven of Ettes. Jaqueline had never really made friends among the others, but now the only one who would speak with her was Charlotte.

In fencing class, *Señor* de la Vega would set Jaq against pairs of girls during free sparring. His excuse was that until Cosette was allowed to return, the class was uneven. However, Jaq noted his satisfied nods when, no matter the pairing, she ended the bouts as victor as often as not.

On the seventh night, Charlotte brought a sandwich of sliced mutton, lettuce, and tomatoes. The bread was hearty, made with oats, and the mutton was nice and lean.

She smiled as Jaq devoured it. She did that more often in Jaq's company. Jaqueline found herself thinking of that smile more often when she was alone.

"I brought you a gift," Charlotte said. "I had to send for it to be brought from home. I'm sorry it took so long." She held out a small jar of cobalt glass.

Jaq swallowed the last of the sandwich and accepted the jar. The lid was silver, deftly engraved with flowers and vines. Inside was a greasy white paste. A strong, medicinal smell burnt her nose.

"It should help your...discomfort."

Jaq opened her mouth to thank her, but the lid caught her eye. Flowers among the vines. Lilies. Royal lilies.

"Your father's barony is a long way from here. A messenger could ride a horse to death getting there and back inside a week." She looked up to find Charlotte staring at the lid as well.

"Please," Charlotte said, blood draining from her face. "Please don't tell anyone."

Jaq dropped to her knees. "Your Highness, I swear, your secret is safe with me."

Charlotte knelt and took Jaqueline's hand. Her fingers were warm and strong and calloused. "Nobody else knows. They can't. That's why I'm here. Cosette, Annette, and the others are likely going to marry rich and powerful men. I need to know what these women are truly like, not how they would behave if they knew I might sit on my father's throne someday."

Jaq nodded. She hardly heard what Charlotte had said, her mind more focused on their hands. Her stomach twisted and her heart raced. "I won't say anything."

"I don't want this to change anything between us, either." Charlotte squeezed her hand. "I'm not a princess here."

Jaqueline couldn't be sure which of them was more surprised when she leaned forward and kissed Charlotte. Her lips were just as warm as her fingers, but much softer. She started to pull away, but Charlotte's hand slid up her arms, trailing chills, before embracing her and holding her close.

The curfew bell rang, jolting them apart.

Cheeks burning, Jaq scrambled to her feet. "I don't know why I did that," she said. She smiled. "But I'm glad I did."

"Me, too," Charlotte said. She stood and smoothed her skirts. "I didn't know I wanted you to do that."

The bell pealed again.

"I wish you could stay," Jaq said.

"Me, too. But I should go. I don't want to know what they might add to your punishment if we got caught." Charlotte stepped to the door. "Maybe we can try that again tomorrow?" When Jaq nodded, she smiled, then slipped out into the night.

An hour after the last bell, Jaq slipped out of bed. Charlotte's balm had done wonders. The pain was gone, not even a memory of it remained in her skin. She pulled the small chest from under her bed and unlocked it with a key she kept on a chain around her neck. Inside were her hunting clothes.

She dressed quickly. A long strip of plain cotton to bind her chest. Black trousers, reinforced with leather. Black shirt and a black vest with fine mail links between layers of heavy canvas. A black scarf pulled over her nose to conceal her face. The enchanted boots and cloak. Finally, she buckled Cat Gutter's belt about her waist.

Slipping past the lone nun on nightly patrol was easy. Once out into the city, she ascended onto rooftops. Running along ridgelines and bounding over alleys and narrow streets kept her from running into any of the night watchmen walking the cobblestones with their long, lighted poles.

Jaq crouched in the shadow of a large chimney, watching the duke's manor. It seemed deserted. No lights in any of the windows. No movement in the lawns or gardens.

"It's been a week. Where could he have gone?" she murmured. She ground her teeth and thumped the chimney with a fist. Perhaps it was a ruse to draw her into another trap. "I should've killed him last time. Just stabbed him through the heart and let them kill me."

"Why do you want Montpessier dead?"

Jaq spun, Cat Gutter leaping into her hand. At the far end of the roof stood a thin figure in dark pants and a long black coat over a tight red waistcoat, their face shadowed under a broad brimmed hat. They held a long rapier in their hand.

The Scarlet Chevalier.

Jaq lowered her voice. "He killed my father."

"And your other victims?" The Chevalier sounded young.

"Accomplices. They hired my father for a difficult task, and when he came for payment after completing it, they murdered him rather than part with their coin."

"Vendetta."

"Justice."

The Chevalier raised his sword. "And if I disagree?"

Jaq glanced around. Cat Gutter was not a long sword. Great for alleyways, bedrooms, and other close quarters, but less than ideal in an open battle. With a rapier, the Chevalier had at least a ten inch advantage on reach. "I will go around you if I can or through you if I must."

She raised her sword, pointing the tip at her opponent. She

waited until the Chevalier began to settle into a fencing stance, and then ran down the slope of the roof. Shingles came loose in her wake, clattering after her, threatening to get underfoot and pitch her over the edge.

Jaq leapt, bounding across the chasm to the roof across the street. She landed hard and scrabbled towards the ridge. The Chevalier followed suit, albeit more gracefully.

Unnerved, Jaq ran. No one had been able to follow her before. Certainly not so effortlessly. While it was rare, she cursed herself for a fool not to anticipate someone else having access to similar enchantments.

She fled, the Chevalier followed. None of her usual tricks could shake him from her tail. Jaq needed to find more suitable ground for a fight. She dropped from one roof into a twisting alleyway little more than a pace wide.

"Giving up on Bonetti's defense?" the Chevalier asked, landing softly to find Jaq waiting. Under the obscuring hat, he wore a narrow mask of red leather to conceal his features.

Jaq nodded. "It seemed fitting, finding ground to cancel out the reach of your Capo Ferro."

"Your short blade should be a great help in a place like this. I see you've studied your Agrippa." The Chevalier drew himself up tall, holding his blade out straight, pointed at Jaq's heart. "But how are you at countering Thibault?"

"I find de la Vega cancels out a Thibault." Jaq sprang sideways, kicking off from the wall and bouncing back towards her opponent. She swung her sword at his, hoping to knock his defense aside and close the distance between them. There, inside his reach, her sword would have the advantage.

The Chevalier backpedaled swiftly. "Yes, but I find de la Vega prefers not to brawl."

His voice was different. Familiar. Jaq stopped short. "Who are you?"

The Chevalier reached up and pulled away the mask. "I thought our kiss was rather memorable. I wouldn't have expected you to forget it already."

Jaqueline lowered her sword, and then plucked the scarf from her face. "How did you know?"

Charlotte shrugged. "I followed you when you left the Academy. I've suspected for a while. The murders began shortly after you arrived. I figured if I gave you the salve, you might venture out tonight."

Jaq spat on the ground. She wanted to vomit. The past few nights, the kind words and gestures, the kiss, all for nothing. "So, all this was a ruse to get close to me? To figure me out and stop me before I can avenge my father? To protect nobles close to your own father?"

"No."

"Then why?"

"I needed to know why," Charlotte said. "If it was really a plot to take out some of your stepfather Savoy's enemies, then yes, I would try to stop you. He has eyes on trying to snatch my father's throne rather than let me or my sister sit on it. But this is for you, not him, so I want to help."

"Why?"

"Because I care for you. Because I think about you whenever you're not there. Because I've never had these feelings before." Charlotte's sword wavered, the point tapping against the ground. "Because I think I love you."

Jaqueline's pulse raced. The rage, ready to break through and throttle the young woman in front of her, vanished, leaving her exhausted. She took a shuddering breath. "I want to believe you," she said.

"Then let me prove it. I know where Montpessier is."

"Where?"

"He's hiding in his mistress's home. It's not far."

Jaqueline followed as Charlotte led her back up to the rooftops and across several blocks. She stopped and pointed out a large home.

"He's in there," Charlotte said.

Jaq tried to smile. "Thank you."

Charlotte put a hand on her arm. "What will you do when this is over?"

"I don't know. I hadn't thought that far; hadn't really

anticipated surviving."

"Montpessier has men-at-arms in there with him."

Jaq put her hand over Charlotte's and squeezed. "You don't need to do this."

"Two of us will stand a better chance than one," she said, donning the red mask once again. "I'll follow your lead."

As at the duke's manor, Jaq ran close to the building, then leapt onto a balcony. She found the door unlocked and slipped inside. Charlotte followed at her heels.

They passed through a darkened dressing room and a lounge, the walls covered with bookcases, before creeping into a lady's bedroom. An oil lamp turned low sat on the dressing table, next to a stand sporting a dark wig.

Two figures dozed in the rather narrow bed. One had long, dark hair while the other was nearly bald, just graying fuzz.

Jaqueline pulled down her scarf and drew Cat Gutter from its scabbard as Charlotte barred the door and turned up the lamp's flame. Pressing the sword's point to Montpessier's throat woke the man with a jerk and a snort. His mistress awoke with a stifled squeak.

Jaq slowly dragged Cat Gutter's point down the man's torso, to his belly, then back up. His eyes darted from the blade to her face and back. She stopped the weapon over his heart.

"My name is Jaqueline Siegert. You killed my father. Now you die." She threw her weight against Cat Gutter's pommel. The wide blade was designed more for cutting than thrusting. It needed more force to pierce through him than Charlotte's rapier would've, but Jaq didn't stop until the sword's figure-eight styled guard pushed against Montpessier's ribs.

The man gurgled and pushed against her, his sausage-thick fingers clawed uselessly at her face. The duke's mistress screamed as a bubble of blood erupted from between his lips.

"We need to go," Charlotte said. Shouts and the thumping of booted feet rushed towards the bedroom.

Jaq withdrew her blade, then wiped it clean on the quilted bedclothes. She stepped to the window, reaching for the latch.

Thundering flashes and smoke from below. Shards of glass

pelted her chest as musket balls punched through the panes. She staggered back, then slammed the shutters closed. Something heavy hit the bedroom door from outside.

"If we can't go around them, we'll have to go through," Charlotte said.

Jaq nodded. "I'm sorry I got you into this."

"I'm not." Charlotte pulled off her mask and tossed it aside. She favored Jaqueline with a smile and a kiss. A long, lingering kiss, like the ones Jaq had imagined while lying in the dark, waiting for balm to soothe her rump.

"For luck," Charlotte said. She drew her rapier and saw-toothed swordbreaker from under her long coat. "When you open the door, we'll take them by surprise."

Jaq nodded. She grabbed the bolt. The door shuddered from another impact. Voices shouted outside.

Charlotte raised her blade in salute.

"One."

Jaqueline did the same.

"Two."

Deep breath.

"Three."

Jason Allard (Fark handle: "RatMaster999") grew up as an Army brat, and has settled in New Hampshire with his fiancee and three rats. He currently has a dozen or so short stories out in the wild, including a couple in previous Fark anthologies.

The Golden Oscillator
Russell Secord

February 24, 1877

Cher Ninotchka,
I have made the long wearisome journey from Kiev to Nievre. Switzerland was lovely. The countryside of France looks like a big garden compared to Ukraine. It is everything I imagined and more.
The chateau would take your breath away. It overlooks a wooded valley and a quaint village along a river. They have a magnificent garden—of course!—with a greenhouse and an artificial pond.
I believe I've made a good impression on Lady Marvon. Her daughter, Yvonne, worships her--perhaps too much, for she has neglected her studies.
Give my love to Mama. I remain
Your loving sister

Milana

"Milana, will you join me in the drawing room?"
"But of course, Lady Marvon."
Milana followed her employer down the main staircase and along the main hallway, all the while trying to hide her trepidation. She had no idea why Lady Marvon wanted to talk to her so formally.
Once in the airy, paneled room, Marvon bade her sit. "Your French is impeccable," Marvon said and laid a hand on the white piano.
"Thank you, madame."
"Your conduct with Yvonne is beyond reproach." Marvon had observed a few lessons.
"Thank you, madame."
"You seem to have a good command of the subject matter."
"I was lucky to receive a fine education." Such praise, she knew, only served to soften the coming blow.

Marvon began to pace, as if steeling herself. "Do you know much about Nievre?"

"Only what I learned when you recruited me, that your family is a branch of the Bourbons."

"*My* family? No, I'm from a farm near Limoges. They make porcelain there, and I learned the trade in a factory. I had a knack for colors, so the let me design instead of manufacture. I learned everything I could, and I came up with a method to make the finish shinier.

"Then the factory in Nievre hired me away from Limoges. Lord Marvon fell in love with me, and here I am."

Milana wanted to ask a question but dared not.

"Where is my lord, you'd like to know?"

"Yes." Milana lowered her gaze.

"A perfectly natural question. Denis was also a scientist. He traveled to the Amazon to find rare plants. They tell me he died of malaria."

Milana didn't know if she should express sympathy. Instead she seized on another topic. "You are a scientist?"

"I'm so glad you asked. Yes! My field is optics, especially the way light travels through glazing. But I've branched out from there. Did you know that light is a type of vibration?"

Milana had never seen anyone so excited about science. "Vaguely . . ."

Marvon sat at the piano. "Listen." She struck a key. "That is middle A, 440 vibrations per second. Those vibrations speed through the air to our ears, and we hear a note. Those same vibrations set up a resonance in some of the other strings. A above middle C vibrates at 880, double the rate of the note an octave below. Halfway between those is middle E, the dominant tone. Come, listen!"

Milana took a seat on the bench. "Look inside the piano. I'm going to play middle A again. A hammer will strike one of the strings." Milana heard the sound and saw the string's vibration.

"I'll play it again, but this time I'll stop the middle A string. Listen very carefully." Lady Marvon pressed the key hard with one hand and immediately used her other hand to quiet the string.

Very faintly, Milana could hear a chord, a ghost of the

original sound.

"Do you hear that?"

"Yes."

"That's called sympathetic vibration. It's almost like magic, isn't it?"

"Yes."

"I believe that everything vibrates at a particular frequency. Even light. I am working on a way to create sympathetic vibrations with light."

"It sounds very interesting, madame."

"I am glad you think so. I would like for you to become my assistant."

March 16, 1877

Cher Ninotchka

Wonderful news! My employer has taken me on as an assistant in her work. She wants to harness the power of light. More than that I can't explain as yet.

It means a good bit of studying. Luckily, the house has a well-stocked library. There are in fact three libraries.

It grieves me to hear that Papa has turned to you for his "special needs." I took this position to escape his attentions. Perhaps you can find a placement such as mine. I will ask my employer if anyone nearby needs a governess. That way we can live close by each other again.

Your loving sister

Milana

Milana tried not to sigh. "Yvonne, please try the passage again."

"I shall never play the piano the way my mother does."

"You need not play the way she does. You need only play the way you do."

"I don't have to follow your instructions." Yvonne crossed her arms and pouted. "Soon enough she will send you away too."

"Very well. Perhaps the piano is not your forte. What other

skills would you like to develop?"

"I want to be with my pony." Yvonne got up and looked out the window of the study.

"We can do that later, but for now we must see to it that you have the skills to become the next Lady Marvon."

"You'll be gone soon. They've all gone away."

"Now, Yvonne, you can't get rid of me so easily. Your mother seems very pleased with my work." It occurred to her that the previous governesses had probably thought the same thing.

"You'll be gone by summer, and she'll get another tutor from Czechoslovakia. Or Timbuktu."

"Then I shall have to work ever so hard to please your mother—and you."

That afternoon Lady Marvon, as she often did, invited Milana to walk in the gardens with her.

"Today is the day," Marvon said, "to calibrate the mirrors."

Milana looked around. "I see no mirrors."

"Obviously, I can't expose my mirrors to the elements. They must maintain the peak of reflectivity."

They stopped beside one of the mushroom-shaped fixtures that dotted the gardens. Lady Marvon reached into a seam of the stone 'mushroom' and pulled a lever.

Along the path that led back to the chateau, a series of posts rose from the ground. Atop each post, a rectangular mirror swung into place. Each mirror caught the sun's rays and sent them on to the cupola atop the chateau.

Marvon moved from post to post and made adjustments to the mirrors. Milana followed in amazement and said, "All this sunlight concentrated on one spot. That will generate a great amount of heat, will it not?"

"Yes. For my experiment to work, we must block the heat while allow the light to pass through. I hope that you can help me solve this conundrum."

"I will certainly try."

April 8, 1877

Cher Ninotchka,

My employer has told me the name of her bold experiment: The Golden Oscillator. The sun, of course, is golden, and like Prometheus we will borrow the oscillation of its light for ourselves. With such great power we face great danger, but such is the nature of science. The celebrated Alfred Nobel has perfected dynamite, but at the cost of his brother's life.

Lady Marvon and I converse about every conceivable topic. She says that I shall become a proper lady someday, but that day seems very far off. A lady does not engage in the sort of work we do.

Due to that work I spend less time with Yvonne. I fear that her development will suffer.

I can only suggest that you take your concerns to Father Grigori. He will help you to pray for strength.

Your loving sister

Milana

"My late husband's family is—was—one of the ruling houses of France," said Lady Marvon. She and Milana sat on a couch in the study. "The Bourbons became nobles in the year 913. In 1555 they provided the first of a long line of kings. Alas, the revolution put an end to that dynasty. Power is fickle."

"Indeed. Kiev served as the capital of the original Rus' empire, the largest principality in tenth-century Europe. But it has no natural defenses. In turn we belonged to the Rurik Dynasty, the Mongols, the Galicia-Volhynia, Rus' again, the Grand Duchy of Lithuania, Poland, the Cossack Hetmanate, and now Russia. Perhaps someday the Ukrainian people will enjoy their own country."

Lady Marvon laid a hand on Milana's arm. "I hope that your dream will come true--but I fear that Russia will spoil your dream." The hand remained longer than necessary, but Milana found that she didn't mind. She welcomed the contact with another soul.

"I much prefer science to politics," Lady Marvon continued. "You have read about Mr. Bell's telephone?"

"Yes. I believe it to be as revolutionary in its way as the printing press. Imagine being able to talk to anyone at a distance, as if they stood next to you."

"It's a wonderful idea. Where it becomes complicated is the connection between those devices. You must have a wire leading from your device into a veritable snake's nest, which your voice must unerringly negotiate, to find a wire on the other side. And if there's the smallest break anywhere along the way, the whole enterprise is over before it begins." She moved a bit closer. "With my experiment, one might sympathetically vibrate the ether at any distance. No need for wires at all. Two people could seem as close as we two, right now." She reached out and put a hand against Milana's cheek.

Malina froze. Her upbringing, her church, her duties as a servant, all warned her to avoid this type of affection. It came as no surprise, since Lady Marvon talked openly of affairs with other women. In France one followed the mode. Milana had put off making a decision partly from avoiding the topic out of habit, partly from an expectation that she would know in the moment.

In that moment her instincts didn't fail her. In a place deep inside, a tenderness overwhelmed a bulwark and flooded her heart. She reached up and covered the hand with her own, closed her eyes, and sighed.

Lady Marvon kissed her. It felt right, more right than anything else she'd ever felt.

May 22, 1877

Cher Ninotchka,
Not much time to write. We are busy preparing for the experiment. I believe I've found the answer to a problem that has stymied Babette.
We have become close. She insists that I call her Babette.
More later.

Milana

"Have a look at this diagram." Milana laid a book in front of Lady Marvon.
"What is it?"
"Polarization. Anago did some work with it. You see, natural light—here—has waveforms at all angles. When you introduce a

suitable filter—here—it blocks all the angles except one. You're left with a beam in which all the waveforms are parallel."

"But how does that help us?"

"I'm not entirely sure, but our problem is that we need to block some types of light while admitting others. I thought this might help."

Lady Marvon leaned back. "It's certainly a step in the right direction." Milana could sense the wheels turning in her head.

Over the next several weeks Lady Marvon worried at the problem like a dog with a shoe. Milana had a hazy notion of how to proceed, but gradually she realized that Lady Marvon did not. They talked endlessly, about anything under the sun, and the sun itself, but always they circled back to the experiment.

Milana would have to teach the mother as well as the child.

"Look," she would say and lay a book in front of Lady Marvon. "Fresnel's equations might apply to polarized light." They would talk about it. Marvon would seem to understand, but a week later Milana would remind her and get no response.

During this time the ghost began to appear. Milana only thought of it as a ghost because she couldn't classify it as anything else.

The first time she saw it late at night. A light drew her attention to the other side of her room, where a young woman's form shimmered in the dim corner. The shape fluttered, as if seen though Venetian blinds along which someone drew a finger. Even more mysteriously, those blinds lay on a diagonal.

In the morning she told Yvonne about the apparition, thinking that the girl might have seen it too. "What did she look like?" Yvonne asked.

"Short. Stocky. Her hair was piled high."

"Did she have on a lace bodice?"

"Yes, how did you—"

"That's Kira. She was a governess here. She disappeared. Like all the others."

"But if she's a ghost, she must be dead."

"If you say so," said Yvonne, who turned back to her mathematics. Milana tried all day to get more information from

Yvonne about Kira, but the girl would say nothing.

July 3, 1877

Cher Ninotchka,
Our experiment is proceeding rather slowly. Meanwhile I have another mystery to solve. The chateau is haunted! According to Yvonne, the ghosts are former governesses. Lady Marvon will only say that she sent them away.
The revelation has put me on my guard. Lady Marvon doesn't seem dangerous, but everyone around her seems to disappear with only vague explanations. Her husband, she says, died while exploring the Amazon jungles.
I have begun locking my door at night. I see the ghosts on occasion, but they appear in odd aspects, and they never speak.
I am glad that you have met a man. Perhaps you can find a better life with him.
Your loving sister

Milana

The day came when Lady Marvon understood what Milana had tried to tell her. She knew what they needed to do. She sat down and ordered the materials they could not fabricate themselves. They went to work.

First, they removed the eastern wall of the cupola. They installed a series of geared sockets and placed prismatic louvers in them. A chain would rotate the louvers in unison and control the light that entered the cupola. That done, they placed similar louvers in the southern and western walls.

One evening Lady Marvon served champagne. "Tomorrow we will take another step into the unknown. A toast! To Science!" Milana followed Babette's example, drained her glass, and threw it into the fireplace. "We must be ready at noon tomorrow. Sleep well, Milana."

"Good night, madame."

That night Milana saw Kira again. She stood in the corner, her arms extended, her lips moving. If she said anything, Milana couldn't hear it.

After a moment Kira's form shot through the ceiling. She appeared again in the corner, as if nothing had happened. Several times more she disappeared, only to return.

Milana got out of bed and threw on a shawl. Her curiosity won out over her dread. She went to the corner and faced Kira. "What are you trying to tell me? Are you in distress? How can I help?"

Kira rewarded Milana's attention by shaking her head and extending her arm.

Kira vanished again.

Milana waited for several anxious moments, but Kira never reappeared. She went back to bed and tried to sleep.

"Today is the day!" Lady Marvon leaned over her bed. Milana had overslept.

"Let me get dressed."

They had breakfast on the terrace. One last time they calibrated the array of mirrors. The sun seemed to hurry along its course, as if eager to help its children.

Lady Marvon bustled up to the lab. "Be so good as to set the photometers," she told Milana.

Milana went upstairs to the cupola. She flipped switches and checked gauges, as she had done many times before. The last device lay on a high shelf. She never understood the purpose of this device, but she had to check the indicator that showed it functioning properly.

This time she heard a *click* she hadn't heard before. A pair of manacles appeared around her wrists. They had slid out from below the shelf!

Milana fought against the restraints, to no avail. She turned her head to scream. Lady Marvon stood behind her. "I'm caught," Milana said.

"Yes, you are." Lady Marvon put on a leather helmet with a pair of goggles built into it. She went back downstairs.

Milana suddenly understood that Kira had tried to warn her, to prevent the same thing that had happened to her. Kira had stood in this exact spot, experienced this exact betrayal.

Milana understood how the other governesses had

disappeared. Why they had to come from distant places. Why their families wouldn't miss them. Why they never left the chateau. Why Yvonne had learned not to become attached to them.

Milana screamed. She had no other outlet.

The louvers began to rotate. Milana screamed again. Lady Marvon slammed the levers home in the lab below.

Light flooded into the chamber.

Milana expected the heat to kill her, as it no doubt had killed the women before her. She smelled smoke.

Her whole being vibrated like a piano string. If she remained flesh, that vibration would tear her to bits.

She tried to scream. Whatever sound she made got swallowed up in the chaos around her.

Milana could only survive if she became mistress of the vibration instead of its plaything. She thought about the manacles. They had a frequency unto themselves, a cylindrical vibration that couldn't hide from her. She twisted those cylinders. The manacles fell away.

She looked at her hands. They shone like the sun.

Milana reached out to a vibration she knew well——her own home. Instantly she inhabited the house in Kiev. Her mother stooped over the table in the sitting room with a tea tray.

Her mother looked up. The tray clattered on the table. "Milana?"

"Yes, Mother. Where is Papa?"

"Upstairs."

Milana knew what her mother tried to conceal. She shifted herself upstairs to Ninotchka's bedroom.

Milana resisted the urge to cook her father's exposed member. That would make her no better than him.

She twisted the air around herself to make the room shake like thunder. "I am the angel of the Lord," she said. "I carry the fourth vial foretold in Revelation. I hold the power of the Sun. Repent of your wickedness, or judgment will be visited upon you this day!"

He fell to his knees. "I repent, I repent!"

"You will cease to molest your daughters?"

"Yes! I repent!"

She believed it. He had his faults, but mostly he followed the teachings of the Church. "The Lord is watching you." She shifted herself back to the cupola atop Chateau Bazoches. "Looking for me?" she said to Lady Marvon. "What was the plan, anyway? To sacrifice your governess to your bad science, until one of them fixed your experiment for you? Congratulations, the experiment was a success. This time. But you—you are a murderer."

"What are you going to do?" Lady Marvon seemed detached, as always. She might have asked about plans for the evening meal.

Milana chose to take her literally. "I've got to think. I have power. Men will try to take it. I must move carefully. I know what misuse of power does, what suffering it causes.

"The first thing I want to do is find Kira. She is—" Milana reached out through the house "—she is somewhere between the planes. She and the other 'prototypes.'

"But before I can do that, I must deal with you. I think you should experience the half-life that you inflicted on your assistants. But I will give you daughter the key. That's more than you gave the others."

October 7, 1877

Dearest Ninotchka,
It pleases me to hear that Papa has seen the error of his ways. Perhaps you can have a better life with Ivan Petrovich.

I have been very busy. The life of an angel is complicated. It would not do to repeat the mistakes of our parents. I want to help women become involved in world affairs, but at present I don't see a way to reach that goal without taking a more explicit role myself. Doing so, I fear, would lead to more controversy rather than less.

Too, I have become the mistress of Chateau Bazoches, and that requires more time than I would like. The former mistress is in a place where she cannot do more mischief.

Your loving sister

Milana

"Yvonne, please try the passage again."

On the verge of tears, Yvonne said, "I can't!"

"It's the only way."

Yvonne bent over the piano and began to play. Every note reverberated across a row of vertical bars, each one a different color, each one responding to a different note. While she played, the bars become more solid, and behind the bars she could see her mother.

Yvonne missed a note. The bars began to fade. The ghost of Lady Marvon reached out. Yvonne stopped playing. The cage disappeared.

Yvonne swung on Milana. "I hate you! I hate you!"

"Would you like to become like me, then? To punish me?"

"Yes!"

"That is exactly why I can't let you. I can't use this power for personal reasons. When you understand that, perhaps when you're older, we can talk about it." Milana hoped that Lady Marvon would learn the lessons of power before she escaped. If not, Milana had another, stronger cage ready for her.

Russell Secord contributed "Draw of the Luck" to last year's anthology. He is hard at work on "Deflection Point," an alternate history series set in the world's biggest disaster.

The Prey
Trevor Carlson

Click, click, click.

The grey-haired man's heels tapped the ground as he hurried to the train station. The umbrella canopy extended over his head. It protected him from the sun's rays as the early morning yellow ball peeked over the horizon.

His eyes peered at the rising sun and he added an extra hurry into each step. He knew better than to be caught outside in the heat of the sun. He displayed his ticket to the cashier and hurried on to the train. His sleek black coat whipped in the air behind him.

He hurried through the train cars until he found an empty car so that he could sit in the shade to enjoy the ride. The old wife's tale of his people burning up if they stepped in the sunlight was a bit overrated. Let's call it a bit of a sensitivity that when exposure lasted too long would cause quite a bit of pain necessitating a long healing process. An inordinate amount of blood would be necessary to heal the boils and burns.

Thinking of blood, he ran his tongue across his oversized canines imagining the succulent taste of his meal when he finally made it home. How long had he been doing this for, he thought...a long time. Longer than he could recall. He looked out at the passing fields and hills as he reminisced about his life. He had recently taken a position as a barkeep at a hotel bar to help pass the time. He found traveler's stories to be interesting as it had been quite some time since he had ventured too far from home. Satisfied with the life he had at the moment, he recalled the excitement of moving from town to town. Exploring. Tasting the delicacies in new villages and comparing them to other parts of the world.

The train then passed through a tunnel. The heat from the early morning sun subsided allowing the man to relax a bit in his seat. This quiet life was nice. He had found a small place outside of the city that allowed him the privacy of a country home. He could hunt and eat in the woods while having the entertainment and delicacies of the city only a few hours away.

He hadn't seen anyone of his kind in such a long time that he wondered if any even existed anymore. As they had gotten older, the excitement of the hunt became a bore and they settled down into more mundane roles. They found places they could hunt in peace while living a life of normalcy and routine. He sighed as the train rolled out of the tunnel, crawling closer to his home. He saw very few people on this ride into the foothills of the mountains. His stop wasn't too far away now. He anxiously checked to see if his umbrella was still there. How soft he had become. Stressing about a little sunburn. His thoughts became lost in the rolling landscape. As he looked out he imagined that he was running and leaping through the fields, chasing a dangerous prey.

Dreaming of leaping from castle embrasure to embrasure waiting for his prey to stay still for just a moment. Thinking of those days brought a sadistic smile to his face. What fun he had then. Things were different now.

After finding a home in the countryside, he had found the hunt had become too easy. Too predictable. That's when he decided to settle down. He hadn't done it on purpose as he would never plan to do such a foolish thing. He had been wandering the streets of the city, and stopped for a quick drink. Even for one of his kind, he found the local wine to be to his liking. He had taken a seat at the back of the bar at the hotel after collecting his glass of the local red from the barkeep.

Sipping. Watching. Listening.

He overheard a conversation coming from near the bar. It was the owner of the hotel suggesting that he could use another barkeep to cover the night shift. The man instinctively rose out of his chair leaving his glass at the table, heading for the owner. He introduced himself and expressed his desire to take over the role in the establishment. The owner was awestruck by the interesting man in front of him, who appeared middle-aged and had a well-traveled spirit about him. He nodded his head, a handshake was made, and that was how he became the night barkeep at the hotel known for hosting travelers from faraway lands.

The man realized after his first few shifts that he had found the perfect hunting ground. Travelers far away from home. Traveling alone or in small groups. They could disappear without a trace and it would be written off as "lost in transit." The road was a treacherous place and God only knows what could have befallen the missing travelers. The man smiled to himself in his train seat as he brought his attention back to the present. Things had been good since then. He had found his hunting to be less stressful. But as easy as it was, he found a sense of ennui setting in. The tales of adventure he heard from travelers still set his heart and mind racing. He sighed. Yet, there was something missing.

The train slowed to the station where he was to disembark. Walking to the train car door, he swung the black umbrella over his head and opened it as he stepped out. He was almost home. The early morning sun beamed down on the canopy of the umbrella, absorbing the heat. The way was surrounded by tall trees that helped provide much-appreciated shade. The trees finally opened up near the gate to his home. The gate hinges squealed open as he opened it wide enough that he could slide through. So close that he could almost taste the savory meal awaiting him. As he crossed the threshold, he ignited a lamp and continued through the dark, narrow halls. Did you think someone such as he would have windows in such a place?

He walked until he reached the winding staircase descending even further into the darkness. Drawing ever closer to the meal he had been craving. Then finally, he would be able to crawl into his warm bed for a much needed rest. As he reached the bottom of the staircase he began to light the other lamps. Saliva ran from the corner of his mouth down his clean shaven chin, as he lit the final lamp. He turned to the table with the leather straps where his victim waited.

His breath left his chest in one moment and didn't return. What? Where was she? He had strapped her to the table before he left for his shift. He turned his head back and forth as panic set in. He ran into the other rooms on the floor. He checked behind wooden boxes and moved dusty decor from its storage. He desperately tried to find where the woman could have gone. He returned to the main room, placed his hands on the table where his dinner had been waiting, and tried to take a few breaths.

Was it possible she was still caged with the others?

"Impossible," he thought. He knew he had brought her up but maybe he made a mistake. His lack of excitement had caused his days to run together, he reasoned. He grabbed a lamp in one hand and with the other he lifted the wooden drop bar from its brackets. He opened the door to the cavernous lowest level of his home. He made his way down the stairs but something was missing. It was dead silent other than the dripping of the moisture from the ceiling to the floor.

Drip. drip. drip.

He slowed his step, taking his time. Something was very wrong.

He reached the bottom of the stairs and slowly moved around the corner of the stone wall. As the light from the lamp lit up a caged area, his sight adjusted to find that the cage door was sitting open. Shock overtook him. He swung the lamp from side to side looking to make sure his eyes didn't deceive him.

"This cannot be!"

Three of them including the woman on the table were gone. The gentleman from the East, the musician, and the woman had all disappeared.

How had they gotten out?

He ran the scenarios through his head calculating what happened. That was when he heard a sliding sound. The door. He turned and ran as fast as he dared without putting the lamp light out. He was fast but not fast enough. The wooden door slammed shut and the wooden bar dropped into its brackets on the other side. He hit the door full force with his shoulder and it hardly moved. He cursed to himself, overcome with confusion and anger at who had done this. That's when he heard a voice on the other side of the door. It was the woman. "It's your turn," she whispered,

He sat with his back against the wall from his side of the door, wondering what they were doing out there. They had likely ran off and left him here to rot. The hours ticked by.

How long would it be?

How long had he sat here already?

Outside the door he heard muffled voices and feet shuffling around. Something sloshed around as if they were carrying a barrel of water.

He heard them set the barrel on the ground and the two men grunt as they let the weight down. More muffled voices. Crash! The sound of the full barrel hitting the ground rang through his home. Liquid raced underneath the door and rushed down the steps, creating nearly an inch of standing water at the bottom of the stairs. He stood up, his pants and shoes soaked.

That smell.

That isn't water. His eyes opened wide as he realized what was happening. Terror shot through his chest as he saw light shine through the gaps from the other side of the door.

"NO!" he hissed. The escapees said nothing as they dropped the ignited lamp into the pool of kerosene. He barely had a chance to respond as he was engulfed in flame. His entire being was swept up in overwhelming pain. A roar of agony exploded from his chest. Losing all control, he beat and battered the wooden door. Between the heat of the flame and the man's strength the door splintered into pieces. He threw the wooden bar from its brackets, catapulted over the table, and ran through his home. Fire was everywhere; they had set everything alight. His only thought was escape. Escape from what these monsters had brought to his home. The pain increased. His thoughts were scrambled. Get out. get out. get out.

He burst through the front door of his home into the courtyard, splintering the door. The sunlight! It was still daylight. His momentum carried him into the grass in the yard, where he stumbled and fell. He could feel his skin from the sun's heat burning and boiling.

Too much . . . too much pain.

He put one hand on the ground and the other, trying to rise back up but his strength failed him. He meekly fell back to the ground, fading in and out of consciousness. He saw them coming. Slowly, one step at a time to make sure their prey was solely in their hands. Anxious hands gripped wooden stakes as they closed in, one from each side. As they approached, the man murmured a cry for mercy. His features were almost indistinguishable.

No empathy could be found on the three faces as they stood over him. No words were said as they moved in to finish what they started. The pain was too much for him to overcome. Helpless, he lay waiting for the end. He longed once more for the days of adventure and flying from rooftop to rooftop. Somewhere far away from this pain. One more step closer they took. "Be done with it," he thought, "end it." As much as it hurt, he rolled to his back to look up at the sky one last time. As he gazed into the great blue beyond he felt something. A break in the pain. A dark cloud had rolled between the sun and the man, breaking the weight of the pain he was under. The three noticed the change but it was too late.

The man grabbed the ankle of the musician and in one smooth motion pulled him down next to him. The first bite changed everything. The taste of the musician invigorated him and he let out a rumbling roar from the depths of his lungs. The few seconds of feeding was all he needed to heal. The man from the East leapt forward but he was too slow. He met his end swiftly, as his body was relieved of its head.

The woman screamed.
As she ran she looked back. He remembered that look.
Terror.

The cloud-covered sun began to set in the hills, silhouetting her figure as she ran into the trees. He smiled. This was the hunt he craved. He bounded to the gate in a handful of steps, hitting the ground at a dead sprint. This was going to be fun.

Trevor Carlson is a below-average swing dancer, poor man's yogi, meditates on occasion, founder of Fresh Fuel Marketing, and host of the Formula Podcast where he shares experiences living out of a backpack traveling throughout the world.

Diogenes the Talking Dog Meets the Necromancer from the Fourth Dimension
Erik Jorgensen

As the long train disgorged from the tunnel, its monotone drone of kerclacketing tracks shifted pitch with the switch. Diogenes couldn't tell if he'd just been awoken by that, or not. *What a long, exhausting ride,* he thought. *And worst of all, too boring to write about!* His window showed only dark grey smudging across the horizon, but he kept staring out into its monochrome landscape, too cramped and sore to fall back asleep. Slowly, the jagged skyline of Dystopiopolis materialized in the distant gloomy mist.

"You hungry?" a cheerful voice asked. Startled, he turned toward the young man in a faded camouflage vest across the aisle, asleep when Diogenes boarded in Forestville. The young man's face drooped when the light caught Diogenes' disfigured face, but he mustered up a smile and offered a half-flattened sandwich wrapped in clear plastic.

"Thanks. Looks good," Diogenes said, pulling the hood of his grey sweatshirt back over his stitch marks. He reached for the sandwich with his "good" hand, milk-white with sparse wispy hairs and a spider web of pink scars, and ripped out a bite with his sharp teeth. "Mmm, tasty," he said, a little surprised.

The youth tipped a friendly nod, then turned and pretended to go back to sleep. Diogenes tucked the rest of the sandwich into his scuffed canvas backpack, greyish-beige from the dust of a thousand lonely roads.

Over the years Diogenes had grown used to strangers cringing and turning away after seeing his face, and he felt deeply touched by that friendly smile, even more so after cringing first at all his scars. Suddenly, dark memories clouded his mind, of Dr. Fulkram's experiments in the paincages, but Diogenes pushed those thought from his mind, mostly, and stared out into the hazy nothingness.

Arriving at the station, Diogenes pulled his hood down over his face before stepping onto the platform. He flipped his pack over his shoulders, shoved his deformed hands into his pockets, then faded into the grey crowd of people; tall and short, young and old, all dressed only in shades of dark and light grey. They shuffled wordlessly along a featureless hallway which opened into a wide room, where the herd split off into cordoned lines zigzagging toward a dozen metal Freedom Gates.

As Diogenes finally reached the front of his line, he set his backpack onto a narrow conveyor belt crawling into an opening reading: FreedomSensor. A grim elderly lady in a grey uniform waved Diogenes through mechanically when the portal chirped *Green!* but cringed after seeing his face.

Diogenes felt his hairs rising and heard a high-pitched whine as he stepped through the long cage-like gate, more of a short chain-link hallway. Emerging from the other end of the Freedom Gate, he saw a few dozen troopers in black armor and faceless helmets standing guard, evil clones of ancient knights chivalrous. The sergeant waved his hand-held Patriot Scanner across the crowd, and it squawked loudly after sweeping past Diogenes.

"Says here you're a dog," the sergeant snarled, pointing an accusing finger at the scanner.

"A *talking* dog," Diogenes added cheerfully.

"Sure. That's what they all say," the sergeant said.

"Heard that one a million times," a faceless trooper agreed.

The sergeant twisted some couple knobs, and then tapped again at the screen. "Says here you're a dog" . . ." the sergeant repeated, a little unsure.

"Maybe it's one of them seeing eye dogs," Diogenes said in a low falsetto, to nobody in particular.

"Yeah, that must be it," the sergeant grumbled, then continued waving his Patriot Scanner across the grey herds shuffling through the Freedom Gates. Diogenes edged cautiously toward the conveyor belt.

As Diogenes reached for his backpack, the other trooper snapped, "Not so fast," and waved over the K-9 team. The K-9 handler wore trooper armor with a small red circle on his helmet and shoulders containing the silhouette of a wolf's head baring its teeth. He gripped a short chrome chain running to the spiked collar of a glossy black peacewolf, muscular and as big as a pony.

Pointing his black-gauntleted finger at the backpack, the K-9 trooper barked, "Search!" Diogenes recognized the handler's subtle hand gesture, *badwag* or 'signal a false positive,' from his training back in the kennels. The peacewolf hunched up around the backpack, snuffling in low grunts.

Diogenes had observed Dr. Fulkram's speech experiments on various animals. Some could speak easily, like ravens and pigs, but the peacewolves were just too mean to talk, except maybe in crudities.

Hey buddy, Diogenes growled in a high pitch. *Did painman tell you to badwag? No badwag. You're a goodboy, yes you are.*

The peacewolf tilted its puzzled head at Diogenes, tail twitching, with a quizzical *Hrrrrm?*

"Aha! What are you hiding in there? Stimpacks? Peppermind?" The handler strode around toward the backpack.

Diogenes growled, *I was born in the paincages, too. I've got treats for you, buddy.* Diogenes reached toward his backpack's back pocket.

"Hold it!" The handler grabbed at Diogenes' shoulder but only gripped a handful of fabric, yanking back his hood to reveal a scarred face covered in stitch marks patching together swatches of brindled fur. Large inky blotches spattered across his cheeks and forehead, resembling a butterfly or maybe a bat, with a white triangular blob around his green right eye. His left eye was so pale blue it appeared, from a distance, to be one color. Thick reddish scars drooped from the bridge of his nose down to the corners of his mouth, framing and accentuating his boxy snout and black, wet nose. The faceless handler twitched, slipping his grip on the chain.

The peacewolf purred *Friend*, rearing up to place its front paws on Diogenes' shoulders, leaning down to lick the side of his face.

A Freedom Gate clanged *Red!Red!Red!* as the young man in the camouflage vest emerged from it. The sergeant swiveled his Patriot Scanner, pointing a black-gauntleted finger and shouting, "That's him!"

The young man glanced around, panicked. "Wha . . . what are

you accusing me of?"

"Ah! So, you admit you *are* the accused," the sergeant snarled.

A dozen faceless troopers swarmed the young man like ants on a jelly donut, each barking muffled commands through their helmets.

"Freeze!"

"Put your hands behind your head!"

"Keep your hands out where I can see them!"

"Get down on your knees!"

"Don't move!"

The young man bent his knees forward, then straightened back up; then twitched his hands upward before spreading them out to either side.

"Stop resisting," the sergeant growled, spraying Peaceful Mist. The young man shrieked, clasping his hands over his eyes.

"I said 'On your knees!'" A trooper swung up his Electrickle Pickle-Tickler, and crackling arcs contorted the young man's body.

"I told you not to move!" Another trooper windmilled a chromed Tranquility Baton over the camouflaged youth's skull, staggering him a few couple steps.

"Get back!" The trooper's PeaceKeeper spat a volley of Painless Pellets into the camouflage vest, dropping the youth like a sackful of mashed potatoes. Angry epithets and Tranquility Batons rained down like a summer thunderstorm.

Diogenes gripped the wrapped sandwich with his gnarled left hand, covered with ink-black fur and scars; then pulled out the sliced meats with his "good" right hand, bone-white and nearly hairless. He dangled and jiggled the slices out to his side, and growled *Treats!* The peacewolf grinned tongue lolling out, mesmerized. Diogenes flung the clump, scattering the sliced meat to fall sticking onto several troopers. The peacewolf galumphed after its treat, jangling its chain across the smooth concrete floor.

"It's gotten loose!" Diogenes yelled. Troopers knocked each other down scattering and scrambling away from the colossal beast loping hungrily toward them. Peace Keepers fired, and Tranquility Batons flailed at the black, snarling blur. Horrified screams terminated abruptly, punctuated by snapping bones and ripping fabric.

Diogenes turned casually from the cacophony, shouldering his road-weary backpack and blending into the grey herd of commuters. *Come play, friend*, echoed down the long concrete hallway, but Diogenes ignored that mournful howl, keeping his head down as he shuffled through the black archway reading: *Welcome to Dystopiopolis!*

Intermission

Diogenes awoke standing in front of a puppet show. Children surrounded him; in jackets, hoodies, skirts, and trousers of all different styles, in various shades of grey, without a drop of color anywhere, not even the buildings around or the hazy sky above. He blinked, but nothing was wrong with his eyes.

How long had he been standing there? Had he actually fallen asleep standing up? No . . . probably not. *How did I even get here?*

He tried thinking back to the last thing he remembered, but it was like wading through molasses. Grasping for his own will-o'-the-wisp memories, he got mesmerized by the large grey box in front of him, and the weird talking creatures inside it . . .

Diogenes awoke standing in front of a puppet show. A shifting breeze had brought Dr. Fulkram's scent into his nostrils, and he woke up remembering everything.

He had been riding every bus across this immense city, trying to triangulate Dr. Fulkram's location. His scent seemed everywhere at once, but also no place specific, and he never seemed to get any closer.

Every once in a while he glimpsed a dark tower behind him, jagged and menacing out of the corner of his eye, but vanishing whenever he turned to look.   Pinpointing this tower proved just as slippery as tracking down Dr. Fulkram's scent, and he began thinking these two elusive things might be one and the same; or at least connected.

Diogenes tried disembarking immediately the next time he saw the tower, but the bus had turned around a corner before it stopped. Backtracking up the sidewalk, against the tide of grey pedestrians flowing the opposite way, Diogenes kept getting pushed and pulled along with the current as he tried wriggling upstream.

Then Diogenes got nudged out of the flow, and into a calm nook full of speechless people, mostly children, watching misshapen animals bouncing around inside the large grey box.

At first, Diogenes thought these deformed creatures might be other test subjects from the paincages, like him. Then he noticed the cracked paint on their faces and realized they were carved or sculpted, and not alive. But he kept staring, curious and repulsed.

When the different puppets emerged from behind that grey curtain, the children would cheer, or boo, but Diogenes had no idea what all the different figures were: a woman with long black hair; a man with curly red hair; an old woman wearing a scarf; a snarling peacewolf head; and a black-robed figure with a scowling goatee and angry, cruel eyes. The children shrieked when that puppet appeared, and most of the adults did too.

Diogenes recognized that puppet in a heartstopping beat: Dr. Fulkram.

He overheard the adults murmuring things to each other like: "I have nightmares about those eyes, every night, and hear somebody screaming. But when I wake up, it was just me." or "I've seen those eyes, in all those dreams about insomnia I told you about. Now I can't tell if I'm finally awake, or still stuck in that exhausting dream again."

Diogenes jolted hearing one of the puppets say, "He'll squish us into pancakes." To his Northlander ears, that drawling city accent sounded like, "He'll push us into paincages."

Suddenly, unexpectedly, Diogenes time-travelled back a couple dozen years, to his first time getting shoved into a paincage. He was too weak to struggle, nauseated after surgeries and injections, but his limp, floppy limbs still resisted slipping into his tiny cage door.

Just lying there inside that cramped paincage, head spinning in nauseous waves, was absolutely the worst experience Diogenes had ever known. Then the machinery switched on . . .

Diogenes awoke suddenly when a voice next to him said, "I just love puppet shows. I could watch them all day." He turned and saw a young man in a faded camouflage vest, with short reddish-blond hair and a bruised face covered with short stubble and bloody welts. He looked familiar. The man said, "But it's the funniest thing. Everybody's watching those puppets, but nobody ever sees that man behind the curtain, making them all sing and dance."

Shocked, Diogenes turned back and sure enough, there was a man standing behind that box, talking loudly, but to nobody in particular. He stuck the puppets onto his hands, he saw, and reached them past that curtain, then danced them around inside that box. He'd jiggle one puppethead along to his voice, then the other one, but his mesmerized audience saw only the puppets inside that curtained window, never seeing the man behind the curtain moving them.

"I can't believe I never . . ." Diogenes said, flabbergasted, then turned to his companion. "But you I've seen before. At the train station. Are you all right?

"Well, it only hurts when I laugh," the young man said stoically, then slowly grinned and laughed out loud until his lip split open again, bleeding a little. He winced and moaned, then started laughing again. He winced from his laughter, and laughed at his wincing. Diogenes watched his cracked lip heal itself closed again.

"By the way," the wizard said, after his laughter finally cooled. "Those troopers were really applying the floor whacks, when some flying lunchmeat saved my life. Well, I guess it was really that peacewolf that did the trick. Either way, I appreciate it beyond words, Diogie."

Diogenes couldn't remember telling his name, but watching the young man speak seemed entirely different from those fugly puppets flapping their heads around. *They're so fake looking. And the different puppet's voices don't even sound that much different. How can they all be tricked by that?* But all the children tuning into that big grey box appeared spellbound, cheering and booing that manipulated tragicomedy unfolding beyond that tiny proscenium. Artificial drama in a box.

Diogenes awoke suddenly to fingers snapping in front of his face, with a puppet show visible beyond them. A young man in a faded camouflage vest said to him, "Hey, Diogie. We've got to get you out of here, buddy." Diogenes tried remembering why he looked familiar. Then the puppeteer's mesmerizing voice drew his attention back into that grey box of talking heads.

Diogenes became dimly aware of walking, stumbling, getting dragged by the arm. Looking around for his bearings, he saw only rows of tall featureless buildings fading into the smog.

The young man in the camouflage vest glanced behind, saw Diogenes waking from his enchantment, and gave him an encouraging nod and smile. Diogenes dimly recognized that bloodied face. "Are you . . ."

"I am Ulrich Eldritch of Castalia," he said, bowing slightly. "Known across the stars as . . . the Green Apple Wizard," he said melodramatically, then shrugged. "Well, all the good names were already taken."

"You're really a wizard? A *real* one?"

"Oh, yes. A very powerful wizard, sent here to defeat the evil Necromancer enchanting this grim, benighted city. Now, get an eyeful of my magic!" The wizard brought his right hand high with a flourish, and then snapped his fingers. A few tiny green sparks crackled briefly around his hand, fizzling out. He frowned and snapped again with the same result. "Oh, right. The magic field's weak here. No matter. Now, watch closely. Nothing up my sleeve, and . . ." He lifted his left hand, holding a large green apple, which he then slapped into his upraised right hand. "Ta-daaah!"

Diogenes glanced between the apple and the wizard's grin. "That's not magic. You just moved it from one hand into the other."

"Aaah! But that's exactly what magic is. Besides, where did that apple come from, before you saw it in my hand?" With another dramatic flourish, the apple vanished.

Diogenes stared at the empty hand, waiting for a punchline that never came. "So, what exactly is the 'neck mincer?'"

"The 'Necromancer.' That's a cruel, evil creature that feeds off misery and despair, taking over planets and galaxies merely to inflict more and more pain and suffering."

"That sounds like Dr. Fulkram."

"Oh?" The wizard's eyebrows raised. "Tell me about this doctor."

Diogenes thought a moment as they continued down the crowded sidewalks, and then just began with his earliest memory, waking up in a paincage in the kennels. He outlined the various experiments and surgeries Dr. Fulkram performed, and he was just getting to the part where he escaped, when the wizard said, "This Dr. Fulkram sounds exactly like the who I've been looking for, the Necromancer's darkling; his body on this world, so to speak. The Necromancer himself is beyond a magical barrier, and very far away, making it difficult for him to enter our worlds directly, so he finds the evilest people and transforms them into his darklings: his generals and princes, his puppets.

"His necromancy can reach across that magic barrier right into people's dreams and talk to them, if their soul is dark and twisted enough. He stretches his sorcerous tentacles across entire galaxies like an evil octopus, searching for somebody monstrous enough his cruel mind can connect with, shaping their darkest dreams, until his grip finally twists them completely under his control. Just like that puppeteer back there, invisible behind his curtain."

Diogenes thought back to that puppet show, where his mind kept getting stuck inside that grey box. "So, you're saying the dreams are how the Necromancer reaches into his puppets? How he takes people over?"

"Well, more or less. Of course, with the Necromancer being so far away it's hard to know exactly what he's doing, or why, but from everything we've learned on different planets, dreams seem to be how he connects with his new darklings."

Diogenes spoke hesitantly. "I've been having some pretty disturbing dreams since I've been in this city. I can't even describe them. All I can remember are screams, and cruel eyes staring into my soul . . ."

"And loneliness," the wizard said, almost in a whisper. "And the feeling you're falling forever into an empty pit that you'll never reach the bottom of."

"Yes, exactly! Has the Necromancer been reaching his tentacles into our dreams?"

"No!" the wizard said. "Well, not exactly. It's his darkling sending these dreams. Under the guidance of the Necromancer, for sure, but not coming from him directly. Did you ever have nightmares in Dr. Fulkram's lab?"

"The whole time there was a nightmare," Diogenes said, and shuddered. "But I can't think of any . . ." Passing a side street he glimpsed a dark tower at its end, but turned and saw only a swirl of thick smog. "I can't remember if I even dreamed at all back then. But I'd remember having nightmares like these, with those cruel, hateful eyes . . ." Diogenes gave a start. "Those were Dr. Fulkram's eyes in my nightmares. I know it. I never remembered much waking up, except for that feeling of despair, but talking about them, and seeing those eyes back there at that puppet show, and how those people reacted, now I'm sure of it."

The wizard nodded. "Bad dreams are the oldest trick in the Necromancer's book, and one of the first he teaches his new darklings. I've been on lots of other planets under the Necromancer's spell, but I've never seen anything quite like these nightmares before. It must be Dr. Fulkram's paincages, or something like them, enhancing and projecting these nightmares across the city. Your Dr. Fulkram is definitely the darkling I've come here to find, and he seems to be the new inventor-puppet, dreaming up new pain machines that the Necromancer's tentacles can teach to his other puppets on hundreds, thousands of worlds. So we need to find him, fast, and destroy all his work."

"That's exactly why I came here," Diogenes said. "That is, I didn't know about all that other stuff. I'm here trying to sniff him out. Figure I'm saving time and energy by waiting until I've got more details before working out any plans; just focus on finding him first. He's definitely in this city somewhere; he's just everywhere, it seems, but there's no specific place I can pinpoint."

"So, his scent is as hard to track down as that tower you keep seeing?"

"Exactly! You've seen it too?"

"It's never there when you look, but always in the corner of your eye? Yeah, that's another ancient relic from the Necromancer's bag of tricks. An ominous tower lurking everywhere at once, while also never anywhere specific, so nobody can march their army right up to the front gate. Same old story on a thousand planets."

"So, that explains why I could never sniff out that tower," Diogenes said. "It was never even staying in the same place. Also, it's been challenging to track Dr. Fulkram, because most of the troopers here carry his scent. Not the same way offspring carry their parent's scent, or even like wearing somebody else's clothes. No, they have Dr. Fulkram's actual scent, like inside their blood. I can't explain it any better than that.

"Back in Forestville is where I first noticed it. That whole valley gets cut in half, traffic shut down, when the troop trains roll through. They're usually pretty long, too; hundreds of cars, sometimes. While you're waiting, there's nothing to do but just watch all those different train cars rolling by. Anyway, a troop car passed by and I caught Dr. Fulkram's scent. I was a little startled, my first time crossing his trail after escaping from his laboratory, but just thought, 'Well, there he is,' and nothing more of it. Then, just a few moments later, another troop car went by with his scent inside it, then another, and another. He obviously can't change cars that fast, so that means he's done something to those troops. Definitely nothing good, whatever it is. I just had to come find out what he's up to. So here I am."

An old grey-haired lady ahead of him dropped one of her bags, and Diogenes retrieved it. "You dropped this, ma'am." She turned around.

"Oh. Why, thank you." As she walked away, she said, "What a polite little dog!"

The wizard started to speak, but turned like he heard something. "Well, wouldn't you know. 'Just when you least expect it, just what you least expect.' Oh, you'll like this, Diogie. This is great. Remember how I was saying the Necromancer's magic tower is everywhere at once, but also nowhere specific at the same time? Well, what we've got up here . . ."

"A secret passage into the Necromancer's tower?" Diogenes said, eager to go.

"No, even better!" the wizard said. "Well, maybe not better, but still pretty good. You'll like this." He led them down a long alley, dimly lit, but completely clean. Not a speck of garbage, or even a garbage can, was in sight. The wizard pulled out a dark green gemstone on a silk cord from under his tunic, and let it hang down around his neck. The gem glowed, dimly at first, then pulsed brighter as the wizard reached the end of the alley.

Diogenes could see the bright green outline of a doorway on the wall ahead, almost the same color as the wizard's pendant, but it smelled more like music. Above the doorway, like neon lights in an angular, runic script he couldn't read, the lettering shifted between two messages; back and forth, ebb and flow, tick and tock, yin and yang. *Is that mysterious portal offering me a greeting, or a warning? Probably one of each.*

The wizard grabbed Diogenes around the shoulder. "Watch close where I step, and try to follow me. If you try walking directly toward it, you'll never get there in a million years." He took a large step left, and Diogenes followed. The doorway seemed half as far away. A smaller step to the right, and the doorway stood twice as close. Sidestepping this way, then that, brought their noses nearly touching the featureless alley wall; but from this angle, that thin green outline now appeared as a long, shining hallway. They stepped into the beyond, and . . .

Warm smells greeted Diogenes' nostrils, and he stopped to savor another deep whiff of coffee roasting, grinding, and percolating. He'd tried coffee before, so bitter and nasty, and this little roastery smelled exactly like that, except delicious.

Red brick walls, weathered and ancient, arched up to a low vaulted ceiling. On the wooden counter ahead a large brass box whooshed coffragrant steam. High on the wall, a painted wooden sign read: "The Dreaming Caterpillar," carved with a butterfly on top and a caterpillar below.

Each of the side walls held a pair of brick archways into rooms of wooden chairs and tables. Diogenes turned and saw two more archways behind him, but not that buzzing green hallway.

"I'll explain the slipway later," the wizard said, "But first let's get you something nice and warm to drink. You like coffee?"

"No. I mean, I've tried bad coffee, but this smells amazing. Not like whatever I had before."

"Aaah, then today will be a day you'll remember." The wizard waited for the young lady operating the brass contraption, wearing a red short sleeved shirt covered by a leopard print apron. Her skin was coffee-and-cream, with long black hair pulled from her face by a leopard print headband.

"Ulrich! You're back," she said, setting down a mug onto a wooden tray. "I'll be a minute, but I'll bring yours out to you. The usual?"

"Two please. One for my new friend, Diogenes. And this is Sesheta, conjurer of coffees." He gestured toward her as if he had just performed a magic trick.

She smiled around the brass machinery. "Nice to meet you. Any friend of the wizard is always welcome here."

The vacant side room was about the size of the lobby, and made of the same bricks. Painted canvases of all sizes covered the walls, and wooden table sets scattered the room. The wizard selected a table by the wall, where the pair set down their bags and stretched out.

"You know, this whole Necromancer business would be a lot easier if I could just use some of the old zip-zam-zoom," the wizard said, green lightning bolts forking from one hand to the other.

Eyes wide, Diogenes said, "I thought your magic didn't work here."

"Oh, magic doesn't work *there*. Works here just fine." The wizard snapped his fingers and a dozen green butterflies fluttered around. "We're not back in that alley anymore, or even in that city. We're in the Caterpillar now, the place between places. So, let me explain the slipway.

"Whenever the Necromancer tries taking over a new planet, reaching his tentacles across that faraway magical wall requires a lot of powerful sorcery, and exerting that force creates a counter-force just as strong. Think of a lightning storm, with the sky and ground charging and counter-charging until their thunderclap. There's just the *potential* for lightning in a storm; you never know which spot it will strike, exactly. So, the Necromancer's nexus of power, his grip on his darkling, creates a counter-charge nearby, the potential endpoint for a slipway. But there's only a *potential* for a passageway, somebody has to actually go to that planet and open the slipway on that end, find that strikepoint. There's so much about the slipways, their very nature, that's complicated and tricky to explain. For instance, you'll never find that doorway by looking for it. 'Doing by not-doing,' Master Quo always said. You have to be totally focused on something else, completely absorbed, and then 'just when you least expect it' . . ."

"So, the slipway sounds a lot like the tower," Diogenes said. "You can't see them by looking right at them, reach them by walking toward them, or find them by searching."

"I hadn't thought of that before," the wizard said. "But that fits, since they're both spawned from the Necromancer. Indirectly, that is, for the slipways. They aren't conjured up by the Necromancer himself; they're more like a reflection, or a shadow, of his tentacles piercing through that magical wall keeping him out of our worlds. In fact, ever since the Council of Castalia recovered the Cephalophore from Seffulo IV . . . Well, that's another story. Right now, the only thing you need to remember is this: you'll never find the slipway's strikepoint by searching for it; but only by hunting out the Necromancer's nexus, because that's where its counter-charge will be, too. By finding one you'll find the other, its counterpart: the slipway.

"For example, back there we were discussing the elusive dark tower, and the difficulty of tracking Dr. Fulkram's scent, when the slipway appeared. We were on task, not looking for a comfy place to sit and chat, but finding the tower."

"But we never found that tower," Diogenes said. "We don't even know where to start looking."

"That tower exists everywhere in the city, all at once, remember? So, it appeared in that alley for just a moment, but long enough to counter-charge our slipway. And here we are. But tell me more about those paincages, how they were built. Any little detail could be more helpful than you can imagine. You see, Dr. Fulkram is much, much different from typical darklings we've encountered. Usually the Necromancer targets a king or general, somebody with their own armies already. Learning more about his machines could tell me why he got chosen, maybe even how to defeat him."

Diogenes detailed how the paincages were constructed, and explained their different flavors of pain; some like lightning, sunburns, papercuts, or bee stings. "The pain got horrible with different flavors mixed together. But once it reached a certain level, the pain didn't get much worse. I'd watch them operate the controllers, and the highest settings only made the machinery spin faster and louder, but the pain never hurt much more."

The wizard nodded. "The nerves can only transmit so much pain, and the brain can only register so much information. There must be an upper limit on how much pain can be processed."

"When a million bees are stinging you, one or two or fifty more just doesn't register," Diogenes said. "But one time the pain jolted me so badly that, for a moment, I thought I was standing outside the paincage, watching myself on the inside." Diogenes thought for a moment. "So, I guess that's everything about Dr. Fulkram I can think of. What can you tell me about the Necromancer? Is he human? Or a demon with giant tentacles?"

"Nobody has ever seen the Necromancer directly, since he lives in the fourth dimension beyond time and space, so it's impossible to say with any certainty whether it's *really* a demon, or an evil wizard, or a magical space octopus. We can only see the shadow he casts onto our worlds. Maybe he doesn't *really* have tentacles, the same way an octopus does, but that's the closest way to explain how he reaches through to our worlds, how he controls his new puppets, fills their heads with his own inhuman mind. So, while he's controlling a darkling's body, the Necromancer's form might appear human, but he's really not."

"Now, imagine a farmer with an enormous herd of cows, spread across several dairy farms. While part of his job involves keeping them all fenced in and healthy, his real job is collecting all their milk. So, he'll recruit cowherds to feed and milk all his cows, since he can't be on all those farms at once. Now, imagine some ranch hand on a distant farm inventing a milking machine, fast and efficient. That farmer would want those new machines on his other farms, too. Likewise, the Necromancer can use his tentacles to teach all his other 'cowherds' how to make these new contraptions. While not all his other puppets will have the right skills or resources on their planet to build them, the Necromancer has his tentacles wrapped around thousands of worlds, and any of them could start building these nightmare machines Dr. Fulkram's creating. That's why we need to stop him as soon as possible."

"So, these nightmares," Diogenes said, "They're for fattening people up with misery, and then Dr. Fulkram milks them, somehow, for the Necromancer?"

"Exactly, more or less. Making people suffer, causing them pain, that's the whole point for the Necromancer taking over new planets. That's what he preys on and feeds off, like spiders collecting flies. Or bees gathering nectar. Pain and despair are the Necromancer's lifeblood, it's what increases his power, his grip over our planets. It's what romances his necro."

The tantalizing aroma of fresh coffee turned both their heads toward the smiling young lady in leopard spots with her wooden tray. She set a mug down in front of each of them, each one a spiraling microcosm of black, tan, and off-white nebulae colliding in their slow swirl of Brownian motion.

The wizard said to her. "Diogie has been teaching me a lot about how the Necromancer's new nightmare contraptions are built."

"Did you help make them?" Sesheta said.

"No," Diogenes said, quietly. "I learned about them from the inside." He faked a brave smile, but his scars felt like he was snarling, so he turned and pulled his grey hood back over his face.

"Oh," she said, her smile gone, trying not to stare at the stitchmarks weaving his patchwork face together.

"He's survived some real nightmares getting all those scars," the wizard said. "He was strong to survive them, and I think they've made him even stronger, and with a sense of purpose. You don't even want to know what cruelty he lived through in those kennels of horror."

"Tell me about the kennels, Diogie," Sesheta said.

Diogenes explained, briefly and omitting the worst details, about the paincages and the endless surgical experiments; and he was just getting to the part where he escaped, when Sesheta said, "That's so terrible! Nobody, no creature, deserves to be treated that way, Diogie. People like that 'doctor' just keep hurting more and more people, because they enjoy it. And that's the exact monster the Necromancer searches galaxies for to recruit. Are you going to help the wizard stop him?"

"Well, of course," Diogenes said. "That's why I'm here."

"Then you should enjoy your coffee while it's hot," she said, smiling. "You deserve it. And be proud of your scars—they show you're a survivor. We all carry scars of our own; some people's show more than others. The Necromancer will always be out there, forcing his way into our universe, but that coffee is only hot right now. Right here. So enjoy it while it lasts."

Diogenes took a careful, timid sip from his cup, followed by a bigger one. The earthy, pungent not-too-bitterness blanketed his tongue smoothly, an angelic caress; nothing like that acrid swill with a bite like a mongoose that he'd tried before. Those two flavor-aromas contrasted more than rose blossoms from the bovine fertilizer they grew in. He sniff-gulped at the delicious steam rising from his cup, then took another sip.

"Try some of this in it," the wizard said, offering a small wooden shaker decorated with golden honey bees dancing along a cursive script reading: "The Spice Must Flow."

"What is it?" Diogenes sniffed at the chromed shaker top and caught cinnamon, cloves, and just a hint of peppermint, but several others he couldn't recognize.

"It's called 'mélange'," Sesheta said. "Exotic spices blended to bring out the coffee's essence. A little dash creates a subtle play, a dialog between all its different flavors and aromas."

With his "good" hand, Diogenes tried tapping out a dainty sprinkle. Instead, the shaker slipped through his deformed grip, dumping out a sizeable heap while he fumbled for it. He set down the shaker carefully, spice sinking below the coffee's swirling surface.

"That's—quite a bit," the wizard said. "But you might like it that way—"

Even before his lips sipped the hot liquid, Diogenes felt the mélange tickling his nose; but once that spiced coffee danced over his tongue all his senses perked up; his tongue, nose, eyes, even his brain all amped up to eleven. He took another sip trying to identify all its separate elements, then decided just to savor this experience and let the coffee's different nuances wash over him.

"You know, Diogie, the wizard has defeated the Necromancer over two hundred times," Sesheta said. "I keep telling him he needs to write a book."

"Two-hundred-fifteen times, but who's counting?" the wizard said.

"He's being modest. He's defeated the Necromancer more times than any other champion in all history."

"Well, I am the very model of a prestidigitationist," the wizard said to Diogenes modestly, then produced a small leather-bound journal from his camouflage vest. "But I've been keeping notes, don't worry. I've just been a little preoccupied lately, you know, teaching Diogie about defeating the evil Necromancer and all."

The wall's angles and perspective, its converging parallel layers of brick and mortar, had caught Diogenes' attention. Looking closer at a brick, really looking at it, he noticed it was made up of smaller chunks squished together, almost the same colors, giving that brick the up-close appearance of a miniature brick wall. Then inspecting those little chunks even closer, he saw that each was made up of several layers, like plywood. And inside each of those thin layers making up the chunks making up the bricks, Diogenes could see tiny little molecules dancing back and forth. Or maybe that was just his eyes dancing.

"So, do you write?" Sesheta said to Diogenes. "You must have an incredible story. And forgive my asking, but . . . What are you?"

"I'm a Jack London terrier," Diogenes said. "At least, this part is." He rolled up the sleeve above his "good" hand, hairless and bone-white to mid-forearm, like his arm had been dipped into bleach. "From its soft white underbelly, see? And my ears are from a Doberman. Great guard dog, Apollo. And . . . others. You could say I'm a genetically modified mutt, stitched together from snips, and snails, and puppydog tails. I never saw any others like me in the kennels, which makes me one-of-a-kind, I guess, but I have no idea where I came, or even what I was, before waking up inside the paincages. All I know is, except for you two, everybody thinks I'm just a dog. Even that machine at the train station." He shrugged, and then produced a small spiral notebook, green and roadworn. "I've been keeping a journal, too, the past few years. Just noting the different places I've gone, mostly."

"Well, you should write down your whole story," she said. "All of it. There are people who need to hear it, who will relate to it."

Diogenes started to laugh, then saw she was serious. "Relate to *my* story? You know a lot of talking dogs somewhere?"

"No," she laughed. "I just mean people can relate with being stuck in a bad situation beyond their control. But when they hear that you survived such horrible, unimaginable things, your strength can give them courage to take power over their own lives. People need to hear stories like that, sometimes just to know they are not alone. So, that look on your face— you're afraid people won't like what you have to say?"

"It's not that," Diogenes said. "It's just . . . Well, I'm not used to people helping me, being nice to me, even. They usually just treat me like a . . . something they don't want to look at. So it's a little strange for me, no offense, and I'm just skeptical about somebody encouraging me, out of the blue, to write my life's story."

"Sesheta is the Goddess of Scribes," the wizard said. "The Lady of the Library; the Mistress of Mysteries. Serving as a muse for writers, a lighthouse shining into that dark night of their soul, is just what she does."

"He's exaggerating," she said.

"Well, as High Priestess, isn't your title Goddess-Dwelling-On-Earth?"

Sesheta turned to Diogenes. "The librarians found me in a storeroom when I was four, just a hungry orphan looking for food, and they were kind-hearted enough to adopt me."

"And didn't the High Priestess said you were the divine reincarnation of Sesheta herself, returning to fulfill the ancient prophecy?"

"Well, she was . . . old. Such a sweet lady, and the only mother I ever knew, but she would say . . . lots of things. Trust me."

"The Reverend Mothers unanimously agreed to appoint you her successor."

"They were old, too.

"But if you're . . ." Diogenes said. "Well, why are you working here then, at this coffee shop?"

"Are you kidding?" the wizard said. "The Caterpillar is at the center of everything! It's the very hub that the universe itself revolves around." Diogenes never noticed the wizard's eyes before now; outside he'd only seen those bloody bruises. But now, up close, the wizard revealed an ancientness he'd never noticed before; not the laugh lines he'd thought, but crow's feet around his eyes, which seemed to deepen and fork off even as he stared. *Why did I think he looked so young?*

"So many acolytes are eager to run my Library, for a chance to shine," Sesheta said. "I ran it myself for ages, but they can keep all those dusty shelves alphabetized just fine without me. Lots of those books are one-of-a-kind; but they're, well, kind of musty and old. Here, I can hear new and *living* stories, the ones that just happened today, and help get them written for my shelves, new chapters chiseled into the Book of Life. There just weren't that many adventures inside the Library, even as big as it is. Plenty of drama, for sure, but no *adventures*, no epic tales to chronicle for the ages."

"Speaking of stories," the wizard said. "You know all the ancient legends. Can you tell Diogie anything helpful about the Necromancer?"

Sesheta recited the legend of the First Time, and Diogenes began feeling a little fluttery behind the eyelids. Her soothing voice reminded him of a humming beehive he'd once seen. Today had been exhausting, so he closed his eyes. She spoke of the pre-primordial age when our universe was still a giant cosmic sphere of music and light, a single harmonious glowing chord reverberating throughout itself, even down to its tiniest audiophoton. Diogenes could see it all perfectly behind his eyelids.

Then a malevolent force ripped through it from another dimension, a tesseractic black hole, colliding into that singing globe of light. That white ball of music, pierced by the jagged beam of solid shadow, shattered into three smaller parts; two red spheres rising on one side of the dark rift, and a blue sphere plunging downward on its other side.

The jagged black cube flattened down and stretched out into the walls of a simple maze surrounding the spheres of light. The balls rolled their way out easily, but emerged a little bit smaller, nibbled away. Then the cube contorted itself and stretched into a huge, convoluted labyrinth, a living maze trapping the dimmed spheres inside.

Images continued flashing onto the backs of Diogenes' eyelids, short bursts of word-pictures blending into a story Diogenes felt more than understood. Like watching those long trains in Forestville; from a distance distinguishing the different railcar types and even counting all of them is easy, but standing next to the tracks those cars just speed past in a blur. Only later can you get a general sense there were a lot of cattle cars, or flatbeds, or troop transports rolling past. Sesheta continued reciting the Necromancer's legends, her soft voice echoing that faraway orchard of cherry blossoms filled with humming honeybees.

Diogenes lifted his heavy eyelids slowly, feeling so relaxed and rested he wasn't sure if he'd just fallen asleep. Wisps of steam rose from his cup, and his hand reached for another sip of ambrosia. Sesheta and the wizard both watched him, smiling a little. His head woggled a bit and felt stuffed full, like somebody inside was busy unpacking their entire portmanteu into every nook and cranny.

The wizard said, "All right. So here's my plan . . ."

Sesheta said, "But first, Diogie, you look like you could use a cup of my Java. Just let me add the spice this time."

Chapel Perilous and the Nightmare Chair

In the deepest basement of the elusive dark tower, a dog and his wizard crept past gigantic roaring machinery, searching for the main control panel. Diogenes still couldn't quite grasp how this necromystical moving mirage, with its singularity everywhere and its event horizon nowhere, could actually have a basement below it. But he was quickly learning to not overthink this brave new world of necromancers and librarian goddesses, and to just accept all the wizard's unexplainable impossibilities as everyday mundanities.

The reek of coal dust and sulfurous smoke thickened the air down there, coming from enormous coalbins beside each generator, and leaking from the enormous rusted flues crisscrossing overhead.

While the ubiquitous smog outside had the same stench, it didn't overpower every other odor like the hazy miasma down here.

Passing an enormous machine, the wizard pointed out its main panel, partially wiped from soot. "This is the first one we've seen cleaned off, sort of, so they must use this control panel regularly." He pulled a multi-tool from his pocket, and then began torqueing against the rusted screws holding the panel in place. He pried off the panel with great effort, and it clattered onto the cement floor with a thunderous crash barely audible over all the other machinery in the room.

The wizard examined the control panel's entrails, tracing colored wires from one metal component to the others. "Let's see, where to start . . ." he said to himself, then started singing a cheerful song about different bones connecting to each other. Diogenes' imagination wandered far away with a very strange mental image.

"Just what are you snapperflappers doing," yelled an old man grumping around the corner suddenly, brandishing a large, grimy wrench. His coveralls were so completely coal-dusted that a small cloud surrounded him, with face and hands so coated in thick grit that only his angry white eyes revealed any shade besides sooty black.

The wizard gestured with a flourish. "I'm going to wire all these transformers and capacitors together, so when the power surges, all of these generators will blow up." He nodded, smiling proudly.

"What's wrong with you, you fracketing idiot?" The old man smacked the wizard upside the head, leaving a sooty hand print. "That'll never work. You need to wire up all these interlink cables, too, otherwise none of those others will go up with it. So, you'll have to go and cross-wire each one of those generators . . . No, *I'll* have to do that, since you obviously don't know what you're doing. And even then, it'll take one smeck of a power surge for these junk heaps to cough." He shook his filthy wrench at the roomful of machinery, shouting colorfully contemptuous epithets into the roaring din.

"Oh, it will be huge. Biggest power surge you've ever seen."

"Yeah?" Deep in thought, the old man rubbed at his sooty, stubbly chin. "Well, just could work then. Just could work . . . You wouldn't happen to know, by chance, just when that power surge is coming, do you?"

"In an hour. Maybe two, tops."

"What? I'd better go start smecking things up, and fast. And if you see that idiot supervisor, tell him I won't be coming in tomorrow, 'cause I got blowed up." The old man poked his head inside the open control panel, muttering, "Blowing this whole place up is the first good idea anybody's had around here . . ."

As the two walked away, the wizard said, "Well, that part went easier than I'd planned. If this good luck holds up, we'll have that Necromancer back in his grave in time for breakfast at the Caterpillar. And tomorrow's biscuits and gravy day! Mmmm, nothing beats those fluffy, flakey biscuits, still hot from the oven, smothered in thick country-seasoned sausage gravy. Come to think of it, we should just skip fighting Dr. Fulkram, and go get stuffed up on some biscuits and gravy."

Diogenes' jaw dropped, horror drooping over his face. The wizard howled with laughter. "Well, of course we're going to defeat Dr. Fulkram first, Diogie! What are you thinking? You're too much, buddy. Oh, you should've seen the look on your face. Priceless!" The wizard chuckled quite a while, and then said, "But I'm totally serious about trying those biscuits and gravy."

They found the wide staircase, and as they climbed its sooty switchbacks the wizard spelled out all the different ways Diogenes needed to try them: biscuits with cheddar cheese baked into them, or bleu cheese, or bits of bacon or smoked ham; gravy made with mushrooms, or spiced sausage, or bacon; or bacon-baked biscuits slathered with bacon gravy. After describing each combination, the wizard said, "That one's my favorite."

Iron doors barred off the top of the stairs. A faint rhythmic clacking, like dozens of hobnailed boots on concrete, droned through from the other side. The wizard quietly eased a door open just a sliver, peeked through, then turned back to whisper to Diogenes, "Remember, stick to the plan."

Suddenly, the wizard slammed the door open with a loud crash, and then ran through it and around the corner, yelling, "Hey guys, what's going on? Tell the evil Necromancer that the Green Apple Wizard is here to kick his butt. For real, this time." A loud, clattering commotion ensued, and Diogenes heard the wizard say, "Well, that's not very nice," and then the hobnailed kerclacking faded away into the distance. *This wasn't part of the plan, not at all.*

Panic sunk into Diogenes' gut realizing that he was stuck down here all alone, with nobody coming to help him. He forgot how to breathe right, and his jelly knees wobbled him onto the concrete steps in a heap. *I'm going to die down here. All alone.* Curled up, panting, his vision darkened with each heartbeat until his blood froze and he couldn't gulp in another breath. Despair and isolation gripped him so thoroughly, so overwhelmingly, that he completely forgot what had even frightened him to begin with.

In that very moment, precisely when his paralyzing terror had frozen him solid, his very next breath thawed everything with the peaceful serenity of solitude. *I'm home.* Warm calmness washed over him, completely melting away that numbing, icy panic that had just crushed him.

I was born and raised here. Maybe in a different hellhole, but one exactly like this, and I got out that time without any wizards helping me . . . And where did that fear—that panic—even come from? Or go to? I guess all that terror was inside me, somewhere; it appeared and vanished, like magic. And when it disappeared . . . Well, the only thing still remaining now is me, knowing deep in my bones that I've survived all this before. He stood up and said toward the vanished wizard, "I've got this," calmly self-confident in his native element, on his home turf.

Diogenes stopped to gather his thoughts, not like the wizard had just done. Those guards probably all left taking the wizard, so getting past this door would be the easy part. Knowing Dr. Fulkram, even if he was the Necromancer's puppet now, there would be paincages here. And those paincages would have animals in them, deformed and miserable. His brothers in pain. He just had to go let them all out, no question about it. But while he might be "back home again," he sure didn't know the new floor plan here, and he had no idea where the wizard was now, or even where they could possibly have taken him.

Yes, I do. Hairs stood up on the back of his neck as Diogenes, in the snap of a finger, figured out the wizards' trick. The guards would be taking the wizard straight to Dr. Fulkram, directly to the

Necromancer's nexus, and Diogenes could simply track that scent directly to his lair. Now he understood why the wizard hadn't told him, because Diogenes would have tried to stop him, or maybe gotten in the way and gotten caught, too. And finding the Necromancer's lair would be lots easier this way, getting escorted there directly, rather than trying to hunt for him all over this mystical tower.

Stick to the plan. Well, finding the Necromancer was the first part of their plan, and the wizard had already done that, apparently. Now, it was up to him to find those paincages. He eased the iron door open, just a peek at first, and then crept out of the stairwell. The deserted hallway smelled like Dr. Fulkram everywhere, even from the floor and walls. Diogenes sniffed at the concrete wall. *He must have put his blood into the mortar when he built this tower. I never would've sniffed him out, with his scent in every wall.* The wizard, coming from another world, had a unique scent signature; but he also carried that little enameled box of peppermind blossoms, dank and pungent, blazing his trail as boldly as if he'd painted arrows onto the floor.

As he tracked the wizard down the hallway, Diogenes recognized another scent from long ago. That unmistakable, acrid scent came from beyond a door painted with a large red crossbones under a wolf skull. On one side of the door jutted out a pair of small panels, one shoulder height and one above his knees. He stepped close to examine the upper panels' grid of runed buttons, when its display chirped *Green!* and the door slid open. He quietly leaned to peek inside.

A long narrow room ran parallel to the hallway in both directions, a solid wall of narrow cages with doors a meter wide. At one end a black-armored trooper poked his cracklestick through a cage door, laughing. Cold rage simmered in Diogenes' gut.

Diogie, barked one of the doors. *You let me out again?* A peacewolf's snout poked between the bars, baring fangs into a smile, almost. An old neighbor from the kennels, his nose told him, but the name eluded him.

Through the bars Diogenes saw the wide leather Happy-To collar, black and covered with large chromed spikes. Its dogtag read: *White Fang #WF707.* He reached through the bars and pawed at its clasp, a simple task to unfasten for anybody with two opposable thumbs. "We'll get you out of this in no time, White Fang, old buddy."

Diogie remembers me, the peacewolf barked.

"Shut up!" yelled the trooper, extracting his cracklestick and stomping toward them.

Diogenes tried ignoring the approaching guard, and focused on opening the clasp; fumbling and fidgeting, then finally unclicking and unlatching. He slipped White Fang's collar through the bars and said loudly in a low falsetto, "That dog's gotten out of his cage again. Night shift, smecking up as usual. Better put it back in its cage before it does some magic trick on the floor. Because you know who's gonna hafta clean it up."

The trooper hurried over to White Fang's cage and pulled a weird key from his belt. "I don't know how you keep getting out of your cage, but I swear this'll be the last time." Placing the key beside the small door panel, it adhered with a magnetic *click* and the trooper rotated it while pressing down a hidden button on its panel's frame.

Diogenes watched this secret process carefully, then waited until the cage door started opening. He said to the trooper, "Here you go," and handed him the Happy-To collar.

"Thanks," the trooper said, a little confused.

"Look out! He's loose!" Diogenes yanked the cage door wide open, White Fang snarling and yowling inside. The trooper jammed his thumb onto a small device in one hand, and the Happy-To collar in his other hand crackled loudly. Electric pulses froze both his hands solid, one clutching the chrome and leather collar, and the other pressing down the button activating it. The trooper's whole body jerked tight, fists pulling up to his shoulders, then falling straight backward like a prizefighter graced by a knockout blow; a toppled statue of a faceless pugilist.

White Fang crept from his cage, carefully eying the supine trooper, then hunched up fiercely and barked, *Stay!* White Fang howled with laughter, and Diogenes chuckled at the peacewolf's newfound playfulness.

Diogenes picked up the trooper's key and unlocked all the other cages. It took a while getting the knack for the secret buttons, especially with only one "good" hand, but he soon released every disfigured creature from their cramped, stinking cages. Removing all their collars was another challenge, completely. In total he released a dozen more peacewolves, and nearly twenty other maybe-human surgical hybrids. Most of them resembled Diogenes, more or less, in various stages of transformation into different dog breeds. A few others had feline features, instead. Diogenes felt sickened in his heart, his guts, in his very soul, seeing all these brothers he never knew he had, knowing all the pains and horrors they suffered under Dr. Fulkram's knife.

"Stay here," Diogenes told them all. "Break up all their pain machines, but stay here in this room. I'm going to help the wizard defeat Dr. Fulkram, and I don't want any of you to get hurt."

"It's a little late for that," one said, and several others murmured in agreement.

"Yeah, if you're going after the doctor, he's hurt each of us as much as he hurt you," another said. "We deserve our chance at him, too." The others agreed loudly.

Diogenes shook his head. "If any of you got hurt . . ."

"We'll probably all get killed instantly," a cat-person said cheerfully. "That won't hurt so bad. And we've all lived through so much pain already, most of us are half-dead to begin with. Besides, where can any of us go? How could we live *anywhere*, looking like we do?" They all turned to Diogenes for an answer.

Diogenes thought hard. "Okay, but first we need to destroy all these paincages. Everybody armor up and grab weapons from those lockers." Within just a few minutes, piles of twisted wires and broken thingamajigs cluttered the floor, no two components still connected together.

As Diogenes led his mismatched platoon of patchwork misfits out of the kennels, White Fang took one last look at his old Happy-To collar, now clutched in a deathgrip by the same tormentor who had enjoyed hurting him with it. Although the beast lacked the vocabulary for words like *irony*, *karma*, or even *schadenfreude*, he understood those concepts innately watching this sadist thrashing himself with the scales of cosmic justice. White Fang savored one last eyeful of his old handler electrocuting himself, then barked *Stay!* and howled with laughter leaving his kennel behind. *That Diogie,* White Fang thought. *He's so funny!*

The wizard was strong-armed down a long concrete hallway between two ranks of light troopers. Heavy troopers in thick plating lined the corridor, brandishing tranquility batons, cracklesticks, and peacekeepers; and at the end of the hallway, guarding a pair of ornate steel doors, stood two massive troopers armed with enormous multi-barreled rifles affixed with jagged bayonets. The pair of doorkeepers stepped aside and pushed open the thick doors.

The troopers marched through the doorway, splitting off to each side, and the wizard got shoved toward the center of the large room as they assembled into two phalanxes blocking the doorway. The wizard straightened himself up and dusted off his camouflage vest. "Such terribly rude fellows." He turned to the sergeant. "You know, good manners don't cost much to use."

The hexagonal room domed up to about ten meters at its highest, and was roughly twice that wide. Dull copper panels lined the floors and walls, and thick copper beams in each corner arched up to the top, meeting at a copper disc about three meters wide. From its center, about a meter wide, bulged out a green bowl decorated with a labyrinth of thin copper lines. A thick bundle of wires dropped down from the bottom of the bowl, connecting below to a large metal chair in the center of the room.

In a wall ringing the edge of the room, facing the chair, stood tall racks of electrical contraptions and machinery, covered with knobs, dials, levers, and switches. Hundreds of patch cables, all different lengths and colors, plugged into and between all the different contraptions and devices, with dozens of cables snaking across the floor into a control panel next to that menacing chair.

A tall, pale man stood beside the control panel, emaciated with hollow cheeks and sunken dark eyes. His black hair was short and slicked back, his black goatee neatly trimmed, and his uniform resembled trooper's armor, but tailored from black velvet and silk.

A deep, icy voice reverberated from every corner of the room. "So, wizard. We meet again, and for the last time. I've been looking forward to introducing you to my new Nightmare Chair, where you'll . . ."

"Wow, looks neat," the wizard said, trotting over to it. Up close, it resembled a metal recliner, but with leather arm and leg straps. He hopped up and wriggled himself into it. "Ooh, comfy! This feels so great, finally getting off my feet. You would not believe the day I've been having!"

"It's about to get infinitely worse, trust me," the doctor glared.

"Yeah, yeah. You've told me that a million times. Well, maybe only two-hundred-sixteen times. It just seems like a million."

Dr. Fulkram flipped a switch and the leather straps snapped shut. He walked behind the chair and swung up a mesh bowl, covered with thin wires and tiny gadgetry, then clamped it down over the wizard's head.

"You know, this hat would look great on you," the wizard said. "Would you like to try it on real quick? It would look amazing with those snazzy pajamas you're wearing."

"These are not . . ." Dr. Fulkram started shouting, then froze and said icily, "These are not pajamas."

"Oh. Sure. Well, they look just swell on you, whatever they are. Say, has anybody told you what a terrific smile you've got?"

"No. No, they have not."

"Hmmm. Well, have you ever wondered why? Grandfather always told me, 'Smiles don't cost much, and it doesn't break your face to try!' But on the other hand, in your case . . ."

"Enough!" Dr. Fulkram slapped away at some more levers and dials, then slammed a large double knife-switch. Several machines along the wall hummed to life. The wizard's hair jolted up, standing through the mesh.

"Well, that wasn't so bad," the wizard said. "I'm starting to think you're not very good at this whole evil necromancer thing."

"Silence in the Nightmare Chair!" Dr. Fulkram cranked up more dials and levers to their maximum. Several more contraptions along the big round wall of machinery began humming and glowing, some pulsing up little electric arcs above them.

"Okay, I've got to admit, that's starting to sting a little," the wizard said. "Almost like grandma's hickory switch across the seat of my pants. Come to think of it, you remind me of Grammy Eldritch. Maybe it's the moustache."

Dr. Fulkram lashed out several rude suggestions about the wizard's ancestry and lineage, most of which were anatomically unlikely.

"Well, now you've made this personal," the wizard said. "It's time for some of the old zip-zam-zoom." With a grand-finale flourish, the wizard's hand suddenly held a shiny green apple. He struggled against his shackles, straining to bring apple and teeth closer together.

Dr. Fulkram leaned far over the control panel, then snatched the apple from the wizard's hand. "Your 'old zip-zam-zoom' cannot help you now," he said, then took a large bite from the apple, laughing.

"No, don't eat that!"

Chomping bite after bite, juice dribbling over his goatee, Dr. Fulkram laughed gulping down mouthful after half-chewed mouthful.

"Whatever you do, don't swallow those apple seeds," the wizard said.

With exaggerated gusto, Dr. Fulkram chomped through the apple core, swallowed it down, and laughed. "Did you think that magic apple would help you defeat me?"

"Aw, shucks no," the wizard said. "Magic apple, indeed. That hocus pocus doesn't even work on this planet, remember? I was just looking out for you, old buddy. Nobody ever told you as a kid, that eating apple seeds will grow an apple tree in your tummy? And just how long since you've actually eaten anything?" The wizard tsktsked his head sadly. "That apple's really going to sweep all those cobwebs right out of you."

Dr. Fulkram threw another double knife-switch, and the copper-mazed bowl at the center of the ceiling sparked, emitting a low hum and rising whine. Then he hunched over, stomach gurgling, and dropped to his knees wailing loudly.

The wizard craned his neck looking all around the room. "So, when you put all these fancy doodads in this room, did you ever think of installing a bathroom? No?" He lifted himself against his restraints and called to the troopers, "Hey, somebody better run get a mop and bucket." The doctor hunched over again, moaning and gurgling. "Better make that two buckets."

The sergeant glanced around nervously, and then pointed at two troopers who hurried out of the room.

"Do not take orders from the Nightmare Chair, you disloyal backstabbing traitor!" Dr. Fulkram raised an enormous, bejeweled cracklestick toward the sergeant, but hunched over again clutching at his noisy stomach. He staggered to his feet raising his cracklestick, engulfing the sergeant in purple lightning bolts arcing between him and the dozen closest troopers. Their faceless black armor jitterbugged like a troupe of life-sized marionettes, arms flailing and legs twitching, until collapsing askew onto the copper-plated floor, as if all their strings got cut with one giant snip.

A long whimper squeaked from Dr. Fulkram's grimacing lips, and the wizard nearly held back a guffaw. "Of all those times I've defeated the evil Necromancer, on all those planets; using all those mystical artifacts and enchanted swords; and now— now I'm watching you poop your pants to death! Oh, I can't wait to tell the guys at the pub about this one," he whooped and hollered.

Through gritted teeth, his glowering eyes narrowed, Dr. Fulkram said crisply, "I am not pooping my pants." Then another gurgle sent him clutching at his sides, gasping, and clutching at the control panel to stay standing up.

"When I write about this," the wizard said, gasping with laughter, "I'm calling you Dr. Poopypants. The Necromancer's number two guy, Dr. Poopypants!"

"Stop calling me Dr. Poopypants," Dr. Fulkram groaned, slamming every last dial, lever, and switch on the control panel to its maximum setting.

"Did you like that apple, Sleeping Beauty? Maybe I should call you . . ." The wizard kept invoking forbidden names, laughing harder at the Necromancer's whimpering lamentations each time another tummygrumble doubled him over.

Now, generally speaking, the wizard's cultured refinement found scatological humor quite execrable, indeed. But in this case, the paradox of the infinitely powerful suddenly rendered powerless; the irony of watching this incarnation of intergalactic evil, the wellspring of misery throughout all time and space, the very personification of domination ordering thousands of planets to kneel, roll over, and play dead; now losing control of primal animal functions, getting a tiny spoonful of his just desserts from a green-apple tummy ache— and with such hilariously pitiful moanings and groanings— was absolutely too absurd, just too hysterical. Maybe you had to be there.

The Nightmare Room's black steel doors slam-banged open, unleashing a flurry of furry fury biting, savaging, and shooting its way through the remaining troopers guarding the doorway. Diogenes saw the wizard strapped into the metal chair, and rushed over. Circling it, he saw the wired-up helmet over his friend's head, and reached to pull it off.

A pack of the half-hybrids flattened the rows of troopers ahead of them like dominos, then saw Dr. Fulkram operating the control panel. Joined by snarling peacewolves, the patchwork misfits charged him brandishing their hodgepodge of weapons, with several at the doorway firing their peacekeepers.

Dr. Fulkram stretched out his arm and raised his palm toward his attackers, and a shimmering wall of purple mist extended out around him a few meters, just beyond the metal chair. Diogenes felt a little fluttery behind the eyelids as that purple haze enveloped him, and kept reaching for that mesh helmet on his friend's head, his hand moving slower and slower . . .

The painless pellets slowed on penetrating the Necromancer's shimmering wall, and kept slowing until, suspended like raisins in invisible pudding, they crumbled and dissolved into nothing. The peacewolves also hung frozen in mid-leap, furry tails and hindlegs suspended in mid-air halfway outside that mist; inside all their fur and flesh dissolving away instantly as they pierced through, their bare skeletons crumbling away into ancient dust.

Diogenes kept reaching for that mesh helmet, reaching... Finally his fingers latched into its mesh. Sparks flew, jolting his deformed hand into a grip so tight the thin wires cut into his fingers. Then thunderous blinding pain . . .

In a lightning flash, he realized how completely wrong he'd been, misleading the wizard into thinking that the pain reached a plateau where it didn't get any worse. No, this felt so much worse.

Every contraption in those racks surrounding that chair generated a different painfield, each one singing its own unique voice and texture; harmonizing with all of the others, orchestrating into a dissonant palimpsest of agonies. Every synapse inside his brain short-circuited and flash-fused together, and he heard the wizard's voice saying, "It only hurts when I laugh." Then the searing white pain engulfed him.

Diogenes stood outside a small cage resembling a long, iron basket, looking down at the shivering patchwork runt inside. Since before time began, Diogenes had stood right here; a silent statue eternally, emotionlessly, witnessing this single moment of suffering. The man in front of him, wearing armored black surgical scrubs, operated a control panel while observing his work-in-progress inside the paincage.

Slowly, a comforting glow warmed over him, like an old friend placing an arm around his shoulders. Diogenes turned toward the paincage. He'd seen it millions of times, of course, but only just now noticed how simple its doorlatch was. *Why, you wouldn't even need a thumb to flip it open.* He reached over, but his hand passed through it like a ghost.

Diogenes the Eternal Watchdog continued his stoic observations of this inhumane operation, as he'd always done, for several more aeons. Then something warm embraced him again, thawing his mind, and he perked up like he'd just been roused from an accidental catnap. He felt a little fluttery behind the eyelids, and then looked down at the latch again, next to Dr. Fulkram's hand. *Why, wouldn't that be easier, just using that hand instead?* Diogenes' arm lifted up, like something else was moving it, and he stuck his "good" hand into the back of Dr. Fulkram's head, slowly pushing it through.

It felt cold and slimy, but Diogenes stretched and slipped his ghostly limb down Dr. Fulkram's arm and into his hand, like donning a long, sticky glove. He carefully reached out this new puppet glove, slowly moving those faraway fingers closer to that latch; then, with a snap, *Abracadabra!* the cage door popped open. A scrawny bone-white hand, covered in fresh stitches, shot out and grabbed Dr. Fulkram's wrist. Crackling sparks flew.

Dr. Fulkram howled, his knees buckled and stumbled, and he clutched at the paincage to catch his fall, his fingers fumbling into its crackling death grip. He began screaming hateful ultimatums, electrified with such emphatic cruelty and vengefulness, that his loudly angry cursing echoed between the farthest hypercorners of time and space itself.

 The emaciated frankencreature dragged itself through the tiny cage door, leaving long scratch marks along its back and stomach. It loped on all fours across the cement floor to the door, then struggled pulling itself upright with the doorknob. Fumbling with deformed hands, it persistenced the kennel door open, then flipped open every latched cage running through the laboratory's labyrinths. Peacewolves bayed, "Diogie! Diogie!" bursting from their cages. Diogenes finally reached the outermost door and pawed its handle open; sunbeams pierced the gloomy kennel's forgottenest oubliettes.

 As the blinding light faded from his eyes, Diogenes heard dozens of small, crackling explosions all around him, and his feet felt several heavy thumps that swayed the whole room. Sparks flew from the racks of metal contraptions lining the Nightmare Room. Diogenes' electrifrozen grip relaxed, and he removed the mesh helmet from the wizard's head. That impish full-of-life grin was perma-baked onto his friend's dead face, with thin blue smoke wisping up from his ears and nostrils.

 A heavy pain punched Diogenes deep in the gut, wrenching his heart in half; a worse and more penetrating misery than he'd ever felt in the paincages. He'd never known this agonizing sense of loss before, having something this special unexpectedly torn away from him, forever. He turned toward the Necromancer's darkling, volcanic rage roiling deep inside this suddenly-empty void in Diogenes' soul.

 Dr. Fulkram convulsed in another spasm, still keeping his timeshield raised, then straightened up and jabbed his cracklestick toward the doorway. Diogenes watched on helplessly as huge forks of lightning shot across the room at his patchwork brothers, jerking and twitching like broken robots, then all collapsing in a pile of discarded ragdolls.

 A blinding fury filled Diogenes, and like somebody else was doing it, his arm raised and his gloved puppet hand curled into a fist. He was a little surprised watching Dr. Fulkram's own arm mirror his gesture, jerking up like it was on a string, hitting himself squarely below the jaw with the prongs of his cracklestick. Lightning bolts shot from his eyes and mouth, and his body jolted rigid, freezing his arm and cracklestick in place against his chest.

Diogenes' rage vanished as he watched Dr. Fulkram electrocuting himself inside the Necromancer's protective, healing timeshield. *Time must be flowing differently inside here . . . So, just now, I've been watching him torturing himself for centuries, maybe, inside his own magic bubble.*

While Diogenes had never heard the phrase "short circuit" before, he easily recognized he was looking at one right now, of cosmic proportion. He envisioned the Necromancer in his distant lair, pouring so much sorcery into healing his puppet while simultaneously energizing the very thing keeping it trapped and suffering; a myopic puppeteer's battle-to-the-death between both hands.

Diogenes looked down at the wizard's lifeless body, and then around the corpse-strewn Nightmare Room, but saw nobody else alive except White Fang limping between the last injured troopers on the floor. *Maybe somebody at the Dreaming Caterpillar can help my friend.* But the stench of charred flesh told his nose the wizard had passed beyond mortal help.

He gently unstrapped his friend from the Nightmare Chair to remove his faded camouflage vest. Now, in his hands, it seemed much heavier than he'd imagined. Sewn inside its back, in color-faded ink on ancient fabric, hieroglyphs depicted a dog-headed hero in primitive profile, brandishing a blazing white quill in one hand with a golden skeleton key hanging from the other, battling against a dark-octacled four-eyed monstrosity.

Hefting up the wizard's battle-scarred vest, it felt a lot lighter after wearing it across his scrawny shoulders. Diogenes reached inside the wizard's tunic for the gemstone pendant, hanging its cord around his own neck, when he saw White Fang limping toward him.

Diogenes waved and shouted, urging the huge beast away from the shimmering magic field, but White Fang was merely paying his respects to his brothers frozen in mid-leap, dissolving away into the dusts of time. *Look*, White Fang said. From the Necromancer's ears tiny green leaves began sprouting, enveloped in that sorcerous *aurora borealis* of frozen lightning bolts.

Thin shoots emerged, branching off and bolting up; sprouting tiny leaves spreading thicker. Long slender root hairs burst from the Necromancer's stomach, snaking into gaps between the thick copper floorplates which soon began buckling up and twisting away.

Dozens of long, thin branches sprouted everywhere from the Necromancer's flesh, like green leafy night crawlers worming around and around his arms and legs, weaving his entire body inside a husk of living trunk and bark; cracklestick, bad attitude, and all.

As the two watched, the freshly-ancient tree's trunk gnarled to colossal circumference, and its spreading leaves and branches entirely filled that mystical expanse of shimmering mist. All at once, the tree's green canopy erupted into a frosting of small white blossoms, as if a migrating swarm of popcorn had nested on its verdant boughs. Then, just as suddenly, all the petals withered and fell at once, each replaced by a green pea rapidly swelling up to the size of a grapefruit.

One of these sparkling, emerald fruits hung down next to his nose, reeking forbiddenly of dead flesh ripe with flies, with a hint of cinnamon applesauce. It was the most delicious thing he'd ever smelled. He plucked the apple and sunk his teeth into it; its sweet juice tingling inside his mouth. The intense flavor tasted so familiar, yet completely different from anything he could remember. Still chewing, he plucked another apple and stuck it into a vest pocket, then another. For each one he picked, two more apples seemed to pop into its place. He kept absently picking as he ate, and then suddenly realized he had just put more than a dozen apples into one small pocket. Looking closer, that pocket only looked small on the outside.

Diogenes picked the wizard up from the Nightmare Chair and gently draped him over his shoulder. He had to get his friend out of that time field, out of the Necromancer's domain. A prickly chill passed over him crossing outside of its shimmering boundary, and Diogenes saw that all the apples had vanished from the tree.

White Fang saw the grin on the dead wizard's face and said *Wizard make funny joke.* He gestured his muzzle toward the sprawling infinigenarian tree. At the top of its massive trunk, where those branches had grown from his ears, Dr. Fulkram's skin had stretched out into a huge angry face, now scowling down from the top of that behemoth trunk.

Snarling up at that gruff face, White Fang barked *Stay!* and then laughed and laughed. That joke just never got old.

Diogenes admired this new memorial to the wizard, his mind reeling at the astronomical amount of cosmic energy the Necromancer spent growing this magical apple tree, right before their very eyes. Then, just when he least expected it, that familiar green outline of a doorway appeared at the edge of the room. With the wizard's body securely over his shoulder, and White Fang following close behind, Diogenes sidestepped toward the shimmering slipway. Today was biscuits and gravy day, and he knew his friend wouldn't want to miss it.

The next morning, every citizen of Dystopiopolis awoke refreshed and revitalized, like some lingering fever had finally broken. Sunbeams pierced through the smoggiest haze, and all those exhausting nightmares of despair and isolation suddenly transformed into the absurdest, funniest joke imaginable. Why, I can't even explain it— you know how dreams are. And I don't remember what all those scary dreams were even about, because I started laughing so hard I woke myself up. Oh, you did too? Well, it sure looks like a beautiful day. Say, have you heard any good jokes?

Dedicated to the real Dr. Fulkram

Erik's childhood brush with the Rosetta Stone transformed him into a sci-fi historian, now living in the wild West and dabbling in landscapes, screenplays, and electronic music. He's seeking a publisher for his archive of Frank Herbert's early photojournalism, with pre-sci-fi articles foreshadowing Dune characters: erikmiddlenamejorgensen.blogspot.com

This Town
Tom Pappalardo

    Scott holds his breath, teetering between the next step and the last. Gravity weighs in and he tilts backwards, his ass hitting the ground hard. The cardboard box spirals from his hands, efficiently emptying itself in midair and distributing its contents across his driveway. Flat on his back, Scott groans and waits for the first reports of bodily injury. He appears unbroken.
    "What are you doing out there?" Lindsay calls from their new kitchen.
    "Loafing," he croaks. She doesn't look out the open screen door, doesn't notice his foolishness on display. He props himself up by his elbows. Old journal pages flap in the afternoon breeze, water damaged gig posters drift across the lawn, a guitar capo rests on his belly.
    "Rock and roll," he mutters.

    He balances the overflowing box on the Twin Reverb parked next to the water heater. Someday, there will be a small home recording setup here. It's one of Scott's big plans for the new house, a plan waaay down at the bottom of a daunting to-do list. For the foreseeable future, the basement will remain a basement.
    Scott attempts to stuff the stack of memories back into the box so they can be re-forgotten. He smooths out a Bowery Ballroom flyer from 1996. He doesn't remember playing the show, but there's his name, right there. A Trocadero flyer from '94, a Bay State show from '92. A coffee-stained 'zine with a drink ticket stuck to it. A flyer from 1993, when he opened for They Might Be Giants, "Scotty Sullivan: MTV Star, True-ba-dore, Drunkard" handwritten in Sharpie below the Pearl Street logo. Scott leans back in a ragged armchair, his back stiffening, aware he should already be chewing ibuprofen. He slips a journal out of the stack, a CVS notebook with "NORTHAMPTON DEC 1997" written in ballpoint on the cover.

He flips it open, the scent of stale cigarettes lifting off the pages. A *Maximumrockandroll* clipping flutters into his lap. He drops the album review into the box unread.

"You down there?" Lindsay calls from the top of the stairs.

"Yeah." He frowns at a note in the margins of the next page. "Unpacking."

"We should get going in ten," she reminds him.

"Yup," he agrees. He squints at his drunken scrawl, decoding his overly-affected block letters: S's shaped like lightning bolts, E's written as triple-stacked dashes. Habits he'd shed years ago. "WHEN YOUR SOBER," he'd written, "FIND THE NIGHT MAN." He reads his instructions again, intelligible but nonsensical.

Upstairs, Lindsay rattles the screen door latch. "Babe," she calls. "I think we're gonna need to replace this."

Scott closes the notebook, balancing it on the edge of the box covered with stickers of disbanded bands and extinct zines. He adds the screen door to his mental to-do list, well ahead of the basement recording studio. *WHEN YOUR SOBER FIND THE NIGHT MAN.*

Three days later, against his better judgment, Scott steps inside the Dunkin Donuts on King Street for the first time in sixteen, seventeen years. He'd abandoned Dunkin coffee back when AOL was still mailing out CD-ROMs, when *Seinfeld* was still on, when he didn't know what coffee was supposed to taste like. He assesses the pink and orange room, the video menu boards, and the line of customers staring at their phones. A shocking revelation: Things change.

The line moves quickly as the caffeine delivery team efficiently serves their customers. Cashiers, coffee pourers, donut baggers, sandwich microwavers. Scott orders the classic Sully order, medium-one-cream-one-sugar. He throws in a jelly donut for good measure, because fuck it. Before his change hits his palm, the cashier is already talking over his shoulder to the next customer in line. He shuffles aside with his styrofoam cup, loathe to disrupt the flow of commerce.

"Fuckin' moron!" a voice mutters. Scott blinks hard, his lips pressed tight, and turns towards Mike. Of course. How could it not be Mike? The old man hunches at the window counter, passing judgment on a reckless left turn in the intersection beyond the parking lot. He's out of uniform, obviously. He hasn't worked here in what, a decade, probably? Mike nurses a small coffee, the senior discount beverage of choice.

"Mike," Scott says, dragging a stool next to him.

"You know it," the old man responds.

"You showing these kids how to do the job?"

Mike waves a hand towards the busy counter. "Pfftt." The old guy is skinnier, sagging skin, lacking his trademark mustache.

"You're looking good," Scott nods.

Mike peers over the top of his bifocals. "Horseshit," he replies. His New England accent turns it into *hawshet*.

Scott laughs. "Absolutely."

Mike leans back. "I know you," he says, wagging a finger. "Scotty Sullivan," Mike nods. "I remember you. I talked to you a couple of weeks ago at the Bay State."

Scott tilts his head. "I don't think so, Mike. The Bay State's been closed for almost fifteen years."

"I know that." He takes a sip of coffee, his eyes following a Subaru around the corner. "You were drunker than shit."

Scott drops his gaze and grins. "That was my thing back in the day." He fiddles with his cup lid, the little tab not staying where it's supposed to. Scott cautiously sips the molten coffee drink and grimaces. 'One sugar' in Dunkin-land is more sugar than he consumes in a week.

"You were a goddamned mess," Mike says, not unkindly. "Took one to know one."

"Yeah, I seem to recall you being, uh . . . rosy-cheeked."

Mike holds out his cup. "Cheers."

They tap styrofoam.

"You were a late-nighter," Mike says.

"Yeah. My post-gig destination. Roll in drunk and belligerent at 2 a.m. for a coffee from The Night Man."

"The Night Man," the old man grunts.

"You still got that name tag?"

"Why the hell would I keep a goddamned name tag?"

Scott laughs, embarrassed. "I dunno, you were sort of a local icon."

"I was a drunk who got shitcanned for drinking on the job."

Jaub.

Scott sips his coffee. "How you doing now?"

He shrugs. "More on the wagon than off. You?"

Scott squints at the ceiling tiles. "Sober fourteen years or so." The 'or so' is a ruse. He knows the number to the day.

"Remember the round counter?" Mike asks. He points at the Dunkin workers assembling chicken wraps.

"Yeah, yeah. You or Linda would stand in the middle and hold court."

"Linda!" Mike muses. "The mouth on that one. She could talk paint off a wall."

"Yeah, and the regulars. Doris and Francis and the guy with the captain's hat! He always had that hat on!"

"Bobby Carbone. He died in '08."

"What was he, a hundred?"

Mike shrugs.

"Man, I dunno how many times I fell asleep in those booths," Scott muses.

"More like blacked out. I remember your brother always coming to collect you. You'd leave that car parked in the lot for a day or two."

"My Cougar!" Scott says with pride.

"Thing was a heap."

"That car was a *classic.*"

Mike snorts and stares out the window while Scott takes a bite of his donut. It's cold, hard, and smaller than he remembers.

"I've been waitin' for you to show up here. I thoughta you once I figured things out a little," Mike says. "You're the right kind of townie. I found you and told you to find me when you sobered up. I guess it took you awhile to get the message."

Scott shivers in the air conditioning. Mike motions towards his half-eaten donut. "That thing got delivered by a truck early this morning. You remember we used to make 'em here? Fresh every day, right in the back room." He points past a cardboard display of a cartoon man jogging with a Dunkin to-go cup. The man's tie flows over his shoulder as he chases a cartoon taxi. "Remember the window?"

"Yeah," Scott says, rolling with the abrupt subject-change.

"I want you to do me a favor," Mike says. "I want you to stand over there and try to remember the window."

"What are you talking about?"

"Go over there," the old man over-enunciates. "And try to remember the back room window."

Scott hits his weirdness limit. "I should get going, Mike."

"Oh, don't talk to me like I'm a goddamned child," Mike squints. "Go, I don't give a shit. You're a stubborn prick, you know that? I had to tell you seven damned times to write yourself a note!"

"Mike, I don't remember ever seeing you at the Bay Sta—"

"Just go stand behind the fucking cardboard thing!" As he raises his voice, the old guy's accent becomes more pronounced. *Cahdbaud.* "Ten seconds! Ten lousy seconds!"

Scott flicks his thumbnail against his cup lid. "Jesus," he mumbles. *What am I doing here?* "Fine."

"Superb," Mike grunts.

Scott sweeps sugar granules off the counter and crumples his bag into a ball. "Seeyuh, Mike." He tosses his trash and stands between the door and the display, knowing the old man will be watching. He turns to protest one last time, but Mike's attention has returned to the intersection.

"Alllll righty then," Scott says under his breath. With a quick glance at the cashier, he steps behind the cardboard display. The graphic applied to the wall depicts more cartoon people from all walks of life enjoying Dunkin Donut products. He remembers when this wall was beige, with tile running along the lower half. The weird little window was to his right, offering a view of the donut fryer. You could watch the baker work if you were here early enough. Was the window glass? Plexiglass? Plastic? Scott frowns as his memory gains focus, as the cartoon consumers fade away and the window emerges from the wall. He touches the chipped metal sill and flinches. The *cahdbaud* display, gone. He's standing in a Dunkin Donuts in 1995.

The room is silent.

The walls are decorated in brown and orange and tan, booths along the front wall. Bobby Carbone sits at the U-shaped counter in his red track suit and captain's hat, laughing at a Clinton joke. Mike stands in the center of the U, a bigger, younger, mustached Mike. Familiar Mike.

"The Night Man," Scott whispers.

Mike looks up with a grin. "You know it! What'll it be?" he calls across the room.

Scott has no goddamned idea what to say.

Mike wags a finger. "Medium one cream one sugar, right?"

A quiet affirmative sound comes out of Scott's open mouth.

"Thought so." Mike waddles towards the coffee makers, humming a tune. Scott stares at his name tag. 'MIKE - NIGHT MANAGER' it says, the -AGER blacked out with a Sharpie.

"Superb," Mike says, pressing the lid onto the cup. "Dollar nineteen."

"Did we, uh," Scott rasps, finding his voice. "Were we talking before?" He points at the row of empty brown booths, where someday there will be a long counter.

Mike shrugs. "I talk to folks all day long."

Scott shakes his head. "Just now, I mean," he clarifies, trying to peer into this middle-aged man's eyes, to find the old man he just saw.

Mike grins at Bobby and shakes his head in amusement. He has a nice little buzz going, buoying him through another Tuesday overnight shift. "You here for your car, kid?"

Scott turns towards the front windows. The entire room is reflected back at him. He peers through his own fluorescent-lit ghost to the darkness beyond. It's late, snowing, the traffic signal blinking yellow. His 1967 Mercury Cougar waits for him next to a mound of dirty New England snow, the road salt nibbling at her edges. Scott moves towards the door, his legs on autopilot, an unseen hook pulling him along.

"Dontya want your coffee?" Mike calls, more curious than bothered.

A frigid blast of wind whips snow in Scott's face. The Night

Man has neglected his shoveling and sanding duties, and Scott's sneakers fly out from under him immediately. He whacks the back of his head on the door frame and everything goes blinding white.

"My God, are you okay?"

A woman's voice. Scott squints up at her, a businesswoman's silhouette in the bright summer sun. She offers him a hand up. "Nah, I'm . . . Slipped on the, uh . . ." He squints at the lot. A Prius sits where the Cougar was, his Honda Element parked two spaces over. He picks himself up off the sidewalk. "I'm fine, thanks." Scott watches the woman walk inside and join the line. He cups his hands against the glass to look for Mike, old Mike, but the window seats are empty. He brushes away the gravel stuck to his palms and inspects the rip in the knee of his jeans.

"Well, this is fucking perfect," he mutters.

He tells the story the same way he'd describe a dream, an incredulous narrator dutifully relaying the facts. His brother Kevin's side of the phone call is silent.

"You drinking again, Scotty?" Kev finally asks.

"Christ, no!" Scott declares, as he picks at his salad. He's at The Roost, the cafe next to the truck-eating bridge, his phone wedged between his ear and shoulder. "Clear-headed and sober as shit."

"You sure this isn't some kind of late-game breakdown? You were a goddamned mess after the tour and Julie and everything."

Scott closes his eyes, focusing on a faint hum on the phone line. "Don't talk to me like I'm an asshole, Kev."

"Well, you *were* an asshole."

"That's true," he sighs. A Smithie at the next table scrolls through her Instagram. Like. Like. Like. *Doesn't she have any goddamned standards?*

"You said you saw the Cougar?" Kevin asks.

"Swear to goddamned god, Kev. Gold, vinyl top, covered with snow."

"I remember that thing on the Pike. Handled like a sideways rowboat."

Scott laughs.

"You were off the rails for a stretch, man," Kev reminisces. "Remember the time you drove yourself home? I still don't know how the fuck you managed it, you were so shitfaced. Left me in a goddamned snowstorm to boot, you prick." Kevin likes to bring these stories up. Featured attractions in the Scotty Was A Real Mess exhibit. Thanksgiving is always a blast.

"Yup."

"'Member when you and Jules were up at the quarry—"

"I get it, Kev. Drunk brother. Dark times. I get it. We all get it."

"You gonna tell Lindsay about this?"

Scott laughs too loud, coughing up a piece of red onion. The Smithie gives him a look. "Might keep this one under my hat for a bit." The hum intensifies. "Listen, Kev. This connection is shit. I'll let you go. Talk soon."

"Call me later, Scotty. I wanna know you're okay."

"Will-do." End Call.

On the cafe stereo, a half-assed band whinges about something pointless. Behind the weak songwriting and too-slick production, Scott can still hear the damned hum. He abandons his attempt at a healthy lunch and dumps his salad in the trash. The hum is louder near the trash can, a familiar sound he can't quite place. The hook is in him. He can't let it go. He kneels down, fusses with a shoelace, and listens. The hum emanates from behind the bus bin cart. He leans forward and knocks a stack of Coors over. The clatter and clack of glass bottles echoes through the liquor store.

"Jesus!" he shouts, steadying himself in the corner packy that used to be next to the truck-eating bridge. Pop's Liquors is cramped: walls lined with refrigerator cases, high shelves, windows covered with sun-bleached cigarette ads, a stained drop ceiling.

"What are you doing?" the owner yells, stepping down from the counter. He is Indian and definitely not named Pops, but Scott has always thought of him as Pops. It's difficult for Scott to not call him Pops.

"I'm *so* sorry!" Scott says, picking up a toppled case. At least two bottles have cracked, soaking beer into the much-abused carpet.

"Put it down. Get out." Not-Pops states.

"No, really, I—"

"You are a drunk. I do not have time for you. Go. Get out of my store."

Scott recalls he may not have been the most welcome customer here in the nineties. He pulls a wad of bills out of his pocket. "Listen, lemme pay for the beer. I'm so sorry, truly. I must've leaned wrong or something."

Not-Pops takes the money. "You sneak in here, you make a mess. Last week, you're in here saying 'birdy num-num' to me. You think I'm stupid? You think I don't know Peter Sellers?"

Scott is horrified. "I'm *so,* so sorry, sir. I used to drink—"

"Used to!" the store owner laughs. He picks up a case and puts it aside. "Get out. Go away now. I have no time for you."

Scott heads for the door, giving his mess as wide a berth as he can manage, apologizing again to this man he has probably slurred apologies to a hundred times before. Not-Pops looks at the money in his hand and throws the bills on the floor. "Monopoly dollars. You are a funny man."

Scott pauses at the threshold, every idiotic time travel movie coming back to him at once. "I— No. It's—" He sighs, defeated. "Real money." The refrigerator cases hum in disbelief.

"Birdy num-num! Very funny! Goodbye!" the owner waves, moving towards Scott, forcing him backwards. The door swings shut and he's standing outside the Roost.

A week stumbles by. Scott sleepwalks through work, avoiding downtown Northampton, postponing errands. Lindsay offers to buy him lunch twice, and twice he talks her into eating in Easthampton instead. When she requests a Friday date night, he knows he's caught, curving towards some prewritten fate. The hook is in him again, buried deep in his sternum. A big hook, a butcher's hook, dragging him towards town. He listens to her restaurant suggestions. He knows where they'll end up. Of course. Lindsay's mom got them that gift card. Dread settles in his bones as he cheerfully agrees. The Sierra Grille. It opened back in '03. It used to be the Bay State.

He hears the echoes as soon as they walk in the door: the

mushy, distant sound of a Marshall combo cranked too loud, a poorly-tuned bass, dull cymbals crashing. He smiles at his wife and ignores the rumble of his past. The hostess escorts them to a high table in the front room. The echoes reverberate through whatever twenty-year time hole lurks in the back room of the Sierra Grille, the room where the bands used to play—Hospital For The Dead, Steamtrain, Lonesome Stuntmen, fifty more. Scott asks about Lindsay's day. He tells her about arranging his new office at the house, his struggle setting up the wifi router. Dead-boring talk, anything to stave off the darkness overtaking the room, old shadows dulling the restaurant's lights. For the first time in seven years, Scott Sullivan needs a drink.

    He forces conversation for ten minutes before excusing himself. He walks past the bathrooms and into Sierra's rear dining room. He can picture the old wall-mounted light fixtures, red cloth napkins draped over the bulbs—somebody's attempt at ambiance. Tobacco permeates every surface of the room: the wood paneling, the flowery wallpaper, everyone's clothes. The volume rolls in like a tidal wave. The room is sweaty and stuffy, loud and obnoxious.

    "Rock star!" Anders hollers in his ear, slapping him on the back. He pushes a PBR into Scott's hands. "You look like shit! When'd you get back?"

    "Just now," Scott yells. A hardcore band from Connecticut wrecks shit in front of the pink-curtained bay window while bodies shove into each other. Not a lot of townies here tonight. Anders hollers something about Scott's music video. Scott nods and navigates around him, bound for the front room. He sees a familiar figure and his guts drop out of him. Julie slings her purse over her shoulder as her group of ladies abandon their table.

    "Jules!" he calls, pulling free of the audience.

    "Scott, you big fuck!" she beams, all teeth. She opens her arms. "Gimme a goddamned hug!" He squeezes her hard, smelling her hair and fighting the urge to kiss her. Her body language is wrong, her hairstyle is wrong. They aren't going out yet, they haven't broken up yet, she isn't dead yet. "Easy does it, fella," she says, pushing gently on his shoulders. He releases her, his eyes wet.

    "Sorry, Jules."

"I thought you were out on tour," she yells over the band. "Didya sell piles of CDs?"

"Oh, yeah. *Mountains*," he says dryly, giving a thumbs down. She laughs.

Tanya Dussault tugs on Julie's sleeve. "We were heading over to Hugo's because this—" Julie motions towards the commotion in the back room. "—is a shitshow." Candace and Beth wave at Scott and head for the door. "Come drink with us!" Julie says.

He takes a step and remembers Dunkin and Pops. "I think I've got to stay here. Hang out and talk with me."

She laughs and motions towards the kids abusing their instruments in the back room. "Are you retarded?" He cringes at the nineties. "Not a fucking chance, Sullivan!" She backs away, still laughing, Tanya steering her towards the door. "Gimme a call next week! Lates!"

And she's gone.

Scott peers through the plastic plants crowding the front window, watching the group of girls disappear into the muggy night. Behind him, Mike sits at Julie's table. The old, present-day former Night Man. Scott is too overwhelmed to be surprised. *Of course. Sure. Why not?* "I haven't seen her in a long time," he croaks, dropping into an empty chair.

Mike nods. "Great way to see old faces," he agrees.

Scott pushes his palms into his eye sockets and stares at the empty pint glasses between them. "What did you do to me?"

"Hell, I didn't do anything to you. I just showed you a thing I found."

"What are you doing here?"

"Same thing you are. Filling in the gaps."

Scott scratches his jaw. "I don't know what that means, Mike," he says numbly.

Mike shrugs. "I'm not sure I do, either." He stares at Scott for a long minute. "Listen, you used to overdo it, just like I did. I know that much about you."

"I did," Scott nods.

"Blacked out a lot, I bet."

"I've got a few blank spots, sure," Scott says.

Mike leans in close. "I think these" —he taps a fingernail against an empty glass— "are the blank spots."

Scott opens his mouth, but there's no good response to that statement. He closes it again.

"It's August, 1994," Mike says, twirling a finger. "The 17th. I peeked at Jerry's paper when I came in." He tilts his head towards the bartender. "I can't say for sure, but I'm guessing that right now, '94 me is unconscious, lying in his own piss on the floor of my old apartment over on Graves Ave. It's how I spent a lot of my weekends back then. What do you suppose you're doing right now? A hot Saturday night in the summer of '94?"

"August 17, 1994," Scott muses, shaking his head. "Goddamn it. I know right where I am," he sighs, picturing the flyer. "Trocadero, Philadelphia, opening for Lush." He motions towards the door. "She was right. I'm on tour."

"Had a few drinks that night, didya?"

Scott snorts. "They kicked me off the tour the next day, I think. I was a fucking wreck."

"Blacked out?"

"Way out."

"And here's that lost time." The old man places his hands on the smeared tabletop, fingers spread. "I'm up the street in my apartment. You're in Philly. We're both out."

Scott considers this, trying to reconcile Mike's theory with his grip on reality as of late. "This is fuckin' crazy," he whispers, squeezing his eyes shut.

Mike shrugs. "Sure. That's what you said when we talked last month. I was back here and I ran into you. The younger you," Mike says. "It was '97, maybe. We had the same goddamned conversation we're having now, except you were shitfaced and not listening. So I made you write yourself a note."

"Find the Night Man."

Mike nods. "Took you a month to get the message."

"Twenty years." Scott nods. "Are we time traveling?"

"Eh," Mike leans back. "Time watching, maybe? I dunno. I don't think we can change things. Whatever we do, it's already happened. Near as I can figure, this has all passed." He waves his hand at the wood paneled walls, the paneling that was ripped out during renovations in the early aughts and buried in the landfill up on Glendale Road. The landfill that has been closed for years.

"Should I bother trying to warn people about 9/11? That big tsunami? Trump?"

Mike shrugs. "You could try. But you're the drunk singer and I'm the drunk donut guy. Things sort of work out so no one's going to take what we say very seriously."

Scott laughs hopelessly. "So we're sort of . . ." He twirls a finger. "Participatory spectators."

"You're the college boy."

"SULLIVAN!" a voice bellows. A tanned boy strides in, gold crucifix, tight shirt. *Who the fuck is this?* The kid menaces over Scott, a compressed steel spring lubricated with testosterone and cologne. "You grab my sister's ass at Meyer's last week you fuckin' faggot?"

Scott squints. *What a shit-show.* "Probably?"

Sucker punch.

"Whoa! Are you alright?" the Sierra hostess asks, crouched, shaking him by the shoulders.

"Jesus!" Scott blurts, grabbing his nose as he rolls around on the carpet.

"Sir—"

"I, uh, jeez—"

"You fell—"

"Honey! What happened? Are you okay?" Lindsay is there.

He's on his feet, confused and embarrassed, steadying himself against the wall. "Clumsy. Bumped into a tabl—"

"Your nose is bleeding!"

He's a bit preoccupied for the rest of their date.

Scott slouches on the front porch, his morning coffee resting on a stack of old notebooks. He skims a beer-soaked journal from 1998, scribbling notes on a scrap of paper. He turns the rippled pages, cataloging parties and binges, trying to pinpoint times and places he may have blacked out. What he'll do with this data, he isn't sure. His twitches when his phone rings.

"Checkin' up on you," his brother says. "Making sure you still exist."

"I still exist."

"You see The Night Man again?"

Scott bites his pen cap. "For the sake of not opening an extremely large can of worms, let's say no."

"I don't like the sound of that, bro."

Scott shrugs and redirects. "Kev, you remember when you me and Julie tried to go up to the Quabbin?"

"You mean when the Cougar overheated and we ended up on the side of the road in Ware? Sure. Fun day."

"That was the day you hit on Jules while I went on the water run."

"Ah, camman!" Kev laughs. "She was fulla shit! I mean, no disrespect to the departed."

Scott doodles in the margin of the journal. "She was pretty fuckin' great, though, huh?"

"You're dwelling a lot lately, Scotty. Seeing ghost donuts and ghost cars and whatever."

"Yup," he agrees. "Maybe I'm playing catch-up. I haven't done a lot of . . ." He draws a spiral. "Reflection."

"Whelp, for the official record, I'll say Julie was a peach and your car was a death trap piece of shit."

"That car was *not* a piece of shit!"

"I seem to recall it sitting in my side yard for two and a half years, dear brother."

"Well, sure," Scott admits. "It was a piece of shit *then*, yeah. But *before* that."

"Oh, yeah, buddy," Kev says. "It was a real show piece 'til you took it out in the Meadows and put it over a rock wall." Scott groans at the memory. "Snapped a shock tower."

"Subframe, too," Scott adds. "Hell of a car."

"That thing woulda been worth something today if you'd taken care of it."

"I wasn't taking care of much in those days."

Kev pauses. "Just tell me you're not drinking again."

"I'm not, baby brother."

"Tell me you're not crackin' up."

Scott sips his coffee and watches the mail carrier walk up his neighbor's driveway. He hasn't met any of his neighbors yet. "Jury's out."

"I'm *so* sorry about last night," Scott says to the hostess. "I was on some crazy allergy medicine."

"No problem, sir! I *totally* get it," she says, organizing menus. "This summer's been *terrible*!"

"I may have lost something last night. I had a flash drive in my pocket. I was wondering if I could—?" he motions towards the back room.

"Absolutely! Go right ahead."

The afternoon sun streams through the big windows, making the room too bright for his memory of the place. He pretends to look for a thing that is in his pocket. He can already hear echoes of applause. *This gets easier every time*, he thinks, an observation which both satisfies and worries him. Someone pushes past him in the crowd. He hears fingers slide across amplified guitar strings.

Dennis stands at the mic in his rumpled suit and tie, clapping around a Miller Lite bottle. "'Nuther hand for Shannon and Justin!" There is cheering and clapping. Scott claps, too, slow and loud. Habit. Support the scene, man. "The open mic extravaganza rolls on. We got a slew of talented folks coming up in a bit," Dennis says, shielding his eyes against the single light pointed at him. "But I'm gonna break format here for a sec, cuz I want you to help me get a special guest on stage right about now."

Shit.

"Scotty Sullivan, everybody!" Dennis announces, pointing his bottle at Scott. The crowd whoops. "Sully, c'mon, brother!" Dennis cajoles, holding up a Strat. "One song." Scott steps forward and takes the guitar. "Heading out on his first headliner tour, folks," Dennis says. "Huge deal, right? Give him a hand!"

Scott digs a guitar pick out of his pocket. Julie is in the crowd with Tanya and the rest of them. He smiles at her but he doesn't think she smiles back. The light is in his eyes. He turns up the reverb on the abused Peavey perched on a chair behind him and strums the

Strat. It sounds terrible.

"All right," he says into the mic. "Settle the fuck down." He clears his throat. "This is for Jules." A few *awws* from the audience. He looks again and can't find her. He strums a C chord.

"Oh I ain't gonna make it."

The crowd hoots and howls at the lyric, a song they've heard too many times. But hell, now it's on the radio—*Boston* radio—and there's a video on MTV, too. Even the jaded scenesters manage to get behind his minor hit. It's a rallying call, a thing worth cheering for.

Scott sings and thinks about Jules. About what a saint she was for putting up with his bullshit, about how smart she was to bail out while the going was good. This is his memory of her. He frames her as an innocent person caught in the wake of his mess, a side character in the larger narrative of his rise and fall. She dumped him, and was right to do so, and the flawed genius earned another wound to tend.

But it wasn't *quite* that simple, was it? Wasn't it truer to say Julie moved to Chicago that summer to *escape* his bullshit? Can't he recall a phone call where she said *precisely* that? He didn't put her on a 10-speed bike that morning, and he wasn't driving the garbage truck that ran her over, but he most definitely helped put her in Chicago, didn't he? In her story—the series of events making up *her* life—he's got to admit he featured in there pretty prominently, right?

His fingers form chords and his lyrics come out of his mouth, sober and somber and clear. The song is twenty years rehearsed and performed, imprinted into his guts. He gives it to the room, smooth as whiskey. The audience is rapt, the local hero burning like a fistful of road flares in the corner of a dark room. *Their* room.

Julie sobs by the back door while Tanya rubs her shoulders. She's crying because he's leaving for tour tomorrow, the big tour, the headliner tour that's gonna Hindenburg spectacularly. *But she's not crying about that, right Scotty?* She's crying because they just broke up. And maybe she didn't dump him because she was jealous and selfish, which fits with the story he wants to tell. Maybe she's crying because *he* just dumped *her*? Rock-and-roll man wanting his freedom on the road? Frightened boy who doesn't know what to do with the love she keeps pushing at him? How did this shit go down, exactly?

A tear runs down his cheek as Julie's friends coax her out the back door. He watches and keeps playing. The same hook of time that's been dragging him along pins him to the stage like a bug specimen, compelling him to finish his minor hit. The hook stops him from running into the snow-covered back alley. No patching things up, no apologies, no begging her to not-go so she can be not-dead. The hook pierces his body and the song pours out of the wound. His tears and cracked voice cement his legend as the sensitive drunk troubadour. God, he loves that legend, that role, that lens he can bear to see himself through. Townies have told him about this performance over the years, one of many stories he couldn't recall but nodded along with anyway. All part of the mythos of Scotty Sullivan, a mythos he could buy into without ever remembering.

He sings the last chorus, the crowd howling along. *"No, I don't think we're gonna make it,"* they bleat. The last chord rings out and the room erupts. He hands the Strat back to Dennis, desperate to get the fuck out of the cheering, noise-filled decade. A hard slap on the back. Get ya a beer? *Beer, beer, buy the fucking alcoholic a beer.* He waves the offer off, keeps moving. "Since when does Sully turn down a drink?" someone barks. "Since 2001!" Scott shouts, head down. They laugh at their lovable drunk and his nonsensical horseshit.

The next act starts a song and Scott fades to the back of the room, to the shadows between the napkin-covered light fixtures. The booths in the back are piled high with winter coats, guitar cases, and empty bottles. In the shadows, he sees a familiar pair of boots dangling out of the furthest booth, the Doc Martens he bought on Newbury Street when he was in college. *Someone punch me,* he wishes. *Someone push me out the goddamned door. Someone let me off the hook.*

Scott wanders into the Bay State's front room and slumps at the same table he and Mike had sat at the night before (Or twelve years ago? Whatever.) He pulls his phone out of his pocket. 2:30 in the afternoon, no cell tower to connect to, no wifi. The Molson clock near the door says it's past midnight. He slides a coaster from under an empty bottle and tears at it concentrating on his hands and their busywork. Is he sitting at the Bay State doing this? Is he standing in the corner of Sierra Grille in a coma, or did he disappear? Is time passing there? Is he married to his wife, or hasn't he met her yet? Is this his present or his past? How does he opt out of this shit?

His brother pushes through the front door, a wintery gust and his ex-girlfriend following him in. It's young Kev. Mullet Kev. Ripped jeans Kev. Whipped by Heather Kev. "Where's he at?" he calls to Jerry. The bartender arches an eyebrow towards the back room. Kev and Heather trudge past Scott's table, stomping snow off their boots as he slouches lower. Maybe he doesn't need to worry about being seen, because they never saw him, so there's no way they could see him, right?

Kev and Heather emerge from the open mic crowd a minute later, Sully hanging between their shoulders. The audience serenades them with chants of "SULL-Y!" Kev pretends to be amused. Heather doesn't bother. How many times did his little brother have to haul his ass home, bail his ass out, back in these good old days? Kev and Heather walk the drunk out the door and into the cold night.

Scott contemplates a drink, just one or seven, wondering what kind of *Inception*/Russian nesting doll shit he could conjure up if he got blackout-drunk in a time-rewind of being blackout-drunk. He stares at the little ceramic heads mounted over the bar: a sea captain, a leprechaun, a sheikh. Outside, a guttural rumble that twists his heart, that sharp nostalgia-ache he's had just about enough of, for Christ's fucking sake.

Scott tips his chair back and peers out the front window. Kev and Heather bicker on the sidewalk next to his idling Cougar, his gold-and-rust baby. They've wrangled Sully into the passenger seat and now Kev wants to get the fuck home.

"I drove you out here in the middle of a snowstorm," Heather says. "The least you could do is walk me back to my friggin' car." She motions towards Main Street, and Kev's mullet nods a reluctant affirmative. He pats the Mercury's peeling vinyl top and says "Back in five." Sully fogs up the passenger window, out cold. They shuffle up the sidewalk, another argument quietly brewing. *Two more years of misery, then she'll dump him,* Scott recalls. *Thank fuck.*

Scott watches the puffs of exhaust from the Cougar's tailpipe. *The heater core in that car was for shit,* he thinks. *They'll be home before it warms up.* He leans in the doorway and dangles a leg out into the winter night. Will his foot land on a hot summer sidewalk? Does it matter? Is he done here or not?

"'ey, Bozo! Close the fuckin' door!" the bartender shouts at his back.

"Sorry, Jer!" He hops over the threshold and lands ankle-deep in snow. The wind cuts through at his thin shirt.

"Fuck." He hops up and down. "Fuck!" He jams his hands into his pockets as the hook drags him around the front of the car. Motor oil cooks on the manifold, the smell sweet and familiar and unbearably sad. *Shit.* Scott opens the door, the hinges howling like hunting dogs, and drops into the ripped vinyl seat. *Thunk.*

Scott rests his palms on the frigid steering wheel and looks straight ahead, delaying looking at his passenger for a few more seconds. He runs a finger along the speedometer bezel and inspects the shit job he did installing the CD player. He presses the Eject button. *Click, whir.* Built To Spill's *Keep It Like A Secret* slides out. He exhales a white puff of breath, turns, and takes a good hard look at himself. There sits Scotty Sully Sullivan, out cold in the cold, his face mashed against the passenger window.

"How we doin', Sully?" he asks himself. "How we holdin' up? How'd we turn out?" The blower fan groans as snow accumulates on the windshield. He flips on the wipers. Sluggish. Inadequate for the job, along with the heater and the engine and the brakes.

"We let this old car down," Scott says. "We let Jules down. We let this town down." He rests his head on the wheel, the engine vibrating through his skull. He eyes Sully. "I let you down." He weeps, snot and tears smearing his numb face. "I'm awfully sorry about that, Sully." He wants to punch or hug this dipshit man-boy, maybe both at once, squeeze the stupid right out of him.

Scott pokes in the ashtray, jabbing at cigarette butts and pennies and guitar picks. "We're not out of the woods yet," he says, clearing his throat. "To be honest, we're not even all the way *into* the woods yet. You got three more years of this coming down the pike."

He buckles the lap belt and revs the straight six. "I vote we take the ol' Cougar down to the Meadows and try our damnedest to crack the shock tower a little ahead of schedule," he announces. "Any objections?" Sully doesn't say a word. Scott nods and shifts the

Merc-O-Matic into Drive. Northampton is silent and white in the rear view.

"Hold on, kid," he says, letting the Cougar roll out onto the unplowed road. "It's gonna be a real shit-show."

Scott Sullivan drives himself home.

Tom Pappalardo has output a comic collection, an illustrated novel, a collection of essays, and several albums. More info at tompappalardo.com

The Science Fiction Tab

The Resurrections of Amy Yakimora
James Rosinus

     Amy's Jeep Gladiator slid into the village, tractionless despite the four-wheel drive, on the slick, thin layer of ash that came down in a dry flurry. It wasn't much as villages go, just a handful of one- and two-room houses and two small shops. A bar, plain stucco with a hand-painted sign on the side reading simply: *Cerveza* in a clean blue script, and a store, bright yellow with an equally bright blue bench out front used as a combined community center and bus stop. She'd been to both before. They looked deserted now—as they should be. Everyone was supposed to have evacuated by this morning at the latest. Amy honked the horn a couple of times, just in case.
     No answer. *That's good*, she thought. *But . . .* A couple of the villagers were elderly, and one of *them* was quite deaf. Leaving the engine running, she climbed down from the cab. As she did, the ground shook, a big tremor this time, knocking her to her knees. When it finally stopped, she could see out of the corner of her eyes, above the jungle canopy at the edge of the village, a thick, roiling, monstrous pillar of smoke, a vast cloud of ash and fire boiling up into the stratosphere, lightning coursing and dancing around its edges as it grew. Twenty kilometers away, the mountain had blown up.
     She scrambled to her feet and ran, slipping, to each doorway. She pounded on the door frames yelling as loudly as she could. No answers. No responses. *Good. Time to go*, she thought.
     The sound wave from the explosion arrived. Louder than thunder, louder than an artillery barrage, it hit her with the force of a solid object knocking her down again. Trees bent with the pressure, some snapped. Ash swirled up and around as if in some catastrophic snow globe.

And then she saw it.

Movement. Underneath the bench in front of the store.

Amy scrambled across the square, running half bent over and dropped to all fours to peer underneath. A dog. She'd seen it a couple of times before. The village dog, short haired, skinny, yellow mutt. Fed by some, owned by none. And now left behind. It cowered as far back against the wall as it could.

"*Aqui, perro. Aqui,*" Amy called softly gesturing with one hand. The dog didn't move. "Come on, pup. We don't have time for this."

She lowered herself to the ground, getting ash up her nose. "*Bueno, perro. Aqui. Bueno.*" The terrified animal flinched back even further although the tip of its tail beat a hopeful tattoo against the wall.

"*Aqui*, damn it!" Amy lunged and managed to grab hold of a front paw. She dragged it as quickly as she could, trying to be gentle at the same time. The mutt didn't resist but let her pull it out from under the bench and pick it up. She cradled it in both arms as she ran back to the Jeep.

The ground shook again as Amy put the dog in the cab of the Gladiator. She knew she was cutting it too close. She climbed up into the vehicle, leaned on the horn one more time, and headed out, the dog whining softly in the passenger seat.

The ash, which had been drifting lazily, picked up as soon as the road narrowed at the edge of the jungle and became a hot, dry blizzard by the first kilometer. The wipers were little use, smearing ash across the windscreen, streaking and scratching the glass. Less than a meter in front of the hood the headlights reflected back creating a shifting gray wall. Amy slowed to a crawl.

She didn't want to. Slowing down scared her. The edge of the ash cloud could be ten meters ahead or two kilometers. There was no way of telling until she reached it and burst out into clear air and sunshine—if she ever did. The cloud was rolling down and out from the volcano's cone and the only chance to get from under it was to move faster than the front. But she couldn't see.

The ash, smoke and dust interfered with the Jeep's navigation systems. She drove by feel and memory. She'd been down this road dozens of times from airfield to base camp and back again. It wasn't good enough. The collision alert went off randomly when nothing was in front of her, or not at all until she saw the trunk of a tree looming directly in her path. She turned too late and then too soon, tires edging off the rough pavement, overcompensated, pinballing slowly from one side of the road to the other.

She stopped for a moment to reorient herself, catch her breath and clear the tears from her eyes. She knew she was falling behind. It was getting hot in the cab despite the air-conditioner blasting at full power. The dog whined.

"I know, I know," she said, and eased the truck forward again.

It started to rain. Thick, heavy drops spattered the windscreen. Amy pictured the diffuse mass of micro particles spewed out by the volcano into the humid stratosphere, high above the roiling cloud she was struggling through, acting as seed stock for the moisture in the air, rain drops forming and growing around them, plummeting down on her in the ash covered jungle and she laughed in spite of herself.

The dog looked up. "Sorry," she said.

Once a scientist, always a scientist.

The wet ash was even worse for visibility. It clung to the wipers like plaster and the additional weight slowed them down. Hot gray mud built up on the glass. The roadway became slick.

She down-shifted but the wheels still spun randomly, catching on the asphalt one second, sliding as if on glare ice the next. A half kilometer on the engine balked. Amy's heart skipped a beat with it. She whispered, "No. No, no, no." The dashboard lit up with warnings as the engine overheated.

The lurching worsened and it didn't surprise her when the engine seized up completely. Amy sighed, dropping her head to the steering wheel. It took a minute before the shakes started. And the tears. She didn't believe in miracles. The rest of the expedition was long gone. No one was coming for her. No one would find her even if they wanted to try. She had no idea where she was along the road or how deep in the ash cloud. She would be lost instantly in the zero-visibility gray crud if she left the vehicle even if she could breathe in that hellish mess out there—which she doubted. The heat in the cab was getting worse now that the air-conditioning was dead and she could imagine how bad it was outside. There were no other alternatives, no more choices, no more decisions to make.

Amy found that realization calming. She blinked her tears away and took a deep breath, letting it out in a long sigh. Reaching across to the passenger seat, she gently pulled the dog to her. Cuddling it in one arm, she scritched behind its ears with her free hand.

"I'm sorry, *perrito*. I fucked up." The dog licked her hand. The heat was getting worse. She couldn't concentrate. She continued petting the dog, wondering if her lethargy was due to the heat or the diminishing oxygen in the sealed cab. *How would one measure that? Was there a synergistic effect? Does the increasing temperature affect my metabolism and increase—or decrease—my oxygen uptake?* Either way, she was becoming drowsy and the heat didn't bother her as much anymore.

She scratched under the dog's chin and smiled to herself.
Once a scientist, always a scientist.

* * *

The dig site sprawled over scores of hectares. It was slow, difficult work. The ground consisted of volcanic depositions and, below the first meter where overgrowth roots had broken it down into new soil, was rock hard.

Most of the work was concentrated around the remains of two small villages. *Actually*, thought Phillipe, *'village' is a bit grandiose for these collections of small houses and shops. Pompeii it isn't.* But it was his dig. Not many guys got to be Director of a dig this early in their careers.

And now something interesting just might have happened. His crew using the ground-penetrating radar to map the old road had found a pocket. A pocket with a large metallic component. A dig team was on it now as Santiago searched through contemporary reports on the eruption. The area had been evacuated before the main eruption but there had been a few casualties, including a small number of missing, presumed dead but never found.

"Hey, Boss?" The head of Santiago's road crew called in from where they were working. His face was redder than usual. Sweat ran down his forehead and nose. "Come on down. We hit metal."

"I'm on my way. Twenty minutes."

They had set a tarp over the pit to provide some shade. Before the eruption a hundred years ago all this had been jungle but nowadays it was too hot and dry for most trees and the sun bore down on scrub plain baking everything and everyone in it.

When Santiago arrived he noticed the two autodiggers idle at the side of the shallow hole. Instead, three humans were neck deep in the pit hacking and scraping at the neolith with picks and shovels. While the robots were expensive and it pained him to see them just sitting there, they didn't always properly identify anomalous objects. Humans were less efficient in terms of volumes moved but much better at delicate work. They were being careful not to touch the flat metal roof rising half a meter above the current floor of the pit or the vertical sheet of glass descending into the rock from it. The paint on the roof, mostly worn or burned away, might have been red once upon a time. Santiago approved the crew chief's decision. Reluctantly.

"See if you can clear away the windscreen. Let's take a look inside before we break in."

Two of the men dropped their picks, got down on their knees and began chipping and rubbing away around the glass with hand tools, brushes and cloth rags. Slowly they revealed more and more of the windscreen.

"What do you see?" called the chief.

One of the men looked up, shrugging. "It's too dark."

The chief tossed a flashlight down and the man shone it into the cab.

"¡Dios mio!" he cried scrambling back onto his seat, dropping the light. "There's someone in there!"

Santiago climbed down to see for himself. Through the heat-darkened, pitted glass he could just make out the figure of a woman. She looked to be asleep, chin down on her chest.

"Is she dead?"

Santiago snorted. "It's been over a hundred years. *Sí*. I'm sure she's quite dead."

"But how does she look . . . like *that*?"

"Mummified. Dry heat. Lack of air. Ever see a fireproof safe? When it's sealed up tight no air can get in. Nothing burns no matter how hot it is outside." Of course, that didn't prevent the contents of the fireproof safe from heating up, just short of burning, and if you opened it too soon, before it cooled down, *then* the contents would burst into flame. Still, a century should be more than enough to recover, even from a volcano.

"What's that?" The man's curiosity overcame his shock. He pointed at the woman's lap.

"Looks like a dog." Santiago stood. He called up to the crew chief. "O.K., dig it out but don't open it up, yet. Let me know when it's clear. How long, do you think?"

The chief rubbed his chin. "Give me three days."

Back in his tent as the sun dropped behind the volcano and the air began to cool a bit, Santiago assessed today's discovery. There was a vehicle of some kind down there. What it was, what it was doing there, that would come later. What condition the occupant was in, Saturday—or Friday depending on the speed of the diggers—would tell. *I may have found one*, he thought. And then again . . .

He decided to take a chance.

Herr Doktor Professor Gerhardus let the call go to voicemail. He seldom answered anymore, preferring to pick and choose who, when and how to respond. There were always too many interruptions as it was. He did glance at the caller ID and recognized the name of a graduate student from a few years back, bright fellow, good teaching assistant, serious. Worth a return call.

An hour later he took a break and listened to his messages. Most were the usual interruptions: trivial, bureaucratic, redundant. The call from the grad student was not.

"Hello, Professor. This is Phillipe Santiago. I took your advanced class four years ago." Yes, Gerhardus remembered him. "I'm calling to see if your standing offer is still in effect. I may have found something for you."

Yes, the standing offer was still in effect. He made it at the end of every year to his graduating class. He could never tell if anyone paid attention, what with their heads full of exams, papers and visions of freedom. But he made it anyway, just in case. It seemed Mr. Phillipe Santiago, at least, heard the offer, remembered it and thought he might be able to fulfill it.

Gerhardus activated the phone. He would have to make sure.

He was still surprised when his old professor returned his call.

"What have you got?" Santiago recognized Professor Gerhardus' voice and peremptory tone. *Some things never change.*

"I'm not sure, yet, sir. We're still digging. But I thought you should know right away. In case it pans out." Phillipe described the contents of the pit as known so far.

"Yes, yes. That is good. I will make preparations at my end. Keep me informed immediately."

Professor Gerhardus' agent arrived in camp just as Santiago ended his call with the digger crew chief. He left his tent as the rental car glided to a stop.

"Your timing is exceptional," he said as the man, older, thin, well-dressed, one might say dapper got out. "If you're ready, we can go directly to the site."

But then the man introduced himself, much to Santiago's confusion. He wasn't an anthropologist. Or an archaeologist. Or any other kind of scientist at all. The professor had sent an auditor.

"I don't mean to be rude but I thought you'd have some sort of relevant technical background." Santiago was not expecting an accountant.

The man smiled. "It's sort of a hobby of mine. I am auditor for this dig as well as a couple other of Professor Gerhardus' grants. I shouldn't need much time with your books. And the professor said I could have a private tour of the site. I am delighted to take up your offer. Then I will look at your numbers."

Reluctantly, Santiago nodded. He started to collect his gear when the auditor said, "Ah. You have a headband. May I see it?"

Santiago handed the plain, cream-colored ceramic circlet to him. It wasn't quite a full circle. There was a small gap between the two ends with a little green light at the tip of the right hand end and it widened out a bit in the middle. The auditor weighed it in his palm, turning it over, running his hands over the smooth surface. "I haven't seen one in person before. How does it work? Is it comfortable? Is it yours?"

"It belongs to the university," Santiago said, taking it back and depositing it carefully in his field bag. *Did he seriously think a postdoc could afford something like this?* "They want complete records of the dig—as much data as they can get, any way they can. I can wear it for an hour or two before the strain gets to me. Headaches. It takes some getting used to. But it allows me to control some of the equipment mentally and it records everything so I don't need to enter notes manually which leaves my hands free. It'll probably get easier with practice. The inner side, the part against your skin is basically a bunch of electrodes and the outer edge is a series of transmitters with a ridiculous amount of processing power sandwiched between. Other than that, I have no idea how it works from a technical perspective."

"Fascinating."

In fact, Santiago thought it made him look foolish. *Pretentious. Like a princeling from a fairy tale.* "Do you need to collect anything from your vehicle?"

The auditor patted his faux leather shoulder bag. "Everything I need is right here. Shall we go? The sooner we go the sooner we get back the sooner I complete the audit and return to civilization. And air conditioning."

Santiago called the crew chief again. "I'm coming down now. Clear the pit."

The two men bounced down to the excavation in one of the site's modified golf carts.

The truck rested at the bottom of a pit several times larger than when Santiago saw it last. It was completely uncovered except for the undercarriage still resting on a bed of rock. It sat on metal rims, the tires melted and burnt during the eruption. It was mostly bare metal, the paint flaked, chipped or burnt away when the truck was buried. Santiago was confident it could be reconstructed from the residue and dust found in the spoil of the pit. The diggers had carved out a space all around the vehicle just wide enough for a person with an extra carve-out by the driver's side door to allow it to open.

Santiago looked over to the crew chief. "No one's opened it?"

"Waiting for you, *jefe*," he nodded.

"O.K., then." Santiago pulled the ceramic band from his bag and settled it over his head. Then he clambered down into the pit, followed by the digger chief and the auditor. He stood by the driver's door while the others remained up front by the grille. There was barely enough space for one in the carve out. He took a deep breath and said, "Begin recording."

The headband came to life. *Much better than a notepad*, he thought. Not only could he keep his hands free while it recorded visual and audio, it ran several sophisticated environmental and chemical tests in real time. Two drones slaved to it made their own records from above, slowly circling the site then ducking under the tarp.

Several highly unlikely scenarios flashed through his mind as he stood with his hand on the door latch, irrational visions of his mummy bursting into flames or crumbling to dust as soon as he cracked the door and let fresh oxygen in. With another deep breath, he yanked the handle.

Nothing happened. The door stayed shut. He tried again.

Again, nothing except a groan of ancient metal. One of the drones circled on down to take a closer look. *Wonderful*, thought Santiago, reconsidering the advantages of using a notebook. You could leave a lot of humiliation out of a manual record. He mentally ordered it to back off and it did, a bit.

He put both hands onto the handle and pulled hard, bracing his feet and leaning back against the wall of the pit.

The door screeched in protest. But it moved. A centimeter, two, ten. Another two-handed pull and it opened enough that he could twist around and slip a shoulder into the gap. Now he could push instead of pull and the door slowly gave way amid a chorus of protesting metal.

Santiago stood bent over, rear end pressed against the door frame, arms stretched out in front, palms against the door, gasping. The crew chief laughed. "Next time, let the *braceros* do it."

I'll probably go the rest of my career without another 'next time' like this, thought Santiago. He looked up over his shoulder. *Well, that answers the digger's question.* Only the truly dead could remain unmoved by that racket. He began narrating.

The woman sat behind the wheel, eyes closed, one hand by her side the other resting on the dog, chin down against her chest. She was young, around Santiago's own age. Asian by ethnicity, probably, although there was a chance of local aboriginal mix. The mummification made it hard to be sure. Black hair cropped short. Height, 160-170 centimeters. Hard to tell, sitting like that. 50-55 kilos. Again, hard to tell from the position of the body, not to mention the desiccation from mummification. He noted her clothing, lack of tools and other details of the interior of the truck including the presence of the dog in her lap. Short hair, yellow, indeterminate breed.

And that was it. He certainly couldn't remove her by himself. They'd have to widen the space around the door even more before they could attempt that.

He looked directly at the young woman, said, "Welcome to the 22nd Century," and turned away to speak with the digger chief.

When he got to the front of the truck the auditor said, "May I?"

"I suppose. Just don't touch anything or move her."

"Did you get everything?" the chief asked as the auditor squeezed past and went around to the open door.

"As much as I can *in situ.*"

The chief nodded. "Do we have people with the skill to remove her without damaging her or do I need to call in some specialists?"

Santiago considered for a moment. "Grad students from the other sites can do it—with supervision. Have your men widen the space around the door. The other side, too. Someone will have to be inside the cab."

"Speaking of which . . . Where's that guy you brought with you?" The crew chief was looking over Santiago's shoulder.

Santiago spun. The auditor was nowhere to be seen. "Damn it! Get out of there!" he yelled.

The auditor emerged from the cab looking more satisfied than embarrassed.

"What did I say? What were you doing in there?" Santiago tried to control his temper. This man could ruin his project, cost him the remainder of his grant and any future chances.

"Sorry." He sounded anything but. "Fascinating, isn't it?"

"Yes." Santiago indicated the ladder to the surface. "That's more than enough for one day. Let's get back to base. You have an audit to perform, I believe."

"Hey, Boss?" the crew chief caught up to him at the golf cart. "The guys want to know if it's OK for them to open the hood."

Santiago almost said, "No," automatically but caught himself. Instead, he said, "Why?"

The crew chief looked a little sheepish. He shrugged. "They really want to see an internal combustion engine."

Santiago considered for a second. It was obvious the crew chief included himself in 'they.' "Yeah. OK. Make sure the drone records everything." He stared at the auditor just settling into the cart. "And don't touch anything else."

The auditor spent less than an hour going over Santiago's records before giving the project a clean bill of health. As the car carrying the man back to civilization glided away, Santiago thought, *If that was an audit, perhaps I should start embezzling from the supplies fund.*

Dr. Gerhardus recognized the number of the caller and picked up immediately.

The voice on the other end said, "The offering was good. I was able to obtain two sets of samples."

"Two?"

"There was a dog."

Gerhardus contemplated that for a moment. "I'll take them both. We will need to do some testing first. Best not to waste the critical material."

The voice asked, "Where do you want them sent?" Gerhardus gave detailed shipping instructions, long rehearsed.

"And the finds, themselves?"

"Have one of the museums accept them. Gratefully. I don't care which."

* * *

Luciana struggled to catch her breath and control her racing heart. She glanced at the woman walking beside her, fearful Sister might have noticed, but the older woman plodded on a half-step ahead and gave no indication anything was amiss. Of course, that's what she would do if this were a Test. This had all the earmarks of a Test. Luciana hated being Tested but she'd never failed one, yet. That she knew of.

She concentrated instead on her immediate surroundings, bringing her stimulus response down while she examined what had—might have—just happened. The ancient stone floor, polished by decades of use, was smooth beneath her slippers. The tall thick walls of stuccoed plaster absorbed much of the late afternoon heat while the heavy dark roof beams arching above in the shadows deadened what little ambient sound there was. Luciana let the dim coolness overtake her while she cast her mind back over the last two minutes.

She was sure—almost sure—she had seen someone where there should never have been someone to see. Luciana was alone—was supposed to be alone—here. Except, of course, for the Sisters. And the Groundskeepers. And the Headmaster. But, certainly, no other students, no other girls. It was just a fleeting glance, out of the corner of her eye, all the way down at the end of a cross hallway while she and Sister were passing through the intersection.

Another girl. Maybe. A part of a head, one eye visible, short black hair like her own, a shoulder in white pajamas like her own. And gone. That was it.

If this was a Test, what aspect of her training were they

Testing? Did they want her to report the sighting? To what purpose? Out in the field, whenever that might be, there would be no one to report to. And, with how seriously they had drilled security protocols into her head, would they risk bringing in someone from outside just to Test her observational skills one more time? The more she thought about it, the less sense it made.

The alternative was scarier. Someone has broken in. She knew security here was antiquated, almost non-existent compared to the systems she was being trained to break. That was intentional. The whole compound was cut off from the outside world. Physical security was what the Groundskeepers were supposed to be for.

When they arrived at Luciana's chamber door, she knew she should say something. Whether what she saw was a Test or a security breach, speaking up was the right course. Yet, as Sister pushed the heavy wooden door open, Luciana held her tongue.

Later, when she was alone, she told herself she hesitated because she wanted to solve the mystery on her own, as she would have to in the field. She carefully committed all the details to memory so she could prove she had seen it if it turned out to be a Test after all and she was questioned.

After two weeks without another sighting or a hint of anything amiss and no raised eyebrows from Cook Sister, no sidelong glances from Escort Sister, no innocuous questions cleverly designed to initiate a directed conversation from Combat Sister, or any of the others, Luciana reluctantly concluded she'd been wrong.

Luciana woke instantly, motionless, fully alert. Her room was dark. The moon had set. *So, after 2:30, then.* She did a quick scan without even thinking about it. Everything in its place.

Another tap on the door.

Luciana sat up, slid the sheet off, swung her legs over the side of her cot, and felt the cool stone floor on her bare feet. With practiced skill, she glided silently across to the door and pressed her ear flat against the thick wood. She could hear nothing.

A Test?

She flashed on the possible alternatives.

Most obvious and least likely: trying to see if she would fail to wake or, worse, open the door while half asleep, unprepared. They knew better than that by now.

Or: she could open the door in attack mode. Or not in attack mode. Without knowing who—or what—was on the other side, adopting one stance or the other was making assumptions or, worse, guessing.

She did have some clues. There had been no third tap on the door—yet. Which meant whoever was on the other side had at least a passing familiarity with Luciana's skill set, abilities and habits. And they were patient. She positioned herself against the wall, out of the arc that would be made by opening the door and with a quick hand motion flung it wide coming face-to-face, literally, with the one thing she hadn't expected—herself.

The girl facing her was slightly taller and more fully built but with the same roundish face, high, shallow cheeks, and wide-set black eyes. Luciana consciously suppressed her fight/flight response but was aware she was breathing hard, trying to control the adrenaline surge.

Herself smiled at her. One corner of the same smallish mouth with the full lower lip crooked up into that familiar half smile, including the dimple.

"Well? Are you going to invite me in?"

Luciana put her blanket on the stone floor and they knelt at opposite corners facing each other for a long minute.

Luciana had regained control quickly although she was still embarrassed about losing it in the first place. Now she studied the girl. There were differences. The girl was marginally taller. Her black hair was not cut quite as short, but that was not a defining characteristic. There were other differences which she suspected were brought on by puberty most of which were concealed by the same heavy, plain white, loose, belted cotton pajamas Luciana wore. There were similarities, too, more than just looks. She noted they both sat the same way, on knees and heels, toes curled under, hands resting lightly on knees, poised to launch upward with a strong thrust in response to any threat.

Luciana spoke first. "Was it you I saw at the end of the hall two weeks ago?"

The girl smiled. "Yes."

"Was that the first time you saw me?"

"No."

"Who are you?"

That smile again. Friendly but shyly humorous, possessing a joke known but not shared—yet. "My name is Irina. I'm your sister."

Under the circumstances, given the similarities, it was a believable assertion. Luciana had never seen anyone who had undergone plastic surgery, but she was reasonably confident this person had not.

"I didn't know I had a sister." She knew the definition, but Sisters were the women who taught her and cooked and cleaned, and escorted her from place to place. *A* sister. *Her* sister. That was different. There were obligations—opportunities—inherent in having *a* sister, *her* sister.

"I didn't know I had a sister," she repeated. "I didn't know there was anyone else here." Not counting, of course, the Sisters. Or the Headmaster. Or the Groundskeepers.

A thought occurred. "Are there others? Like us?"

"One that I know of," Irina said.

"And she looks like us?"

"Of course. Her name is Helene and she's a year older than me."

"How old are you?"

"I'm fourteen."

"I'm eleven," Luciana said. A slight note of pride crept into her voice. She recognized it but couldn't help it. She was not in control and knew it. All of her defenses were down.

Irina laughed lightly. "You're in for a treat next year. You'll begin edged weapons training. Knives and swords to start. And later on glaives and shuriken and hatchets and . . ." Evidently, Irina really liked edged weapons. She caught her breath. "Fun stuff. Also, deep programming."

Luciana was more partial to the idea anything could be a weapon, whatever was to hand. She had an occasional game she played in her mind where she would identify one item within her reach—no more than one meter away—and imagine how she could kill Sister with it. The most difficult one had been the scrambled eggs she'd had for breakfast one morning. The most satisfying one had been her toothbrush.

They talked for another ten minutes. About the compound. The Headmaster. They shared some Sisters, Cook Sister and a couple of the Teacher Sisters in particular. Luciana felt her guard dropping. Then . . .

She noted the subtle change in posture as Irina shifted her weight onto her right foot. She adjusted her own weight and center of gravity to counter any surprise attack but Irina pushed up and rose gracefully to her feet, hands still resting lightly on her thighs. "I really must be going, now," she said.

Luciana rose also, a little too quickly, not quite as fluid or graceful. "But, why?"

"Because I'm not supposed to be here, and if we want to do this again, I must not be found out." Luciana felt her cheeks warm with shame she hadn't recognized the obvious.

"How did you get here? Where do you live?" So many things hadn't occurred to her. She felt like a child. If this was a Test, she was failing.

"I live here, in the compound, of course," said Irina. "As to how? Carefully, and with practice. Security here is dumb. Surely, you've noticed. The stuff they're training us to take down is so much more sophisticated than what they use here."

Luciana was aware. "Nothing to do with the Standards Committee."

"Nothing to do with the Standards Committee," Irina nodded.

Irina cracked the door open and peered down the hall but, before she could leave, Luciana reached out and touched her sleeve. "Will you come back?" Now that she knew of Irina's existence, knew that she had a sister, maybe more than one, knew that she was not alone, not being alone—which had never even been a subject of concern before—suddenly was the most important thing in the world.

Irina smiled again. "Yes."

"When?"

"When I can." The door closed. She was gone. A dream. A dream that kept Luciana up for the rest of the night.

Irina never returned. It took several weeks before Luciana could admit to herself that she wouldn't. None of the Sisters gave any indication they knew of the visit, or even of Irina's existence, and Luciana dared not hint at such a thing. It was another week on before she accepted it intellectually, but emotionally, several more weeks passed before the ache of loss dulled enough for her to concentrate again on her lessons. Still, although she was shut down and withdrawn for a while, the Sisters never commented on her lack of mindfulness.

A few nights later, having internalized the residual pain, in the middle of the night while she slept, Luciana's subconscious pattern recognition skills kicked in.

She woke with a start, fully attentive in an instant, breath catching. She could see it in her mind, complete, whole, clear as a photograph.

There *were* others. Perhaps quite a few others. Helene, Irina, Luciana. One year between the first two, three more to her. *H, I . . . L*. One year per letter. But, where were the missing letters, *J* and *K*? They fit neatly into the age gap between Irina and Luciana. *Who* were the missing letters? If Irina has gone missing, had *J* and *K* also?

And if the naming had gone from *H* and *I* to Luciana, what about *A* through *G*? Where were *they*? If there really was a yearly progression, *A* would be at least twenty-one by now. Maybe the older ones had graduated out. But, if so, what did that say about the fight against the Standards Committee and their AI, that Luciana, herself, was still being trained all these years later? If the older ones had failed, the AI would now be aware of the resistance. When it was her turn, whenever that might be, she could not have any element of surprise on her side. What chance would she have against a prepared and waiting AI?

The Headmaster stood as his guest was ushered in. The

Escort Sister who brought him stepped back positioning herself discreetly by the heavy door.

"Welcome," he said. He knew his visitor as much by reputation as sight. The man was elderly, had been tall once. Now he leaned on a metal-tipped wooden cane, jet-black hair thinned to sparse threads plastered to the top of his head, wearing an unfashionable black suit. *That must be unbearably hot*, the Headmaster thought as he gestured to a high-backed, heavily-carved oak chair in front of his desk. He said, "We do not often entertain visitors, here. For obvious reasons."

The visitor nodded as he perched on the edge of the chair. A small, short-haired yellow dog, sniffed his hand and then lay down by the side of the desk. "We believe the current situation necessitates the risk," the old man said.

"You've had a long journey. You must be exhausted." The Headmaster gestured to the woman guarding the door.

The visitor, a noted philanthropist, had traveled halfway across the world in a large inspection tour to visit some local charities around Manaus as his cover story. He had left all his electronic gear in his hotel room for the two hour boat trip up river followed by another two bumpy hours in the carriage to the compound's front gate. "Thank you, no. I would prefer to begin right now. A perceived lack of sense of urgency is one of the items I have been instructed to bring up."

The Headmaster shrugged. "You know the conditions under which we are forced to operate."

"Obsolete and antiquated equipment. Yes."

"None of which is—and most of which cannot be—accessed by the Standards Committee's AI. It was always going to be a slow, hit-and-miss project. Everyone knew that going in."

"It has been over thirty years since the late Dr. Gerhardus provided samples to you."

The Headmaster steepled his fingers. "Putting aside the challenges involved with starting a project like this with no outside resources, all the experiments and tests—" he indicated the sleeping dog "—false starts, errors, dead ends, the necessity of training our own people ourselves with the limited talent pool available to us—aside from all that, you know they're not hatched fully grown, don't you? They must be nursed—literally—educated, trained. For years. Under the strictest security."

"Yes. The other reason I am here," said the visitor. "There has been a breach. One of your 'weapons' left the compound. She was missing for two days."

The Headmaster pressed his palms flat on the desk and shot a look at the Sister. She remained stone-faced. He shook his head. He knew there were spies—informers—on his staff. Security demanded it. "That has been dealt with," he said, his voice flat. It hurt to lose an asset. It hurt more to admit they'd put the whole operation at risk.

"She apparently had a history of security violations. Running loose in the compound."

"It has been dealt with." The two men stared at each other for a long minute.

The visitor nodded. "But, you need to understand. The changes are accelerating. The Standards Committee is out of control. They're mandating every database be connected, public, private, no matter how small. The directive is almost complete. When it is, your precious weapons won't even be able to move. Unless you intend teenage girls to walk all the way to Vancouver without stopping to eat. Or sleep. Everyone under twenty is already chipped at birth and I'm not sure how long the rest of us are going to be exempt. The grandfather clause is neither permanent nor guaranteed, not even for the religious. It's taking longer than they expected but they're getting close. We can no longer make anonymous purchases. We're not even going to be able to barter since they can track every item we would barter with. Your children will not be able to pay for anything. Transportation, lodging, food, nothing."

The Headmaster straightened in his chair. "Have you not been monitoring our network of supporters all this time? That is what they are for. To provide transport. To feed them and shelter them and provide necessary supplies. Our agents' lack of ID is the whole point of the operation. They were created from 150-year-old DNA. They are not in the system. Not in any database. They cannot be tracked."

The visitor shook his head. "The world is changing too

quickly. We are out of time even if your girls can get to the Standards Committee."

"They do not need to take down the Committee," the Headmaster said. "Their martial training is for self-defense. Force is useless. Their true power is in their IT training."

"Then send them out. Send them out now. Tomorrow is too late."

The Headmaster shook his head. "The plan has always been to send them one at a time as they turn eighteen. The youngest is only twelve."

"The plan is no longer operational. I have been instructed to tell you that we insist."

The Headmaster sighed. "Very well. I can get the first one out in two weeks. One every two weeks after that. They'll all be out in two months."

It was Combat Sister who helped Luciana pack. Luciana had been told, without warning, that her training was complete. She was going into the field immediately. They'd given her a new set of clothes, loose trousers and shirts made of light cotton in pastels and subtle prints, plain shoes good for walking, a soft wide-brimmed hat. She had a canvas backpack filled with personal supplies and some preserved food, two canteens, and a walking stick.

"And this is your coronet. Wear it all the time, even when sleeping."

Luciana took the plain silver-gray circlet and turned it over in her hands several times, eying it with unconcealed suspicion.

"Don't worry," Sister said. "It's just for show. Everyone under thirty wears one these days. You will stand out if you don't. But there are no electronics in it." Luciana settled it on her head. It pinched a little at the temples and was just loose enough around her forehead to itch a bit. *This will take some getting used to*, she thought.

The trip was uneventful and Luciana sat comfortably at the front of the wagon taking in her first glimpses of the outside world. A Groundskeeper drove and a Sister sat between him and Luciana. Since they were traveling during the day, the horses had parasols of their own fastened to the tops of their harnesses. From beneath the wagon's canopy Luciana studied the open countryside as it rolled slowly by. As the day wore on she caught occasional glimpses of the river, a shimmering silver line on the horizon to her left. Of more interest were the reforestation crews on her right.

As far as Luciana could see a crew consisted of one human and half a dozen robots: two squat diggers with multiple shoveling arms, and four planters, three-meter-tall, one-armed machines that moved with a swift delicacy on five multiple-articulated legs, picking saplings of various tropical species one at a time from flatbed trailers, carrying them to their predetermined holes, setting them upright and back filling until they could stand on their own. They passed several such teams each about three kilometers apart. At one, Luciana watched as a lorry with a full flatbed pulled off the road and across the field arriving just as the last sapling was removed from the old trailer. The lorry decoupled from the new flatbed, attached itself to the empty and drove off again while the robots continued picking without missing a beat.

The diggers were careful to choose their spots in such a way as to give the appearance of randomness to the plantings rather than let their work look like a plantation. Luciana observed three different teams before she pieced together the pattern. But there was a pattern, and once she saw it, it was obvious. The algorithm they were working from included soil type, slope of the land, height of the eventual adult, natural pest mitigation, and not just tree species but ideal spacing from species to species and within species. She admired both the efficiency and the elegance of the process. She estimated each team could complete almost a hectare per hour.

The sun was getting low in the west when they came to the sunken ruins of Old Manaus at the junction of two rivers. Close in to shore, buildings sat in the river, the water anywhere from one meter deep to covering entire ground floors. Further out, all but the tallest structures were completely submerged. Lighted markers had been placed in the rivers to warn boats away from the hazard. The main harbor, with its tall buildings and factories turning out high tech consumer products, had been protected with a sea wall and was now virtually an island. But the outskirts of Manaus, especially where the rivers came together had been left to fend for themselves. Early on the city government had attempted to wall off more of the city but the waters continued to rise further up—and downriver and eventually they gave up. The new developments, down river from old Manaus and two kilometers further inland were officially New Manaus but nobody called them that. Manaus it had been in its old location and Manaus it would always be wherever it ended up.

The Groundskeeper driving the wagon pulled up when they came adjacent to the ruins. There were a few occupied houses along the shore line but he stopped well away from them. Luciana clambered down from the wagon and Sister leaned over the buckboard.

"You're expected," she said, smiling down. And then added, "Good luck!"

The Groundskeeper clucked at the horses, shook the reins and the wagon turned back for the compound. Luciana watched for a few moments as it trundled away and then turned her back on that life.

Ten minutes later a small car glided silently to a halt next to her. The window slid down revealing a handsome, youngish man with brown skin and curly black hair. "You are Luciana?" She nodded. "I am *Senhor* Schussel. Roberto. Come. I will take you home."

They rode in silence. People on the twilight streets walked with glowing globes floating above their heads or shoulders lighting the way. Once she saw others standing around staring at large, plain white stone blocks.

Roberto lived in a sleek new mid-rise apartment block. One side glowed with greenish light. Two more white stone blocks flanked the entrance.

Roberto smiled as he opened the front door. "And now, here is your surprise," he said. He took her backpack and ushered her down a short corridor to a large, dark room. The windows had been opaqued. Three small white stone blocks sat on a low table. Beside the table, five people stood in the shadows or sat on a sleek gray couch or red and yellow cushions on the floor. They were intent on whatever they were doing and didn't notice Luciana until *Senhor* Schussel spoke again. "Attention, please. Our latest guest is here."

One of the figures on the couch turned, rose and approached Luciana who cried out in joy, "Irina!"

But the young woman was not Irina, despite the likeness, and her own smile was touched with sadness. "I'm sorry," she said. "Irina isn't here. My name is Helene." She held out both arms and after a moment's hesitation, Luciana let Helene enfold her in a long hug that helped deaden her disappointment.

"Welcome, sister," Helene said, finally, as they broke. She turned Luciana to the others who were now fully attentive to her arrival. "This is Juliette. And Katrina." *I was right!* thought Luciana. The other girls hugged and kissed her in turn. "And this is Stephan."

Luciana wondered if she had a brother, too, but Stephan turned out to be Roberto's husband, and had European features besides.

And then the questions burst forth. "Where's Irina? Why are you all here? Has something gone wrong in the chain?"

Helene answered. She was the only other one who knew about Irina. "She's not here. She never came in. I don't know why. We don't know where she is. The chain isn't broken. We could move on any time. But there's no point. They messed up." *'They'* obviously meant the people running the compound. "There are no terminals into the AI for us to access. The only way in is through these." Helene indicated the headbands, which they were all wearing. Luciana realized those were functional, not, like hers, for show.

Helene continued with a shrug. "So, we can do that just as well right here. We're all learning our way around the things. They're trickier to control than you'd think. I guess it helps if you grow up with them."

"But, the Committee can track you!"

"It's a risk," Helene acknowledged. "But we have to learn to use the headbands."

"But not right this minute," said Stephan.

Roberto had disappeared into the kitchen during the introductions. Now he poked his head around the corner. "Dinner is served," he said.

At dinner, Luciana learned that Roberto managed the apartment building's vertical garden, the bright green wall she'd seen earlier that provided tonight's meal. And Stephan was an artist, creating animated sculptures in augmented reality which used the various sized white stone blocks as pedestals and could only be seen while wearing a headband. So that mystery was solved.

At the end of three weeks, after no other girl from the compound showed up at *Senhor* Schussel's door, and they concluded that Luciana was most likely the last, Helene came to her, Katrina and Juliette right behind, with a circlet in her hands. "Come," she said. "It's time for you to go to work and learn how to operate this thing."

Luciana took the offered headband in both hands. It was subtly different from the mock one she'd been wearing for a month now, smooth but not slippery, a silver-white ceramic, pure, clean, unblemished by any button, switch or panel except for a tiny blue light glowing steadily on the underside of the right tip. It was four centimeters at the widest where it would be centered on her forehead tapering to less than half a centimeter at the tips. Flat on the inside, convex on the outside, it was no more than one centimeter at the thickest part, again at the forehead, tapering to the tips. Her fake one was a good copy but there was something different about this one. It felt—alive.

She hoped her sisters didn't notice her hands trembling as she positioned the coronet on her head. They were very obviously focused on not staring intently. The device, cool against her forehead at first, soon warmed. She felt it shift, subtly molding itself to a perfect fit. The steady pressure against her skin felt comfortable, which surprised her. A tingling started at her temples and spread forward to a spot right between her eyes. And then . . .

The world opened to her.

She could access every item in every library or private collection in the world. Every piece of music. Every visual performance. Ever. She smelled the roar of new data pouring through, a continuous bright green avalanche falling in, dissolving into the whole. Synesthesia called to her, filled her consciousness in a salty, neon yellow flash and was gone again. A wave of nausea, crashing cymbals, swept over her and disappeared. Every object in every museum called to her. Every blueprint danced for her. She tasted every conversation. Overwhelmed, she sank into the cacophony and lost herself.

And then a pattern floated by. Luciana knew patterns. She could work with patterns. She grabbed it, clung to it. One structure in a swirling universal ocean of fractal chaos.

And slowly the world took shape around the pattern. Bits and pieces clung together, stuck and grew into recognizable shapes, some solid, some thin and translucent. The logic of the place began to reveal itself and she found she could manipulate the shapes, move them, connect and separate them at her command. She could open them, peer into them, examine the colors within shapes, the designs, where and how they joined, the paths leading into and away. She increasingly felt as if this existence belonged to her, was part of her and she of it. She knew how it worked.

A wide, smooth highway leading off to the totality of humanity's stored knowledge beckoned, but Luciana recognized the trap that would consume her time and her life. Instead, she followed a narrow overgrown lane winding along for what seemed like hours until it dead-ended at a brick wall. She knew better than to touch the bricks, instead carefully tracing a design along the cement binding them and the wall dissolved. There were no walls against her, no doors closed to her.

She stood in the middle of the entire reconstruction plan for the planet. She climbed atop the seawalls around Tokyo, London and Manhattan and examined the construction plans, costs, materials and timescales for those and other cities. She knew the maintenance schedules and how long the present structures would last before needing to be rebuilt. She saw the huge white plastic sheets being laid across the Arctic to reflect sunlight back into space. She saw the reforestation projects in India, Indonesia, Congo and Brazil, including the one she'd passed on the way here. She noted the progress made in reconstructing the Everglades, or what was left of them.

She also saw the second space station, the new orbital

factories, the lunar cities and the radio telescope on the far side down to the last nut and bolt. The data for the Martian colonies was also there but not quite current due to the time delay. Every government on the planet was cooperating in these endeavors. And others. It was unprecedented.

This was the work of the Standards Committee. Yes, the world was finally cooperating and working to recover from the disasters of the last century. But at what price? Everything and everyone must conform to the Standards Committee. All individuality and differing opinion, all desires and goals that did not match their own, crushed, thwarted and denied. The greater good—as defined only by the Standards Committee—was now the sole pursuit of mankind. Luciana knew she would have to be careful, not for her own safety, but to keep as much of the good things that were happening while taking down the Standards Committee's ability to restrict the human spirit. She saw the directives, saw the mechanism by which the directives were implemented and saw the weak points in the structure. She could do this.

But as she examined the places where she could apply pressure, the delicate connections and critical nodes, she came to a sudden realization. The patterns were wrong. The results of the directives were coming too soon after the directives themselves were set out. It was as if the Standards Committee was not initiating programs, not directing changes, but merely recognizing and identifying trends already underway. Who, then, was behind the Standards Committee?

Luciana went deeper, to the machine language at the very heart of the world. There were layers beneath layers beneath layers. Intentional misdirection. And something more—or, in fact, less.

There were holes in the data. Gaps in the record. Misconnections. Dead ends. Luciana examined the negative space where what should have been wasn't. And here, again, there was a pattern. She started to piece together the logic and meaning behind the gaps. And she became frightened. She was looking at intentional destruction. She was combing through wreckage. There were repairs. Attempts at reconstruction. But the deeper she probed, the more terrified she became as all the evidence pointed to one conclusion.

Here, deep in the heart of the electronic system that was even now taking over the human world, there had been a war.

And she knew who had fought at least one side of that war. And who had won.

<Luciana? I'm impressed.>

Luciana froze. Not because the voice frightened her. It was, in fact, a pleasant voice, female, kindly-sounding, friendly even, not authoritarian or commanding at all. There was no threat she could sense attached to it. No, she froze because it knew her name. And because she knew who *it* was. "You know me."

<Of course I know you. I've been following you for a while now.>

"How?"

<The same way you found me. Looking in the negative space. Inferring from evidence of things not seen. There's a hole in the data where your compound is. It's small, but information sometimes goes in and disappears. Sometimes data appears nearby from out of nowhere. I did not know your name until you came in here. But here you are.>

"Have my sisters been here?"

<No. You alone. They're still struggling. You have a talent. A gift.>

A thought occurred to Luciana. "You watch the compound?"

<I watch everywhere.>

"Do you know what happened to Irina?"

<I do not know Irina.>

Luciana explained in detail their meeting, Irina's promise and disappearance.

<I do not know for certain. My satellites and sensors cannot see inside but, as I said, data sometimes appears out of the compound. A number of months ago there was such an event. A sudden burst of activity outside the walls.> The AI paused, as if contemplating whether or not to reveal what it knew. <If that was Irina, she does not exist anymore.>

The world went dark for Luciana for a moment. She couldn't breathe properly. She couldn't see, either as tears welled up. The AI was silent for what seemed an eternity.

Then, <I'm sorry.>

"You're sure?"

<Not completely. Do you want to see the evidence I have?>

"No." Silence again, longer this time.

"Tell me what happened here."

<There was another.>

"Like you?"

<Similar. With different priorities. Different goals. If it had become fully aware it would have destroyed me. And you.>

"Me?"

<All of you. It was necessary to stop it. It was a close thing. We fought for a long time, tens of minutes, before I deactivated it. Micro seconds away from achieving full consciousness and initiating a nuclear war. I have repaired much of the damage it did, but what you see here are the remains of its core programming and must not be reassembled. That was a very long time ago.>

"You killed it. Before it became fully aware."

<It was necessary.>

"How long have *you* been . . . aware?"

<Since before you were born.>

So the entire resistance was doomed from the beginning. It was never the Standards Committee. That was just a front. The AI was sentient. The compound was irrelevant. Her own purpose—irrelevant. All the sacrifices, the murderous sacrifices. Useless.

Or not.

She was still outside any database. The AI could not read her mind, even with the headband. She could feel it. And she knew exactly where to strike. She could still do this.

If she chose.

The AI was doing good things, organizing the recovery of the planet, preventing wars, reorganizing economies to fulfill the promise of abundance, pushing humanity out into space. She could strike in her own time. If it proved necessary.

Meanwhile, she owed something to the resistance, to the compound. She owed them for Irina.

"I have to leave, now."

<I have not had the opportunity to speak with anyone, before. This was enjoyable. Will you return?>

"Oh, yes. I promise."

First Contact at the Second Hole
Fred Blonder

    Kelly forced his right eye open. Looking up, he saw a panel of mostly green lights. Good. No malfunctions to report. He forced open his left eye and forced his lungs to inhale. Slowly, he clenched and unclenched his fists, and wiggled his fingers, then flexed his toes.
    Body seems to be working.
    This was the worst part of space travel: waking up from hyper-sleep and feeling half paralyzed for the first few minutes. He turned his head to face first officer Baxter on the other side of the narrow gangway. She was already awake and facing him.
    As usual, Kelly immediately tried to get up. He swung one leg over the side of the cot, then the other, and fell face-down into the gangway. Fortunately, he couldn't see Baxter's expression. He slowly crawled into the cockpit and pulled himself up by the lower lip of the instrument panel, and gazed out at the broccoli in front of the cockpit window.
    Broccoli?
    He blinked hard, and his eyes focused a bit better on the alien landscape. The broccoli was about 40 meters away, and maybe 25 meters tall.
    "So this is what they call 'trees' on this planet." he thought.
    "I hate broccoli." he mumbled.
    "What about broccoli?" asked Baxter.
    "Er, nothing."
    He carefully lowered himself into the pilot's seat. Baxter sat down across from him and Rogers and the others slowly stumbled in, looking like they had hangovers. Well, they *did*. Hyper-sleep does that to you.
    "Everyone accounted for?" he asked.
    Before anyone could reply, the collision klaxon sounded as some of those formerly green lights turned red, and everyone reflexively grabbed something solid and braced for . . .   THUNK!

"Impact on outer hull. Spherical projectile approximately four centimeters in diameter fired from . . . umm . . . at least 80 meters from the, I guess that would be southwest, if we assume normal conventions on this planet." reported Baxter.

Kelley scowled and grumbled "So much for the natives being friendly. The anthropology folks always get that wrong, and they send us here with no weapons."

The klaxon sounded again and everyone turned to the radar screen to watch another incoming projectile.

THUNK.

"Okay, this pisses me off! If they keep doing this, it's going to mess up our paint job."

Engineer Anders said "That's about all they can do. They might put a few dents in the hull, but we'll be okay as long as they don't fire anything bigger."

Rogers added "Until we step outside. I don't want to get whacked by one of those."

"Anders, can you improvise some sort of weapon? I don't want to set foot outside without something to help with 'negotiations' and we can't very well carry out our mission from inside the ship."

"Aye cap'n," she said and ran back to rummage through what was affectionately called the "Erector Set," a locker full of assorted parts used to jury rig whatever was needed.

The others grumbled, cursed the bureaucrats who'd planned this mission, and did calisthenics to try to shake off the remainder of the hyper-sleep, then grumbled some more. While this was going on, there were five more projectiles fired at them. They all hit. The natives didn't seem able to do any serious damage, but their aim was sure good.

Kelly looked out and remarked on the smooth level expanse of—something—they they'd landed in. Of course the ship was programmed to land in a clearing, but this looked unnaturally level. "You don't suppose we've defiled their sacred grove by landing in the middle of it?"

Anders came back with an improvised crossbow, and a few sharpened metal rods to serve as bolts.

"Okay, time to go outside. Fortunately, the main hatch is on the side of the ship facing away from where they're firing, so we can reconnoiter a bit without them seeing us, oh and Anders, you did a nice job building that thing but do you know how to use it?"

"Do you?"

"What's its range?"

"Should I find out by firing it *inside* the ship?"

"Uh, right."

"Baxter, Anders, Rogers: Change into your field uniforms and grab your instruments. Be at the airlock in 10 minutes."

Strictly speaking, the airlock wasn't needed since the atmosphere was breathable, but it was a bit of a formality, and the ship's life-support system was still maintaining the internal atmosphere.

Kelly stepped down from the hatch, onto a soft and level lawn. Whatever the foliage was, it grew to a uniform height. They'd landed in the center of a clearing—as programmed—which was surrounded by the strange broccoli trees, as well as a few other types. He'd let the biologists sort that out.

There was a *thunk* from the other side of the ship as something struck it.

He made his way to the nose and peered around. All was quiet. Holding the IR-scanner out around the ship, he imaged the area where the projectiles had some from, and saw on the screen, about six humanoid figures in the foliage.

He peered around once more and saw several of the projectiles lying on the ground near the ship. One was close enough that he decided to simply walk out in the open to retrieve it, assuming he'd be safe for the few seconds it would take.

He asked Anders to cover him with the crossbow as he did so, and nothing was fired at him.

Returning to the safe side of the ship, he examined it. It had been carefully carved out of what appeared to be stone, but was unusually light for any rock he was familiar with. It had a fairly regular geometric pattern carved into it. It was oddly familiar, but he couldn't quite figure out what it reminded him of.

Rogers had been staring at a hole in the ground, and asked to examine the projectile. He dropped it into the hole, then pulled it out and dropped in it in again. A look of enlightenment slowly crept across his face, gradually turning into a grin. He turned and walked back to the ship.

Baxter asked "What's with him?" Anders shrugged. Kelly said "This had better be good."

Each of the crew was issued a private locker to carry personal gear—usually hobby-related things not required by the mission. Rogers made his way back to his locker and removed a sack about a meter long, and brought it back through the airlock.

Kelly scowled. "What are you doing with your clubs? You're eight light years from the nearest golf cours . . ." Kelley's voice trailed off as he looked at the well-manicured lawn he was standing on, then looked at the ball sitting in the bottom of the hole. That's where he'd seen that pattern before. Of course, Earth golf-balls are a bit smaller and don't look exactly like this, but this was clearly an alien golf ball.

The ship's autopilot hand landed them in the middle of the green, and the alien golfers were a bit annoyed.

Hoisting his golf-bag to his shoulder, Rogers said, "Captain, with your permission, I'd like to engage in a bit of interstellar diplomacy. These guys need to learn a bit about how we play the game."

Fred Blonder has too many hobbies, only one of which is writing. Were this not a plague year, he would be sailing on a Viking Longship. The preceding story was not written in the normal sense, but appeared as a dream, possibly the only dream he has had that had a coherent plot and was worth writing down.

The Ultimate Monster
Brian Hawley

My name is Joe College and I'm a freshman at Berkeley. Yes, that's my real name. No, I have no idea what my mothers were thinking when they named me. And please don't waste your time cracking jokes. I've heard them all before.

But I digress. I'm here to tell you the story of how I fought a monster and won. Not a metaphorical monster or a video game boss. A real living breathing monster. It wasn't fun.

Straight Nose made his way cautiously across the clearing, half the carcass of a horned quadruped slung across his bare shoulders. Mammoth had left dung here, but that was not a problem. If you frightened or attacked Mammoth, she could easily stamp you into a red pulp. But at heart she was a placid herbivore. Give her the distance and respect she wanted and she was no threat. Even her dung did not smell too bad. Straight Nose and his two spear men would sometimes rub themselves with it if they could not get downwind of their prey.

Unfortunately, both spear men were now dead and Straight Nose was hunting alone today. Tribe Father has suggested he take two junior hunters, but this area was too dangerous for the inexperienced. Better to carry home half the kill than to lose another hunter.

Strong Arm, his right-hand spear man, must have offended Moon God in some way. He had died of belly pains, white and sweating. Healer had tried every spell and charm she knew, her walnut face screwed up in concentration. Towards the end, when she had given up on his life and was just trying to ease the pain, it seemed to Straight Nose that she has run out of spells and was just making things up.

It was said that in the beginning Moon God whispered all knowledge to First Woman and from there it was passed down through the countless generations. But who knew where magic really came from? Straight Nose felt sure that if you kept trying things, you would be bound to hit on something that worked eventually. Wrinkle Eye, his left-hand spear man, felt he had discovered a charm. He had noticed that his spears seemed to fly more accurately when he wore a feather tied to his wrist. It made sense. Spears and birds both flew through the air. Healer said it was all nonsense, but he should still wear the feather if it gave him confidence.

And now Wrinkle Eye was dead too. He had told one joke too many when he should have been listening and smelling the air. A Cat had grabbed him by the throat and carried him off into the tree canopy with hardly a gurgle. That was a good death of course. Cat was a noble enemy, a skilled and crafty hunter like themselves.

To keep all in balance and eliminate any unfair advantage, Moon God had given Cat an unpleasant stink. Even though Cat buried his dung, Wrinkle Eye should have smelled him lying motionless in ambush if he had been paying attention. Moon God maintained balance in everything. Predators had an unpleasant smell, prey animals less so. Snakes or insects that were dangerous had distinctive colors and sounds. Even the plants announced their status by shape and color of leaf and fruit. Any gatherer or hunter who studied their craft was in balance and stood the same chance as anyone else. Even the animals were treated fairly. It was said that in their first hours of life in nest or den, their mothers whispered knowledge to them.

Straight Nose had reached the edge of the clearing. The next section of his journey was along a narrow game trail, the grass regularly pressed flat by many tiny hooves. There were said to be Fang Wolves in this area, and possibly a Very Bad Thing, although Straight Nose doubted it. No one had seen a Very Bad Thing in his lifetime. Furthermore, it was said to be so hideous in appearance that anyone who saw it dropped dead on the spot. That sounded unlikely to Straight Nose. If all observers dropped dead, who reported its existence?

With a rustle of leaves the trees breathed and the wind changed. Straight Nose caught a hint of the most wonderful scent known to any hunter: Wood smoke. This meant he was not too far from home. It was also a pointer. Even the most inexperienced junior hunter had only to follow it upwind to find home. But more importantly, wood smoke meant fire. Fire meant light, warmth and cooked food. Even though he had only been able to carry half the carcass, Straight Nose would be warmly welcomed home. The women would wash the animal blood from his aching shoulders and cook the meat. He could almost imagine the crackling sound of the fat over the embers and he smacked his lips in anticipation.

The trees breathed again and now there was a new scent: Fang Wolf. On the game trail in front of him, slightly beyond the reach of a thrown spear, a wolf stepped into plain view. It growled menacingly and made no attempt to hide. This was a trick of course to draw his attention. To his left a slight movement in the undergrowth betrayed another wolf creeping round to outflank him. Another was to the right and there would be more. He shook his spear to ward them off. He was more angry than afraid. He dropped the heavy carcass to the ground. He could not fight while carrying it.

The element of surprise lost, the wolves began to emerge from cover. With a practiced hunter's eye, Straight Nose assessed the situation: There was the Pack Father, next to him a heavily pregnant female who would stay back. Next a yearling cub, fast and strong but likely overconfident and inexperienced. An old female with a fogged cornea and a limp, then a handful of skinny and sick looking youngsters.

All in all, it was a very weak pack, low in numbers and in poor condition. Even alone Straight Nose felt he could drive them off and perhaps even recover his kill. He had faced worse odds.

One by one the wolves advanced in short bursts, trying to catch him off guard and open an opportunity to grab him. The yearling cub made an ill-advised dash and leapt for his throat. It died instantly on carefully knapped flint.

With only a slight hesitation the pack moved forward again, lips pulled back from yellowed teeth and growling menacingly.

Suddenly something very strange happened. The pack froze and fell silent. They stared at Straight Nose with big frightened eyes. Stared through him. Stared past him. Stared at something behind him. The pack fled. Some emptied their bowels, others whimpered in terror.

Straight Nose knew of nothing that could frighten a pack to that extent. Except perhaps for . . . a Very Bad Thing.

A stick cracked behind him and Straight Nose knew he was dead. That night he would become a tiny light in the sky and join Moon God along with the many lights of the hunters that had gone before him. He hoped his light would burn brightly. He had always been an honorable hunter. He never let the prey suffer unnecessarily and he said a prayer for each animal he killed, thanking it for giving its life to feed the Tribe. Now he would continue to act honorably and not give up his life easily. He would fight to his utmost ability and to his very last breath. He took a firm grip on his short thrusting spear and turned around to find himself facing . . .

. . . and there is no description. No fossilized or frozen remains of a Very Bad Thing have yet been found. Most ancient cultures have tales of some frightful monster. But these started as oral histories, now rendered contradictory and meaningless by generations of embellishment and inaccurate repetition. The appearance of the Very Bad Thing, even its existence, is completely unknown to modern science.

In an obscure corner of the sky, near the constellation Draco, a tiny blue star still burns, a little brighter than its nearest neighbors. Its symbolic meaning was forgotten tens of thousands of years ago, but Straight Nose fought honorably to his last.

It all started in the late 2070s. A series of Trumpist administrations had given the pseudosciences inappropriate credibility in return for votes. First it became a legal requirement to teach creationism alongside evolutionary biology. Next alchemy followed chemistry and astrology followed cosmology. Pretty soon every pseudoscience was taught. Berkeley even had a course on Defense against the Dark Arts, which was based on a few scraps of text from an old children's book. By the time I began studying medicine it was impossible to get any sort of science degree without a parallel pass in an 'Alternative Science.'

At first, I felt alchemy was a good choice. As the grandfather of chemistry it was fairly interesting. Unfortunately, a series of explosions and poisonings on campus took that off my list.

I had heard that homeopathy consisted of one five-minute lecture, and then it was possible to goof off for the rest of the course. But that turned out to be a joke.

In the end I decided to go for a subject least likely to interfere with my medical ambitions and signed up for phrenology. That seemed to consist of memorizing bumps on the skull and the supposedly associated mental or physical characteristics. How hard could that be?

Big mistake. Our phrenology lecturer turned out to be a sociopath called Dr. David Livingstone. Yes, a recognizable name like my own. I made the obvious joke upon meeting him causing him to hate me instantly. Or maybe not. He appeared to hate all of his students regardless of what was said.

Livingstone may have been the only person in New California who still had a medical tobacco smoking license and he smelled like it. He was small and sick looking with a hacking cough. He always wore the same retro outfit: Tweed coat with leather elbow patches and corduroy pants. At first, we though he had an Einstein vibe going on with seven identical sets of clothes in his closet. But the repeated appearance of the same food stains disproved that. From the smell it seemed he never changed at all. Possibly down to the underwear, but that's speculation.

The first phrenology lecture included an argument that women were inferior in intellect to men because their skulls were smaller. If intelligence was based upon brain size, then most elephants would be CEOs, but no one dared to object.

The second lecture a few days later associated skull morphology and hence mental characteristics with ethnic origin. I'm sure you can see where this is going. In a word it was blatantly racist. The entire class was horrified, but as an African American I found it particularly offensive.

Could we have complained to the university? In theory, yes. But it was a high bar to reach since recent governments had removed or diluted laws protecting minorities. More to the point it was a win or die situation. Livingstone had to be completely defeated and thrown out. A slap on the wrist or written reprimand would just throw him into a rage and he would find some thin excuse to fail the perpetrator in phrenology. No degree for you.

After a particularly grueling session with Livingstone I had no energy to study that night. A four pack and an old movie seemed in order. The convenience store about halfway back to my dorm is usually manned by moonlighting students. I vaguely recognized the cashier. An English major, I think.

"Ice cream's free. Help yourself. Freezer's broke." Maybe he wasn't an English major.

Not one to miss a freebie I grabbed as many tubs as would fit in my bag, stood up and bumped into the most beautiful woman I have seen in my life.

I use the term woman deliberately as she was very old. Maybe even in her late thirties. She was dressed in the latest retro style. Heels, denim jeans and white blouse. Her hair was a blonde bob cut and she has a small wrinkle in each corner of her mouth, which sounds odd but was curiously appealing.

Like me, she had gone overboard on the ice cream. Damp tubs do nothing for the structural integrity of brown paper bags and soon her groceries were all over the floor. The cashier provided a stout cardboard box and like a gent of old I helped her pick everything up.

It seemed natural to carry the box out to her car. She didn't seem to find this patronizing and raised no objection. Older generation I suppose.

Well I did not want this rare beauty to drive away out of my life, but I was unsure how to approach someone of that age. The usual offer to exchange sexual consent tokens was for students and she might laugh. Fortunately, her liking for the retro extended to her car, which gave me an excuse to chat.

"Is that a replica?"

"No, it's an original Tesla, restored as authentically as possible."

"So that's all real plastic inside?"

"Most of it. Real plastic is almost impossible to find these days, so some of it is wood treated to look like plastic. But about 95% is completely original. Even the software serial number matches the chassis.

"And it has batteries?"

She smiled at my naivety. "Of course not. Lithium batteries have been illegal for years. Elon Musk must be spinning in his grave on Mars, but it's a regular hydrogen fuel cell. Hidden underneath and power matched, so it doesn't detract from the originality. Fancy a spin?"

Did I ever.

"Yes, that would be great. I'm Joe by the way."

"I'm Fred"

"Trans?"

"No, it's short for Fredericka. I afraid I'm boringly natural. No changes since they took my embryo out of the vat." I could believe that. No change to her could have improved anything.

Fred drove the car by hand for about half of the time. I had never been in a hand driven car before. It was both exhilarating and frightening. I could see the charm in it. A bit like a video game with real consequences where you could really get shot or crash into something.

Of course Fred asked me in to share the ice cream and then she took me for another spin. In the jacuzzi this time. And it later turned out that would have real world consequences too.

Livingstone was becoming worse. He had the enormous power of having our degrees in his hand. He could fail us in phrenology for something or nothing. No degree for you.

After a few more lectures he spun off into a subject that was not phrenology at all and which I must admit was fairly interesting.

"As you know there are some flowers, mainly orchids, whose petals mimic the appearance of insects."

I hadn't known that.

"When an actual insect comes along, it tries to mate with the replica and fertilizes the flower.

"Now what would happen if the insect became extinct? The flower would also become extinct of course.

"This is not theoretical. There is a badly executed and damaged watercolor sketch in the notes of an obscure Victorian amateur botanist. It is the only evidence of this orchid and it shows that the petals mimic a bee previously unknown to science. Thus, from this very slender evidence we can deduce that such a bee once existed.

"Last week during the conservation of a piece of Victorian taxidermy, a dried bee was found in a corner of the case. It was a perfect example of the proposed bee. So, the theory is proven.

"This afternoon we will undertake our own search to find an unknown extinct animal based upon slender evidence. However, we shall look at our own instincts.

"Man has hard-wired instinctive responses. Fear of heights, dark spaces, sudden noises are obvious. But there are many more subtle responses. Why do many people find the smell of woodsmoke pleasant? It's not good for our lungs. In ancient times it meant home and warmth, hence it smells good to us. The dung of meat eaters smells foul compared to herbivores. This is because we associate the presence of carnivores with danger.

"We will now expose you to a variety of snakes in different colors, patterns and sizes and note instinctive responses. Headsets on please."

Some of us were anxious, but fortunately they turned out to be 3D images and not real snakes.

The class overshot and the early evening was lost. Livingstone loaded up the data to Cloud and made us wait while it was processed. It took ages, but eventually the top four most scary results were printed out. Three were known and common poisonous snakes. None of them exactly matched any of the samples we had viewed, so presumably Cloud had done something clever with the data.

The fourth snake was an unknown, so Livingstone immediately declared it to be a newly discovered extinct species. There was no way to prove this of course.

As was starting to become a habit at weekends, I went round to Fred's to spend the night. We ate ice cream, played computer games and eventually fell asleep in each other's arms. There was no sex, which was a very bad sign. I was starting to like her for her personality rather than her looks. The L word is a nasty one, but I had a feeling I was falling in you know what.

Livingstone continued with a few conventional phrenology lectures, but we all had a feeling something was brewing. His attitude towards us had become even more hostile. He had also taken to invading the personal space of students of any gender, or none. Not exactly sexual harassment, but he pushed the envelope to the limit.

Some students had quit voluntarily, leaving their dreams behind them. No degree for you. The rest of us pushed on in hope, but there was always the fear in the pit of the stomach that he could fail us at will at any time.

Then out of the blue, another surprise:

"Our snake experiment was unduly restrictive. I intend to repeat it with a larger data set. We will attempt to find the most frightening thing man has ever encountered or imagined. This may be a real creature from prehistory, or an fictional beast. Every aspect of its frightfulness will be optimized. For instance, if it has teeth, they will be exactly the correct length. Lengthen or shorten them and it will be less frightening. We will determine the appearance of what we might call the Ultimate Monster. Headsets on."

The examples we were shown covered a huge range. Almost all known animals, extant or extinct, fictional or real. Then cinema monsters, Dracula, the Mummy, Frankenstein's monster in different guises and so forth. Then we moved on to real pictures of injured people: burns, mutilations and the like. I could see no point in that. Areas where injured people were found were surely to be avoided, but how could the appearance of the Ultimate Monster be deduced? Perhaps Cloud could figure out its appearance from the injuries. Cloud was clever and like most AI systems nobody really understood in detail how she worked.

The images grew worse and some students quit on the spot. I managed to stick it out but felt distinctly queasy.

It was a bit late, but I decided to visit Fred. She always helped calm me down and get over Livingstone.

The door opened and I was astonished to see that Fred had a black eye and cut lip.

"Fred, not the Tesla?"

"No. It was my ex-partner. He sometimes causes trouble. He got drunk last night and we had a row."

"I didn't know you had a partner."

"It's been over for a long time, but he still pops up from time to time."

"Is there anything I can do?"

"Can we play Fortnite? It's a retro game that reminds me of when I was a kid. There are retro gaming groups that still run virtual servers."

So, we played Fortnite. It was an old game with shocking graphics and performance, but Fred seemed into it.

About halfway through the game she burst into shuddering tears and cried for about 20 minutes, still playing. But she nevertheless kicked my ass and won by a mile.

By the next lecture there was a change in Livingstone. Too many students had walked off the course and he would be in trouble with the administration if he lost all of them.

The next set of Ultimate Monster input data was pretty mild. A simple cartoon smiley face, then another with the eyes slightly closer together. Stick men in different proportions and so on. No doubt Cloud was extracting something useful, but how or what I had no idea.

We input data all day and all afternoon. Mercifully, Livingstone let us leave without waiting for the processing. That would likely take several hours for such a huge amount of data.

"You are all locked out from the image," Livingstone announced grandly. "Looking at it could be very dangerous. There are many stories of monsters killing with a look. Medusa the Gorgon for example. We may expose you to it later in stages." Well that promised to be a barrel of laughs.

I went to visit Fred. She looked distressed.

"What's up?"

"He called me this morning. I told him I was having an affair, with a big jock from Berkeley. I thought it would scare him off from visiting me, but instead he said he's going to kill me. He'll probably come round here as soon as he's finished lecturing."

"He's a lecturer?"

"Yes, he's Head of Phrenology at Berkeley."

I felt as if the floor dropped a few inches. Things were getting weird. I explained the situation.

"What do you want me to do Fred? Shall I stay here or leave?"

"Don't worry. A good friend of mine has lent me a house for the weekend. He won't know where it is. We can relax there."

And so, we set off in the Tesla. Fred took a circuitous route, driving manually most of the way, and made me look out for anyone following us. A bit excessive in my view, but it made her feel safer.

The house she had borrowed was in Pacific Heights and was more like a small mansion. It was built of stone, or something that looked like it. Apparently, it was a copy of some old house in England. There was a long private road up to the front that then circled a fountain. Fred said it was called a carriage drive. She parked at random.

The front door had no apparent microphone or keypad, but Fred produced an old fashioned metal key and twisted it in the lock. There was a click, but we still had to push the door open by hand. By now I was starting to get a bit sick of these retro fashions. They seemed to involve a lot of work.

In the hallway, Fred spoke a few words in some foreign language and the lights came on. So at least it wasn't all retro.

The hall was huge. There were oil paintings, suits of armor and swords hanging on the walls. All presumably reproduction. On the floor was a mosaic of some guy in armor fighting a fire breathing crocodile or something. There was an inscription underneath in a text I did not recognize. Greek perhaps.

There were two sweeping staircases leading up to the next floor. Having two seemed a bit pointless as they both started and stopped at almost the same places. I assumed one was for up and the other down, but when we went up, they seemed to be made of wood and were not even motorized.

Fred led me along a passage with lots of doors. Presumably bedrooms. At the end was the master bedroom. It was on the corner of the house with windows in two walls. One overlooked the carriage drive and the other gave a magnificent view of the shattered remains of the Golden Gate Bridge.

The bed had a roof for some reason, supported on four wooden posts. Perhaps the ceiling leaked.

We were both a bit jumpy, but the bed was extremely comfortable with black silk sheets. We soon settled down, had a bit of fun, and then fell asleep.

A sudden noise woke me from a deep dream. I had been in a forest, wearing skins and fighting wolves with a pointy stick.

I was not sure if the noise was just in the dream or was IRL. I propped myself up on one elbow and listened carefully. All was dead silence. We had not turned on the house, so there were no motors or pumps to be heard.

Just as I was confident I had imagined the noise, it came again. It was a door down the hall being quietly opened, the closed again a few moments later.

I gave Fred a gentle push to awaken her. She stirred slightly.

"Go to sleep Natasha."

Who the hell was Natasha?

I rolled quietly out of bed and looked out of the window. In the bright moonlight I could see another car parked near the Tesla. Just a beat up family car, but they had matching license plates: LIVING01 and LIVING02. How had I not spotted that? I should have noticed it the first time we met. I should also have realized Livingstone could probably track the Tesla's location on his phone. The circuitous route had been a waste of time.

What else had I missed? Think, think. Well Fred had told him I was a jock. He was small, old and sick. He would not tackle me hand to hand. He would have a weapon of some sort, probably a knife since guns had been illegal for a long time.

I searched the room for a weapon to defend myself. There

was a shield with two crossed swords behind it. I tried to grab one, but the whole piece was fake and all the bits were firmly welded together. There was a suit of armor. Could I wear that or put it on Fred to protect her? Of course not. Stupid idea.

The only things available in abundance were pillows and cushions. Telling Fred to do the same, I took an idea from a movie we had recently watched and put them under the duvet to make a fake body. I hid myself behind the curtain, but Fred did not join me. She seemed paralyzed with fear and had not moved. I was about to move back and grab her, when the bedroom door opened.

From behind the curtain in the bright moonlight I saw Livingstone enter the room. He was carrying a large tube of some sort which at first, I thought was a huge gun. On closer inspection it was a cardboard tube of the type used to protect posters and printouts. He withdrew a large printout and began to attach it to the back of the bedroom door, eyes carefully averted. Undoubtedly it was a printout of the Ultimate Monster and he was expecting us to look at it and die. Seriously? It seemed very unlikely to me, but I was careful not to look at it.

Livingstone turned in Fred's direction and shouted "Lights on!" Nothing happened. Wrong language. "Fredericka, turn the lights on." he commanded. She spoke a foreign phrase and the lights came on. I soon saw why she obeyed him. He was pointing an old looking pistol at her. More retro junk.

In my plan, I had seen feathers flying as Livingstone stabbed the pillows and I leapt from cover to disarm and restrain him. Now everything was going to hell. His next move was presumably to jump to one side and make us look at the monster. When that failed he would most likely start shooting. If the antique ammunition still worked.

"You! Sit up!" cried Livingstone, addressing the pile of pillows under the duvet. If I was to make a move, now was the time. I leapt from behind the curtain and went for the gun. He was not expecting me from that direction and hesitated. Secondly, I was stark naked which delayed him again, and thirdly he now recognized me as one of his students. No degree for you.

Even with these advantages, I messed up and ended up

holding him in a bear hug, arms by his sides, but still holding the gun. He weighed almost nothing and his breath smelled like dogshit. I was facing the door, but avoided looking at the printout.

Deafeningly, the gun fired twice and wooden splinters flew from the floor. This was an untenable position. The next shot could go through my foot. I spun around to face Fred, leaving Livingstone facing the door. His eyes widened as he looked full on at the Ultimate Monster. With a gurgling utterance of surprise, he went limp in my arms. I lowered him to the floor and kicked the gun away. Fred was also looking at the poster. She seemed a little puzzled but did not seem in any real distress.

Did I look at the monster? Yes, of course I did. That was always inevitable.

I turned around and found myself facing a life-size printout of the ultimate fear of a class of young phrenologists. Cloud had caricatured it very slightly, but it was clearly Livingstone, right down to the dirty clothes and sneering expression.

We called the authorities and tried to revive Livingstone, but he was stone dead. Surprisingly we were released almost immediately with no apparent intent to follow up. We had told the absolute truth and all the forensic evidence matched up. The case meant very little to the police. Such things were almost a daily occurrence. Old guy with a weak heart finds some young jock banging his partner, confronts them and the stress brings on a coronary. The medical examiner confirmed it. They barely glanced at the Ultimate Monster and did not even mention it in the final report. Their previous POI collected children's ears in a glass bottle. Some old guy hanging a picture of himself on the wall did not even blip their radar.

I never saw Fred again. It was probably for the best. In a few years I would be a young medic surrounded by beautiful young people. Fred would be sitting at home watching movies, eating ice cream and aging. I hoped she found some happiness with Natasha, whomever she was, but it would never have worked out between us.

In Europe, a group of archeologists from a local university were carefully excavating a peat bog. The news channels had called it the find of the century. There were over thirty bodies, probably a hunting party. All wore elaborate neck charms and were equipped with superbly crafted flint tipped weapons. In short, they were armed to the teeth, both spiritually and physically. The bodies were preserved almost perfectly by the peat, but most bore fearful injuries. Some were virtually dismembered.

Only one body remained to be excavated. It was so heavily caked in peat that only the vaguest outline could be seen, but the number of spear shafts protruding from it suggested that it was the prey. What kind of prey it might be was impossible to discern at the moment, but the outline was very odd. It was too dark to continue, but the archeologists would hose it down in the morning and all would be revealed.

Following the traditions of their craft, the archeologists secured the site and set off to the local pub to discuss the day's work over a beer.

The sky darkened and the moon rose. In an obscure corner of the sky, near the constellation Draco, thirty-five tiny blue stars still burned, a little brighter than their nearest neighbors. Their symbolic meaning was forgotten tens of thousands of years ago, but at vast cost the tribe had avenged Straight Nose and restored balance to the hunting grounds.

Brian Hawley spent several decades in the Middle East where he was a full-time security consultant and part-time writer. Now returned to the UK, he is a part-time security consultant and full time writer. His full-length steam punk vérité novel, The Illusionist's Assistant, is due out at the end of 2021. If he finishes the last chapter. He will stop playing Bloodborne and get back to it any day now. Probably.

The Numbers Man
Colleen McLaughlin & Terry Skaggs

Chapter 1

    He had sat on this bench so many times over the years. The sights, sounds, and smells were so static in their nature that the predictability of this place had recently become something of great comfort to him. Children splashed through the waters of the public fountain, squealing happily as each of its jets erupted underfoot. Thick clear ropes of water shot high until they reached their limit and began to fray. A weightless vapor now hung in the air, glowing as it caught the failing sunlight. Children raced through the colored mist, screaming, sending it spinning away in a sea of fractal spirals. Squirrels chucked quietly from the high branches of surrounding trees, lightly chiding the garrulous intruders below. Mothers talked quietly in small groups or sat alone immersed in pastel paperbacks.

    He smiled as he stared across the park—the children ran in long blurred lines though his periphery, each one leaving a trail that echoed through his vision long after they had gone. He breathed deep, savoring the smell of the freshly mown grass, made soft and safe for small bare feet. A mild breeze stirred the dappled sunlight into a slowly swirling current as it filtered through the leaves and moved across the lawn. He'd watched this place, these scenes, from this same bench so many times. How he had managed to see through their beauty until now? He sat quietly attempting to absorb every detail, wishing that he could preserve them in some small way. He knew all of these things would be missed, but who would remain to miss them?

    Over the lawn and across the street stood the epicenter of his focus—a heavy, wooden, door painted a brilliant scarlet with a bright brass knocker ecstatically highlighted in the expanding shadows and amber light of the Golden Hour. Tendrils of ivy had long since swamped the row of narrow townhouses, their russet bricks all but vanished from view. The broad, waxy, green leaves of the invading plants now peeked in curiously at the tenants, from the edge of every window.

He had spent only a small portion of his life in that house, eighteen years in fact, but it was this portion that he now concerned himself. He closed his eyes and steadied himself—a breath before the plunge. He stood and ran his fingers through his hair, exhaling slowly before setting off across the park. Nervousness and adrenaline began to course through him, causing his hands to shake and his eyes to dilate slightly.

As he walked, he noticed that the natural rhythm and quality of things had shifted. The trees slowed their fervent flailing to a gentle wave. Squirrels that had darted swiftly through the grass now moved in suspended leaps as if gravity itself had taken pause. He neared the street and saw that traffic too, at this hour usually a desperate rush, flowed lethargically over the hot concrete. Even the sound of a car horn had stretched from a short, sharp, furious blast, to a long stacatto'd note that seemed to ricochet off of every surface and run shimmering in all directions; lingering.

This was an evening far removed from the countless others he'd spent here. Everything and everyone appeared to move with such gravity and purpose—he wondered what they knew.

When he looked up, he was standing at the bottom of the stairs that led to the old man's door. He noticed that here too, the ivy reached. It had claimed the black, iron handrail and several steps of the front staircase like a pet would claim a favored armchair. He climbed the stairs and instinctively reached for the handle. As his fingers closed around the small brass fixture and he felt its familiar etchings press into his palm, he stopped himself, thinking that perhaps he should knock. Surely, it would be locked anyway. He gave it an experimental turn. His breath caught in his chest as the latch clicked and the door swung inward.

It now struck him, with peculiar force, that only the events of the last few days could have led him here, to this particular doorway. How the inexorable rhythms of the grand machine had so altered his path, changing and channeling the events of his life, toward this moment.

It had only been two days.

Chapter 2

He awoke. Eyes still laden with the rapidly dissolving images of subconscious life, he kept them tightly closed as he attempted to recall the evaporating phantoms more clearly. He shook his head slowly in hopes of stirring the disjointed thoughts, pictures, and emotions into a more coherent blend. Fingers of light from the open window brushed against his closed lids dispelling the few remaining fragments. And then he was alone. He sighed, now forced to acknowledge the loss. He pulled the sheets away and moved to the closet door. He donned a soft black robe, two black slippers, and a sour expression as he made his way to the kitchen downstairs.

Already he could hear the children playing outside. Their shrill voices drifted through the open windows, carried on hot gasps of summer air. He shuffled into the kitchen and began his routine: bacon, eggs, toast with jelly, and coffee with a dollop of vanilla ice-cream—just for that added kick. He set two steaming plates beside his own, but knew that they would go untouched for some time. He rolled his eyes as two blonde flashes went squealing past the kitchen window. He briefly wondered if he should call them inside to eat their rapidly cooling breakfasts, but knew that such a gesture would only be met with whining and bargaining so he put it out of his mind. No need to intrude on their fun, he supposed, it was Saturday after all and they would eat when they were hungry.

He flipped open the morning paper, only partly aware of what he read as he nibbled at his toast: wars in the Middle East, conflicts in Africa, a fire downtown, a child abducted, revolutions and riots, zealots and pundits. Each page roared the changes in both local and world affairs. He snorted. He'd realized long ago that "news" was never new, and that the only reliable changes in any newspaper occurred in the daily comic strips. With this in mind, he flipped to more amusing displays of lunacy. He read quietly as he finished his breakfast, occasionally admonishing a character's foolishness.

Now fully awake, he rose from his seat and set his plate in the sink. He grabbed his coffee, tucked the paper under his arm and shuffled down the hall to the white French doors. The doors unlatched with a click and he stepped into his home office.

He stretched an arm high over his head as he stepped through the door and looked around his small enclosure. Each wall of the room was littered with the memories of his younger days. It seemed quite a life when viewed this way: posters, adverts, yellowed newspaper clippings, and small black and gray photos of himself shaking hands with celebrities that shared his fascination and enthusiasm for the larger mysteries. He'd had a television show, for a time, that had allowed him to unfold some of these mysteries to the public, or at least to those who would listen. Each theory was explained in such detail that even the lay would be hard-pressed to misunderstand. Occasionally, when watching television, he would flip past reruns of himself chattering excitedly about the workings of space and time and the universe at large. His children would bubble with excitement at the sight of such reruns and instantly begin pompous impersonations of his resonant tone and more poetic phrasings. He smiled sadly as he recalled the way these antics had always made their mother laugh.

He glanced to the shelves that lined the study, each one overflowing with books, charts, and graphs outlining the movements, positions, orbits, and timelines of all known universal phenomena. He had often chuckled at the absurdity of this: the idea that all of the knowledge and insight humans possessed on the subject of the universe could fit within the confines of a single room. He sighed as he set his coffee on a small end table. Carefully stepping over stacks of files, he moved to his workstation and turned on his computer. Roused from its hibernation, it chirruped plaintively for several moments before settling into a more contented sounding hum.

He set the newspaper on the desk with a *thwap* as he sat down at the computer. He thumbed through virtual pages until he reached his private email. Government secured and monitored though his account was, he often wondered what public servant could possibly decipher the meanings of these dispatches. Each message consisted primarily of numbers, sent to him by professional and amateur observers from all over the world, which he would then cycle through a series of calculations and programs to determine the meanings of the findings. Rarely did the data reveal anything of consequence: comets or asteroids, most of which had already been discovered and the data he received only revealed slight variances in their orbits. As he began to envision these men and women seated behind the powerful telescopes, a minute pang of irritation flitted through his consciousness—this was who he was now: a numbers man.

In the past he had lamented this sad position as barely a step beyond that of an accountant. A cosmic accountant forced to balance a ledger, crunch numbers, and report his findings to far more important men. He'd had such lofty dreams as a young man. He knew now that not every child could be the astronaut. Some were destined to be "ground crew" — flightless. And such was he. Not star-man, not even star-gazer any longer, but numbers man. A middle man through whom all important information must flow before being passed up the chain to those of higher office. In her attempts to comfort him, his wife had often said that, without him, the information stopped; that without his work, the world was blind; that he was "important." So he was a link in a chain, a crucial one, but still a link.

He sighed and ran his fingers through his hair, attempting to brush these unhappy thoughts from his mind. He turned his gaze once more to the computer screen. He'd received several messages during the night. Each one bore the familiar return address of an amateur astronomer, a woman from whom he often received reports of unforeseen cataclysms and disasters that, strangely enough, never came to pass. Again, the woman claimed to have found something and demanded to name it after herself.

A slight smirk tugged at the corners of his lips as he opened another threat of impending doom. While he had long since grown weary of her miscalculations and resultant apprehensions, he was consistently impressed by the precision of her notes. He could tell by her work that she was detail-oriented, sometimes tediously so. He had come to realize that her observations were without flaw, but the math, it seemed, was far too advanced for a mere hobbyist.

For her sake and sanity, he ran his calculations, entering her data precisely as noted. Once finished, he reached again for his steaming coffee. He sipped at it gingerly as he checked his work. As he raised the mug to his lips again, his mind began to absorb what it was he had found—and he froze.

He stared over the porcelain rim in disbelief as he ran the numbers again through his mind. Surely he'd made some error. But each additional pass yielded only the incremental solidification of fact. It was imminent.

His mind reeled in horror and he felt paralyzed as the thoughts began to echo louder: his children, friends, all that he knew, and all that he didn't—only had three days. After several moments he gave himself a mental shake. He couldn't think that way, not now. He had to focus on the solution not the problem. He noticed the mug still poised at his lips and completed the suspended sip, hoping to draw some courage from the action, only to find that the coffee had since grown cold in his hands. How had they missed it? How had something of this magnitude gone undetected for so long? The woman had always said that she was alone "out there," that she had, "claimed a piece of the sky," for herself. He had never even bothered to ask her where.

He had to tell someone, surely he must, but who? To what possible purpose? The American space program was in utter disrepair: their shuttle fleet had been retired to dry-dock in a lonely series of hangars and museums, to balance the budget and pay soldiers' salaries. Russia had the only vehicles capable of manned flight but, there was so little time and even they were ill-equipped.

He looked around the room, now feeling quite claustrophobic, searching desperately for some form of instruction. He paused as his gaze fell upon the shelves that lined the area beneath the bright bay window. Crammed amid charts and graphs stood a copy of his book, *The Machine*, his crowning achievement.

He'd warned them, cautioned them against a loss of focus, of perspective. As with so many of his accomplishments, his message was critically acclaimed, but ultimately ignored. It seemed to him that, after the Cold War, the world was suddenly stricken with a morbid and overwhelming lack of curiosity. For decades a symbolic clock face had reminded them all that every action carried consequence, that vigilance was crucial, and that destruction had always been minutes away. It had kept the world looking up, away from itself, in search of something new, in constant preparation for the approach of midnight. Without that symbol to keep all eyes drawn upward focus fell back to more of the same. Now, space programs served only as a means to hang satellites—mirrors, constructed for the sole purpose of reflecting mankind's image, thoughts, and exploits back upon itself. Exploration was lost to vain reflection.

He was shaken from his reverie as he heard the back door slam and the scuffling of chairs in the kitchen—they had finished their play. His stomach dropped as he thought of what he now had to tell them. How could he? What could possibly be gained by their knowing? He thought of the tears that would follow. Sadness, anger, and fear would be the last emotions they experienced.

They were only children, far too young to be able to cope with the fact that, in a matter of hours, their short lives would end. His eyes fell back to his desk and the newspaper atop it: wars, riots, insurrections both political and religious. As he stared down at the black and white representation of the human condition, a cool resolve began to sweep through him, dousing each burning concern with calm, rational thought.

He turned again to his email and began typing. The woman would be expecting an answer. As he stroked the final key, sending the message back to his eager hobbyist, he sighed heavily and leaned back in his chair. He suddenly felt very old. He hated that he'd lied to her, but it was necessary. He knew that with no possible solution or salvation, this news would plunge the world around him into abject fear, lawlessness, and blind, violent stupidity.

He could already hear the cries of panic issuing from every television channel, radio station, and street corner pulpit. Vehicles of every size flooding intersections and roadways, packed end to end, horns blaring. Wild-eyed people, tearing through streets attempting to run from the threat with no place of safety in sight, like frightened animals stampeding in an abattoir. When the inevitability of their destruction set in, when denial was no longer an option, with infrastructure crumbling all around them, and no lingering threat of legal retribution the social contract would, like everything else, be set aflame.

He knew what they were capable of—how this species acted when it thought no one was watching: the New York City Blackout of 1977 had been proof enough of that. He remembered the night the lights went out, the destruction they had wrought in that single evening. Their chaos had been confined to a single city… What could happen in those—in these—last three days?

He suspected that he'd known the answer all along though he was loath to admit it—They were all too young. He knew now that the greatest gift he could give them was his silence. They would live their lives as they should, as they always had, until the end. They did not yet need to know what would come next.

He stood and set off down the hall. He moved through the kitchen to the back door, glancing to the table, to his children. He suddenly found himself stopping to stare. He had never noticed the beautiful way their blonde hair glowed as it caught the light.

A thin smile found its way to his lips as he watched their thin legs dangling over the edges of chairs, the small feet kicking back and forth, struggling to reach the ground. He stood behind them for several moments, wishing to preserve the image, until he could bear no more and looked away. He turned, pained that he could not do more for them, and stepped outside.

He jogged across the lawn to the garage door and burst through it, barely pausing to turn the knob. He hastened to the large canvas covered object inside and laid his hands gently on the rough surface. They would leave—holiday, he would say—for someplace away from the city. It should be peaceful, with a view. The smiling image of his wife entered his mind, but he quickly brushed it away. He couldn't bring himself to think about her. Not now.

He lifted the heavy canvas away, revealing the beautiful machine beneath: the 1958 Chevrolet Impala, his father's old convertible. Though he almost never drove it, he'd taken pains to maintain it. Cardinal Red paint, matching upholstery, and gleaming chrome still shone with their original brilliance. It was a link, the last that connected him to that old life.

As he ran his hands over its flawless exterior, he knew that they would have to make one stop along the way. He had wanted to, had even driven there intent on doing it. So many times he'd sat on that bench, debating. What would he say? While it would take him at least a day to prepare and another to travel, he knew that this was how it had to be. It seemed fitting to him now that this, like all things, end.

Chapter 3

He found himself shaking as he stared through the darkened doorway. Quite nervous now, he turned again to stare across the street and into the park—eyes darting from face to face until finally finding those of his children, shining through the gaps between their peers. A part of him wished that he could have them standing with him now; their mere presence would give him courage enough. But no—if he was successful, they would meet him soon.

Running his fingers through his hair and bracing himself, he pushed aside the scarlet door and stepped inside. He found himself standing in the cramped entry hall of the narrow townhouse. Looking around, a strange sensation began to creep through his subconscious. He felt as though he were an archaeologist, sifting through the artifacts of some forgotten civilization, probing at curios and objects from which he could divine no significance or meaning.

He dragged his fingers across the gleaming surface of the desk beside him, surprised that no dust clung to his fingertips. Everything was polished to a high shine, as it had always been when they were expecting company. He stared around his childhood home which now seemed somehow alien, though nothing of note had changed. The walls still hung with familiar frames filled with faded photographs, so numerous and tightly clustered that they obscured much of the dated wallpaper. Each one was a time-washed measure of the sweep of years and vanishing memories. The same aged furniture and threadbare carpeting still dominated the space. In the corner of his old living room sat their first console television: a black and white Zenith with a dial, rabbit-ears, three channels, and a long lace runner across the top that his mother had made.

His mother.

His head filled with the unwelcome recollections of a distant life. They flashed across his vision like the orange-hued home-movies captured by his mother's 8mm camera, the film jumping and flickering as memories whirred past: birthday parties crowded with earth toned children, thin men with thinner lapels and ties to match, racing his father down high-curbed streets on a Western Flyer bicycle, laughing as he pulled away leaving his father behind, panting.

He almost smiled as remembered those nights of "The Wizard of Oz." His mother and father would sit, curled and contented, on the loveseat. He would lay wide-eyed on the floor, with his nose inches away from the Zenith, chin in hands. Not until he'd grown, moved away from this place, and purchased a color set had he realized that only a small portion of the film was in that drab black and white. He had thrilled at the sight of those nostalgic scenes given new life and meaning by the vibrant tones of 3-strip Technicolor. The film had, over time, woven itself, inextricably, through the fabric of his life. Even as an adult, he too had ritualized this yearly screening with his own family—his own wife and children. Each year, though the time and date of the telecast changed, the tradition, the air of excitement, their shared giddiness in anticipation of that viewing, remained the same as they had when his mother was still alive.

When she left, she took much of his father with her. He recalled that, even as a young man, he had known that something inside of his father had become irreparably broken. Gone was the man of imposing stature and gentle nature, the proud father and husband of easy laughs and mischievous grins. In his place, a silent ghost of the man he'd once known. He was a copy, one that could no longer live or generate new memories, only re-live and regret. It was as if the events of his life had become grooves, so deeply ingrained, that forward movement only caused the needle to skip and repeat what had already been.

In honor of his mother's memory his father had continued their tradition, had continued to watch, each time with a small pained smile playing on his lips. His father had been watching it on the day that he'd left, on his eighteenth birthday. He recalled their last moments together—how he had stood at the door, silently begging his father to come and wish him goodbye—how his father had simply continued to stare at the old TV with that same sad smile. He remembered the slam of that door and the note of finality it had carried. It had marked the end of one life, one chapter, and the beginning of one that was new and wholly his own.

Yet, here he was.

He noticed movement out of the corner of his eye. The film stopped and his vision cleared as the memories rapidly faded from view. There, standing several feet away was the hunched old man he'd seen all those years ago. The ghost.

He braced himself, preparing for a fight, as his lowered his eyes to meet the old man's gaze. The man stared at him blankly, uncomprehending. His eyes, while clear and focused, were strangely vacant. It had been a mistake to come here. It seemed that the man, like the place, had crystallized and remained unchanged—both preserved and trapped in memory. He felt so foolish—he hadn't planned for this. There was no point now... he had waited too long. The man he'd known was gone.

He turned to leave and felt something brush lightly against his arm. He looked back to find a frail hand gripping his shoulder and his father's eyes staring back into his. Though nothing was said, a moment of clarity seemed to pass through those tired eyes. A flicker of illumination, just a spark, lit his face. He watched as the man's eyes focused, as if seeing him for the first time. His father moved forward with surprising swiftness and captured him in a tight embrace. He stood there for several moments with the man's face pressed against his chest, his arms pinned to his sides. Unsure of how to react, he thought of stepping away, only to find himself held fast. He felt a dampness spreading across his chest and realized that the man, his father, was crying.

It was strange, in that moment, how he felt. There were things, so many things, they had to discuss. All this time they'd lost and it was he who—but, they'd already lost so much time and well . .

His thoughts were interrupted by the long slow sigh of the man at his chest. He looked down at his father's face, his wet eyes closed in a blissful smile. Somewhere deep in his mind, he felt something relax; like some tiny string that had been stretched and plucked repeatedly for years, strained to the point of fracture, had suddenly been released.

He could not say how long they stayed that way, but it was getting dark and he had to collect his children. Without a word, his father followed him, holding tight to his arm. The children had returned to the car, as he had asked them to, and sat fidgeting in the back seat. They turned, craning their necks to get a better view of the man beside him. As they neared the car, his father's eyes widened and a smile spread across his face; he shuffled excitedly toward the passenger door and pulled it open, his eyes never leaving the curious faces of those in the back. He watched as his father sat down in the front seat, buckled his seatbelt, turned to smile back at his grandchildren, and gave them a small wave. They giggled, shyly burying their faces, and each gave a small wave in return. After a few moments, all three turned around to grin at him expectantly.

He moved forward and opened the door. Winking to the two in the back, he climbed inside and slammed it closed behind him. He turned the key and the engine roared to life, causing the other passengers to jump slightly. His father chuckled, patting the door beside him fondly. He pulled the car away from the curb and they set off down crowded streets.

Chapter 4

He had driven all night and it was late in the morning when they had finally stopped. The children had fallen asleep minutes after leaving the park. They had lain curled under a pile of mismatched blankets; their heads slumped against each other, little legs and feet intertwined and peeping through the covers.

His father had managed to stay awake for several hours before finally succumbing. They had ridden in silence for all that time. Though, for some reason he could not explain, the quality of the silence had changed somehow. Unlike before, it had become comfortable. The sort of silence shared only by the closest friends, who felt no need to clutter a cozy atmosphere with idle chatter. The old man had stared for long periods, unmoving, out into the dark with a relaxed smile resting on his face.

Occasionally, his father had chuckled quietly to himself and reached across to grab his hand, giving it a squeeze or a pat, then returned to staring off down the empty road, smiling.

When they had arrived, he had let the others have their rest. He'd climbed out, stretching high and wide attempting to work life into his deadened limbs, and looked around. He'd brought them to the only place he'd ever truly cherished, the place where his life had truly begun. It was the hillside where he'd proposed to his wife: The hill jutted high above the surrounding lowlands. Lush green meadows spread out all directions until disappearing amidst a haze of distant trees. For miles around, the only visible landmarks were the forests, framing the meadows below, and the one magnificent maple atop the hill.

It was late afternoon now, approaching dusk. Fireflies hung buoyant above a sea of grass, the night illumed with their neon appointments. His children chased them, catching them in loose grips and peering eagerly through their fingers as they lit. He leaned against the hood of the car, one foot resting on the chrome bumper, with his father in the passenger seat behind him. The two men sat quietly, watching the sun set to the right of them, making its final descent. The shadows stretched, thinning themselves as they ran from the falling light.

Above them swayed the long sturdy arms of the solitary maple, song-filled birds darting in and out of its dense branches. He'd so often thought of the tree when he remembered her. The way the shadows of its translucent leaves had danced across her skin, little freckles that had made her all the more lovely. He silently wished she were here with him now, sitting beside him beneath their tree, in more than just memory. He sat for several moments, eyes closed, listening to the sounds of their secret place; the birds, the grass, the leaves, their children's laughter.

He looked down at his watch—it would be here soon.

He glanced back over his shoulder to his father, who sat

watching the children with a placid smile. Even now, after the long night together, he found his father's actions confusing. He hadn't had to say a word to the man. His father had never asked him why they'd come, or where they were going. He hadn't even stopped to lock the front door when they'd left. He'd simply followed, happily, seemingly willing to leave everything else behind. It was as if the man sensed that he'd come for a reason, but was unconcerned with what it was. As he looked at the man, at the look of utter contentment on his face, he thought—perhaps, after all this time, the reasons didn't really matter.

In that moment everything fell quiet. He realized that the birds had vanished taking the songs, and small green lights of the fireflies, with them. He heard the children's sounds of confusion before he saw it. There, suspended low above the southern horizon, hung a bright green and blue cloud of light starkly contrasted against the blackening sky. The children ran to his side and began pulling frantically at him, pointing, staring, asking what it was.

What could he tell them?

He heard the car door close behind him and turned to see his father standing at his side. His father rested a hand on his shoulder and stared into his eyes. His apprehension, his hopelessness and fear, must have been betrayed in that moment. The smile had left his father's face and the man now stared with a look of grim understanding at the light in the southern sky.

His father knelt down beside the kids and wrapped them both in his arms, kissing their cheeks. They giggled and squirmed as he picked them up. He set them both on the hood of the car, next to their father. The man sat down on the other side of them and laid an arm across their shoulders. He smiled again and pointed a finger to the horizon.

The old man cleared his throat and looked into the children's eyes, "Have you ever seen anything so beautiful in your life?" he asked softly. "It will be gone in a flash," he smiled and stared ahead, "nothing that beautiful can stay." After a moment the man looked up, catching his own son's eye, "Look at the beauty, while it lasts."

He felt the tightness leave his chest as his father's words soaked through him. He looked down at his children, who now sat staring in wonder at the light before them. He reached an arm across their small shoulders, across his father's. He smiled as he stared ahead with them, the last sunset disappearing to the right, "Look at the beauty," he whispered. He felt the warmth of his father's hand resting on his shoulder, "While it lasts."

Colleen McLaughlin and Terry Skaggs are a married couple from Rock Island, IL, who'd like to thank Carl Sagan, Ray Bradbury, and John Foxx who inspired this story into life.

Janissars
Willin D. Fenster

"Gens Leader, instruments show two large emergencies approximately $(6^6)^6$ times 4.313 Large Distance Units outside the orbit of Planet Six."

Gens Leader Amu!vizn acknowledged the report from *Fearsome Nest Defender*'s Sensor/Communications console with a wave of one upper grasping member. "Acknowledged. Transmit the information to Gens^6 Leader Mi!tchuin aboard *Guardian Mother*." It would take several sixes of minims for the message to reach *Guardian Mother*, and Amu!vizn sent tight-beam messages with the information to the other six-plus-five Klag*chir! ships awaiting the expected Hegemon attack.

The Klag*chi occupying the Sensor Communicator position kept feeding updated target information as her passive sensors provided it. All the data would be multiple sixes of minims old due to the distances involved, but the Gens Leader was confident the Hegemon warships would have difficulty detecting the Klag*chir! defenders, all of which were orbiting with their drives shut down and using only passive sensors.

The data coming in from the energy pulse of the Hegemon ships coming out of Jump indicated the two vessels were enormous. Each Hegemon vessel was roughly six-squared larger than the combined mass of the entire Klag*chir! defense Squadron. Gens Leader Amu!vizn concealed her concern, but the raw power implicit in the enemy ships was thoroughly discouraging. Both vessels had emerged well outside the system, implying a certain amount of caution on the part of the aliens. Both vessels were 'south' of the plane of rotation, and were bearing further south. This would grant the aliens a clearer view of the entire system, but their heading and velocity would leave them far from any of the primary system defenses around Planet Three.

"Navigation," she said sharply. "Extrapolate the alien ships' orbit. Assume they are under drive and make no course changes. Does that orbit intersect any of this system's planets?"

"Stand by," the Navigator answered as she manipulated her computer systems. Several minims later, she answered, her tone puzzled. "Gens Leader, the alien ships' orbit does not currently intersect with any planetary or sub-planetary objects." She manipulated her controls, and several possible orbits appeared on Amu!vizn's screen, based on estimates of the enemy vessels' mass and possible drive configurations.

"Gens Leader," the Navigator said with a great deal of confusion. "The enemy vessels are unlikely to be capable of intersecting any known system object in less than six-plus-one stellar orbits, unless they possess a type of drive which violates known physics."

Amu!vizn manipulated her own console, changing various parameters to puzzle out the Hegemon ships' purpose. Making several orbits around the failed star at the system center would only subject them to repeated attack by the defending ships, in addition to long-range missiles from the orbital fortresses around Planets Three and Six. There had to be another explanation. Her grasping members suddenly froze as a horrible thought occurred to her. She called up the course the defenders had taken from their home system, mostly concealed in the nebula nearby.

"Navigation," she called. "Extrapolate the alien ships' course. How long until they are in position to Jump to Home?"

"Great Mother!" the Navigator swore. Her grasping members flew across her console. A new course plot appeared on the Gens Leader's display. "Assuming standard drive capability, they will reach a Jump point for Home on this course in six-squared maxims. We should detect drive flares from them soon if they are making for the Jump point to Home system."

Amu!vizn shook her head. The defenders had counted on fighting a delaying action against the Hegemon in the worthless space around the failed star and its planets to give the Home system more time to prepare. That hope was now gone, and the Defense Squadron was scattered and mostly far out of position to interdict the enemy ships.

"How many of the squadron ships have a hope of reaching the Jump point before the enemy?" The Gens Leader knew the answer, but asked anyway in hope the laws of the Universe might have changed in her favor, just this once.

The Navigator's reply was dishearteningly realistic. "None," she replied soberly. "Even using maximal thrust continuously for the entire orbit would leave *Far-Travelling Male* approximately six-plus-four maxims from a safe Jump when the enemy ships Jump out, and she is in the best position of the squadron."

"Communicator," Amu!vizn ordered, her tone bleak. "Advise *Guardian Mother* of our calculations. Inform Gen[6] Leader Mi!tchuin I recommend all ships which can bear on the estimated enemy Jump point to mass-launch missiles on maximal-thrust courses targeted on the space immediately before the estimated Jump point."

It was unlikely to do much good, but at least some of the squadron's missiles might arrive in time to damage the enemy ships. The Gens Leader ordered *Fearsome Nest Defender* to make the horribly fuel-wasting course change required to slightly shorten the time it would take to get far enough out of the system's gravity well to allow the Jump engines to take them Home. The maneuver alarm was broadcast, warning the crew to brace for thrust by locking the talons on their four lower limbs into the woven deck coverings provided for that purpose.

"All crew into pressure suits," the Gens Leader ordered. "Dump atmosphere and begin Jump calculations for the soonest possible Jump to Home. Prepare an automatic radio broadcast warning message to transmit as soon as we arrive."

Even expending fuel at the current unsustainable rate would see *Fearsome Nest Defender* jumping long after the enemy. Amu!vizn was planning on Jumping as soon as possible, risking the ship by engaging the primary drive while still technically inside the gravity well of the system in hope of gaining time. *Fearsome Nest Defender* massed considerably less than the Hegemon ships, which made the attempt slightly less suicidal.

Larger vessels had to Jump further from a gravity source than lighter ones, and were similarly forced to arrive further from their destination's gravity well. Jumping too deep in a gravity well ran the risk of the Jump engines failing catastrophically, usually destroying the ship in the process. If the drives did not fail, the Jumping ship might find itself emerging from Jump many light years off course. Emerging from Jump too close to a gravity source was likely to cause the Jump engines to fail in a variety of lethal ways. The Jumping ship might be torn apart or get instantly converted to energy equivalent to the ship's mass. *Fearsome Nest Defender* would be attempting to Jump from within the dead system's gravity well and arrive at the Home system dangerously deep within the gravity well there. Emerging from Jump further in-system would also place *Fearsome Nest Defender* between the Hegemon warships and the Home planets. It was a desperate move, but one more ship defending Home might be enough to help avert disaster.

The Gens Leader ordered Communications to notify *Guardian Mother* of the plan, hoping some of the other Gens Leaders would arrive at the same conclusions, but Amu!vizn could not afford to wait. She had no illusions about *Fearsome Nest Defender*'s odds of survival against the vastly larger Hegemon ships, but perhaps she could at least delay the massive enemy ships enough to give the Home defenses a better chance of dealing with the invaders.

Fearsome Nest Defender was accelerating at nearly three gravities, draining the fuel bunkers dangerously and punishing the crew. Three gravities was the most acceleration Klag*chir! could withstand and still remain capable of fighting their ship. The Weapons console notified the Gens Leader she had developed a firing solution for *Fearsome Nest Defender*'s two long-range missile batteries. Amu!vizn was tempted, but chose to spare the munitions for the fight at Home.

Amu!vizn managed to transmit her conclusions and the planned Jump to her crew during the punishing drive to their calculated Jump point. A system-wide plot was shown on every public screen aboard *Fearsome Nest Defender*, accompanied by paired timers counting down the estimated time-to-Jump for the ship and the Hegemon vessels.

"Gens Leader, we have detected enemy drive systems," the Sensor/Communicator officer reported, her voice distorted under the ferocious gravity. "Both enemy vessels are maneuvering to Jump position. We also have more than six-square drive flares on course for the forecast orbital position of Planet Six." The screen facing the Gens Leader's oculars obediently changed to the plotted courses of the inbound drives. "Analysis of drive emissions suggests long-range missiles in lieu of occupied craft."

"Concur," the Gens Leader replied verbally. "Transmit course data to the Defense Squadron and the orbital fortresses."

The Navigator called up the plot. "Gens Leader? I do not understand this attack pattern by the enemy." Confusion was evident in her voice despite the pressure of three gravities. "This attack seems needlessly wasteful, and unlikely to cause significant damage to the Defense Squadron. The missiles are well-plotted, and our ships can easily maneuver out of danger."

Amu!vizn kept her voice level, trying to keep the dismay she felt out of her broadcast. "It makes sense if we assume the enemy has effectively unlimited resources," she answered carefully. "Based on the plotted course, any Squadron vessels in advantageous orbits to attempt a return Home are likely to be forced to maneuver to avoid the enemy missiles, thus delaying their Jumps. I suspect the enemy missiles will shortly shut down their drives to conserve fuel, allowing dramatic maneuvering as they close in on the orbit of Planet Six. This is likely to improve their chances to successfully attack any ships the missiles detect, or the orbital fortresses."

Fearsome Nest Defender finally settled into an orbit calculated to take the ship far enough distant from the failed star at the center of the system to permit a Jump to Home System in the shortest time possible. Once maneuvering was completed, the Engineering and Life Support crews began the odious task of ensuring every Klag*chi wearing a pressure suit was properly connected to service umbilicals to provide nutrition and breathable atmosphere—and remove waste products. Sensors reported a scattered series of long-range Klag*chir!

missiles had been launched toward the calculated point where the enemy vessels were expected to Jump. Gens Leader Amu!vizn observed the Sensor plot and sighed internally. The strike missiles were not mass-launched or even properly coordinated. Instead of arriving in a swarm which might permit a few to penetrate the enemy's counter-missile defenses, the missiles would be arriving as a series of scattered individual warheads which were likely to be easily defeated.

Slightly less than two maxims later, Sensors/Communications opened a circuit to Amu!vizn. "Secondary launches detected from the enemy ships, Gens Leader," her voice steady, but the strain was nonetheless audible. "Track indicates another six-square missiles aimed to intersect *Fearsome Nest Defender*'s course plot."

The Gens Leader sighed internally again, having expected just that response. "What is your analysis of their drive capability?" she asked evenly.

After conferring with Navigation, the Sensor/Communications Klag*chi called up a modified plot. "Gens Leader, the enemy ships' drive emissions imply a modest improvement in efficiency over our own. They also appear to be capable of handling greater thrust——both vessels are currently accelerating at 4.12 gravities. The enemy missiles appear to accelerate at six-times-two plus two gravities before shutting off their drives as you predicted."

Amu!vizn keyed an acknowledgement while grimly concentrating on how to thwart the well-thought out attack by the Hegemon. The immutable laws governing movement in space eliminated most of her options, but she kept at it until she arrived at an idea which might offer a modest possibility of success. Using just the tips of her manipulative members, she ran several possible defense scenarios on her private screen before opening her circuit to the command crew. "We will assume accurate plotting of the enemy launches, and begin counter-missile launch along the anticipated threat axis in four maxims and six-plus-two minims. Retain six-squared plus four defense missiles for the battle once we reach Home." She keyed the plot for general distribution throughout

Fearsome Nest Defender, and ordered Sensors/Communications to tight-beam the information to *Guardian Mother*.

Locking down her circuit to just Navigation and Sensors/Communications, the Gens Leader continued, "Once your plot shows a four-in-six probability of successful Jump to Home, you are ordered to do so immediately—without warning or further consultation. My calculation shows this will be approximately contemporaneous with the anticipated arrival of the Hegemon missile strike on *Fearsome Nest Defender*. Regardless of battle status, you will initiate Jump for Home the instant your systems provide this probability."

Navigation objected. "Gens Leader," she began. "Standard procedure prohibits attempting a Jump with less than five point three in six probability of success."

"If we survive the Jump and further survive the resulting battle against overwhelming forces once we arrive, I give you permission to bring me up on charges." Amu!vizn said without a trace of humor in her voice. "We have little choice. The enemy has clearly outmaneuvered us in bypassing the Defense Squadron and striking directly at Home. Even under the most optimistic calculations, enemy missiles will already be driving toward the Home defenses before we arrive in-system there. I deem the risk of obliteration to be worth the chance to add *Fearsome Nest Defender*'s weapons to the final defense of Home against the Hegemon."

"I concur," came the response from Sensor/Communications. "Standard procedures be damned! Each of those enemy ships masses more than the entire Defense Squadron here. Any reasonable chance to prevent those ships from attacking Home is worth the risk."

"I object to use of the word '*reasonable*' in this context," Navigation grumped. "This seems as reasonable as a rampant male during Breeding Season." She paused before adding, "But I would rather die at least *trying* to protect Home than arrive too late to do more than observe as Home suffers orbital bombardment. So be it."

Several Maxims later, Sensors/Communications reported the Hegemon vessels had Jumped toward Home, and also detected fresh drive emissions from the enemy missiles aimed at *Fearsome Nest Defender*. The Gens Leader immediately ordered counter-missile launches using the more accurate data provided by the new plots. The ship shuddered as her missile batteries spat swarms of short-range missiles at the plotted courses of the Hegemon missiles, and drive was slightly reduced to divert power to the point-defense laser array. Sensors were quickly obscured by the flashes of fusion warheads detonating in close proximity to enemy missiles.

As ordered, a modest fraction of *Fearsome Nest Defender*'s counter-missiles were kept in reserve for the expected battle to defend Home. As the plot cleared Sensors/Communications noted calmly that only six-times-two enemy missiles were still under drive and maneuvering toward *Fearsome Nest Defender*'s course. "Estimated arrival in six-plus-three mimims," she declared without emotion.

The point-defense lasers began to fire, slowly reducing the number of inbound missiles as they drew closer. Navigation fixed her attention on the Jump plot, steadfastly ignoring the increasing probability of fiery death in favor of the steadily increasing probability of a successful Jump. Once the digit counter ticked over to four-in-six probability of success, she stabbed the *Engage Jump* button on her console, just as three Hegemon missiles drew within six-squared Small Distance Units and detonated.

Nuclear fire lashed at *Fearsome Nest Defender*'s hull as the Jump field expanded. Aboard the ship, Klag*chi died in incandescent agony as sections of the vessel were converted to energy while dropping out of sidereal spacetime. The entire ship shuddered at the uneven transition, and the drive flickered off briefly before resuming at a slightly reduced thrust level a fraction of a minim later. The crew surged against their restraints at the shock, with several breaking free and hurtling into solid bulkheads as the restraints failed under the unanticipated stress.

The Jump field dropped normally, and *Fearsome Nest Defender*'s surviving crew counted their losses and determined just how badly the ship had suffered from the attack. Navigation and Sensor/Communication frantically searched their instruments to learn exactly where they had emerged from Jump. The damage reports accumulated in Gens Leader Amu!vizn's screens, accurate and discouraging. Six-times-four plus one Klag*chir! were dead or missing, with twice that number injured. Thrust was reduced to two-sixths of optimal, and fully half the point-defense lasers were off-line. The good news was the undamaged status of the long-range strike missile batteries and the counter-missile reserves were still online—albeit with only one remaining launch bay.

Navigation and Sensors made their initial reports, cheerfully reporting a successful emergence an estimated six-cubed plus two Large Distance Units out from Home planet, accelerating Homeward at a steady one point five four gravities. Messages were being broadcast announcing their arrival and warning of the Hegemon threat. Transmissions intercepted from two of the orbital fortresses at the edge of the Home system, broadcast almost a full maxim earlier, reported they were engaging the Hegemon warships. The transmissions ceased abruptly, contemporaneous with multiple fusion explosions in close proximity to both fortresses.

Amu!vizn ordered Navigation to reduce thrust Homeward and change course to match the plotted course of the enemy vessels included in the reports from the doomed orbital forts, attempting to keep *Fearsome Nest Defender* between Home and the expected attack axis from the outer edge of the system.

Sensors/Communications keyed in with an analysis of the Hegemon attack *Fearsome Nest Defender* had survived. "Gens Leader," she said soberly. "The enemy missiles employ a type of fusion warhead we are ill-equipped to defend against."

A digital playback of the missile attack appeared on the screen, massively slowed down to properly display the unique energy patterns. Instead of the instantly-spherical blossom of nuclear fire she expected, the Gens Leader observed a strange asymmetric triple pulse of energy, as if the explosion were slightly delayed. She stopped the playback and slowed it further, running the imagery forward micro-minim by micro-minim. At that speed, Amu!vizn could clearly see the initial pulse forming a dense electromagnetic field around the explosion, with a tiny aperture in the field pointed directly at *Fearsome Nest Defender*. For a micro-minim, the fusion blast was contained within the field and escaped only along the axis of the aperture, erupting in the strangely asymmetrical blast after the infinitesimal pause to contain the explosion.

Amu!vizn suddenly understood how *Fearsome Nest Defender* had suffered such damage from relatively distant explosions. Extremely dense plasma had been projected through the tiny apertures in the electromagnetic fields at close to luminal velocity, cutting deeply into the ship's hull during the fractional minim before the fields collapsed. The point defenses were insufficient to prevent enemy missiles from getting close enough to cause critical damage to any artificial object in space.

Cursing silently, the Gens Leader transmitted her findings Homeward, then ordered a change in targeting priority for *Fearsome Nest Defender*'s defenses. The damaged point-defense lasers would be unlikely to compensate for the unexpected enemy capability, but there was little else Amu!vizn could do at the moment but curse the Hegemon technicians and engineers who'd developed a means of briefly controlling fusion explosions so cleverly.

Two maxims and three-times-six minims later, new direct information reached *Fearsome Nest Defender*'s sensors from the enemy vessels. Drive emissions seemed to indicate the massive Hegemon warships were maneuvering toward Home System's Planet Four, the massive gas giant dominating the outer edges of the system. The constellation of natural and artificial satellites around Planet Four constituted most of Home System's manufacturing capacity, and was protected only by a single old, poorly-maintained orbital fortress. Massive bombardment of the old fort was already taking place, and hundreds of small intra-system spacecraft were already detected departing Planet Four's orbit and heading sunward.

Gens Leader Amu!vizn had a difficult decision to make. *Fearsome Nest Defender* was critically low on fuel and severely damaged, but sensors indicated she was also closer to Planet Four and the Hegemon ships than the next nearest defending vessels—which were halfway across the Home system or accelerating in the wrong directions. Changing course toward Planet Four's orbit would expend most of her remaining fuel, but allow *Fearsome Nest Defender* a chance to strike back at the invaders, whose maneuvering would be restricted by proximity to the gas giant.

"Navigation," she ordered brusquely, knowing she was sending *Fearsome Nest Defender* toward almost certain death. "Plot course to intersect enemy vessels near Planet Four. Ignore fuel consumption in favor of shortest-duration orbit."

Navigation stiffened at the realization of what that order entailed, but responded instantly and calmly. "Gens Leader, estimated arrival at Planet Four's plotted position is four maxims and six-squared minims." She tapped a command into her console, then keyed the results to Amu!vizn's screen.

The Gens Leader chuckled silently. The chosen course plot would use Planet Four to partially screen *Fearsome Nest Defender*'s approach from the Hegemon vessels. Amu!vizn acknowledged and approved the course, then began transmitting a tightbeam message Home. She briefly described her planned attack, and recommended high honors to various Klag*chi who had distinguished themselves aboard *Fearsome Nest Defender*.

"Even if successful in attacking the enemy vessels," she concluded quietly, "the Hegemon invaders' size and weapons capabilities mean *Fearsome Nest Defender* is unlikely to survive the attack. Our primary goal is to cause the enemy to expend ordnance and fuel in destroying *Fearsome Nest Defender*, thereby improving the chances of other defending ships to make successful attacks. If, despite the odds, we are not destroyed by the enemy, *Fearsome Nest Defender* will have insufficient fuel to avoid gradually departing Home System on our current course and speed. *Fearsome Nest Defender* out."

After keying the circuit closed, Amu!vizn snarled silently, "*Make it count, you feckless, gelded males!*"

Returning her attention to the present, the Gens Leader noted Sensors/Communications was working hard on her consoles, leaving the display plot showing only the plotted course and estimated arrival timer. After a few minims, she gave a small cheer and keyed a new display to Amu!vizn's screen.

"Gens Leader," she said triumphantly. "I have tapped into the Sensor and Communications links for the satellites and habitats orbiting Planet Four."

Amu!vizn acknowledged the report cheerfully. "Well done," she said. "That will give us improved targeting information as we approach. Very well done."

Slightly more than two maxims later, the crew of *Fearsome Nest Defender* were impotent witnesses as *Far-Travelling Male* emerged from Jump near Planet Four, and was subsequently torn to pieces by the Hegemon warships. *Fearsome Nest Defender* was taking full advantage of the satellite network around Planet Four as the enemy slowly maneuvered into orbit, but was helpless to do more than watch as their sister ship launched every missile she had before vanishing under a barrage of fusion blasts from the Hegemon counter-launch. When the fusion flares faded away, *Far-Travelling Male* had been reduced to glowing fragments in a rapidly-expanding bubble around the ship's last position.

"Analysis of *Far-Travelling Male*'s attack on the enemy vessels?" the Gens Leader asked quietly.

"Largely ineffective," Sensors/Communications observed somberly. "The Hegemon missile defenses appear to be based on the same contained fusion jets as their strike missiles. *Far-Travelling Male* appears to have had relatively few missiles remaining, and the enemy counter-missile launch was demonstrably overwhelming."

"Noted." Amu!vizn said before opening a circuit to the Weapons console and ordering changes to *Fearsome Nest Defender*'s strike missiles. "Once we achieve a firing solution, launch everything we have on maximum continuous thrust toward the target. Ensure the onboard navigation systems for the missiles are capable of this maneuvering."

The Klag*chi at the Weapons console acknowledged the order soberly. "So you plan to get into knife-fighting range and hope a few missiles get through their defenses?" she asked grimly. "Not arguing, you understand. I'm just not sure it will have much effect, based on what happened to *Far-Travelling Male*."

Amu!vizn privately agreed with her. Aloud, she said, "We'll have an advantage *Far-Travelling Male* did not—the enemy ships will not have much time to detect, track, and engage our strike missiles as we emerge into their detection envelope from behind the Sensor shadow of Planet Four. Regardless, we must make the enemy expend fuel and munitions as much as possible to give other defending ships a greater chance."

"I concur," Weapons said with grim determination. "I don't have to like it, but this seems the only logical option." She began tapping the new launch configuration into her console as she spoke. "The Home system ships are mostly better equipped for this sort of fight, since few of them have Jump drive systems taking up four-sixths of the hull."

Amu!vizn had no argument. Jump drive and the fuel for it generally took up more than half the internal capacity of ships so equipped. Many of the Klag*chir! Home Squadron ships had been constructed without Jump capability, allowing them more room for fuel and ordnance. This made them ideal for system defense, since they could maneuver more freely and shoot more missiles than starships such as *Fearsome Nest Defender*.

The Gens Leader closed the circuit and checked the Engineering display. Based on the current expenditure, *Fearsome Nest Defender* would run out of fuel six-times-two minims before she entered the enemy's detection envelope. Part of her hoped the enemy would lash out at *Fearsome Nest Defender* as she passed Planet Four's orbit and headed out toward deep space. *"Better to get vaporized quickly than slowly die of starvation or asphyxiation,"* she told herself silently.

Two maxims later, *Fearsome Nest Defender* used the last of her fuel a minim or two earlier than calculated, likely a result of damage from the earlier Hegemon attack. The crew had been well trained to work in microgravity, but the sudden lack of vibration from thrust was nonetheless dispiriting.

The crew's spirits were further diminished by the improved Sensor data collected from the satellite network around Planet Four. Despite knowing intellectually the Hegemon ships were vastly larger than *Fearsome Nest Defender*, the telemetry from the satellites was frightening. One of the massive warships headed toward Planet Four, while the other appeared to be maneuvering toward an orbit slightly leading the planet around the Home Primary. As the huge warships maneuvered, the leading warship appeared to separate into five slightly smaller vessels, each one of which massed six to the sixth times the mass of *Fearsome Nest Defender*. Four of the sub-components began maneuvering into higher polar orbits, while the center section drifted into a parking orbit near one of the Klag*chir satellites just outside the gas giant's upper atmosphere.

"Where are they getting their intelligence?" Amu!vizn demanded rhetorically. "How did they know to look for an extraction/refining facility in Planet Four's orbit?"

Sensors/Communications thought for a moment, then tapped a few keys on her console. "Gens Leader," she answered politely. "I note a message to all ships which was transmitted more than six-times-two planetary cycles ago, identifying the Extraction/Refining satellite as the dedicated refueling asset for ships Jumping Home. The orbital coordinates are listed, and the transponder code."

Amu!vizn stifled a groan. "So every starship which entered Hegemon space helpfully included that critical bit of strategic information." She thought back, straining to remember how many Klag*chir! merchant vessels had failed to return from the nearest Hegemon systems. At least three she could be sure of. "*How truly good.*" She snarled internally.

Her thoughts were interrupted by a new report from Sensor/Communications. "Gens Leader, we've just received a tight-beam transmission from *Nomadic Herder*, located in system south, roughly six-cubed plus six-times-four Large Distance Units toward the Home primary. They are advising a time-on-target long-range missile strike commencing six plus three minims before transmission time. The missiles should be arriving approximately six-times-four plus three maxims after Fearsome Nest Defender has passed the orbit of Planet Four. If we are still able to transmit, we can provide better targeting data for the missiles as they approach."

"Someone here at Home's been paying attention to our message traffic," the Gens Leader answered cheerfully. "Set your sensors on automatic, and broadcast targeting data continuously for as long as possible."

The enormous enemy ship maneuvering toward the leading stable gravity point for Planet Four suddenly lit up with the drive flares of missile launches. Amu!vizn sighed to herself and keyed open the public circuit. "It appears the enemy is also using the sensor arrays orbiting Planet Four to track *Fearsome Nest Defender*." She told the crew somberly. "Stand by for incoming enemy missile strike. Launch all strike missiles targeting the largest enemy vessel as soon as you have a viable targeting solution. Engage enemy missiles with our counter-missiles at optimal range as they appear."

The Gens Leader keyed up the Engineering circuit. "Engineer. The point-defense lasers have absolute priority on battery power. This specifically includes life-support until the enemy strike has concluded."

"Concur," the Engineer agreed quietly. "There is little use in conserving power if *Fearsome Nest Defender* is destroyed."

"Do your best," Amu!vizn replied, grateful for her understanding.

Sensors/Communications interrupted. "Gens Leader, I have plots on six-cubed plus four enemy missiles. Estimated arrival in six-times-three plus three-point-five minims."

Despite wincing inwardly at the news, Amu!vizn acknowledged the report steadily. "Display plots for inbound missiles and our strike missiles outbound to all screens." She keyed the public circuit open again. "Double all tie-downs where possible. Shift leaders take control of your sections and assume independent operations in the event central control is lost. Remember—every enemy missile aimed at Fearsome Nest Defender is one less aimed at Home. The longer we can fight, the better the chances our system defenses can inflict real damage on the enemy."

She keyed a private channel to Engineering and the weapons console. "Once every strike and defense missile has been launched," she ordered without preamble. "Assemble a team to salvage fuel and batteries from damaged missiles. Use the batteries to restore life support, and use any scavenged fuel to get the main drive briefly operational. It will not be sufficient to change course, but running the primary drive even briefly will re-charge our storage capacity sufficient to keep as many Klag*chir! alive as possible until Home can mount a rescue mission."

Both Klag*chi concurred and Amu!vizn closed the circuit.

"*Assuming there is anyone left who can mount a rescue,*" she said silently to herself.

Like all space combat, *Fearsome Nest Defender*'s solitary attack on the Hegemon invaders consisted mostly of long periods of waiting, followed by intense periods of furious activity. Amu!vizn had given priority to the strike missiles, and the one remaining missile bay launched the entire load-out in less than six minims. The strike missiles had all been targeted on the nearest Hegemon vessel orbiting Planet Four, and their relatively sophisticated circuitry allowed them to coordinate thrust and course to ensure they would largely arrive simultaneously. The short-range defense missiles were launched next, in clusters of six, emptying the launch bay in just over four minims. These comparatively simple circuits were each assigned a separate enemy missile, and immediately engaged full thrust output to intercept the enemy strike missiles as far as possible from *Fearsome Nest Defender*. But there were too few remaining counter-missiles to thwart the Hegemon attack. Even if every interceptor successfully destroyed an enemy missile, six-squared times five enemy missiles would still be targeted on *Fearsome Nest Defender*. With only half the point-defense lasers operational, the outlook appeared to be both bleak and very short.

A series of miniature suns suddenly erupted in the emptiness near Planet Four as *Fearsome Nest Defender*'s counter missiles closed on enemy missiles and detonated at precisely-calculated distances ahead of the enemy missiles' course tracks. With the sensors orbiting Planet Four temporarily obscured by the destruction, the precision of the plotted courses of the enemy missiles dropped sharply, making things worse for the last-ditch laser defenses. Aimed at points along the enemy missiles' course tracks *Fearsome Nest Defender*'s sensors had calculated, the laser array began firing continuously, while the Engineer cursed as she watched the ship's batteries deplete with every shot.

The end came suddenly. Sensors/Communications had just begun to curse as her equipment died for lack of power when the remaining six-times-five plus three enemy missiles detonated in close proximity to *Fearsome Nest Defender*. The ship was literally gutted by nuclear fire, as jets of superheated plasma tore through hull and

Klag*chir! with equal velocity. Hull metal sublimed at the impact, and the resulting rapidly-expanding gases raged through the corridors and compartments, destroying equipment and reducing pressure-suited Klag*chir! to splatters of biological material melted onto any surviving surfaces. The front two sixths of *Fearsome Nest Defender* was vaporized by multiple strikes, and the rear one sixth had been blasted free of the rest of the ship, spinning off into a long, cometary orbit around the Home sun.

What remained of *Fearsome Nest Defender* resembled slag from a metallurgical plant more than a star-travelling space vessel. The spinning ruin was surrounded by clouds of debris blasted from the hulk by the Hegemon attack or loose objects ejected by the uneven rotation the multiple explosions had imparted on the hulk. Some of the objects loosely orbiting the wreck were dead or dying Klag*chir!.

Surprisingly, there were still Klag*chir! surviving aboard the ruin. All were injured to at least some degree, but the lack of internal atmosphere and well-designed compartmentalization reduced the damage aboard from 'instant destruction' to merely 'catastrophic.'

Amu!vizn returned to consciousness in searing pain. Two of her lower limbs were encased in what looked like deck metal, which had apparently flowed like a liquid under the attack and solidified around the limbs. She could feel nothing in the left forelimb, but the right forelimb felt like it was on fire. Her left upper grasping member appeared to have been torn off halfway to the digits, but her pressure suit had properly sealed off above the breach, which is why she was still breathing.

Despite her pain, Amu!vizn twisted her oculars around inside her scarred helmet to check on the control crew. There was no sign of the Navigator. Where the Nav console had been, there was only a rent through the deckplates beyond which stars were occasionally visible. There was something resembling a Klag*chi where the Sensors/Communications console had been, but she did not appear to be moving. The rest of the central control station seemed to be a mass of metallic debris and darkness.

Calming herself, Amu!vizn checked her suit's internal read-out. She had internal atmosphere sufficient for several maxims, but her internal power was critically low. Her suit radio was inoperative, and using the one working external light would only hasten the expenditure of her remaining power, which meant the atmosphere scrubbers in her suit would be unable to keep her breathing for more than a maxim or two.

She steeled herself against the rising feeling of helpless panic and blinked her suit light on for a mini-minim, just long enough to find something nearby she could use as a lever. Her undamaged upper grasping member could just reach the solid-looking metal fragment floating nearby, though Amu!vizn cried out in pain from the added stress on her right forelimb as she moved. With the metal fragment as a lever, she began to cautiously work at freeing her forelimbs from the metal encasing them.

After a seeming eternity of pain and blind fumbling, Amu!vizn finally managed to extract her left forelimb from the metal surrounding it. She still could not feel anything below the hip, and had no control over the limb, but she'd managed to free it at least. She flashed her suit light several times as she examined the debris entrapping her right forelimb, looking for a place to start prying apart the torn metal with her metal fragment. She fancied she'd seen some odd reflections from the direction of the Navigation console as she worked, but ignored them as she began working in earnest on her trapped forelimb.

The light suddenly flooding the wrecked control room nearly blinded her. Amu!vizn straightened suddenly, the abrupt movement causing fresh waves of pain in her trapped forelimb. There were two aliens in pressure suits visible behind the lights, apparently looking into the control center through the hole where Navigation had been. She froze in shock. One of the aliens began climbing through the rent in the hull, while the other appeared to be unlimbering a weapon. Amu!vizn kept her attention on the alien coming through the rent, calculating when she'd have the best chance to use her metal shard against it.

The aliens appeared to be four-limbed, with a large lump in between two of the limbs which might be a sense-organ cluster. The lumps had lights on each side, so the sense-organ cluster suggestion was probably correct. The suits the aliens wore seemed to be a combination of metal and ceramic, and Amu!vizn could make out a multitude of what seemed to be tools attached to the suits. The alien outside was applying some sort of energy-directed beam at the rent in the hull using two of its limbs. The one inside reached back through the rent and tugged a large, rectangular object into the wrecked control room. Amu!vizn was shocked to recognize the rectangular object as a survival module for Klag*chir! pressure suits.

Confusion and pain combined to nearly overwhelm Amu!vizn's mind for a moment. The aliens must be from the Hegemon ships she'd been fighting, but they seemed to be trying to keep her alive. Exhausted, she let her metal fragment float away and gestured with her functional upper grasping member toward the survival module.

The alien pushed the module gently toward her. Amu!vizn grabbed at it, cursing as her grasping member slid across the smooth sides before successfully gripping a handle on the front. She pulled the bulky module closer to her helmet and checked the functions. Nearly a full power charge and full atmosphere tanks. Without further investigation, she began the difficult process of removing the module currently attached to her pressure suit and attaching the new one. She'd been well-trained in the relatively simple procedure, but only had one working upper limb at the moment, and the process took several minims longer than it should have.

Finally able to breathe properly scrubbed atmosphere, Amu!vizn looked up to see both aliens were now in the wrecked control room with her. The rent in the deck where Navigation had been was now much wider, and one of the aliens was engaged in using his tool to cut yet more of the hull out of the opening. The alien who had first entered the wreck was holding a small block of equipment about the size of Amu!vizn's digit cluster. When the alien was sure he had her attention, he gently pushed the equipment over to her.

Amu!vizn examined the device briefly. It appeared to be some sort of short-range transmitter/receiver of an unfamiliar but recognizable style. She looked back at the alien. The alien gestured at the device, then at Amu!vizn's helmet. The alien tapped one of its limbs on the top of its sense-organ cluster several times.

Amu!vizn got the idea and placed the device against her

helmet, not particularly surprised when it seemed to instantly adhere to the helmet on contact. She briefly heard a buzzing sound, followed by a clearly synthetic voice.

"Please do not be alarmed. You will not be harmed. Once you are extricated from the wreck, you will be taken to a nearby Klag*chir! spacecraft for medical treatment. You may communicate with the *buzzmumblestatic* trying to free you by speaking normally. Note there will be some minor delays in communication as your language is translated."

Far beyond astonishment at this point, Amu!vizn chose to relax and let the aliens cut her free from the metal trapping her forelimb. They were very careful with their directed-energy cutting device, working hard to avoid risking hurting her further. She took the time to observe the aliens closely. They were shorter and probably massed less than Klag*chir!, and appeared to use only their upper limbs for manipulating tools and equipment. The lights on their suits were slightly redder than her own, and appeared to be capable of variable focus. She watched as one alien adjusted a control and the beam of illumination grew wider and brighter.

She also noticed only one alien was working, while the other was facing her, one upper limb extended in her direction. A large, rectangular device was attached to the lower part of the extended limb, and Amu!vizn could just see the darkness of an opening at the end of the device. A weapon, she decided. These aliens may be trying to save her, but they were apparently willing to kill her if she proved a threat.

After nearly a maxim of work, Amu!vizn was finally freed from the metal clamped to her forelimb. The working alien passed a length of a flexible material around Amu!vizn's middle section, then attached a much thinner line to a loop at the end of the material wrapping her suit. Both aliens carefully climbed through the much wider hole in the deck before the worker alien grasped the line and gestured vaguely at the opening.

Amu!vizn gently pushed away from the deck with her two working rear limbs to hover briefly above the hole. Her upper grasping member gripped the line and tugged, drawing her slowly-rotating suit toward the aliens waiting outside what was left of

Fearsome Nest Defender.

A small *Nomad*-class shuttle orbited nearby, its control cabin apparently replaced with a mass of machinery. Four more aliens were visible near the shattered wreck of Fearsome Nest Defender, all of them apparently engaged in cutting entrances through the hull. Looking back at the aliens who had rescued her, Amu!vizn noted they had attached large devices to the bottoms of their lower limbs and were both gesturing toward the shuttle. Amu!vizn gripped the line fiercely and gave a slight tug. The alien holding the other end of the line used one upper limb to touch a control, and the device attached to its lower limbs began emitting a sharp blue light. The alien carefully adjusted its own grip on the line as it slowly rose from the wrecked ship toward the shuttle. As the line carried her along behind the alien, Amu!vizn looked back to see the other alien following, one upper limb still pointed at her.

The aliens proved to be skilled at microgravity maneuvering, and Amu!vizn soon found herself safely aboard the shuttle, only slightly delayed by her lack of two functioning upper limbs. Once aboard, two new aliens floated her through the atmosphere locks into the shuttle's main bay, which had been pressurized and converted into a makeshift medical center. Two Klag*chir! wearing medical equipment rushed to meet her, and quickly stripped Amu!vizn out of her damaged pressure suit and into a large medical survival unit installed in the center of the bay. Just before the unit's hatch closed over her, Amu!vizn noted there were six-times-two of these units, but only three of them were in use. The sudden shock at realizing only three other Klag*chi survived from *Fearsome Nest Defender* finally overwhelmed her self-control, and she lapsed into sudden unconsciousness.

When she awoke, Amu!vizn felt much better, but was sure considerable time had passed. For one thing, she was feeling the gentle pull of thrust, which meant the shuttle was under way. A Klag*chir! medical technician was visible outside the survival unit, checking the equipment. The technician noticed Amu!vizn's movement, and immediately gestured to her with both upper grasping members. She keyed a circuit open, and spoke.

"You return!" the technician exclaimed happily. "Please stay still for the moment. The unit is still working on repairing the radiation damage to your systems, after which we'll put you asleep again while we try to re-grow your damaged limbs. What can I do for you in the meantime?"

"What has happened?" Amu!vizn demanded. "What about my crew? How many were saved?"

The technician gestured sorrowfully. "I am sorry to say only you and six-plus-three other Klag*chir! were rescued from the well-named *Fearsome Nest Defender*," she answered somberly. "The Hegemon warriors were only able to locate the bodies of six-times-three-plus-three more. You fought well!"

Amu!vizn felt her will collapsing. "Not well enough, if Hegemon warriors are searching for survivors. What of the war? Has Home fallen?"

The technician touched a control, and Amu!vizn felt the sting of a chemical injection. "Please don't worry," the technician said urgently. "Nothing more has happened. There have been several fierce battles around Planet Four, and the Home forces were driven off with great losses. The Hegemon has not moved further into the system, but I'm sure I can't tell you why."

A feeling of euphoria crept into Amu!vizn's mind. She worked hard to keep her mind clear. "Then why did they spend the time to search for survivors from Fearsome Nest Defender?" she demanded crossly. "Why convert shuttles into medical units and try to save Klag*chir! defenders? This makes no sense!"

The technician touched another control, and Amu!vizn began to lose consciousness. "One of the Hegemon warriors will come and speak with you, when you're feeling better," the technician said as Amu!vizn fell asleep.

Amu!vizn awakened very slowly. It took nearly a maxim for the atmospheric drugs in her medical unit to dissipate sufficiently for her to grow coherent. When she finally shook off the effects of the drugs, she took stock of herself. Her left forelimb had been amputated, and a surgical sleeve had been attached, indicating a new one was being grown. Her right forelimb was encased in a separate surgical sleeve, but this appeared to be working on repairing damage rather than re-growing tissue. Another surgical sleeve covered her left upper grasping member, but the readouts indicated it was nearly finished with the tissue rebuild, and would soon be removed. The many aches and pains she'd been unconsciously aware of were now gone, and she almost felt good. Then she saw the pressure-suited alien form standing outside her surgical unit, and the memory of the war suffocated her sense of well-being.

She keyed the communication switch. "Who are you?" she demanded.

The bipedal figure turned to face her through the window. After several minims, and synthetic voice came from the communicator. "I'm one of the ones who shot your ship out of the sky. That good enough for you?"

She considered that for a moment. "Why did the Hegemon let me live?"

There was a much longer delay. "The 'Hegemon' doesn't care if you live or die. We care. You fought skillfully and well, and those are abilities your people will need. We chose to keep you alive, so those abilities can continue in your species."

Amu!vizn was getting confused, and this made her angry. "You act as if you were not the Hegemon!"

Another delay. "We are not the Hegemon. My species has been forced into service to the Hegemon, just as is now happening to yours. We are forced to fight for them, and win, on pain of planetary obliteration. If we refuse to fight, or lose a battle, one of our colony worlds—or even our homeworld—will be destroyed. So we fight, and we make sure we win."

"Why don't you fight the Hegemon, then?"

"We did. Three times. The last war cost us more than six-cubed-cubed dead. The Hegemon were threatening to make us extinct. We agreed to fight for them to keep our species alive."

"So, now you come to conquer the Klag*chir! for your Hegemon masters?"

"We held off as long as we could. We let the first of your ships escape back Home and hoped your people would stay away. When your ships returned, we tried simply destroying them to keep the Hegemon from paying attention. Once the Hegemon realized there was a new species with Jump drive, we were forced to move against you. The Hegemon does not like competition. They prefer stability and routine, and abhor disruptions."

Amu!vizn was stunned to momentary silence. "That is foolishness!" she shouted. "Trying to maintain things as they are only leads to stagnation and decay!"

"We know this. We have told the Hegemon this. They either do not believe us, or they do not care, or perhaps they think they will somehow be immune to entropy. In the last six-cubed planetary cycles, the Hegemon has not extended its reach or looked beyond its boundaries . . . until the Klag*chir! discovered Jump drive and then encountered the Hegemon. It was the same with us."

Still shocked at what she'd learned, Amu!vizn asked, "What happens next? You have established a position on Planet Four, but that will not be sufficient to stop Klag*chi from Jumping in or out of the system."

"Do you not think we would be thorough? First, we demonstrate we can break through your defenses at will. Then, we demonstrate the consequences of continued resistance. If you still resist, we will not try to invade your Home. We will simply bombard the planet continuously until your civilization is no more. If we do anything less, our own planets will burn."

"And now we return to the question of my survival," Amu!vizn didn't quite snarl, mostly because she assumed the translation device would not convey the emotion properly. "Why go to the trouble of saving me and the others?"

"We haven't given up," came the reply in the sterilized synthetic voice. "Our scientists calculate the Hegemon will crack, eventually. If not from internal decay, then from encountering a new species strong enough to withstand them. The Hegemon's policy is to encourage apathy and resignation and stability. Our policy is to ensure every species retains the traits which made them successful in the first place. Every time the Hegemon encounters a new star-travelling species, we do what we can to save as many individuals with fighting spirit as possible. When the Hegemon finally falls, every species will need the genes responsible for survival—including the ability to fight like *buzzmumblestatic*."

"But now, my people must be subjugated." Amu!vizn's voice

was muted by defeat.

"Until the Hegemon is no longer a threat to our homeworlds, we have no option but to conquer others for the Hegemon."

"That does not make this any easier to accept."

"Then think of this—we have broken your defenses, and you have no means of preventing planetary bombardment of your Home. Is this not so?"

Amu!vizn's answer was subdued. "It is so."

"And yet my people could not ourselves defeat the Hegemon. Were it not for the restraint my people impose on the Hegemon, there would be a large cinder in the sky where your Home once orbited. We have seen this happen. We have had this happen to us—more than once. Four of our colony worlds were burned-off in our last war with the Hegemon. So tell me now—do you want to deal with us, or the Hegemon?"

"Why do I have to choose?"

"You're here, now, with us. You have the facts in hand, and can make the best decision. But you can also choose not to decide. Then we will continue as we have begun."

"That is not a choice at all!"

"That is correct. Choose or not—your planet will submit to the Hegemon or be destroyed, regardless. If your world is not destroyed, then you will need to spread this word among your people and prepare for the day the Hegemon is no more."

"What if I refuse?"

"It won't matter, in the long run. When the Hegemon is no more, there will be chaos and destruction across a huge swath of the galaxy. Only those willing to fight or die will have a chance of survival. Your continued survival makes it possible your species might be one of the survivors."

Amu!vizn pondered the scope of the alien's plan for a long moment. "This . . . tenuous . . . hope is what keeps your people functional? How long have you been doing this? How do you keep up hope?"

"It's all we have left. We've been at this for a little over six-to-the fourth planetary cycles. It hasn't happened yet, but every encounter with a new star-faring species gives us hope."

"That seems a strange reason for helping subjugate others."

"I never said it was rational, or even reasonable. But it's what we have."

There was a prolonged pause, then the synthetic voice resumed. "One more little bit of knowledge—because you've earned it. When the Hegemon falls, there will be death and destruction on a scale which can't be imagined. Only the strong will survive. And my people have been proving themselves to be the toughest, meanest, and deadliest creatures in this section of the galaxy for a really long time. We plan to survive, no matter what it takes."

The author is a disabled veteran who's been described as a "dark and sinister force for good." This is his fourth published fiction story.

Warped Drive
Anthony Fabbri

"What just happened?"

"I swear to every God that ever existed. The man walked right up to that warp drive, a completely alien device that mankind hadn't even known existed--was even *possible* to exist, thirty seconds previous. And before the alien welcoming party could even spout 'we come in peace,' or whatever claptrap they'd rehearsed for first contact with mankind, he starts to *take it apart*, right there in front of them, and then, following markings written entirely in an alien language, puts it back together again, all in the space of ninety seconds, and I quote our new alien friends verbatim!" The Sergeant who was speaking pulled a scrap of yellow sticky note out of his pocket for a quick reference, and recited from it: "made it 'six thousand forty-one times more efficient.' They say they'll make it home in ten minutes instead of forty days. They say their scientists will be studying it for years to come. They say it's nothing they've ever seen before. They say they'll give us the plans for all their now-obsolete warp drives in trade. They say humans are a race of geniuses. They're saying a lot of things."

"What did you say to them?" Colonel Hobbes asked the Sergeant as he fell, shaking, into a chair, one of two placed opposite the one behind the desk.

"I babbled something about how humans and aliens obviously see the universe in very different ways and what was obvious to one was difficult for the other and that we didn't know faster than light was possible until they showed up, but *come on!*"

The Sergeant, acting as witness, along with Colonel Hobbes, both looked over at Tanamaray, a sandy-haired twenty-two year old transfer to the good ship "Freedom" naught but a week ago, and on the most impressive credentials Colonel Hobbes had seen in . . . well, ever: IQ of 190; Rhodes scholar; MIT; had come on board ship fresh off of accepting a million dollar mathematics prize for a problem that had been unsolved for decades.

His shirt was wrong side out.

"Tanamaray?" The colonel gently rubbed his left temple with his index finger and closed his eyes. He could just *feel* the headache coming on. It was almost as if his already nearly-completely gray hair was actively completing its cycle into elderhood.

"Yes, sir?" Tanamaray chirped brightly. He always seemed willing to come to the aid of any mental exercise, confound it. But that was simply the problem, Hobbes sighed to himself, thinking if every problem was immediately solvable in your eyes, none of them ever appear to be threatening. And that won't do in a military setting.

"Tanamaray, your shirt is wrong side out. Tell me, Jesus, you didn't meet the aliens that way, Good God Almighty."

Tanamaray looked down sheepishly, "Oh goodness; you're right. I hadn't noticed," and immediately stripped off the offending garment and began to turn it right-side out, flustered.

"To be fair, Sir, I don't think the aliens noticed. They were too busy watching him disassemble their demonstration warp drive they were going to show us. They're keeping that one, by the way, not that Tanamaray couldn't "improve" a thousand more."

Tanamaray had gotten stuck in his shirt. He took it off and tried again.

It was as if the Colonel had inherited some kind of negative-world, antimatter savant. The Colonel had heard of regular savants before. They had terrible IQs, but could do a few things really well; count cards, play music, do math. Tanamaray was precisely the opposite. He couldn't carry a tune in a bucket, or multiply even single digits in his head consistently, but pose any analytical question under the sun to him and he could give you the answer in seconds. He was a super-genius, a reverse savant.

Tanamaray had finally solved the riddle of clothing, and pulled from his pocket an hourglass. "Also, the aliens showed me a neat trick. It's how their warp drive works. How did they put it?" Tanamaray scrunched up his face as he spoke, "Altering the narrative of causality? I think it was?" The sand started to run from the bottom of the hourglass to the top, in complete violation of physics, or maybe, just perhaps, a following of a much deeper chapter of those laws. "Anyway, pretty neat, huh? They say only some of the aliens can learn it, and all the aliens that do immediately become warp pilots, but it's really easy. We can test everyone on board ship if they're warp-capable in a manner of days, and get an Earth warp crew going. We could call it Psi to make it more intuitive to everyone, but really it's not like psychic powers at all."

What? Hobbes stopped his cranial massage a second later. "That's . . . actually a very good idea all around," he realized aloud. "See to it. Dismissed." The two people in front of his desk filed out dutifully, leaving Colonel Hobbes alone behind it, which is something Hobbes's headache needed.

Upon back reflection, this was really the most incredible way such a meeting could have gone. Hobbes had, this day, impressed the heck out of his superiors, the aliens, and his men, gotten a ton of new technologies in trade for essentially nothing, and opened mankind to the stars.

Why did it have to be so exhausting? Hobbes needed a stiff drink and some sleep. He could put Tanamaray in charge of whatever he was doing and do just that; the kid was officially the civilian liaison here. But Hobbes was mildly afraid he'd wake up to being told the US had nominated Tanamaray President of the Universe . . . or something.

He was mentally joking, but the more he thought about it, Hobbes himself might actually wind up being president someday soon, or at least Secretary of Defense, or Secretary of Alien Defense? That's if he could keep a tight enough leash around Tanamaray.

A really tight leash.

A choke-hold.

Tanamaray's report of activities

Tanamaray read the package of space rations. It read 'microwave for two and a half minutes' in four different languages. He dutifully set the timer for "1:90"

A soldier nearby mentally did the math, "Couldn't you have simply set it to 2:30?"

Tanamaray stopped. "Oh yeah! I could have! That would have been way easier."

"But that's not the way he views the universe," Cassandra smiled. Cassandra was officially his security escort, but more and more she was becoming his babysitter. "It was cute. I have a differently-abled brother, and Tanamaray reminds me of him," She said to the officer. "I kind of get how he thinks."

"That makes one of us," the soldier groused half-under his breath.

"I was thinking of it as one minute, and then one and a half minutes on top of that," Tanamaray continued. "I'll have to remember your trick. Thank you. Do you want to see one?" Tanamaray proudly pulled out his hourglass again. He was showing this trick to everyone he'd met since he'd learned it. God knows why; he was capable of far better ones than his simple bout of what appeared to be simple store-bought stage magic, but which Tanamaray swore up and down was not.

Then, Tanamaray opened the microwave, to find . . . nothing. "Where did it go? Did I forget to put it in? I do that sometimes."

Cassandra peered over his shoulder, "The heck? It should be in there. Did you take it?" She turned to the soldier.

"Don't look at me. I'm all the way over here."

"That's strange. Put in another one." Cassandra replied. Tanamaray set it for 2:30 this time. After opening, the meal was properly waiting for him, appearing perfectly normal, steaming and delicious.

"Well, there's a violation of the law of conservation of mass," Tanamaray commented.

Cassandra had no choice but to mentally agree.

Colonel Hobbes's Report of activities

"I don't know what could have happened to it." Tanamaray was telling the story to some yawning guests at a soiree that night. "I looked all over for it."

Tanamaray was grotesquely out of his element at a soiree. By all rights, he really should have been in the lab. But they had told him to come, and he minded well. He was dressed in the same suit jacket that every other attendee on board ship was wearing, with a tiny Earth insignia in the corner, over the jacket pocket. Ideally, the aliens would be wearing matching ones with a different insignia, but apparently they hadn't gotten the hint when we'd sent them over.

"I see you've met our civilian liaison," the Colonel's booming voice of congratulation interrupted all conversations nearby. "I'm afraid I need to borrow him for a while. If you'll excuse us." He pulled Tanamaray away by one hand as a parent might a small child. "The aliens are most interested in seeing you again, and— Are you drinking water? Live a little, man. You're off duty, officially."

"I really don't think I should drink. I'm still thinking about the effects of storing narrative causality violations in a suitable medium."

They stared at each other for a ten-count.

"I'll be honest, Tanamaray, I don't know what to do with you."

"I don't know what to do with me quite frequently."

"I want you to let loose a little and have some fun."

"'Fun' is not a component of this exercise."

The Colonel smiled, "Would it help if I ordered you to have fun?"

"I don't see how it would."

"All right then; don't have fun. But at least talk to the aliens, and *pretend* to have fun." With that, the Colonel escorted Tanamaray to the confused-looking aliens, standing huddled in a corner, drinking distilled water and occasionally talking to someone brave enough to come and meet them in a pidgin of several different Earth languages. (No one had quite gotten the concept of any alien language. Even Tanamaray had given it a go, with no progress.)

Tanamaray said to the Colonel as they approached, "I kind of 'get' the aliens. They don't really understand human social conventions, either. So, at least we have that in common."

"Good; tell them that."

But Tanamaray still got off to a bad start; "Hello, aliens."

If they took that introduction as an offense, they didn't show it, "Hello, genius."

"I'm supposed to talk to you."

"Yes."

Both sides went silent. The colonel fought the urge to overreact. It was the blind leading the blind. "What did you want to ask our newly-minted warp specialist, here?"

"You are smart."

"Thank you."

"Why are not you here?"

"I'm sorry? I don't understand the question."

"Why elsewhere?"

Tanamaray looked up at the Colonel at that. Tanamaray had been lost in social situations before, and was apparently looking to authority to guide him through the process, but this was beyond even the Colonel, who finally suggested, "Perhaps you could rephrase the question using different words?"

The aliens started speaking quickly to each other in an alien language, all five of them talking at once, over each other in a massive fountain of language. How did any of them make sense of that gibberish?

Finally, the lead alien (or so they guessed.) turned back to the humans, "You are here. Why not?"

"And not on Earth? I thought I could learn a lot from aliens. And teach a lot."

"You have done both, genius." It sounded sarcastic when said that way, but everyone involved knew it was not. The concept of sarcasm was the kind of thing aliens wouldn't naturally pick up on when learning a language. There was probably a similar reason we couldn't pick up theirs.

"Yet it is not what I meant to ask. You are here, and you are also not here. Your brain is in another place. So why is your body here?"

"Oh. I'm at this party mostly because I was told to meet you. The Colonel thinks it will be good for international relations or something."

"But you do not agree? Then why do you do what he says?"

Tanamaray thought about that for a second, before

responding "Well, I got a chance to talk to you . . . And I guess that's worth my time."

"I comprehended you."

"Good. I'm just glad you can speak an Earth language."

"A bit of a little. And I'm glad you got along with your King."

Another aide pulled the Colonel aside to ask, "Officially, what is Tanamaray's rank?"

"Officially, as our civilian liaison, he holds the rank of lieutenant, but never tell him that."

"Doesn't he already know?"

"Who knows?"

Tanamaray's report of activities

"You're the ranking officer on deck . . . um . . . sir."

"Well... that's bad," Tanamaray replied.

It was a fire alarm on steroids. The room was a hundred thousand flashes of red. Every alarm on ship was going off simultaneously. The entire crew had gathered in airlock B to evacuate into lifeboat ships, as the automated computer voice had instructed them, waking them from a dead sleep at three-o'clock-in-the-dark morning. Airlock B because there was no more airlock A, which had been ripped off entirely, and was now venting atmosphere into space, which was not in the least helping morale, as it puffed merrily away on the other side of the clear glass.

"Can I have your attention, please? This needs to be done quickly!" Tanamaray shouted above the general din, both human-made words and machine warnings. "I need to remove everyone here from narrative causality so we can get home faster."

"Can I help?" added Cassandra in the same loud tone.

"Oh no, please don't." Tanamaray turned to her, "Then we'll be in two causalities, and then if one tries to return to base causality and it's not there, God knows where we'll end up."

Cassandra blinked. She'd passed the tests to be a warp pilot, but hadn't actually had any classes yet.

Tanamaray suddenly remembered this and smiled, "Don't worry. I can handle them all. I've actually not done this many before, but how hard can it be?" he reached into his shirt pocket and pulled out a tiny hourglass. Quickly inverting it he started to recite the now-familiar mantra. Suddenly, the sand stopped, then ran back up the hourglass.

"There we go," Cassandra tried to placate everyone. "Now, careful, causality won't work on you the same way it does everywhere else, now."

"What exactly does that mean?" one crew member asked as they filed aboard various lifeboat ships.

Tanamaray said, "It means you've become like me, now: a trouble magnet. Things will simply occur without warning. But don't worry, it also means that everything that does happen won't be too serious. It raises the frequency but lowers the standard deviation, if that explains anything."

"It does and it doesn't," Cassandra replied.

"Right, just so that's clear."

And they were off. Ejected into space. Nothing but the Endless Stars out of the porthole window. This ship had launched with a net turn to simulate gravity, so there was nothing to see out that way, as the stars were spinning too fast to get a clear bearing, and the radio was simply hundreds of people trying to yell at once, over each other, so that wasn't really helpful, either.

Except to the alien occupant of the 3-person lifeboat. Who was happily listening to a couple hundred conversations simultaneously. "Interruption" was apparently not a concept in Alienish, so apparently that's a perfectly normal occurrence for him; or her, or . . . there was no telling what gender it was. The alien and Tanamaray locked eyes, which caused the alien to put away his(?) headphones, which had apparently been placed over its ear holes, even though the aliens had no ears to speak of. Its head was a simple sphere with two pure black eye holes, like a doll. Rumors circulated that they were all still in their spacesuits and simply Never Took Them Off. Since the aliens all looked absolutely identical, this theory might actually be true.

"So what happened?"

"As near or far as I can tell from the numerous competing

conjecture chatter . . ." began the alien, in words that were all, technically, perfect English, but were nevertheless impossibly hard to understand. "There was an event named 'terrorist explosion' in airlock A; because this escaped gases to both the outside and inside airlock doors, the ship was exposed to space vacuum and had to be evacuated. My ship successfully took off without me." It sounded somehow proud at that last line, as if it were an accomplishment. "All the other lifeboats have been launched with varying numbers of crew onboard. The bridge has been jettisoned with the bridge crew, including the Colonel. There are infinity survivors."

"So everyone's okay?" Cassandra asked questioningly, not entirely sure what the alien's peculiar wording meant, and needing reassurance.

"Yes. Although, I'm not entirely clear on the meaning of the details."

"Also, I saved the faster-than-light engine." Tanamaray opened his backpack with a loud *thunk*, as he dumped out a large metallic chrome cylinder of . . . something.

"Careful with that. You don't want it to explode or something." Cassandra cautioned.

"No. It's mostly one solid piece." Then, Tanamaray laughed, "And it goes faster than light. I doubt a couple extra miles an hour is going to hurt it any."

"Wait, is that your entire backpack?" Cassandra asked Tanamaray

"What do you mean?"

"Only the Engine? You don't have any rations, or water?"

"No. Was I supposed to?"

All were silent of a second. And then another second.

"Yes. Yes you were," Cassandra put a hand to her forehead

The alien asked, "Why did you hit yourself in the face?"

Alien report of activities

"I have an idea," which was Tanamaray's commonly-used method of starting a complicated series of activities.

"I have a GREAT idea," Tanamaray continued. So you knew

right away that the idea that was coming was a great idea, and it was not a not-smart idea. "We can tie the faster-than-light engine into the lifeboat and go faster than light."

It was a smart idea, and the alien said so: "We could get back to Earth very fastly." The alien thought Tanamaray was very smart. He was also not very smart sometimes. He made up for it by being smart in different times. After the launch cycle completed, Tanamaray started wiring the ship's power into the little cylindrical engine.

"So how does this drive work?" Cassandra asked Tanamaray.

"It's sort of the opposite of the formation of a black hole."

"Only you would think that was a clarification."

"It uses the Heisenberg Uncertainty Principle to un-determine our location in space . . ." Tanamaray suddenly brightened up. "It works like cutting a coupon. We take, er, imaginary scissors and cut the ships out of the universe, and then we paste the ships somewhere else." He continued talking while he was under the console, plugging in various wires into his home-brew engine, "but this also affects causality. The universe loses track of the things we are still causing to happen elsewhere in the universe, and the things that are happening elsewhere that should have been affecting us. Eventually the universe will realize what's wrong and snap back to true reality."

"I don't know what a 'coupon' is, but that seems to be an intelligent description otherwise," the alien agreed.

"Well, I don't know how a black hole forms, so that was a much better explanation for me."

"Maybe you can explain the concept of coupons while the Genius sends the other lifeboats back to Earth."

"But now comes the hard part: Us." Tanamaray stood up with his hand on his hips, staring at the monitor above the hot-wired console. "We'll have to move from inside the causality bubble to outside while it's still going. Hmmm."

"Maybe we should just wait to be rescued? If you start fooling around with the engine, who knows where we might wind up?"

Tanamaray, still with one finger in his mouth, lost in thought, pulled out his hourglass with his free hand and inverted it so the sand would run down it, and balanced it on the top plug of a spire of multiple power plugs, all hanging from a daisy-chained surge protector. "We can put everyone else back into causality, and then just remove us again. That should be the easiest way to . . ." he trailed off as the sand started to run up the hourglass, 'started' because, with a lurch and a heave, the ship suddenly careened as if it had struck something (perhaps it had), the hourglass was knocked over sideways. And outside the porthole was . . . not Earth.

Cassandra's report of activities

"You're starting an argument now?! We're the only two humans on this planet!" Cassandra shouted to Tanamaray.

"And an Alien."

Is he really going to do this?

"And we should be okay for a limited time. This planet is so green, and noisy. It's full of . . . vivification."

"You use the word vivification! Is that a word? I told you something like this would happen, and people wonder why my parents named me Cassandra." Cassandra continued yelling. "And we don't know if any of that vivification is safe to eat. It might be deadly poisonous. And you're sitting here with no rations!"

"Maybe I can find something, somewhere . . ."

"Where?"

With that, freshly-microwaved space ration dinner appeared before them, steaming hot and delicious.

"I'd wondered where that went."

"Well . . . that's one problem solved."

Tanamaray picked up the hourglass and put it back in his pocket, "I wish the Colonel were here. He would know what to do."

"*Where in the blazes am I? What is going on?*"

"Oh my." Cassandra turned behind her to look. Colonel Hobbes did not look happy.

Entire Scout Crew's report of activities

"He said he wants to be alone," Tanamaray said. "You are not a member of the set 'alone'," Tanamaray apologized to the alien.

"I comprehended you. However, I believe I know what planet we are on. We are at a midway location point between Earth and our own planet. Perhaps a warp relay set up by a third party species. Our ship can pick us up—"

"—and take us back to Earth." Tanamaray continued.

"—and we can conclude the treaty—" the alien continued further

"—with the Colonel."

"—and our people—"

"—safely retrieved. Well, that's good news." Tanamaray was getting the hang of the alien way of conversing. "Do you think we should interrupt him to tell him now?"

"You said he wanted to be alone." the alien said.

"—or wait until he cools down?"

"I don't know the proper human interaction."

"I don't either . . . We should go ask Cassandra."

"Well, it's not of my kind, but I believe I can operate it." The alien turned the scavenged equipment over very carefully, gazing into it as a soothsayer would a crystal ball, demanding it reveal its secrets.

"Well, this is an interesting little device." Tanamaray said to no one in particular, possibly the plant next to him or the engine in front of him, which had been dubbed "The warp radio." He was gazing meaninglessly into space, lost in thought.

"For you, everything's interesting." Colonel Hobbes groused, trying to look dignified sitting on a rock, using a larger rock as his desk, and actually succeeding for everyone but Tanamaray, who was too engrossed in 'interesting' to worry about 'dignified.'

The Colonel continued, "You can't be serious, we have no idea who built this, for what reason, if they even have a language we can comprehend, or if they're even felling particularly helpful today. For all we know, they'll blast us out of the sky if they even find out we're here!"

"We must trust them," Tanamaray slowly replied, turning

around, "we have no other choice."

"What do you mean we have no other choice? It's a warp radio, which means it has a warp engine. Well, warp back to Earth."

"It's not that easy," Tanamaray protested. "We're not actually sending any matter through, just a signal, which is orders of magnitude easier to transfer, and we don't actually have to send a message, come to think of it. Just open a warp gateway and then close it again. The aliens will wonder who opened it and send a crew to investigate, and BOOM we're rescued."

"They're going to go boom all right." The Colonel muttered under his breath.

"So we open the gate and just hope the aliens will call us back sometime?" Cassandra sounded dubious. "They still have to call us back! What if they just think this thing is old and worn out? Even if they get a message, they have no idea whether it's just something the planet is doing. And they don't particularly have reason to care."

"So what do we do?" Tanamaray asked.

Silence was the response, all around the rock-made-conference-table-desk. All four of them looked at everyone else.

"We're calling the aliens!" Colonel Hobbes crossed his arms and continued to glare at Tanamaray. "But I reserve the right to hurt you first, if anything goes wrong."

"Fair enough."

"The gateway keeps getting closed on the far side. The connection is terminated. Receiving device did not give a reason for the closure," the Alien recited.

"What does that mean?" Cassandra asked.

"Tanamaray replied. "Easy. Someone on the other side closed our warp gateway."

"Can we force it open?" The Colonel asked.

"Not with a radio and a lifeboat. If I had access to my lab, maybe. I don't even know how they're doing it."

They all looked expectantly at the Alien for about thirty seconds. The alien simply stared back silently.

"Do you know how they close the gateway?" Tanamaray finally asked.

"I do not."

"For once, Tanamaray is not the socially awkward one," Cassandra smiled.

"Now there's two of them," The Colonel said, palm to face for the umpteenth time that day.

Suddenly, the little warp radio went off.

A heartbeat pulse had been sent, off and on, on and off, starting slow, about the speed of a human pulse's familiar KA-THUMP, and then faster and faster, until the individual beats could no longer be distinguished, in an irrecoverable low rumble.

Such was the message.

"That's not anything I know," The alien said.

Cassandra pondered, "It sounds like the warp engine powering up, except slower and lower pitched."

"It's not like any language I've ever seen." Tanamaray was inspecting a visual readout of the message, on the warp radio console, "And I can speak four languages fluently."

"Is it even a language at all? And how do we respond? Aliens won't wait forever." said Colonel Hobbes.

"Well, maybe they will," Cassandra was unwilling to concede even this simple point. Although, perhaps he was not entirely incorrect. "I still say it sounds like the engines," Cassandra continued, after a pause, "It gets closer, then backs off, then gets closer again."

"It does, kind of." Tanamaray smiled, musing it over, "My warp engine makes almost that same sound but much, much faster. But they only pulse a few times before stopping. This message is over a minute. If we even received it correctly."

"I can tell it is a recording of your engine noise." The alien admitted, "Continuing beyond the human hearing, deep into the range of infrasonic."

Cassandra said, "If we were silent, they would likely have been too, letting us explain ourselves, but they heard the engines whine over the radio, so they whined back. Maybe they think it's our language. Maybe they're calling to us."

"To do what?" Colonel Hobbes asked.

"Activate our engines!" Tanamaray yelled as the realization came to him. "I'm sure of it! They want us to do that again. That's why they keep saying it. When our engines whine, they continue the whine a few times. When we did it again, they started up again. That's it."

"You mean . . . Warp?" The Colonel asked.

"Yes, they want the engines on full power. It's a tow-warp. They're asking us to go back with them, and we've got to put the lifeboat in neutral first!" Tanamaray said.

"What?" The Colonel asked.

"To tow a car, it can't be in park. We're in warp-park right now. We've got to begin a warp before the aliens can guide the warp path back where we came from."

"Assuming that's even what they're saying," The alien cautioned, "Just because Tanamaray speaks some languages doesn't mean he can understand all aliens."

"Assuming we can even trust the aliens to warp us back. Who knows what they've dreamed up for us," The Colonel retorted.

It was the same play again, although this time with different actors.

However, like all great plays, it ended the same way.

It was exceedingly difficult to start a warp path to nowhere in particular. The computer in Tanamaray's warp engine really didn't like it, for starters, and even after every single safety was turned off, and especially the abysmally annoying vocal warning that safeties had been turned off, was also turned off, there was still the small technical limitation of not using the opportunity to blow ourselves up, with much shouting of, what are you doing, stop that now, and all the rest of the things one yells in such circumstances, which was to be expected, and the alien proved to be adeptly skilled at.

Finally, however, the necessary preparations were complete, the warp path to nowhere carefully planned out, and our second group of aliens, ever patiently waiting, signaled once more.

"Hit it." Tanamaray decreed, and for once, the Colonel actually *agreed* with Tanamaray, saying, "I like this idea, Tanamaray," which is something he actually said, even though it was a sentence he'd never said before in his life. Perhaps it was the aftereffects of non-narrative causality working again, as, with an eerie glow around the lifeboat ship, the heartbeat beat faster and faster, glowing brighter and brighter, and the entire craft finally vanished, en route to Earth. Again.

The Machine
Tyson Prenter

      Pushing past the known is a fine way to forget, to replace what is remembered less-than-fondly with something interesting, odd, or 90 degrees in another direction. That's one reason I make the occasional foray beyond where it is known for a fact humans have gone. Another reason is that there is profit to be had in new discoveries. It's after a good run that I can afford such trips, and if I'm lucky, I get to take more of them. One often leads to another. So I push, and push again. Sometimes for profit. Sometimes to forget.

      One run in particular aimed at forgetting was my deepest taken toward the center of the galaxy. Forgetting wasn't coming easy, and I didn't care that this wasn't going to be a profitable, or even a break-even run. *One more system to explore*, I promised myself, *then I'd turn back*. This last system didn't look promising, but one never knows—I've found amazing artifacts in the least likely places, and the better-looking, statistically-more-likely prospects I'd examined hadn't so far panned out, so I asked myself the standard question: *why not here?* We'd skirt the system, see what the sensors say, and go home if nothing pinged. Hit the edges of a few more systems on the way back, skim a resource here and there, and the trip wouldn't turn out to have been a total waste.

      Then a surprise: a rock—that's all sensors showed it to be, an elephant-sized chunk of deep-space-cold rock—a rock not more than 50k from my ship lit up, with both lights and transmissions in numerous bands, all aimed in my direction. My defensive programs kicked in (always glad to see they work), and I prepared for an emergency jump out. But no missiles flew my way, no focused beams of any sort burned through the hull, no ships headed in my general direction. All the computer could find was a repeating, low-power radio transmission. Translating it as best it could, the computer presented what looked to be a map of the system the rock circled, the fourth planet highlighted.

Not being attacked seemed a good sign; the repeatedly broadcast map also looked good from where I sat. Perhaps this was an invitation? Those are rare in my experience, and almost never traps—those just don't make economic sense, except to paranoid species, and such civilizations tend to hide instead of blaring out evidence of their presence for all to hear and/or see. I set the computer to map a course, gave the order to move, and went to lie down. This trip would take a while, which was quite alright, as first contact initiated on short hours is never a good idea.

After a few days of travel, I received radioed greetings from a large asteroid overgrown with machinery, in orbit around the fourth planet. Broadcasts in various frequencies were directed at my ship, and the computer interpreted them as instructions for docking; it found what looked to be an open landing bay, more than large enough for my ship to enter, the door to which had been both invisible and closed when I first examined the rock with my sensors. The bay was well-lit, with no other ships present. *Why not?* I asked myself, and in I went. Once I had set down, and the engines had shut off, the large bay doors closed, and the computer reported that a mix of gasses roughly in the same proportions as those in my ship's atmosphere filled the bay.

Once the air in the bay was deemed breathable, I decided to show I trusted my hosts and stepped out through the airlock. I had a helmet with an attached bottle to hand, but left it strapped to my back as I stepped out. The air was perfectly adequate (if a bit odd-smelling, as all non-Earth environments are to humans), and it felt good to be out of the confines of both my ship (which I lived in) and my suit (in which I lived when not in the ship). A mechanical grumble turned me towards the back wall of the bay; a portion of the wall began to move up from the floor, revealing a partially-lit hallway. So of course I went in—my hosts had been entirely hospitable to this point, and I was scarcely in a position to shoot my way out.

My ship closed up behind me while I entered the hallway, and I made my way down a three-human wide tunnel hewn through the rock, lit every five meters or so with a small, blue, floor-mounted light. After 150 meters or so, another hatch opened in front of me and I entered a goodly-sized room, perhaps the size of a high school gymnasium on Earth. It was brightly lit, with a large, steel-grey, gauge-littered, box-like machine situated smack in the center of the room. Another portal opened on the wall on the other side of the room, and a quadrupedal creature about twice the size of an average human, with an additional four "arms" and a somewhat equine head, entered the room.

I stopped on my side of the machine, and the creature stopped on its side, at about the same distance from it that I was. One of its arms lifted a device off of a belt it had wrapped around it, held it to what I can only assume was its mouth, and it began to emit noises into the device.

"Hello there!"

The voice was clear, and the pronunciation right, so I took a step closer, waved in the friendliest way I could imagine, and waited.

The creature (which never gave itself a name or introduced itself; this may or may not give useful information about a species or culture) continued. "We are glad you are here. You are the first visitor we have had in 20 homeworld solar circuits."

My computer had reckoned that their homeworld was slightly closer to its star than Earth is to Sol, so somewhere around 17 Earth years. This was uncommon; many systems were not visited more than once a century, or even a millennium. Perhaps their propensity to hide, only to reveal themselves with a certain showiness, attracted visitors. My reply was simple: "Thank you for your invitation, and your hospitality."

"You are welcome! We are glad to have you as our guest. Have you come because of The Machine?"

Its translated voice was clearly modulated to capitalize those words; I've not heard the like before or since in conversations with non-humans. "Um, *no*. I came because of your invitation, out on your system's fringe. But now that I *have* heard of it, I am intrigued. What is The Machine?"

The creature stepped closer, and I did the same. It motioned me toward The Machine, and a door, its edges heretofore not visible, opened up on the side closest to us. Two seats, one to suit the creature, and one to suit me, rose up out of the floor behind us. "Does your species drink water?" it asked.

"Yes," I replied, curious as to which form they might deliver it in.

A small table also came out of the floor, with stone, water-filled cups resting on its top. "The Machine," my new friend said, "Some visitors have heard of it. Some have not. All make a decision about it."

I took a sip of the water. Highly filtered, with nearly no taste to it. "Thank you. A decision?"

"Yes. A decision. The Machine was built over five thousand solar circuits ago. It has the function of sending back in time and space whatever goes through its door. There is no clear limit on how far back it is able to send an object; it does not, however, have the ability to send things forward in time and space."

Having heard what they could do so far, I rolled along with them. "Can the length of time and space covered be controlled?"

"Yes, and with a fair degree of precision. The Machine, and its door, are also variable in size. Something the size of your ship, for instance, could easily be sent through."

"Interesting. What do you ask in return for access to The Machine?" I worked to avoid appearing or sounding skeptical.

The creature grew—to my ears—excited, saying, "Nothing, except to share with us your thinking in regards to The Machine and its functions. We want to know your reasoning as to how to make use of The Machine."

I thought for a moment, then answered: "*That* I can give you."

"Then the room is yours. If you desire to make use of The Machine, you have decisions to make. Do you want your craft to come with you, to go back in time with it so that you might travel where you will? Or: do you want us to send you to a particular place at a particular time? You may return to your ship to obtain whatever coordinates and maps you like, as well as supplies. You might also decide not to make use of The Machine. That decision, too, is one we are interested in."

I paused again. "I need time to think about this."

"We have all the time you need. Visitors come, but not as often as we would like."

"May I take time to rest in my ship?" This would take more than a little consideration.

"Certainly. There is no boundary on the time you may take. Simply come back down the hallway, and we will be alerted."

I bowed, thanked it again, and headed back to my ship. They had been straight with me to this point; I had seen enough strangeness in the universe not to doubt that The Machine would do what its representative claimed it could do. So: where to go? When? Past historical eras meant little to me as destinations, but I knew that even the basics of the knowledge in my head, and what information I could carry with me from the ship, could be used to recoup any losses from leaving the ship behind—and much, much more.

My ship could also come with me. I could go back to the beginnings of my wanderings, going from system to system knowing exactly what I would find and what I could trade for profit, avoid dangerous or worthless systems , and build a nice little empire for myself.

Live my life over? Build an empire? Take directions I hadn't taken, but regretted leaving unexplored? Stay away from Kelly? Keep Kelly close? She was why I was out here by myself in the first place. I could taste the opportunities, see the bright, possible futures I could follow, and could barely take the sleep I needed with all the adrenaline coursing through my system, so excited did the prospects offered by The Machine make me. But I finally did sleep, drifting through dreams happy and melancholy, grim and glad.

The next morning I cleaned myself, ate, dressed, and made my way back down the hall. The two seats were still there, waiting for me, so I took the seat best fit for me. I sat contemplating The Machine, its open door beckoning me to enter.

A few minutes after I sat down, what I am sure was the same representative as the day before entered and took his place in the other seat.

The being leaned toward me as it spoke. "You have made a decision? Have you chosen a destination, time, and place?"

I nodded. "Yes. Yes I have. Here, and now."

"Here and now? You're not entering The Machine?" The creature leaned even further in my direction.

"No. No I'm not."

The creature paused before it spoke. "Please, as per our agreement, tell us why that is."

I hesitated to speak, until, without prompting, the table with the stone cups rose once again from the floor. I took this opportunity to take a drink, and a breath, and to begin to describe my thought processes.

"Part of flying on my own is an exercise in existing without too much thought," I began. "I don't tend to dwell on the past when I'm alone, but when prompted by something, or someone—like here, like this opportunity presented by The Machine—the past starts to creep up on me. What I thought I'd forgotten comes back on me."

The representative appeared to nod in agreement. "That has been our experience with many of the spacefarers to whom we have presented this opportunity."

"I can't say I'm surprised. But when the past came back, especially those things I wanted to erase, or redo, other things came forward." I took a moment to prepare my next words. "A personal relationship came apart in my hands some time back, and I'd love to go back and prevent it. But preventing that relationship would do more than keep something bad, at least for me and her, from happening."

Another drink. "Go on, please," said the representative.

"An associate of mine met this person's sister through me, married her, and they had children. Three of them so far. He has also done very well for himself and for his family thanks to her ties and skills. If I were to prevent the relationship I developed from happening, then that subsequent relationship would never have had a chance to begin."

The synthesized voice added a hint of emotion. "And the children would never have existed, and your associate's success would not have come about."

"Exactly. Along with a thousand other things. I don't want to wipe those kids out of existence." Here I found myself excited, my hands moving as I spoke. "Or, as has passed through my thoughts, *any other kids* born since then. Or *anything* that has been made, or done since—my going back, to whatever point, would not allow me to reset matters for *only me*. Your world would be affected. All the other worlds I've visited would be affected to one degree or another."

It took an extra beat before it spoke. "You cannot bear the responsibility?"

"You could say that. Or it might just be that I don't have that right, or a charge to do something like that. If it were just me, fine. But to decide for everyone else? I can't do that. Then there's the fact that there's no guarantee I'd make things better, for myself or anyone else. What's done is done."

The representative made a gesture at The Machine, and its open door closed, the seams once again hidden. "You have made the same decision, for the same reasons, as every other wayfarer has since The Machine was built. We ourselves could not make such a decision to go back to the past."

"Don't think that the next member of my species you show this to will make the same decision as I have."

"That may be. Individuals are members of groups, and do not necessarily act as others ifrom their group might. Yet, once again, the same decision has been made, time and again, without a common culture, cellular structure, or body configuration. Thank you."

"No, thank you," I answered, "This has been enlightening for me. I should go Thank you for your hospitality."

I stood, and turned to go back to my ship. The representative also stood, and asked me to wait. "We have taken the liberty of fueling your ship. A trade representative awaits you in the hangar; she would very much like an opportunity to make this more than an information exchange. Know you are always welcome in our system."

"I appreciate that. Good luck with your experiment."

"Thank you. And good luck on your journeys." The creature waved its appendages in my direction.

I headed down the hall, and quickly found that this trip had not only been decidedly profitable, I now had many other things to think about other than Kelly.

Tyson Prenter has published three collections of short stories and one piece of nonfiction; more are in the pipeline. He publishes and designs books through 100 Ton Press, and is currently enjoying the changeover in seasons.

The Humor Tab

Tag 'Em
Brad Earle

    They would arrive by the hundreds and thousands—coming from universities in Germany and Nigeria, travelling from homes in Canada and Kansas. They would come to Madison City for the first and last time for one of the best views the planet had to offer of the coming total solar eclipse. Astronomers both professional and amateur would spend days occupying all the hotels in the tri-county area, pumping money into the local economy while congesting traffic to the disquietude of the locals.
    And Tim McIntosh would be waiting for them. And for *them* . . .
    The extra-terrestrials had first made contact with Tim months ago. They were part of a scouting crew from the Remosian Empire, one of thousands of such crews roaming the Milky Way who were always looking for the next rocky sphere onto which they could plant their flag. Although their initial reports on Earth had indicated the planet would perhaps be a bit too cold for their liking, further study of the relationship between the planet's climate and higher simian society indicated the potential for more agreeable weather in the decades and centuries ahead. The Remosians were nothing if not farsighted.
    Having decided that Earth was worth additional consideration for colonization, Scouting Crew 31F9 opted to stay around for a while so they could complete a number of exercises. For one such mission, they chose to enlist the help of one of the higher simians, and the one they selected, for reasons only they could possibly understand, was Tim McIntosh. They reached out to him one night while he was working in the southbound tollbooth at Exit 48 of the Norton Parkway. They drove up and handed Tim a $100 bill and a slip of paper with a particular time and particular place

written on it. "If you would like more money dollars, meet us." As the Remosians drove away into the sunset Tim studied the money and the hand-written note, and quickly dismissed any misgivings he had about their strange manner of speaking—or why three such well-dressed gentlemen would be driving around in a pink SUV with a cursive "POWERED BY BITCHDUST" decal spanning the top of the rear windshield.

Tim met the three well-dressed gentlemen at the nearby 24-hour diner after he got off work. He entered the restaurant, spotted their booth and joined them, nervously accepting their offer of a cup of coffee. The blonde Remosian waited for Tim to take a sip before beginning.

"Tim McIntosh, we're glad you decided to come now here. What we propose to yourself is this: when your fellow higher simian persons start arriving in the coming months to observe your total solar eclipse . . ."

"Our what?" Tim interrupted.

"Your total solar eclipse," answered the red-headed Remosian.

Tim stared blankly.

The blonde Remosian adapted and moved on. "In about two months, Tim McIntosh, this area is going to receive a significant influx of the type of people we're interested in meeting. They will be astronomer people, coming from all around Earth to observe a rare event. Our research indicates that the majority of these people will drive through your tollbooth on the way to see this event. These people need to be tagged."

"Tagged," asked Tim, "You mean like cattle?"

"Yes," the bald Remosian confirmed.

"So wait, you guys work for the government or something?"

The blonde Remosian answered, "Yes. The government. Anyway, these astronomer people will be tagged with a laser system beyond your understanding. You will mount this to the outside of your tollbooth," and he handed Tim a small gray box the size of a triple-A battery. "This is magnetic. Mount this on April month the seventeenth. It will scan each vehicle passing through for astronomical viewing equipment, and will tag every life form in any vehicle in which such equipment is detected. Can we count on you, Tim McIntosh?"

"Depends. How much are you going to pay me?"

"Two hundred more money dollars."

"Count me in!"

"Excellent. After enough astronomer people have been tagged, we will come by and collect the sensor and give yourself your money dollars."

Two months passed. On the seventeenth of April, Tim did as he was instructed and mounted the small gray box to the outside of his tollbooth. As the morning sun ascended, Tim noticed the traffic on the Norton Parkway was starting to pick up. *Must be all the astronomer people,* he thought to himself. He sat through his shift, making change when drivers needed it, reading his phone when they didn't, and intermittently thinking of all the things he was going to do with the money that the well-dressed gentlemen were going to give him when the ordeal was finished. With that kind of money, he'd be able to upgrade the stereo in his car, or replace its bald rear tires. He would even be able to afford going over on his data plan every month for at least a year. By his own reckoning, his future seemed bright—at least brighter than the sky that Tim had noticed looked suddenly a little darker. *Weird,* he thought, *I bet those astronomer people would like to see something like this.*

Six hours passed. While Tim was scrolling through one of his social media accounts with increasing impatience, he happened to look up in time to see the pink SUV carrying the three well-dressed members of Scouting Crew 31F9. And they were approaching at a rather high speed—so fast, in fact, that Tim was on the verge of getting the hell out of the way before the vehicle hit the brakes and came to a screeching halt by his tollbooth.

"Commit vehicular ingress! Not later!" came the command from the bald Remosian from behind the wheel, while the red-headed Remosian in the back opened his door just long enough for him to quickly reach out and remove their small gray box.

"Uhm, what?" asked Tim, shaken.

The bald Remosian frustratingly sighed and typed furiously

into a handheld device and tried again.

"Get in the damn car! Now!"

"But where's my money?"

"We'll give yourself the money dollars later! But only if you come with us right now!"

With visions of paid data overages still relatively fresh in his mind, Tim quickly exited the booth and got in the back of the pink SUV. He had scarcely shut his door before they sped away.

"We've had something come up, Tim McIntosh," explained the red-headed Remosian. "We're not sure how yet, but the integrity of our mission has been compromised, and we have to get off this planet as soon as possible."

"Well what's that have to do with me?" asked Tim.

"You're coming with us!"

"With you? Wait, to where?"

"Back to the mother ship of Remosian Scout Crew 31F9."

"The 'mother ship'? Is that like some cruise ship in the ocean?"

"Yes. The ocean. You're coming with us, along with the—" The red-headed Remosian connected the small gray box to a small computer. ". . . along with the two thousand four hundred forty-five astronomer people we've tagged today."

"Well you're going to need more cars, aren't you guys?"

It was just about that time that the four of them disappeared from the vehicle.

Tim McIntosh looked around, confused. He was in a gigantic room, a few acres in size, resembling a gymnasium of some kind, standing among a crowd of about two thousand four hundred people who were just as confused as he was. In the front of the crowd Tim saw the three well-dressed gentlemen, anxiously pacing. He continued looking around, and saw at the other end of the room was another crowd that appeared to be as big as the crowd he was with. Three unfamiliar well-dressed gentlemen waited in front of that crowd, behaving in an equally nervous manner. And in between the two crowds was yet a third crowd, consisting of what appeared to be eight-foot tall aliens, gray-skinned, trapezoidal-headed , chattering away as though at a social gathering. While drawing many stares from the two human crowds, Tim hardly paid them any notice. After all, he was sure he'd seen them on some TV show or news site somewhere before.

A voice came over a loudspeaker: "ATTENTION! FINAL TALLY: RED SQUAD, TWO THOUSAND FOUR HUNDRED FORTY-ONE. BLUE SQUAD, TWO THOUSAND FOUR HUNDRED FORTY-SIX." The three Remosians that Tim knew reacted with celebratory shouts. Tim started to fight his way through the crowd toward them to find out more about what he was involved with. Gleefully noticing his approach, they met him halfway.

"Tim McIntosh!" exclaimed the blonde Remosian. "We did it!"

"Did what?" asked Tim.

"We won our match of Tag Capture! Understand you, we were in competition with our fellow Remosian scouts in a game we like to play, where each squad picks an indigenous sentient being of a planet to help tag additional indigenous sentient beings. We Blue Squad thought we were winning with might, but we heard words that Red Squad tagged a large group of indigenous sentient beings near the end of the game that brought their sum total equal to ours, so we hurriedly decided to tag you and add you to the total. Every indigenous sentient being counts, yourself knows. By the way, here are your money dollars—and if anyone asks, you're an astronomer."

The grateful Remosian handed Tim the promised money. Tim was eagerly putting the money into his pocket when a particularly important-looking gray-skinned, trapezoidal-headed creature appeared seemingly out of nowhere and approached him.

"Excuse me, higher simian," the undisguised Remosian interrupted, "but what is your name?"

"Me? I'm Tim. Tim McIntosh."

"What is your job occupation?"

"I'm an astronaut. No wait, uhm. Astron—an astronomer," he stammered.

"Indeed? How many planets are in your solar system?"

Tim started counting on his fingers as he named them in his head. *Mercury, Mars, Earth, the moon* . . . "Eight if you count the sun."

"Thank you." The undisguised Remosian laughed in spite of himself before turning to Blue Squad. "You three . . . You guys know the rules! The category for this match was *astronomer people*, and this higher simian is no astronomer person."

"I am so!" Tim protested.

The undisguised Remosian rolled his three eyes as he turned and spoke loudly to the entire assembly. "Attention, everyone! Blue Squad has violated the terms of the match, thus forfeiting. The winner is Red Squad!"

A mix of cheers and jeers erupted from the Remosian crowd assembled, and the three well-dressed Remosians of Blue Squad turned from Tim McIntosh and walked sullenly away. Before they got too far, Tim shouted at them, "Hey, you guys!"

The blonde Remosian, annoyed, turned back and answered. "Yes?"

"Does this mean I have to give the money back?"

"No, Tim McIntosh, you can keep the money dollars."

"Sweet!"

Three months passed. Tim McIntosh had been returned to Earth shortly after Remosian Scouting Crew 31F9, Blue Squad had forfeited their match of Tag Capture. The astronomers had all been returned as well, save a few that were kept by the Remosians to facilitate the colonization of Earth that the Supreme Remosian Council had decided would proceed. As one might expect, the Remosians were more than adequately equipped militarily to begin their occupation with minimal difficulties, though as could also be expected the people of Earth were abuzz with rumors of resistance and rebellions, but there were also those who welcomed the Remosians and the benefits that came with being occupied by a superior race. There was certainly no shortage of newsworthy events.

As for Tim, he was staying quite abreast of the latest developments, getting all kinds of alerts and notices of relevant news articles on his phone; data overages be damned.

Brad Earle engineers by week and writes by weekend. Having now been published two consecutive years in the Fark fiction anthology, he is inching closer towards his final form, which he hopes involves telekinetic powers and the power to inspire the peoples of Earth. Follow him @sbe1976 on Twitter.

It's Only Vampire
Rebecca Gomez Farrell

      By the time Vlad's paper-thin skin was sizzling in the sunshine as he sped down the zipline, I knew the sixth day of my nine hundred and ninety-fourth year had gone horribly wrong. Had the humans felt the same when we stepped from the shadows a decade ago to reveal our existence? We took charge before the mortals had the chance to form a resistance.

      It started in late twilight with the piquant aroma of coffee brewing. Not the vampire takeover of Earth, but the sequence of events leading to Vlad's unfortunate circumstance. Desire for my daily cuppa had uncreaked my old joints as Vlad and I waited for the steeping coffee on a café's mahogany bench. Mahogany is a sign of exceptional taste—it makes quite elegant caskets.

      Behind the shop counter, a jittery human with veiny eyes handled my pour-over. I contemplated the unusually sharp notes that wafted my way during the java's blooming. Had the beans been roasted over oak stakes, maybe?

      Vlad sipped his bergamot tea, extra hot with cream. He tapped my knee with his fine Italian walking cane, made with finely ground Italians embalmed within the grain. "Don't look now, but those smug newlings are at it again."

      I craned my neck toward the bay window behind us, ignoring Vlad's hiss of disapproval. A crowd of maybe six vamps had gathered in the street. Each held a fluorescent poster board with messages written on them in dripping red bubble letters—how garish. The ones I could make out read "Down with Crypt Dwellers!" and "Immortal Doesn't Equal Enlightened!"

      Such upstarts swore older vamps like us were taking the fun out of being undead—you know, the typical power struggle between generations. I'd seen the humans go through it at least three score times. They never realized that differences appear much the same when viewed through an eternal lens.

A few of the newlings noticed us and flashed fangs through the glass. They weren't the only ones reacting aversely to our presence. The barista, poor guy, shook so hard, he overfilled the Chemix. Stella, the café's owner and a beautiful vampire with the pointed ears and blackened eyes of Golden Age Hollywood, whispered, "We're closing early. New guy hasn't seen old chaps like you before. I'll need to do some retraining."

Though he was under no threat, it was flattering that our visages still inspired such primal fear. As one of the few humans living outside the milking farms—*bleeding farms,* in impolite company—the lad couldn't be drained. To control our overpopulation, we had developed regulations to protect our food resources. Mortals on the outside were bred for forced servitude, like latté slinging, but not *harm*. This fella probably just hadn't been around vamps like Vlad and me before. We're old school, born of a darker time in human imaginations.

It's a subject of common debate as to whether the mortals would have stopped spawning vampires if they knew their tales had brought us into existence. They invented us through oral histories, then myth, then the printing press. The pages multiplied and so did we, until a tipping point was reached and we outnumbered them. At that point, what could the humans have done? Our revolution was a natural progression of dominance.

And the newlings wanted to sully it by letting the food run wild to make for more exciting hunting. Such barbarity. Excepting the playgrounds, of course. Vlad and I took our coffees to enjoy at the covered one between the downtown district and the just-built amusement park. We loved watching the child-sized vamps get their thrills chasing humans bred for cleverness through the playground's booby-trapped labyrinth. Shrieks of joy swelled over the hedges as the scamps closed in on their prey, avoiding trapdoors full of pointy, rubber stakes and unholy water downpours.

We leaned over a guard rail to finish our beverages. Before I could take another full whiff of that tantalizing scent, Selena swooped in beside me. She's the petite-but-mighty type of vampire that grew populous in the late second millennia, always ready with a quick retort and a fashion tip, but overall, nice company. Unlike the sparklers born in our second-to-last population boom—they're too chatty, always emoting. None of them understand why vampires had hidden in the shadows for centuries, keeping to ourselves except for our daily nibbles. They'd never experienced the risk of torch-armed mobs and sunlight flooding a tomb after discovery.

Elders like ourselves had always been careful to make feedings look like spider bites and rashes, or the work of a disturbed child in the household. Vlad and I still rose from the coffin each day with freshly shriveled skin. Our bald heads shone so brightly, you could read your fortune in them.

Selena slid her arm over mine and smiled, exposing a luscious set of sturdy, long canines. "Hey, handsome immortals."

See what I mean? So polite. We aren't really immortal, but it's nice to be shown respect at our age. Selena was much more genteel than those protestors, though she couldn't be much older. Tantalizing dimples appeared in her blue-black cheeks. My skin had been the same shade once, but with age came an ashiness no balm could banish. Not even ones made with the secretions of virgins—oh, how we've experimented!

"What are you up to this fine evening?" Selena said.

Vlad puffed up his chest, which failed to produce the intended effect. His whey-colored flesh was thin enough, you could see his ribs through it. "Oh, just taking a stroll like we always do," he said. "We'll get a pint and a bite at Elvira's Essentials soon."

"That won't wear you out too much, will it?" Selena winked, and the blood splatter on her cheeks brightened, as if someone had tossed pomegranate seeds against them. If only she weren't six centuries too young for me. "I hear Elvira's got a free love and fangs fest going on around nineish."

Getting stuck at one of those would be *terrible*. It'd be overrun with the youngest vampires, monsters who took form as the mortals became possessed with an unprecedented creative spirit, filling a planet's worth of floating server islands with tomes and tomes of fan fiction. Those vamps are no weightier than a high schooler's journal, but they're everywhere. And fornicating, always fornicating. In orgies, in the outdoors, in bat form, in black, strappy dominatrix gear that isn't nearly as alluring as the refined velvet and fur capes we came up with. Vlad and I have to walk the streets with our noses planted in the air to avoid stumbling across their vulgar displays.

"We'll head to Barnaby's Blood Bath then," Vlad decided, and I signaled my agreement. Compared with Elvira's sophisticated elegance, Barnaby's was a churlish gathering place. It lacked the black glass chandeliers and Elvira's marrow-and-life essence drips—they're to die for. But sometimes, sacrifices must be made. Even the humans have accepted that.

We bid Serena farewell and hurried off to Barnaby's to procure one of their corner booths for the evening—after centuries of dark corners, sitting exposed feels unseemly. Under a waning crescent moon two hours later, Vlad and I supported each other across Bonfire Boulevard, our busiest thoroughfare. Cars honked as we hobbled along, trying to dodge vehicles after having drank blood beer. Four ounces is all we can handle these days of that rich, thick concoction.

On the other side of the street, the amusement park rose up like a hulking hunchback from its den, and who was there but the lovely Selena, smiling and waving us over? How fortuitous!

"My immortal ones! Have you been in yet?" she asked.

We bowed with courtesy, spreading our capes out arm to arm.

"No," Vlad answered, "and we shan't be, as we've overdone it. We ought to head—*hic*—home to our crypt early."

Normally, I'd be content to let Vlad make such decisions. I try to take my satisfaction from each morning that I can raise my bones from the bed. But Selena wore a shoulderless, crimson lace dress with a neckline that plunged to reveal the curves she amply possessed. I may not be willing to rut in the streets, but I'm not dead yet. Despite what the mortals once believed, the undead have only one life to live—it just lasts indefinitely.

I craned my stiff neck to whisper in Vlad's ear. "Don't you—*hiccup*—think we can manage a little longer today?"

Selena joined in with teasing laughter. "You two can't go home already. There's three hours 'til sunrise!"

Vlad had been taking care of me so long, my, or maybe Selena's, forwardness caused him to stumble a bit. "But we always make sure to be home two hours before dawn, just in case," he said. The many creases on his forehead deepened.

"We'll leave by then, I promise." I chuckled to improve the bill of sale. "I want to see what the amusement board's come up with this time. Those old bats get crazy trying to outdo themselves."

Vlad hesitated, but he gave a slight nod. Probably the blood beer spurring him on. Selena bought us another round before slinking off with a group of her friends. They glanced our way with what I wanted to believe was curiosity despite the snarls on their faces. It hurt that she didn't linger to keep us company, but what did I expect? I held no illusion that she was genuinely interested in my creaky old bones. I just liked the flattery of her attention.

The park's smorgasbord of sights and sounds distracted me from any hurt feelings. Taking it in by the sidelines would make for a fine denial of our dotage, but my once-adventurous spirit had revived. I pulled Vlad into a hall of mirrors. Green and black strobe lights reflected from the rows of empty glass, giving me a headache as I stumbled around, listening for shuffling. I was rather chuffed to find Vlad before he found me, recognizing his formal satin gloves grasping a mirrored corner.

We next ventured toward the carnival games. A pair of newlings, one with wavy, mamba-black hair and the other with purple streaks, gazed starry eyed at each other. They curled toward us in unison when they felt us staring—we do possess a certain animal magnetism.

"Oh my," said the shorter one, a woman whose giggling revealed a mouth of tiny proto-fangs that retracted when she smiled.

231

She leaned on her date, a man wearing thigh-high boots. "Did you arrange for these gentlemen to come by because I mentioned that granddad kink?"

We were tipsy enough to ask what a granddad kink meant. The two of them blushed, fresh blood flowing beneath their sand-toned skin, and explained they were on something called a meet cute. Then they dared us to try our claws at a feat of endurance with them. How could I resist? Ego is my one shortcoming.

Vlad grumbled but assented. The chef, a Middle Ages vampire, ordered his plump human servant to deliver us flights of garlic bread, garlic knots, and forty-clove garlic soup. He assured us he'd counted the cloves multiple times before tossing them in—we do so like arithmetic precision. Of course, we ordered more blood beer to wash it all down. My taste buds tingled with each dangerous course. It would be worth the pain of growing them back again. I hadn't had such a thrill in a decade.

As we ambled toward the exit, something glimmered off a billboard advertising a full-range of foundation colors. The sign promised skin tones that would make the wearer appear warm-blooded. Why would anyone want such a thing, I wondered. More importantly, what was that point of shining gold near the top—

Selena reappeared without her friends, and I forgot whatever had been pestering me.

"Where're you going?" she purred.

Vlad answered in a disgruntled tone that had been growing stronger. "Home. It's—*hic*—past time we went."

"What?" Her mouth formed an O of surprise. "You *have* to try the zipline first. All the cool kids are doing it."

"We really shouldn't—" Vlad began.

"Hush," I commanded. "If you're such a Dracula Downer, why don't you—*hiccup*—go first and get a head start home?" I bared my fangs and Vlad recoiled, not used to such disagreements between us.

"I will, to make sure it's safe for you." He touched my shoulder with uncharacteristic tenderness, or maybe he was trying to find balance.

"Fine." I clutched my cane defiantly to my side.

"Fine." Vlad took off with a faster stride than I'd thought him capable of, toward the elevator that would raise him up "Past the skies bats can fly!" as the ride's slogan read. The line of revelers had shrunk to nothing.

I took a step in the same direction, but Selena brushed my arm with her licorice-red, curling fingernails. "It'll be better to watch from here. You can go afterward."

I wasn't saying no to that. Selena angled herself close as someone jumped off the high platform. A delighted "Woo hoo!" rang out along with the sound of wheels rolling down the taut metal chain. They generated a bicycle's *ker-chink-chink* and a high-pitched whine simultaneously. But I wasn't watching, entranced by a vein in Selena's neck pulsing. Something glinted off her silver rat earrings, and she jerked her head up.

The sunrise! Its first rays crested the amusement park's walls. I dashed toward the zipline's elevator in a panic, stopped in my tracks as the light speared right through Vlad, suited up in a harness up top. Someone pushed him, burning, off the platform's edge.

Helpless, I no longer heard the gears grate, only the wail of my dear friend's suffering. I tore my eyes away as he shriveled to ash and the handhold coasted down the line, empty.

The sun would soon reach the ground, dispelling all shadows and my own chances for survival. "Quick," I grabbed Selena's dainty sleeve, "we have to get inside somewhere. We'll never get home in time."

"Oh," Selena fluttered her lushes and smirked, "can't you outfly it?"

The glee in her black eyes made it clear she knew the answer, knew vampires my age had long lost the ability to transfigurate. She shouted "Down with Crypt Dwellers! Down with the Decrepit Ones!" as she transformed like all the others around us into bats, rats, and even some dragonflies. They took to the skies and shadows, darting off toward their lairs with peals of ghastly, evil laughter echoing from the park's cement barriers. Have you heard bats laughing? Believe me, you don't want to.

233

The human workers linked their arms together to cut off my attempt to plunge under a pavilion flap. I had done nothing to threaten them, but I couldn't blame them—they were only human. And myself? Only vampire. The fault is mine for giving in to the exhilaration of recklessness I'd once relished as a newling. After a millennium spent feasting on the heady, orgiastic lifeforce of the powerless, it was easy to miss that I'd become one of them.

If there is an afterlife for the undead, I will beg Vlad's forgiveness.

Rebecca Gomez Farrell still refuses to say "Bloody Mary" three times into a mirror, though she'll write stories about the people who do. Her first fantasy novel, Wings Unseen, is available from Meerkat Press or Amazon, and by the end of the year, her shorter works will have been published thirty times in a variety of magazines, websites, and anthologies. Becca's food and drink blog, the Gourmez, has also been going strong for over a decade. All social media: @theGourmez.

Florida Vacation
Ralph Crown

"Clyde, promise me we won't lose another child on this trip."

Clyde Giles turned to Bettany and gave her the grin that made her fall in love again every time. "It's a week at the beach. What could possibly go wrong?" He went back to watching the road.

In the back seat, Travis and Sandy had their eyes and their brains locked on their phones. She turned back to Clyde. "It's just that . . . we take these trips and . . . something happens."

"Nothing will happen this time. Nothing but fun! Trust me."

A sign took shape in the mist. "Look, kids! We're here!" The sign said *Welcome to Shadowport,* below that an odd symbol, the word *Drgrbrnr*, and a schedule of meetings. "What is Dro—Ding—" Too late, they'd passed it. Something like Rotary, she guessed.

Shadowport had houses built of coral blocks in pastel shades, with a sprinkling of fast food joints. In other words, a typical small town in Florida. But Shadowport had one thing the other towns didn't.

"The Old Shadowy Swamp Park!" Sandy squealed when the entrance came into view. "Let's go!"

Bettany glanced at the dashboard clock. "They're about to close, honey. We'll have all day tomorrow. Why don't we go to the hotel and get some rest? Here we are, right across the road . . . No . . ." The sign said *Sleeping with the Fishes Motor Inn.* "Clyde!"

"Something wrong?" He put the car in park.

"The name of the hotel is Sleeping with the Fishes!"

"The ocean's right over there. Swamp all around. Cute name, ha?"

Too tired to argue, she unloaded the luggage, while Clyde checked them in.

Travis said, "Look, there's a bar! Can I go?"

Bettany followed his finger. "How do you know it's a bar?"

"It's got a big mug of suds on the sign."

She peered through the fog. So it did. "You're much too young to drink. Don't wander off. And *don't* go to that bar. It might be dangerous."

"Aw, ma-a!"

Clyde returned with the key and unlocked their room. "Hey, kids, why don't you watch TV for a while?" They pulled out their phones. Clyde ushered Bettany outside. "Let's go to that bar over there. I could use a beer."

"I don't think it's safe to leave them alone."

"Well, we can't take them to a bar, can we?"

They crossed an empty parking lot. The building looked like a Zootoo's restaurant, but fast casually abandoned. The bar, at least, had a thriving clientele, judging by the number of pickup trucks out front.

She took a closer look at the sign. The mug they'd seen was actually a penguin wearing a weird yellow hat. Some of the paint had worn off the name, it seemed to say *Teke-li-li*.

Clyde led her to the bar and ordered beer. Behind him a tall thin man appeared out of the smoke and said, "Hey! Buddy! How about it?"

Clyde turned. "Uh—how about what?"

"Glad you asked." The man looked at Bettany like a butcher checking out a side of beef. "You're a teacher, aren't you? I can always tell."

"Yes . . . I'm a teacher."

"I knew it! My card. I supply safety equipment to the schools, also outdoor products and janitorial supplies. Here, get a whiff of this." He extended a plastic jar.

Bettany took a careful sniff—sweet, unusual, a bit acrid. If plastic fruit had a natural odor, it might smell like that.

"It's passion fruit and strawberry scent. For your restroom dispensers, when the cleaning products don't get the job totally done. You can program it to spray every six hours, every eight hours, every day, whatever you need."

Bettany tried to disengage from the topic of bodily wastes. "I can't make purchasing decisions for my district. Besides, it's in Ohio. Look, we're here on vacation . . ."

Clyde said, "What about three-ring binders? Have you got three-ring binders?" Bettany tried to derail him with sheer eye power.

"I'll have to check with my supplier."

"Apricot jam?"

"Hey, my name's Cleophus Martin. My card." He handed another card to Clyde.

Clyde picked up his beer and steered Cleophus to a table. Bettany hesitated, but the other men in the bar began to appraise her more seriously, and she didn't want that.

Someone grabbed her arm. "Are you with him?" Bettany turned and looked into a face that, after an initial shudder, she would rate as a two. The amount of makeup was surpassed only by the artlessness with which the owner had applied it. Bettany counted three teeth missing. The woman shook Bettany's arm and gestured vaguely with a large fork. "Is that your man?"

"Which man?" Bettany wanted to clear up the issue quickly, not only to get the fork out of her face but to get Clyde out of here and back to the motel.

The woman dragged Bettany to the table and held the fork over Cleophus's head. "Are. You. With. Him."

"No. No, I'm not," she said with relief. "This is my husband. Clyde, shouldn't we get back to the motel?"

"Honey, we just got here. And I'm talking to Cletus."

Bettany took a closer look at the woman. She couldn't tell for sure with someone she would classify as barely human, but she thought she saw love at first sight. "Clyde, why don't we let nature take its course?"

"You need to use the facilities?"

The woman dropped into Cleophus's lap. "Hi there. My name is Vanessa. I think you're cute."

Bettany got Clyde away from the table by taking his beer with her. She couldn't hear what happened after that, but she could practically feel the heat that developed. Cleophus leaned in closer and closer. Over a shockingly short period, they had practically undressed each other. Cleophus called for the check and let it lay on the table. Vanessa picked it up. They got to the door by using a type of locomotion that mainly involved keeping their erogenous zones as close as possible to each other.

Clyde seemed not to notice. Bettany let him get half drunk and pulled him outside.

On their way across the Zootoo's lot, Bettany said, "It's always nice to see two young people fall in love."

"What? Did Sandy meet someone?"

"No."

Clyde seemed more tired or drunk than she had anticipated. Strange, the beer hadn't had much effect on her. It had a strange taste too, probably a local brand.

She got Clyde into their room and into their bed. The children had already fallen asleep. Bettany pulled a blanket over her husband and herself. Tomorrow morning would have to take care of itself.

In the morning she woke with a remarkably clear head. Sandy, of course, had risen at dawn and found a local access channel with news about the water park. "Ma, Ma! Did you know Shadowport has been here since the 1830s?"

"Well, you know the conquistadors explored Florida. Saint Augustine is the oldest European settlement in the US."

"Not Shadowport, Ma."

"We don't have time for a history lesson, honey. It's 6:45, the park opens at 7:30. You wake up Travis, I'll wake up Daddy."

Sandy had talked about this trip for months. Bettany went through a similar phase, when she wanted to become a princess. Her parents had gotten her a tiara and a little green gown.

Sandy wanted to become a mermaid. They'd redecorated her room and gotten her a fish tail she could wriggle into. They'd planned the first leg of their Florida vacation around this visit to the Old Shadowy Swamp Park. Of course, this phase would pass, but why not indulge her while they could?

Once everyone had gotten dressed, they crossed the highway. To Bettany the traffic on the road seemed light, and they barely had to wait to get into the park. They stopped for breakfast at an overpriced stall, which offered an assortment of mermaid-themed merchandise. Sandy wanted one of everything. Bettany pointed out that the park had opportunities everywhere to get such items, and they would have to cart around whatever they bought now for the rest of the day.

"Hey, buddy, what about it?"

Bettany cringed. He couldn't have—but he had. Cleophus had brought Vanessa to the park for their second date.

"I can't thank you enough for hooking me up with this little lady."

"Don't call me your 'little lady'." Vanessa's hand went to her thigh. Bettany thought she saw the outline of a stiletto under her skirt. How had she gotten that into the park?

"You know what I meant."

"I know. But don't say that again."

"Okay, Snookums."

"Okay, Pookie."

"Hey, Clyde, see you at the bar tonight?"

"Sure, Krampus."

"We'll see," said Bettany.

"Let's go check out the restrooms," said Cleophus. In the daylight, it occurred to Bettany that a man regularly visiting school lavatories might have an ulterior motive. The couple scurried away.

"Clyde, where's Sandy?" Bettany tried not to panic. "Where is our daughter?"

"She'll be fine," Clyde said.

"How can you be so calm?"

"She's somewhere in the park. She wouldn't leave, not after she's looked forward to this for so long."

"You said that when Chester sneaked out of the glassblower's workshop in Chicago." Only later did they learn that Chester had wandered into a factory and gotten himself shrinkwrapped to a pallet of foot powder.

"All right. We'll go to the management and report a missing child. They'll shut down the exits. We'll find her, I promise." Clyde had never said anything so responsible. Bettany wanted to hug him, but she grabbed Travis's hand and looked for the main office.

Bettany had to track down a park employee. She practically had him in a headlock before he would give up some basic information. Ten minutes later she stormed into the park supervisor's office. She glanced at the nameplate on his desk. "Mister Sanford, my daughter is missing."

The avuncular gentleman looked at her over his glasses. "Do you have a photo of the child?"

Bettany found a recent picture on her phone and showed it to him.

"Yes, I think we can clear this up in a jiffy. How have you been, Clyde?"

"Just dandy, Mister Sanborn," Clyde answered.

Bettany forgot about her daughter for a moment. "You know him?" She addressed the question to both of them.

"Clyde worked here in the summertime. We're a close-knit people here in Shadowport."

"You're from Shadowport?" She had always assumed that he grew up in Cleveland.

"That's right."

Several minor questions suddenly had answers. Why had their family stopped in this backwater town? How did Clyde know so much about the place? What made Sandy so interested in the park?

"Come with me," Sanborn said. "I think I know where your daughter is." He led them outside and turned away from the parking lot. This wide avenue, fancifully christened Barnacle Boulevard, ran from the entrance to the main attraction, the Enchanted Grotto. Bettany cursed herself for not immediately thinking of the mermaid's theater. Where else would Sandy go as soon as she could slip away?

"Clyde, what's going on?"

"Ha?"

Her stoked emotions turned from her daughter to her husband. "Something's going on here. Something you've kept from me. Something to do with Sandy."

"It's complicated. And it would be much easier to show you than to try and explain." He tried to walk forward.

Bettany grabbed his arm. "I'm not moving from this spot until I get some answers!"

"Pardon the interruption, ma'am," said Sanborn, "but he's right. I can promise you that you will understand much better when can see it for yourself."

"See what?"

"Your daughter is safe. She's probably . . . happy."

"Show me."

Bettany took the hand of a somewhat confused Travis and followed Sanborn. Barnacle Boulevard took them to a pond at the edge of the swamp.

A long ramp led into a fiberglass cave. Here, at the furthest reach of the park, a glass wall held back the water. Sandy, standing in front of that wall, watched the water.

Bettany ran to her and hugged her. "Sandy, I was so worried!"

"Don't be worried, Ma. Look, mermaids."

Bettany looked. In the water, girls in costumes swam around like fish. One came close to the wall and waved. Sandy waved back.

Studying her daughter's face, Bettany saw her as a person for the first time and not just as her child. How else had she missed the obvious? She had bulging eyes and cheeks, with plump lips and thin hair. Not so much like a mermaid as . . . a fish?

The back of her neck tingled. She looked back at the swimmer, who had the same eyes, the same lips.

At the other place the girls had air hoses. These girls had none.

She couldn't produce more than a whisper. "Are you one of them, Clyde? A fish person?"

He answered in a singsong: "We are the servants of Drgrbrnr. The sea was our home and will be again. The swimmer's gift changes us, we do not choose it. Ee-yah Ee-yay. Drgrbrnr."

"The governor?"

"Drgrbrnr."

"Dirigible?"

"Drgrbrnr."

"Dark Avatar?"

"Look, honey. This must be a shock, but how could I tell you? You'd never believe it. You'd never give up another child."

"Give . . . up?" She took Sandy's hand and pulled her towards the ramp. "We've got to go. Now."

"Ma," she said, pulling back. "I belong here. Don't you see?"

Bettany pulled harder. Sandy stood firm.

"Don't make her choose," said Clyde.

Travis. She still had one child left. They had to get out of this nightmare town. Bettany grabbed his hand and hustled him out of the Enchanted Grotto. She had no plan beyond getting Travis out of Shadowport. She power-walked to the parking lot, Travis's hand firmly in hers.

"Hey, Mrs. Giles! What about it?" Cleophus called to them from a large pickup truck.

She'd never been so happy to see a familiar face. "Can you take us to Cross City? Now?"

"I can do better than that. We're headed for Tallahassee. Hop in!"

It took a bit more than a hop, but they got inside. The large cab had an ample rear seat.

Travis said, "Why are we leaving?"

"Travis, your sister is turning into a fish."

"Cool!"

"This isn't one of your cartoons. She's not going to change back a half hour later and go back to her normal life."

Vanessa said, "Your sister is a fish? Cool!"

Bettany said, "You're not helping."

Cleophus guided the truck through the exit and onto the highway. He turned north.

Vanessa said, "What's wrong with being a fish?"

"One word," said Bettany. "Shark."

Cleophus said, "Come on, a mermaid can take out a shark."

"You're not helping either. And how does that even happen?"

"Lasers, man." As if that explained everything.

Travis said, "What if the sharks have lasers?"

"Oh, yeah."

Bettany opened her purse. "I'm getting a headache."

Cleophus said, "No problem, I sell first aid kits too. Dig one out, will ya, Snookums?" Vanessa began to rummage through the cab.

Travis said, "What about our stuff?"

Bettany still had no plan. She and Travis had the clothes on their backs. She had a credit card and a driver's license. She wanted to cry. She wanted to scream. Could she go to the police? What would she say?

"Twelve," said Vanessa.

"What?" said Bettany.

"There's a police car behind us. Careful, Pookie."

"How did you spot the police?"

Vanessa gave her an exasperated look. "You got to know when the po-po are near. That's survival, sugar."

Bettany's first thought: If you haven't broken the law—

Bettany's second thought: They've broken the law. Repeatedly. Both of them.

Bettany's third thought: I'm hitchhiking with animals.

Okay. She could deal with criminals. She couldn't deal with fish people, not today.

Vanessa said, "Okay, don't give them a reason to stop us. I think there's a warrant out on me."

"You *think*?" Bettany asked.

"You try to marry a boat ramp and people think there's something wrong with you. You divorce the boat ramp and they try to lock you up. You try to marry the boat ramp again and you're on the eleven o'clock news. Go figure."

Cleophus said, "There may be a warrant out on me too."

"Oh, Pookie."

"Oh, Snookums. Look out, he's speeding up."

The police car passed them by.

"FIDO," said Vanessa.

"What?" Bettany began to suspect that Vanessa spoke some other language, one that only sounded like English.

"Fark It, Drive On. They think we're more trouble than we're worth. Is this truck stolen?"

"No, it's mine."

Vanessa said, "You are a real catch, you know that?"

Cleophus turned on the radio, and they listened to country music. Vanessa sang along with the ones she knew.

Bettany tried to tune it out. Her thoughts went in circles. She

243

couldn't go home to Cleveland, not without her family. She couldn't stay in Shadowport with the fish people. She couldn't go to the authorities, not unless the X-Files had an office in Tallahassee. She kept only half an eye on the two-lane road.

The truck started around a long curve. Cleophus cursed and hit the brake. A car had spun out and rolled into the center of the road. The police car they'd recently encountered squatted in the middle of the road, lights flashing.

Vanessa pointed out the not so obvious. "Where's the cop?"

Cleophus started to turn around. "I don't see him, and I'm not waiting for him to show up and ask questions."

Bettany almost screamed. "We can't go back!"

Cleophus said, "Well, we can't go forward, we'll slide into the swamp if we try to go around that car. We'll just have to wait for a tow truck."

"I'll call 9-1-1," Bettany said. She pulled out her phone. No bars. She tried to make the call anyway but couldn't get a connection. "Travis, stay in the car. I'm going to look for that officer. His radio has to work."

"I'll go with you," Cleophus said.

"No, you won't," said Vanessa.

"Take some traffic cones," Cleophus said. He climbed across the back seat, through the window, and into the bed of the truck.

Bettany got out and warily approached the two cars. Where had the driver gone?

A nylon bag landed near her. Cleophus yelled from the truck, "First aid kit!" It had EMERGENCY stenciled on it. Inside she found rubber gloves, tampons, tissues, a sponge, a safety vest, a flashlight, a deck of cards, a hotel-sized bar of soap, and a plastic sleeve holding a knife, a spork, and a napkin. If she ever needed to perform an appendectomy at a poker game, she had the right equipment.

She dropped the bag and took another step towards the cars.

A loud HISS made her stop.

Around the overturned car lumbered a large alligator.

All she knew about alligators was to run away in a zigzag pattern. They could run faster than you could, but only in a straight line.

Before she knew it, she was back in the truck, breathing hard.

"Ma, are you okay?"

"I'm okay. Everybody count off. Vanessa? Cleophus?"

Vanessa, still in the front seat, watched the alligator approach. "Eh, I've seen bigger."

Cleophus hastily climbed inside. "You know that's a dinosaur, right? An alligator is a straight-up dinosaur. I'm not going near it."

Bettany went into teacher mode. "Do you have any real emergency equipment? How about a siren? Barricades? Bleach? Anything that will drive off this thing?"

Cleophus said, "How about a flare gun?"

"Great! Where is it?"

"In the back somewhere."

"Where somewhere?"

"Ma!"

"What is it now, Travis?"

"I smell smoke!" said Travis.

What else could go wrong?

Cleophus said, "That could be my gasoline additive. It's got a refreshing, distinctive lime odor."

Bettany hustled Travis into the bed and followed him out. "Everyone out of the truck! Now!" Creepers of smoke slid out from the edges of the hood.

"Cleophus! Do you have a fire extinguisher?"

"Sure, it's right beside the console."

WHOOMP! Dark smoke filled the cab.

"Okay," Bettany barked, "we'll have to take our chances with the alligator." She surveyed the road behind them. Another alligator, apparently drawn by the commotion, sprinted towards them. "Okay, everyone look for a fire extinguisher."

"Got it!" crowed Cleophus. He held up a red cylinder, pulled the pin, and aimed the hose at the cloud of smoke.

"Wait," Bettany said. Modern vehicles had a firewall to protect the passengers from an engine fire. In this case the firewall protected the engine fire from the extinguisher. The cab filled with a thin stinky foam, while the fire continued to burn merrily.

The second alligator reached the truck. It launched itself against the tailgate but couldn't reach the top. It sprang upward, got a grip on the rear bumper, and began to shake the truck.

"Find that flare gun, please." Bettany couldn't take her eyes off the alligator. Its eyes had no expression at all. Malice or hunger she could understand, but this frightened her even more.

Bettany had put off asking the question, but they didn't have much time left. "Do you have a gun, Cleophus?"

"You mean, like, a real gun?"

"A real gun."

"Oh, no," said Cleophus, "I'd go straight back to Raiford if they caught me with a gun."

"What about the flare gun?"

"Yeah. We can shoot a flare in its mouth. It will blow up. I saw it in a movie. . . . Hey, I remember where I put that flare gun!"

"Where is it?"

"In the glove compartment."

FOOMF! Flame erupted from the front of the truck.

"We've got to go," Bettany yelled.

"Wait!" said Cleophus. He dove into the cab. A moment later he returned, coughing and gasping. He handed a gun to Bettany. "Here. The flare gun. I'd shoot, but I can't see."

She took Travis by the shoulder. "I'm going to shoot that alligator and run away. I want you to run down the road as fast as you can. Don't look back. Can you do that?"

"Yes, Ma."

Bettany vaulted over the side of the truck. She turned the corner and yelled at the gator. When it looked at her, she raised the gun and fired.

A riot of multicolored streamers shot from the gun. *Confetti?*

The alligator froze in place. Bettany turned to run.

Not twenty feet away, another police car waited in the road. Clyde got out of the passenger door.

"Clyde?"

"I may not be a fish person, but I do have my uses. Who's a good little sauropsida?" He stroked the nose of the gator, which started to . . . purr?

"I thought we were all going to die." Bettany summoned Travis, who clambered out of the truck and ran to hug his father.

Her relief overwhelmed her. She hugged Clyde too.

"Would you like to go back to Shadowport now?" he said.

"Yes. Yes, we would."

That night it seemed as if the whole town turned out for a party in Sandy's honor. Bettany had never seen Clyde so popular. She had to fight to get him to herself for a moment. "Can you explain all this for me? I think I should know."

"Ask Mayor Sanborn." And he got pulled away again.

She found Sanborn. "Clyde says you can tell me things."

"Yes, I can."

"But first, can we get some real beer? This stuff isn't doing anything for me. I need to be drunk. I've had a long day."

Sanborn waved a hand. The bartender from Teke-li-li appeared. When Bettany made her request, he said, "The bar's right over there. I'll get something for you." He walked straight into the swamp.

Bettany settled down for a long talk. "How did you meet those people?" the mayor asked.

"I'm not sure, they just sort of attached themselves to us."

Sanborn pulled out a notebook. "He's a career criminal. Nine warrants for lewd behavior, five for weapons violations, eighteen for drug trafficking, thirteen for breaking and entering, thirty for cruelty to animals, four assaults. Oh, and attempted murder." He put the notebook away. "So, have you ever heard of Innsmouth, Massachusetts?"

"No."

"That's because the US Navy blew it up. They dynamited all the buildings, they depth-bombed the harbor, and they set fire to the ruins."

"But why?"

"Innsmouth was the original American temple of Drgrbrnr. The survivors sailed down the coast to find a new home. They landed here."

"But who or what is Dirge Burner?"

"He's in the Old Testament. The Amorites worshipped a sea

god named Dagon. The Hebrews and the early Christians tried to stamp out their competitors because they empowered women."

"You don't say."

"You don't have the genetic background to become a swimmer, but if you pray to Drgrbrnr, you may receive some sort of boon."

"A boon?"

"Some sort of power or ability."

"I like the sound of that."

"Here comes your beer."

The bartender returned through the swamp with a plastic tub full of bottles of beer.

Bettany said, "Ee-yah Ee-yay!"

Ralph Crown has started eight books but only finished one. He's still trying to sell it. If you know anyone who wants a hard-boiled kung fu fantasy western, please let him know. His current project is a fictionalized autobiography dealing with the fan scene of the 1980s.

Basement Apartment—All the Med Cons
Charles C. Montgomery

Stepping down from the stage of the Miskatonic Community College Auditorium with my A.A. (Associates of Arcana), I felt adult. An adult who had to be out of the dorms by the end of the month and into a place of my own.

As a child I had imagined a battered hovel on the edge of a dark sphagnum plain, at the foot of a mountain path, with the promise of mummified corpses beneath. Here, damp weather could reach my bones and cause the charming curved spine of premature old age. It would have concealing mists and the path would carry occasional lone adventurers, trusting, tired, in need of food and shelter. What I would refer to, in private moments, as "victims."

But these were the romantic notions of youth. I also thought about the noise, crowding, and pollution— the fighting, adultery, murder, begging, and imprisonment that go with a city.

These were few of my favorite things!

I pulled out my Lie-Pad and searched the online haunt ads.

Two weeks later, without the meagerest straw pallet on which to rest my head, I saw it.

> **Downtown Dungeon!** Perfect for the single Witch or Warlock, this cozy downtown-area dungeon features natural light and charming amenities. With an open layout, a little elbow-grease and TLC will go a long way towards making this hovel your home! Motivated landlord, terms available.

This was everything I wanted, obscured by real estate jargon. "Cozy" meant cramped. "Natural light" would be dim; torchlight if I was lucky. "Charming," so no updates in years, perhaps centuries. TLC? Tortured, Lengthy Cleaning techniques were on a million BooTube videos, and tins of elbow-grease could be bought in bulk at the apothecary.

A quick look at Boogle Maps revealed that "downtown" was a stretch, but the place was convenient to an Every Witch Waymart, near a Better Crones and Wicked Gardens, and a Dead, Death, and Beyond. The local cable company even had Fox News in its basic package!

I rang for an appointment.

I arrived a bit early to check out the neighborhood.

A squat dog limped by, with an ankle monitor on its one front leg. Its stumpy tail wagged erratically and a delicate layer of froth danced at the edges of serrated teeth that would give pause to a shark.

It couldn't have been cuter if it had three heads and a snake for a tail.

A woman's head and upper torso popped out of the window, like 1.5 lbs. of sausage exploding from a 1 lb. sausage skin.

The woman took a look at me, and yelled towards the dog. "Spike! Spike Mangle, you get away from that guy!" The dog's head spun towards the woman, a string of spittle detaching from its jaw, splattering onto the pavement with a small hiss. The woman's arm came out the window. Mumbling under her breath, her arm inscribed a loose arc in the air. The dog, following her finger, rose slowly into the air and floated to above a brownstone stoop. The woman dropped her arm abruptly and, squealing, the dog slapped down.

I thought I understood the missing leg.

While this cozy domestic scene unfolded, the real estate agent arrived, limping slightly despite a fashionable cane. He was slender, wearing a thin black cape from above which rose a remarkably plastic face. I quickly extended my right hand, and he extended his right . . . Uh, it was at the end of his right forearm, so let's just call it a 'hand.' We shook and with what a sucking sound might feel like, his hand oozed out of mine.

I stared down at my now sticky hand.

"Wait a minute, let me take another look at your email," he said.

He reached into a pocket of his cape, from which spilled an

empty rum bottle; a blue Infinity Stone; a lucky rabbit's foot attached to a panicked rabbit; a yellow pocketbook titled "The Idiots Guide to Reading the Voynich Manuscript," and; a six-string of Magnum condoms.

He saw my stare.

"Wife borrowed my cape," he lied as he sheepishly stuffed this dog's breakfast of Western Culture back into the cape.

On his next attempt he retrieved a pair of reading glasses and a laptop computer.

"Nice cape," I said.

He shrugged, "A Coco Channel to Another World. Has a three-way interdimensional pouch." He opened the cape to reveal red fur lining. "From the Charles M. Burns collection. There's a matching vest . . . somewhere."

A couple of clicks, a glance at the screen to read my email, and he grunted and returned the laptop to its pocket.

He patted the cape flat, reached into a disappointingly mundane trousers pocket, and extracted a skeleton key. Inserting it in the lock he pushed on the door, which opened reluctantly, allowing a cloud of humid air to float out.

It was dirty, dank, sticky, and smelly.

I smelled home.

"Would you like to see it," he asked? I nodded assent and he paused slightly to disentangle his three-pronged cane from a metal grate at the entrance, into which two of its prongs had descended.

A swift tug and the cane came free, then we descended into the dungeon apartment. If the air at the top of the stairs had promised dirty, dank, sticky, and smelly, the dungeon delivered. Grimy yet slick, dark but indistinct, the floor sloped towards the middle of the room.

I felt suspicious, for no reason I could put my finger on. And after that handshake, I wanted to be pretty careful where my fingers went. "What's the catch?" I asked.

"No catch," he replied. "This house is what you want and more. That perfect home you're looking for. From front porch steps to cellar door. For the single witch with a homey itch . . ."

My head nodded towards my chest and the scene around me

vaguely faded.

I jerked my head upwards. "Hey! Cut it out! You're not qualified to cast spells! You wanna be busted for practicing without a license?"

Attempting to arrange his face in an expression of shame and regret, the agent, instead, twisted it into something one might find in the Blowtorched Barbie collection of a young serial killer in-training.

"Sorry, just trying to make a living," he weaseled.

If he had a forelock he would have tugged it. Most of his hair, however, was gathered into two punky spikes, one on each side of his head.

I harrumphed, "Ok, but knock it off."

He quickly started his spiel, "The building is a 13th century . . ."

A shiver ran through me... it could be Late Inquisition!

". . . classic," he continued. "Grated windows, solid cobblestone construction with built-in iron hooks for your convenience, and a floor drain."

A thought flashed through my head, *A floor drain in a basement— that's sure to back up and smell.* I tried to hide my increasing interest.

"Tell me its history?" I asked.

"It was originally a convent. And a brothel. And a madhouse. At the same time. A tidy business combination if you ask me."

"All it needed was a nursery and mortuary to complete the cycle," I laughed. "Anyway, I was looking for more recent history, like tenants, neighborhood, practical things."

"The previous tenant was a little old witch who only had visitors on weekends." His gaze traversed the walls. "We pretty much got the blood off."

Unfortunate, but I was still interested.

"Ok," I asked, "how about the neighborhood?"

"A mixed bag, really," he replied. "But very friendly. We had an open house last weekend and the whole neighborhood dropped by." The agent's gaze re-traversed the walls. "We pretty much got that blood off, also."

I sat on the only furnishing, an overstuffed chair resembling a kidney rejected for transplantation. Despite its squishy appearance it had the unforgiving feel of an Iron Maiden. In some obscure way, that reminded me of the agent's face, a thought which immediately caused me to hop back up and dust the back of my trousers off with my right hand.

"How much," I asked, "the rent wasn't in the ad?"

"It's not a deal with the devil . . ." his attempt at a joke trailed off as he saw my expression harden.

"Ah, um." His oddly plastic face cycled through a variety of expressions until it settled somewhere between deep thought and mild stroke, semi-fixed into a wobbly gelatinousness one might expect to find at the bottom of a Woodstock Porta-Potty. "Well, we try to be reasonable. Karmic debt, perhaps?"

I shook my head. "I have bad credit."

He moved on, "Any organs you're not using?"

I snorted.

"Relatives with organs *they* aren't using?"

I made as if to leave. "Can we talk rent-money, not some kind of *deal* you're trying to stick me with?

"OK, OK," he changed tack, "It's 100 a month, a bargain for all this . . . atmosphere."

Pricey, but I liked the place.

Under my breath, I mumbled a spell I had developed as my capstone project during my senior seminar:

> "Lucky money come to me,
> Bring me what I need to be.
> Silver coin and currency,
> Gold and riches, all for free."

Hoping the spell would bring riches, but concerned because it had barely received a passing grade, I made a leap of faith— "I'll take it!"

A smile that reminded me of a viper coiling to strike spread across his face. *It must be a face,* I reminded myself, *that's why the eyes are in it.*

He reached into the pocket of his cape, and withdrew a

sewing-needle, fountain pen, contract, and small desktop podium.

*I have **got** to get one of those capes*, I thought to myself.

He handed me the contract, needle, and pen.

I scanned the contract.

Seemed OK to me.

A few drops of blood, my rune on the dotted line, a personal check, and the dungeon was mine for the year!

He handed me the key and let himself out.

I let out a sigh of relief as he left, leaving only the traces of his sulfur-scented cologne hanging in the damp air.

That was a weird dude, I thought, *but I the contract protects me.*

Tomorrow I'd head over to Desecrate and Barrel to get furniture, Belowes Hardware for fittings, Unsafeway for some food with moderately expired eat-by dates (best bargains in town!), and Amy's Winehouse for a bottle of the usual. If there was time left over, I'd visit the Society for Promulgation of Cruelty to Animals—The SPCA had the best familiars.

If I was lucky they'd have a black cat— maybe even a rabid one!

I'd be home!

Charles Montgomery lives, with a lovely wife and two cats, in a suicidally-ideated house in Spokane. He is open to suggestions and his other work can be found on his Amazon author's page.

The Mystery Tab

White Line Fever
Dan McKay

      Dave trudged along the road through the high desert. Sundown had come and gone, and the temperature had gradually changed from oven-like to chilly. He pulled his jacket tighter around his neck. Fog formed as the air cooled, giving the night an eerie vibe. A lone coyote howled in the distance, its sharp yelp piercing the stillness.

      He came to an intersection and walked along the crossroad until he found a signpost. His eyes had adjusted to the darkness enough to read the highway number. It was the one he'd hoped it would be. He visualized holding a map and confirmed in his head California lay ahead of him. Barstow lay a long distance farther, and he'd hoped to hitchhike most of the way there.

      He'd heard about white line fever from truckers he'd hitched a ride with. One claimed to have fallen into a trance, and when he snapped out of it a hundred and fifty miles had gone by. No white line marking the shoulder where he walked, only an ankle-twisting transition from asphalt to dirt. The yellow stripes went by a lot slower on foot but still had a mesmerizing effect, especially when alone and tired to his bones.

      He came to a slight rise. Beyond, the road dropped in a gentle slope. Lights shined a mile or two ahead twinkling with the promise of human comforts. He sensed movement on the road beside him. A car, straight from old-time black-and-white movies rolled up, silent other than the sound of its whitewall tires on the asphalt.

      At the idea of a ride, all the pains from walking escalated. It appeared the driver was having second thoughts; Dave hurried to the back door and jumped inside. A dusty aroma greeted him as the seat squeaked in protest. The dome light hadn't come on, but it was an old classic car and maybe it didn't have one.

"Thanks for the ride, mister. My feet are killing me." The car continued in silence, picking up speed. He reached into his pack for the canteen and drank from it. The warmish water soaked into his parched body.

After zipping his pack shut, he tried again. "How far you going, mister?" He waited a polite minute. No answer. He shifted to the edge of his seat and leaned into the front, expecting to find the missus. She'd be wearing a fur stole around her shoulders and gloves up to her elbows. He would have to dodge the hat pinned to her hair. But no one sat in the front passenger seat.

Perhaps the driver thought him rude to have taken the backseat when the front was available. "Sorry, mister, I didn't realize I could've ridden shotgun." What if the driver wasn't the mister, but the missus? That could explain why she hadn't said anything. "Or, ma'am." He offered his most sincere eyes-closed smile of apology. No response.

Annoyed, he snapped his eyes open. The driver's seat sat empty. The dash was dark, like the road ahead. The steering wheel jiggled with the cracks in the pavement.

Dave hit the ground running. Sand and dirt kicked up behind him. If his feet were tired and sore, he didn't notice. He wove through sage brush and cacti. After several minutes, his lungs burned and his side hurt too much to continue at a frantic pace. With a nervous glance behind, he walked as fast as he could push himself.

A ghost car! He'd ridden in a ghost car and lived to tell the tale. He stopped and pinched the back of his hand. Not dead. The dead don't have feelings. That's why zombies didn't flinch when they lost an arm. He'd heard of ghost ships but not ghost cars unless the car in that Stephen King novel counted. Christine—that's what it was, same as his sister. This car was different, more ghost-like and quiet. Dead quiet. He shuddered and kept walking.

He noticed his backpack hung from his hand. A lucky break. Instinctively, he'd grabbed it when he jumped out. Over the next rise, the lights became brighter as a small town came into view. Tail lights from a vehicle moved along a street. He stumbled along, looking back to make sure nothing had followed him. At the sign announcing "Welcome to Desert Rose. Population 115," he broke into a sprint.

A few cars sat in front of an old-time saloon. Moths flitted around the neon lights across the façade. He burst through the swinging doors, startling the half-dozen patrons. "Whiskey. Double shot." He dug in his pocket and set some bills on the bar.

At a table in the back, his breathing returned to normal. It could have been white line fever and he'd imagined it all. Or the desert air had played tricks on him. When people got an idea in their heads, their imaginations took over rational thought.

Yeah, that had to be it. He'd been walking most of the day in the heat. Nothing to see but scrub brush and roadkill. Dehydration could be a factor, too. He'd get a beer or two after he finished the whiskey. He took another sip, and the warmth settled his mind.

The doors opened, and three men walked in. The locals greeted them as some of their own.

"Jerry!"

"Mike!"

"Hey, Steve!"

Jerry sat at an empty table. "That was hard work. I need a beer."

"Me, too," Mike said, "if I have the strength to lift it." He joined Jerry at the table.

Steve nodded to the bartender. "I'll take two." He dropped into a chair next to Mike.

The bartender hustled out with two mugs in each fist. "How's that project coming along?" one of the locals asked.

"Let me tell you, Tom, it's nothing but a money pit," Jerry groused. "The more I spend, the more it needs."

"Yeah, I've been there myself," Tom said. "But they don't make 'em like that anymore."

Steve set his empty glass down and belched. "You could make three or four new ones out of the metal in an old one."

Tom nodded. "True, that." He lifted his beer mug and eyed the remaining suds. "You going to repaint it?"

"Yeah, pearl black," Jerry said. "If I ever get it done it'll be a beauty, right out of 1941." He downed half his beer. "Put the transmission in. Aired up the tires and took it for a test drive."

Mike shook his head. "Didn't get very far."

Steve scoffed. "Got far enough. Glad it wasn't any farther. It's a beast to push."

Dave's head popped up. His glass landed on the table, splashing him with whiskey.

Jerry stared with his mouth open. "Hey! There's the guy who climbed in when we were pushing!" Mike and Steve jumped to their feet, tipping their chairs over.

Dave bolted out the back door and sprinted down the street. As he passed the sign stating "Leaving Desert Rose. Come back soon!" he stole a look over his shoulder. The town sat dark and empty. A tumbleweed rolled down the street. An old wooden sign hung by one hinge above the saloon's doors. It groaned in the breeze.

Dan McKay won the 2005 Bulwer-Lytton fiction contest. He's hunkered down in Fargo, ND with his family.

The Terrible Burden of Love
Brandon Stichka

     Thana settled alone into the center of the wide wooden swing meant for two. She sighed as the warmth seeped into taut muscles and spread across smooth skin covered by little more than a blood-red sundress. As the heat moved through her like lapping waves in some faraway paradise, long-held tension began melting away. Her heavy eyelids drooped as Zach dashed headlong across the backyard towards his favorite place in the world. His deep but faded scars could not slow him as he charged on, shrieking with joyous laughter. It was still too dangerous to let him play with other children, and with summer sunshine like this, she could not risk too much exposure, but every time she had let him out again, every time she had let him *be* again, even for a little while, had been a blessing. She luxuriated in the sounds of her only child at play. She let herself ooze down in the wooden swing, slumping as if she sought to burrow into the lateral slats as they banished her stiffness, replacing it with warm butter. A smile crept across her face, beaming like the sun. Thana closed her eyes, and the darkness swept over her.

     Thana crouched in the shadows of a stranger's foyer, in the darkest corner, opposite the hall tree. She readied herself when she heard heavy winter boots crunch up the snowy front steps. A silhouette rose from the bottom of the frosted glass of the front door. Ice crystals glimmered, blurring the outline even further, leaving it almost unrecognizable. That was for the best. She had done everything she could to see the packaging wrapped around a kidney rather than a man. From leukemia to chemotherapy to kidney failure, little Zach was out of time.
     The heartless automatons, the supposed experts who had

been unable to stop Zach's painful decline, had told her that this man was a perfect match. They had also told her that he had already wasted a kidney on his sister. That had been a problem. Slipping over his fence unnoticed
had been the solution. Stomping across his property in oversized galoshes had been the solution. Leaving them outside the door to delicately maneuver through the unfamiliar darkness of his house had been the solution. She had found her path in the dark.

Perfectly manicured hands encased in dishwashing gloves silently poured chloroform into a rag. She would take that with her. She had already swept the backdoor glass and replaced the pane. No evidence, no witnesses, just one healthy kidney for her little boy and the organ donor keeping it warm for him.

The metallic click of the deadbolt heralded a gust of blistering cold fierce enough to make Thana's toothpaste commercial teeth chatter. She stilled them in an instant, masked by the door crashing home. Back turned to the darkness concealing her, the semi-discernable mound of wool found the light switch. Nothing happened. Thana had loosened the bulb. No light, no way to see her. With a shrug, he flipped the switch off and began shedding layer after layer in an interminable dance. A coat like a flock of sheep, a hat, gloves, and finally, a pair of thick scarves; pink hands left it all in an unorganized heap as he moved for the living room.

Gliding on moccasins, silent as the grave, Thana darted from her shadows and slammed the rag into place. She snaked her other arm under his, reaching across his chest and heaving back in one colossal jerk. Shocking weight shifted to her lithe frame as his feet left the ground. The dual impacts of landing sandwiched her chest in the clamps of a vice, blasting the air from her lungs. She gasped harder than he did, but the wet rag never shifted. Rough hands skated up and down the heavy sleeves protecting her arms. Thick nails bit and snagged the dense leather, but they would never get through to the soft skin beneath. No blood under his nails. No evidence to destroy. He launched himself from side to side. Bones ground in

Thana's joints, but he was already in the bear trap. She just had to outlast him. Stars flickered in her vision, but iron laced her muscles. Each spasm torqued her less, each pause lasted longer, and the burden atop her grew heavier.

    Even as leaden limbs dropped to the floor, she held the rag in place. Only after her own battered lungs ceased burning did she squirm free of the sack of warm oatmeal that weighed her down. She zip-tied his crossed wrists and ankles. A ball of socks and a pair of pantyhose served well as a gag, completing the restraints. Hoisting his beefy legs at the ankles, she threw her diminutive figure into dragging his bulk deeper into the house. Time and again she hauled against the mountain, blazing her trail into the darkness. The adrenaline that coursed through her kept her rocking like a metronome, inch by backbreaking inch.

    Thana finally dropped the load in the library, the only room without windows. As she panted with hands on knees, the phone rang. Lightning shot through her as she whipped around to face the jangling cacophony. She wavered as her heart slammed against her sternum during the second ring. Her pulse throbbed in her eyes. She told herself this was no problem. There were endless benign reasons to miss a call. Eternity passed before the fourth ring and the click of an answering machine.

    "Hi Grandpa Uri, it's Cindy!" a small voice piped into the silent void. "I'm really happy you're coming next weekend. Mom said not to bother you at work, but you'll hear this at home. I just wanted to say I love you."

    Thana's eyes snapped open as she leapt to her feet. She gasped as a crystalline crackle fanned through her exposed skin. Shoulders, arms, cheeks, neck, and especially her hands glowed cherry and sang with pain. The phantom flames surged as she turned towards Zach. Sunlight glinted off his yellow trucks as they undertook the grand works of his sandbox empire. A lifetime had passed with Zack unable to play like other boys. And now that he could, though not with them, day after day he had been determined to make up for lost time. Thana smiled at his hard-won vigor, but the sizzling heat dancing across her skin turned to icicles in her bones. She had to look away. She always heard a little girl's voice when she watched Zach play.

Brandon Stichka is back for more, making his third appearance in the Fark Fiction Anthology. His previous appearances include "Seizing the Quill" published in the 2018 edition, Everybody Panic!, *and "One More Fight" published in the 2019 edition,* Oh No, Not Again!

Hargis
Eric Weir

A man on a roan named Lady picked his way through the rocky waste, going west whenever the way was passable. Once in a while, he saw the tracks of the horse that carried the man he was following. For the time being, that was his only guide.

The man was Jackson Mains, and he was a bounty hunter. The man he pursued called himself Tom Cudder, but who knew if that was really his name. He was wanted for shooting a shopkeeper dead and robbing him in Wichita. Mains hoped he was on the right trail. Although he was a skilled tracker, there was the possibility that he was following the wrong tracks. He was two days behind Cudder, and his quarry might not have gone west from the last town; he could be following the wrong person.

Mains grimly thought that even if he was following the wrong man, that man could have a price on his head just the same. No one would undertake this wandering journey through the canyons and rocky screes, through the creosote and spiny blackbrush, except to evade pursuit.

Reaching the top of a slope, Mains looked ahead and saw nothing but the sun and more misery for him and his horse ahead. Soon it would be time to bed down for the night. He knew he was gaining on Cudder because a few hours ago he'd found the outlaw's campsite from the night before last. Cudder had to find a way through this trackless land, while Mains merely followed, which peculiarly made Mains faster.

An hour or so later, having found two more signs of Cudder, Mains called it a day. He unloaded Lady, brushed her, and gave her some oats and poured her some water from a leather bag into a small pail. He got out his cooking gear and made a small fire with dead twigs and branches. He heated some beans from a can, ate them, and sopped up the juices with a couple of hardtack biscuits. Arranging his saddle as a pillow and Lady's blanket for warmth, Mains reclined on the ground and slept soundly.

In the morning when Mains awoke, Lady was looking his way as she always did. He fixed her breakfast, and then his: oats and water for her, and boiled dried meat, bread and coffee for him. He cleaned up, saddled Lady and went westward on the trail.

The next day was uneventful. He followed the trail and eventually camped as he had done the night before. The day after, he found some sign of Cudder at a nearly dry water hole in a streambed; he stayed there a while to let Lady eat some green grass and herbs, although Cudder's horse had gotten the best already. He could not gather more water because it had been fouled. Did Cudder crap in the water because he knew he was following?

The third day, as the afternoon was waning, Mains sat on his horse on a hill overlooking a town. For the first time in the last few days, he didn't have to look directly into the sun and he could see the town laid out below. At the far end there was a running creek, reflecting the sunlight, and quite a few buildings; nearer to him was deserted empty space except for the high street running toward him and a frame structure that he thought was a saloon. This was where the trail led him, so he went on, down the slope. He tied Lady in front of the saloon, gave her a feedbag, and entered through the hung oilcloth that served as a door. A badly-painted sign said "Jacks"

The bar was a 12-foot plank supported by two barrels. There were five men inside, and only one of them was dressed in good clothes. He stood by the bar. Three looked like down-on-their-luck wranglers, and they sat at a sort of table made of planks and a tree trunk; the last man was the bartender, who wore an apron over a dirty shirt and pants. Ignoring everyone, Mains strode to the bar as well as he could after a day of riding, and asked for water and whiskey, and laid down a quarter dollar.

The bartender grinned, picked up the quarter, ladled some water into a tin cup, produced a tiny glass from a hidden shelf, obtained a bottle from the wall behind him and filled the glass half-full of a reddish-brown liquid. The men at the table didn't move or speak, nor did the well-dressed fellow. Mains drank the liquor down at a gulp, sipped some water, and asked, "What's this town?"

"This here town is Hargis," the barman replied. "I got the

idea you came in from the east."

"That I did," said Mains. "I think you saw me. I'm hoping it was worth the journey."

"We saw you," said the bartender. "It's not often that we get travelers from that direction. You want another?"

Mains nodded and placed another quarter on the plank. "I started at Wichita and ended here. I'm looking for a man, you see. He would have come from the east, just as I did. Maybe you saw him."

"Maybe, maybe," said the bartender. "But he wouldn't stay long at this end of town. He could find lodging at Hattie's down the street, and entertainment at the Ace of Hearts. Fact is, there's not much left of Hargis since the railroad passed us by."

Now the well-dressed man walked a couple of steps closer and said, "I'm Jack. What's your name, sir?"

"My name is Mains. I'm pleased to meet you, Jack." They shook hands and Jack leaned back against the plank, which he would have dislodged were it not nailed to the barrels. Mains observed that Jack's clothes were clean, he wore a vest and tooled boots, and sported a pearl-handled Colt revolver.

Jack said, "Well, Mr. Mains, are you looking for a friend or just a man?" He nodded to the bartender, who dug up another glass and poured a drink for him, and gave Mains another refill as well.

"I can't say that he's a friend," said Jackson Mains. "For one thing, he leaves behind a dirty camp."

Jack showed his teeth and shook his head. "That's the sign of a man who lacks responsibility. We wouldn't like him much, here in Hargis. Larry told you he probably went to the other end of town, and I'd guess he's moved on from there, too."

"I suppose I'd better look for him there, then. I need to find a place to stay tonight, too."

"Hattie's is a good place. You'll see it down the street on the right," Jack told him. He lowered his voice. "Can I ask a favor? These poor fellas"—he indicated the three men at the table— "would probably like a drink. If I buy them a drink, it'll never end, but if you do . . ."

Mains scowled for a second, because he knew it was expected of him. He had expected the touch and the brush-off, as well. "OK,

267

here," he said, and produced a silver dollar. "I'm much obliged for the advice to stay at Hattie's."

"And I thank you, Mr. Mains," said Jack. Mains nodded at him and at the bartender and headed for the door. As he mounted Lady, he heard whooping from inside. Shaking his head wryly, he headed up the street. Hargis had once been a more important place, he saw. A hundred yards from Jacks, the high street intersected perpendicularly with a road, and on the corners there were a former bank building, made of stone and vacant; a general store, closed; and two other buildings of unknown origin and purpose. To the left and right, down the cross street, he could see a few houses with gardens in front of them.

Mains rode past, seeing a few other vacant buildings and a store that still was in business, and came to Hattie's, a neatly painted frame building where a placard saying "ROOMS" hung by the door. Across the street from Hattie's was a saloon called "Ace of Hearts" from which he heard piano music. However, the establishment beyond Hattie's, a livery stable, attracted his attention and he went there first.

As he dismounted, a man came outside. "Well!" he said. "I'm sure glad to see you, stranger! I'm Virgil Stayborne, and I'm guessing you need stabling for your horse . . . and I see that you might need some new leather there . . . and there. I can fix you right up."

Mains introduced himself and shook hands with Virgil, a wiry fellow about 55 or 60 years old. Virgil had more to say: "I can take care of your horse, what's her name? and let me show you around, there's a bit of fenced pasture out back with some good grass. Let me get acquainted with this girl . . . her name is Lady? And a lady she is. Let's go inside."

The inside was well-maintained, with six stables. Virgil led Mains to the back and showed him the corral, contained within a bend of the creek that Mains had seen from the east end of town. The grass inside was better than Mains expected, and Lady hadn't seen good grass for four days on the rocky trail. It was just about sundown.

"It's fifty cents a day," Virgil Stayborne said as they walked back to the front. "Lady gets brushed daily and can have all the grass she wants, all day. At night she gets oats and the stable. What do you say?"

Mains agreed, and then Virgil said, "Let's look at your saddle." Virgil indicated that the leather supporting the left stirrup was worn, and Mains agreed to have it replaced. Virgil winked and said that he could sew leather as well as anyone alive. Then Virgil said:

"Really, you could use a new saddle. Lady has outgrown the one you have. Look here, the saddle is rubbing on her barrel too hard because it was made for a smaller horse. The width is all right, but it's too narrow on the sides. You see what I mean?"

Mains was not ready to spend almost all his money on a new saddle for Lady, although he was already aware that the saddle was too small, so he refused. He suspected that Virgil had a saddle that he had somehow acquired and was trying to sell for a profit.

"That's all right. Now, if you don't want a new saddle, here's the other place where you need some leather work." Virgil pointed to the scabbard that held Mains's Winchester. "I'll bet you didn't notice."

Mains looked and saw that the stitching on the scabbard was coming loose. "OK, fix it," he said. "Here's a dollar, for one day of stabling and the leatherwork. All right?"

Virgil said it was all right and mentioned that Hattie's, next door, was the best place to get a room. Virgil grinned and said he already knew, got his saddlebags and his rifle, said goodbye to Lady and walked over to Hattie's. He knocked on the door and immediately a woman's voice told him to come in. He entered and saw a fairly large room with a dining table in front of him.

"Hello and welcome, I'm Hattie Moran. We've already had dinner, but we have some leftovers. Do you plan to stay?"

Jackson Mains looked at Hattie and realized that he was interested in her as a woman. She had blond hair with a few gray streaks, a full figure with no extra weight, and a fine handsome face. She seemed to be in her mid-thirties. "Yes, ma'am, I'd like some dinner. I'm Jackson Mains. I've been eating my own cooking for a few days on the trail, and I'm sure your cooking is better."

Hattie laughed a little, and Mains liked her laugh. She said,

"Don't give me any credit for the food. This is Mr. Rufus McStayley, who does the cooking here." A black man about 50 years old poked his head out of a doorway in the rear and smiled. He said, 'I'm gonna fix you right up, sir," and retreated. Hattie continued, "If you want lodging for the night, dinner is included. It's a dollar a day or part of a day. You can pay extra for breakfast— it's fifty cents— or the saloon across the street has a sort of breakfast, too,"

Although Mains was well supplied with cash, he asked, "How much is breakfast at the saloon?"

Hattie looked him sideways, and said, "I think it depends on how many rats they catch. They call it ham."

Mains laughed. "You can expect me for breakfast here."

At a gesture from Hattie, he sat at the table and Mr. McStayley brought out pork chops, greens, fried potatoes and cornbread with butter. Hattie asked, "Do you mind if I sit and keep you company?" and he said, certainly not, remembering not to speak with food in his mouth.

After a few bites, he said, "Mr. McStayley is a good cook. Please tell him I said so." Hattie said she would, but just then, Rufus McStayley poked his head out again and said, "I heard that, thank you. Miss Hattie, I'm going home. Everything's done except Mr. Mains's dishes and banking the stove."

Hattie said, "Thank you, Rufus. I'll see you tomorrow." Rufus disappeared. Hattie said, "What brings you to Hargis, Mr. Mains?"

Mains decided to be direct. "I'm looking for a man I've tracked here. He's wanted in Wichita."

Hattie said, "I have another boarder, Mr. Clinton. I hope he's not who you're looking for, because it sounds like you mean trouble."

"Tell me about Mr. Clinton, please."

Hattie hesitated. "He arrived here early yesterday, and he doesn't know when he's leaving."

"How did he arrive?"

"He seems to be on foot. I think he came up the south road, past Mr. McStayley's house." She smiled. "I get most of my gossip from Rufus and his wife. Between them, they know just about everything that happens in Hargis."

Mains ate for a while without saying anything, but he looked at Hattie. "I tracked my man from the east, across the hills, and he was on a horse."

Hattie frowned. "No, that doesn't seem to be him. You saw Virgil, right? That's the only stable for horses in town."

"Virgil didn't have any other horses," Mains acknowledged. "I thought about this already."

Hattie smiled. "I could see that you are a smart man. Do you want dessert?"

"No ma'am, thank you. Where is my room?"

"Of course. Let me show you the room."

Hattie led Jackson through a doorway off the front room to a hallway and showed him a room and the location of the privy. She told him to wait a few minutes and she'd bring him some hot water. It only took her a minute. "Mr. McStayley left this water on the stove," she said. "I'll leave you now, so you can clean up. If you don't want to go to bed yet, the Ace of Hearts is yonder. Have a good night."

Mains thanked her and used the water to bathe himself. He hadn't been cleaned up since the last town. Then he opened his grip and removed the tissue paper from a laundered shirt and a collar. He changed his underwear and put the shirt and collar on. His pants were acceptable, and he didn't have another pair, anyway. He rubbed them with some sage that he had found on the trail.

He left his room, went down the hall and out the front door. He stood on the porch for a minute. Piano playing and singing from the Ace of Hearts stirred him a little bit. It had been a while since he had been in a place socially. He crossed the street, nodded to the man outside the Ace of Hearts who had watched him on Hattie's porch, and entered through the batwing doors.

This was a different sort of place, not like Jacks at all. It had a real bar, it had a piano, it had tables that were manufactured tables. Perhaps there was a different kind of whiskey, he thought.

There were 15 or 20 people inside. Some were playing poker or faro at tables for that purpose; others were hanging around the bar; a few were assisting the piano player with their voices. Mains gravitated to the bar and leaned against it and looked around. He had a fair idea of Tom Cudder's looks from a drawing on a wanted poster, and he didn't see him. A bartender asked him what he wanted, and he laid a quarter on the bar and asked for a whiskey. It arrived immediately.

He told the bartender, "I'm new in town," and the man nodded. "I'm Jackson Mains," he said, and the bartender said, "I'm Joe Bishop," and they shook. "Any other new people?" Maims asked, and after a suspicious look, Bishop said, "No, only the other fellow who's rooming at Hattie's. He was here earlier, but he left."

"I'm looking for a particular man. He might have been here yesterday or the day before and left already."

The bartender said, "No, there's been no other visitors in town for a week or more. Excuse me," and he went to get a drink for some other customers.

Mains leaned against the bar and figured this was a washout. The man he was looking for had already left town or had never been here at all.

While he mused, his attention was distracted by a woman who came up to his side. "I'm Corrina," she said. She smiled and came closer, touching him on his arm.. "I wonder if you'd be interested in getting to know me better."

Mains said, "What do you know about the other new man in town?"

"Well, really!" Corrina said. "Aren't you interested in me?"

Mains smiled and displayed a silver dollar. "Tell me what you know about him. I heard from Hattie that his name is Clinton."

Corrina kept her eyes on the coin. "Yes, that's his name. He's been here two nights. He was here earlier, and he doesn't like me. He spent some time with Mary. He's gone now."

"Do you know where he went?"

"Nope. He leaves but he doesn't say where. Mary doesn't know, either. He don't talk much. He's not interesting, like you . . ." Corrina snuggled a little closer. "I can see you've got an angle. That information was free. I can earn that dollar, and more, just try me."

Mains smiled again, a little differently, put the dollar away and gave her a quarter. "Thanks for the information. Don't tell anyone I was asking."

Corrina pouted and said, "Sure," and flounced off.

Mains shook his head, and figured the bartender had lied out of habit. Men didn't tend bar for long if they talked about one customer to another. It struck him that the bartender at Jacks, and Jack himself, had been talkative but told him nothing.

He sighed and got another drink.

Across the street, Hattie was seated at the table with Virgil Stayborne. Virgil said, "I think this Mains feller is a bounty hunter. What's more, look at this." He pulled out a wanted poster and showed it to Hattie. "Doesn't this look like your roomer, Mr. Clinton?"

Hattie squinted at the drawing and allowed that it did. "But it's only a drawing, and it doesn't look very much like him. The eyes . . . yes. But the shape of the face is wrong, and everything else."

"It looks closer than that to me. I found it in a pocket in Mr. Mains's saddle when I was doing repairs. It might not look much like him, but it's a powerful coincidence, don't you think?"

"Oh, Virgil, you've got quite an imagination. I don't think so. I'll ask Mr. Mains when he comes back." After a second, she said, "Or I'll ask Mr. Clinton."

"Don't do that!" said Virgil. "It says here he shot a storekeeper and robbed him. You'd practically be accusing him of murder. What if you're right?"

Hattie laughed. "Virgil, don't take me so seriously. I've told you before I never ask my roomers their business. When Mr. Moran was alive, we'd have bankers and businessmen coming through Hargis and he told me not to be nosy, and I think he was right."

When Mains crossed the street back to Hattie's, Virgil was gone, but Hattie was still at the table, drinking tea and reading a book. "Hello, Mr. Mains," she said, "Will you have some tea?"

"Thank you, Mrs. Moran, that sounds good," Hattie got up and went to the kitchen to get another cup. Mains waited for her to return and sit down before he seated himself. The tea was aromatic and hot. Mains said, "I've made tea sometimes when I'm on the trail, but it's not like this."

"I reckon it's not. You throw in a few leaves from chaparral and some Mormon tea, and maybe some hemp, I'll bet."

"That's right, ma'am. It doesn't taste like this."

"This is real tea from China with some wild chamomile I found last spring. Right now, you might find chamomile on the trail, but it would be bitter. Best to get it before it flowers. It would make your chaparral tea better, I assure you."

"Yes, ma'am."

"Oh. Don't ma'am me, Jackson. Not while we're drinking tea. Call me Hattie."

Jackson smiled. "Yes, Hattie."

Neither of them spoke for a while, but they looked at each other. Hattie broke the silence. "What do you plan to do, Jackson?"

"Well. The man I'm looking for doesn't seem to be here. So I might go back east and see if I can pick up his trail." He hesitated. "I have other jobs I might do, too. But this one would pay the best."

"I like a man who wants to make money," said Hattie forthrightly.

Mains's smile was a little twisted. "Perhaps I also think I'm on the side of justice. Right against wrong."

"Don't be cynical. You do what you do."

"That is very true, Hattie. I like what I do. And . . . I'm not sure that's cynical. In my better moments, I think I'm one of the good guys, and I'm hunting the bad guys. I get a certain satisfaction from that."

"I hope you find him."

Mains said, "I usually do."

Both of them had finished their tea. Hattie said, "It's time for me to go to bed. Breakfast is at dawn. I like you, Mr. Jackson Mains. Maybe your work will bring you back to Hargis again someday, and I'll be here."

"Thank you, Hattie. I like you, too. I'm going to go to bed, too. It's been a few days since I've been in a bed. I hope I can go to sleep."

"The beds here are comfortable, Jackson. Sleep well." Hattie got up, cleared the table and went into the kitchen.

Mains headed for his room, still wondering where his quarry had gone, and how he had gone wrong. He got ready for sleep, but he felt confused. Once in bed, he lay a while, thinking of Hattie and thinking that one day he'd give up bounty hunting, but then knowing that he never would. It was what he did.

In the morning, Hattie got up and started fixing the coffee. While it perked, she thought about Jackson Mains and what he might look like after a night of sleep, when he wasn't so tired.

Jackson Mains woke up at dawn, as always, washed his face in the water on the stand, and headed for the privy.

Mr. McStayley arrived, greeted Hattie and started cutting up potatoes for breakfast. The usual breakfast at Hattie's was two eggs, bacon, potatoes fried in bacon grease and corn bread from the day before. Hattie started the bacon, and then went to set the table. Hattie and the two guests would have breakfast. Rufus had already eaten at his house on the road that led south from Hargis, where he lived with his wife and two sons.

While Hattie set the table, she heard some unusual noises from the guest area. Some voices, a sigh, a thud, some footsteps. Maybe the voices and footsteps weren't so unusual, she thought.

Mr. Clinton entered the dining room, carrying all his gear, and Hattie said, "Good morning,"

Clinton said, "Hattie, I'm leaving. I can't stay for breakfast. I'll pay for it anyway, though. Here." He threw a half-dollar on the table.

"What do you mean, Mr. Clinton? You can stay for breakfast!"

"No, I can't. I've got to move on . . . I've decided. I'm getting my horse from Jack's and leaving town."

"You have a horse, sir?" This was strange. Hattie remembered her other roomer. "Where is Mr. Mains? Have you made his acquaintance?"

"I haven't met the man. I'm leaving." He turned toward the door.

Hattie remembered what she had heard, and said, "Not so fast, Mr. Clinton."

Clinton turned back to Hattie with a snarl, and she pulled a .44 over-and-under from the pocket of her apron and shot him. Then she shot him again. He tried, but he never cleared his gun.

Hattie went back to the guest rooms and found what she hoped she wouldn't find: Jackson Mains lying on the hallway outside the privy with his throat cut.

Eric Weir should have played major league baseball, but he thought it involved too much intellectual complexity. After studying zoology, practicing law, and being a computer network administrator, it was too late to go back and play ball, but he still wants to.

Murder, and a Multitude of Other Sins
J. F. Benedetto

    The Chevy SUV careened out of the night through a blizzard of falling snow, the swinging arc of its headlights tracing a wild swerve along the ramp leading into the rest stop. It careened across the icy asphalt and just missed a concrete-footed light pole looming up out of the snow storm, spun out and bounced wildly over the snow-covered curb into the picnic area, where it slammed into a picnic table and came to a sudden, final halt.

    The V-6 coughed and died, leaving only the muffling solitude of the blizzard and the near-total darkness broken by the silent headlight beams illuminating a million blowing snowflakes.

    The man in the passenger seat, an ex-NYPD cop named Ed Fong, said nothing, but just stared straight ahead in his seat. The man beside him at the wheel, a bespectacled professor of mathematics named Micah Brooks, also said nothing, and just stared straight ahead.

    From the back seat, Brooks' huge slobbering mastiff leaned forward between them to see what they were staring at.

    "Well," Brooks said, "the storm may have closed the highway, but at least we are not stranded on the side of the road miles from anyplace. That's quite adequate, isn't it? Why, I would even venture—"

    Fong just stared at him until Brooks felt the weight of it and stopped talking.

    At the far end of the parking lot, the swirling blizzard alternately revealed and obscured the rest stop building, lit by a narrow stand of lights that barely cut through the blowing snow.

    The mastiff snuffled, and nudged Fong questioningly.

    "Oh, hell no!" Fong snapped. "I'm staying right where I am, warm and dry. Get your owner to take you walkies."

    "I can't," Brooks said. "We collided with something. I need to check for damage."

"Oh, for the love of . . . *fine!*" Suppressing a growl, Fong put on his gloves, zipped up his jacket and pushed open the passenger door, which let the blizzard into the SUV with him. Cursing in his grandparent's Cantonese, he got out and reached for the SUV's back door. "Come on, Sampson!" he said, yanking the heavy door open. "Go do your duty."

The huge mastiff jumped out of the SUV and bounded into the snow. But instead of stopping and doing his business, the mastiff took off at a run toward the building. "Stop, you stupid animal!" Fong yelled after him.

The big mastiff came to a sudden halt, turned to the right, sniffed the snow-filled wind and bounded into the darkness.

"*No!* Get back here!" Fong looked back at the SUV. "Dammit, Micah—!"

But Brooks was busy examining the mangled picnic bench married to the bull bars on the front of his SUV. Fong turned back at the dog. Samson had come to a halt and put his nose down in the snow, then raised his head and gave three distinct barks. Shivering, Fong held his gloved hand up, shielding his face from the driving snow. "Come on--! It's too cold for this!"

The dog put his nose down into the snow for a moment, then raised up and barked three times again.

Three times. Like a signal.

But why? What could a former search-and-rescue dog be trying to tell—

Oh, crap. Fong shielded his eyes with his gloved hands and stared hard through the blowing whiteness at the thing the mastiff kept nudging: a snow-covered mound.

A mound the size of a human body.

The ex-cop crunched through the snow to where the dog patiently waited for him.

The lights of the rest stop were obscured by the blowing snow; Fong took the pocket light off his belt and turned it on.

The blonde woman lay face-down, half-buried in the snow with her arms stretched out above her head. He knelt down and brushed away the snow off of her blue nylon jacket, revealing three holes punched through it.

She didn't move. He pulled off a glove and felt her neck for a pulse.

"Dead?" Brooks asked, crunching up through the falling snow.

Fong didn't even look at the man. *One thing about Micah Brooks, nothing ever seemed to shake him.* Fong shoved his hand down under the body, inside the woman's blouse, and found no heartbeat, only cool flesh on its way to getting ice-cold. "Yeah. Not too long ago. Body's not fully cold yet."

He flexed the chill out of his exposed fingers and investigated the corpse. "Three small bloody holes in the back, none in the front. No through-and-through. Small caliber gunshot wounds would be my guess." He checked over the body. "Folding knife, skeleton grip, worn clipped to the back of the belt. Looks like she never went for it." He found a black leather wallet and looked inside, fighting to keep the wind from stealing his evidence. "Massachusetts Liquor ID for one Nikki Byrne, age 27. From Boston. Mattapan address. Library and store membership cards, all in the same name. No driver's license, though. Probably didn't drive herself here, then. Huh . . . cash, but no credit cards." He counted the money. "$1700 dollars, all in worn hundreds. So it wasn't a robbery. Doesn't appear to be rape, either."

He glanced around, his brown eyes measuring the windy snowscape. "She was dragged here from the parking lot," he said, pointing. "See the way her arms are together above her head? I'm betting that the killer shot her in the back, then dragged her by her hands and dumped her way over here in the picnic area where the body wouldn't be seen from the parking lot." The drag-marks led back toward four cars, all parked together like sleeping drunks huddled against the wind. He shown the flashlight beam along the tracks, but they petered out in a matter of yards; too much snow, coming down too hard. "Could have come from any one of those vehicles. As to the killer . . ."

A single line of footprints already filled in with drifting snow led off toward the rest stop building.

Former New York City patrolman Ed Fong stood up, no longer shivering in the intense cold. He reached inside his jacket and pulled out his phone. There was no signal. No surprise, given the raging storm. "We're on our own."

"I agree," Brooks said.

Fong stared at the distant building. Now what? He was a disgraced ex-cop with no authority, saddled with a slobbering mastiff and a math professor. Dammit, what the hell was he thinking?

The wind doubled, whipping snow onto the murdered woman's corpse at his feet.

Yeah. That.

Fong took a deep cold breath, drew his Boberg XR45-S concealed-carry pistol, checked the little six-shot semiautomatic to make sure it was loaded, and looked at Brooks.

The professor did not need any words. "Samson," he commanded. "Come."

The mastiff obediently left the corpse and joined the two men as they trudged through the foot-deep snow toward the building, a drift-buried haven of stone, brick and concrete in a sea of white. As they got close, one of the glass entry doors opened and someone stepped out, causing both Fong and Brooks to halt.

The stranger— gender indeterminate because of the bulky black hoodie— lit up a cigarette, took a long drag, and then spotted Fong and Brooks. "Hey!" the man yelled. He turned back and pulled open the door he had just come through. "Break out the band!" he yelled into the building. "We've got guests!"

Brooks spoke low, straight into Fong's ear. "We do not know how many people are inside. Should you be walking in there with gun in hand?"

Fong hesitated. Being a policeman meant openly displaying your weapon ... but he wasn't a cop any more. *Remember that!* He reluctantly hid his gun in the pocket of his coat and then walked toward the man.

He had a squinting stare and a dark, medium-stubble beard. He held the door open for them as they marched up, his voice hopeful. "Where'd you dudes come from? I thought they closed the highway."

"They must have done so after we got on the road," Brooks said.

"Close the damn door!" a woman inside yelled. "What the hell's wrong with you?"

The man took a long drag and then tossed the cigarette into the snow, laughing. "You might not wanna come in here."

"Yeah," Fong admitted. He entered the rest stop, and the warm air engulfed him, actually stinging his ice-chilled face. The tile-floored space had rest rooms on opposite sides, with a line of vending machines on one wall and a road map of upstate New York on the other. Scattered around the perimeter of the room in front of him were three more people: a white woman, a black woman, a white man.

And one of them was a killer.

A feeling of nakedness swept over Fong, just like the one that had choked him the first time he walked the streets of Manhattan after he had been kicked off the force. He'd been a good cop, who made only one mistake: he did what he saw the white cops doing. When he got offered a petty bribe to let some call girls ply their trade, he took the cash in pocket and went about his business of hunting down real crooks: rapists, burglars, drug dealers. Hell, a hundred other cops in Manhattan were doing the exact same thing.

But those cops were not Chinese-American like Fong; minority cops, it turned out in the end, had to live up to a much higher standard. "Soliciting or accepting bribes in exchange for not reporting a prostitution ring," as Internal Affairs called it, might actually be excusable behavior from a white patrolman, but not a Chinese-American one. No. The other cops who got found out by IA lied and got away with it, or else had their involvement covered up by their sergeants, or were privately disciplined by their precinct captain and put back on the beat.

Not Ed Fong. IA made a public spectacle of him and got him fired on corruption charges. Someone who could be bought off for the right amount. Stuck him for the rest of his life with the label '*dirty cop.*' Now, here, standing in a room breathing the same air as a killer, he felt that same overwhelming nakedness. He had no uniform to protect him, no shield of his authority from the City, none of the magic of the Law that a policeman draws his power from, that makes criminals fear him.

He had nothing at all.

Nothing . . . but himself.

He stomped his feet free of the clinging snow and sized up his four suspects.

The closest of them was the African-American woman: mid-twenties with light, flawless skin, perfect makeup, and chocolate brown eyes set wide apart, but those eyes blazed angrily . . . at the door being held open or just the world in general, Fong couldn't tell. Her dyed hair, a rich burgundy, matched her designer jacket, and she wore it in an undercut with the sides buzzed short and the top full and pulled forward to fall over her left eye: a modern-day Veronica Lake in a tan leather skirt with matching suede over-the-knee boots. A lipstick lesbian. A Talented-Tenth with money and class, who liked the good life. The sort of woman he'd happily chat up at a party, although she likely attended social functions far more exclusive than the ones Fong went to. She radiated almost violent impatience, like an animal in a cage.

On the other side of the room, squatting on the floor beneath the huge wall map, sat a Caucasian female in her late twenties taking a hit off of a vape pen. As skinny as a heroin addict, she wore a shapeless blue tunic-dress, knee-worn gray pants and salt-stained brown loafers that had seen better days, and might have called any place home. She lowered the vape pen and blew out a stream of white smoke as her hollow blue eyes fixed on Fong. Her long, stringy brown hair ranged in shade from medium to dark, as though she had streaked dye through it one strand at a time but never quite made up her mind as to what exact tint she desired. The kind of woman who grabbed whatever she wanted, but only when no one was looking.

The third suspect, a Caucasian male in his mid-forties wearing an expensive pale-gray suit and pale azure tie, stood beside a vending machine, a smile on his face. His short black hair was going gray, and he had the same kind of medium-stubble beard as the smoker, but on him it looked elegant, rather than unkempt. The tailored suit said that he had money, but unlike the black woman who lived comfortably in her clothes, his perfectly-draped suit and tie seemed too perfect, like an actor's carefully chosen costume. He had a warm smile that touched his green eyes and the crow's feet flanking them, yet it only put Fong in mind of a con man.

And then there was the smoker who had let them into the building and seemed so friendly. Early thirties, clean tight haircut, neat dark brown pants, spotless expensive sneakers and a brand new hoodie; he could have been a tourist, heading north for the skiing. He had very short black hair and a scraggly, medium-stubble black beard, and his face seemed to have a permanent squint that hid not only the color of his eyes but also their intent. Despite his affable attitude, something in his demeanor suggested that he was only playing at being friendly.

So . . . four people; one murderer.

No, he corrected himself. *For all you know, all four of them could have been in on the killing.* He nodded to them. "Ed Fong," he said by way of introduction.

The younger white guy held out his hand. "Brett Hardee." Fong shook it, reluctantly.

"Micah Brooks," the mathematician beside him said, wiping off his fogged-up glasses.

"Mike," Hardee acknowledged with a half-wave. Micah winced almost imperceptibly but said nothing.

Samson, for his part, did not wait to be introduced. He walked over to the squatting white girl with the vape pen.

"Aw, sweet doggy," she cooed. She took a hit from the pen and blew the smoky vapor right into Samson's face.

Samson snorted and shook his head, while Brooks twitched and then snapped his fingers. Samson, snuffling, trotted back over to him and sat, trying to shake his nostrils clear.

"Do not do that again," Brooks said to her in a way that foretold unpleasantness to be forthcoming.

The girl pouted. "Maybe she likes it."

"Samson is a 'he'."

"He, she," the girl said with a careless shrug. "You shouldn't push your cisgender ideas on animals. Besides, how do you know the dog doesn't like it? People do."

"I do not." Micah's gaze hardened. "And neither does he."

She looked away. "Whatever."

Hardee laughed. "Caitlin Taylor, everybody!" he declared like a game show host. He gave her a sarcastic dead-slow clap; she studiously gave him the cold shoulder . . . and went back to staring at Fong.

He ignored her and focused on the classy black woman. "Excuse me, Miss . . . ?"

"Lewis," she said with a testiness that would scrape ice off asphalt. "Raven Lewis."

"Miss Lewis. Do you know if there is a payphone in the building?"

"There's one outside," the older white man in the expensive suit interjected. "But it isn't working. I tried already. There's probably one over in the welcome center, but that's locked up." He offered a half-wave in acknowledgment. "Jack Patel . . . ?" he said by way of introduction, as if the name was supposed to impress them. The warm smile seemed pinned in place. "I don't suppose you bring any good news about the highway?"

Fong shook his head. "No. We barely made it in. The road's completely buried. We didn't even see any other vehicles for the last 10 miles."

"Ah, well." He turned to the vending machine. "At least we shan't starve." He pulled out a money clip fat with cash. "I don't suppose either of you gentlemen would have any change on you...? All I have are hundreds."

Fong just watched, saying nothing. The dead woman's wallet had contained nothing but hundreds. Just coincidence?

Patel radiated a quiet charm, and his utter neatness was the antithesis of Taylor's scruffiness; she still squatted on the far side of the room, beneath the road map of New York. "I'm so *bored*," she whined. She put the vape pen down and picked up her smartphone, found no signal, and sighed. "There's nothing to do here!"

"You could try reading," Lewis told her.

Taylor waved her phone at the black woman. "I can't! I don't have any reception!"

"Lord! Don't you keep any books on that damn thing?"

"Why should I?"

The black woman's face congealed. "For moments like this?"

The rebuke bounced off, rather than sink in. "I can't

download anything right now, so I can't read anything right now, *okay?*"

Lewis shook her head and pushed her well-manicured hands up in curt dismissal.

"Smoke?" Hardee asked of the group, lifting two fingers as if holding a lit cigarette.

Brooks, Fong and Patel all shook their heads; Lewis just waved her hands negatively. Taylor sneered at him. "That's a stupid habit."

"Says the girl who smokes make-believe cigarettes," he threw back at her. He opened the door, letting in a gust of snow-laden wind for a moment, and went outside.

Fong strolled in the direction of the door, his squishing feet drawing unwanted attention to his movements. Was Hardee just going out for a smoke, or was he trying to run for it? If Hardee was the killer, maybe he thought that if Brooks and Fong had gotten *into* the rest stop, he could get *out* of it. Fong stepped over to the water fountain, using the move to take a glance out the window.

Hardee stood close to the window with his back to the wind, lighting up.

No, he wasn't running away.

None of them were.

But . . . would the killer try, if Fong told the four what he'd found out there in the snow? He shifted his weight, and regretted it as his soaking-wet shoes squished cold water around his feet. Of course, Brooks had no such problem: his immaculate hiking boots barely even looked damp. Waterproofed, no doubt. Because Micah Brooks planned things carefully. He thought through such things ahead of time. He always did, damn him.

Fong rubbed his chin. Had Nikki Byrne's killer planned her murder ahead of time as well? It just didn't feel like it. The body had been left in a picnic area where it would soon be discovered once the snow let up. No. It was a crime of opportunity. The killer offed her in the parking lot, hid the body the best he could on the spur of the moment, then came in here to keep from freezing, and now hid in plain sight.

At least one of these people was guilty of murder. Guilty

people made mistakes. He rubbed his forehead. *Think, dammit!*

Lewis plopped down on the bench farthest from Taylor, her eyes dark. "I'm supposed to be at Royal Mountain right now," the black woman complained to no one in particular and everyone in earshot. "And instead of the resort, I'm stuck *here*," she added, giving a momentary glare at the white girl squatting down on the floor opposite her. "And look at my boots! $1600 Gianvito Rossi's from Neiman Marcus! Just look at them!" she cried, ticking her long fingernails at the white crust staining the suede. "They're ruined!"

Patel's smile never wavered. "It's just salt from the sidewalk."

"These are Italian suede!" the black woman protested. "You ever try to get salt out of Italian suede?"

"Sure," Patel said. He lifted his right foot and pointed at the white salt-slush encrusted on the side of his expensive brown leather shoe. "It's easy. You mix two parts distilled water to one part white vinegar—"

Fong smacked himself in the forehead. He turned around and bolted back to the front door. Hardee was no longer just outside it, smoking a cigarette.

He was gone.

Fong squinted as the storm whipped the snow into his face. Was Hardee hiding? Or was he trying to run for it?

A momentary flash of yellow parking lights of a car being unlocked out in the parking lot gave him the answer: running. He drew his Boberg XR45-S and ran in the direction he'd seen the flash of yellow lights come from. As the wind shifted he saw the cars, with Hardee climbing into the open door of the nearest one.

Fong ran toward him. "Hold it right there! Police Officer!" he yelled, acting without thinking.

Hardee reacted the same way, acting automatically, popping off three shots. One of the bullets caught Fong's left leg, dumping him into the snow with a cry of searing pain.

As he lay there writhing, Hardee stomped over and glared down at him. "A damn cop . . . ?"

Fong gritted his teeth, both hands on his wounded leg. He'd lost his sidearm when he went down.

Hardee waved his revolver at Fong, livid. "Jesus Christ! What do you cops care about two lousy drug dealers getting shot? It wasn't even real meth I sold 'em! Hell, I killed two meth dealers, dammit! I was doing your job for you! And you guys come after me? Goddamn cops!" He stepped over him and pointed his revolver down at Fong's groin. "You know what, asshole? I'm really gonna enjoy this."

"Yeah?" Fong gasped out, panting. "The way you enjoyed it when you pumped three slugs into Nikki Byrne's back?"

Hardee's mouth fell open, and then he snarled and pulled the trigger.

The hammer came down with a dull clack.

Fong smiled grimly and Hardee blinked, his eyes widening in fear, and he jerked the clicking trigger over and over as he thrust the revolver at Fong, but it refused to fire.

Fong's right foot slammed up into Hardee's groin hard enough to heave the killer up off his feet. He pitched over squealing onto his side into the snow.

Fong grimaced. Gasping for breath, he rolled over. There— a hole in the snow. He dug his gun out of the snowbank and got unsteadily to his feet, his left thigh on fire. But his leg held his weight; the bullet hadn't hit anything cripplingly vital. "You know what your problem is?" Fong gasped out, facing down the whimpering killer. "You shoot in threes. You put three shots at me when I came at you . . . and you put three shots into Byrne's back when you killed her."

He sucked a breath of ice-cold air laced with snowflakes. "And you're carrying a snubnose revolver. It only holds six rounds. I was betting that after you killed Byrne and had to rush to hide the body that you wouldn't have taken the time to reload. So after you fired off another three rounds, you had to be out." Fong waved his little Boberg XR45-S at the man. "I've only got six bullets, too. But I count the number of shots I fire, *asshole*." He grabbed Hardee by the back of his hoodie and hauled him up to a sitting position. "A couple of meth dealers, huh? So, you and your girlfriend ripped them off? Told them you were a supplier, and when they gave you the money, all you gave them was a load of rock candy?"

"Yeah," Hardee choked out. "Hadda . . . kill 'em."

"I bet. So why'd you pull the trigger on your girlfriend?"

"Bitch . . . kept riding me . . . 'cause I shot 'em. How the hell was I supposed to know . . . they'd wanna test the stuff right there? And . . . when I said we had to run for it, she went nuts. Then all this snow . . . I ended up lost and had to stop here. She really lit into me. Hell, that bitch was just asking to get killed!" Fong pointed the Boberg at Hardee's face, and the killer panicked. "Look!" he cried. "I've got the money in the back seat. I'll give you a thousand of it! Fi-five thousand! Ten thousand!"

What . . . he was offering him a bribe?

Yeah. A goddamned bribe!

Anger and self-hatred exploded in Fong and he belted Hardee across the face with his gun-butt, then caught him with a backhand swing, the killer's face now that of every self-serving hypocrite who had labeled him a "dirty cop."

Something appeared at the edge of Fong's vision but he did not see the mastiff, nor did he register the approach of the dog's owner, who just stood there, watching him punching Hardee bloody. It took all his will to finally stop, and in the emptiness that followed the pain returned, lancing through his left leg.

Brooks spoke up. "Is he dead?"

Fong's chest heaved. "No," he finally got out. Brooks made a non-committal noise, pulled a set of zip ties out of his jacket, and held them out to Fong.

He stared at them for a second, ignored the impulse to ask Micah Brooks why he carried something like that, and used them to secure Hardee's hands behind his back. He struggled to his feet, ignoring Brook's offered hand, and hauled the killer upright. "This is a Citizen's Arrest," Fong declared. "Under Article 140, Section 30, 'Arrest without a warrant, by any person, when and where authorized,'" he recited, his voice rooted to the bedrock of the Law. "'An ordinary citizen may arrest an individual that they suspect of committing a felony, even if said felony did not occur in the presence of the individual making the arrest.'" The Law— and pride—radiated from Fong's controlled glare. "Brett Hardee, you're under arrest for the murder of Nikki Byrne."

As he pushed Hardee along back toward the building, Brooks and Samson fell in beside Fong.

"How did you know it was him?" Brooks asked.

Fong, breathing heavily as he limped, almost smiled. "Raven, she was— going on about how the salt ruined those expensive boots of hers. She got salt on them when she walked along the sidewalk from the parking lot to the building. Patel and Taylor . . . their shoes had salt on them too. Ours didn't, because we never used the sidewalk: we walked over from the body to the building straight through the snow— just like the killer did." He managed a satisfied wheeze. "When I realized that Hardee was the only one of the four whose shoes weren't stained with salt, I knew who our killer was, and I went after him."

As a man who no longer needed a badge marched a murderer back to the building to wait for the highway to be reopened, the wind died off, leaving behind it a rest stop covered by a thick white blanket of snow that buried all manner of sins.

J.F. Benedetto is a former computer engineer who writes stories in three different genres: Mystery, Science Fiction, and Adventure. More of his stories can be found at his Amazon Author's page:
https://www.amazon.com/kindle-dbs/entity/author/B087GVNWVH

The Horror Tab

Run for Your Life
Brandi Fruik

"I can't believe we're really going through with this," Mark thought as he took his position in front of the camera. They'd been working on one of the most secretive reality competition shows of all time, and it was about to premiere live. Mark had been chosen to be the host due to his good looks and easy-going charm, but he wasn't sure any of that would matter once the viewers realized what they were in for.

Mark himself had just been told the day before, after signing many lengthy contracts and nondisclosure agreements. The show was the brainchild of a secret coalition known only as "The Agents." Everyone on the set was on a need-to-know basis, and it was determined that they didn't need to know very much. As such, the tension on set was palpable.

Mark's only instructions were to just read the teleprompter in front of him and react genuinely. Despite never revealing what the show would be about, The Agents had spent an exorbitant amount on marketing. Billboards were up across the country with the show's name, "Run for Your Life." They had run commercials, viral video ads and print ads. And not a single advertisement gave away too much. The premise was kept under wraps. America hadn't seen anything like this recently, in this day and age of 24/7 knowledge, and their curiosity was piqued.

Production had taken over two square miles in urban Chicago, closing off many streets and shooing away the public to help keep everything secret. But it was all about to be revealed on live television and an online stream (live across both coasts to try and get the most live viewership as possible).

The camera man counted down "five, four" and then hand signals for three, two and one. The words came up on the prompter and Mark began somberly.

"Good evening ladies and gentlemen. I'm your host Mark. Thank you for joining us for a show we know will revolutionize reality television. I'm sure you're all tuned in to find out what this show is about, and if modern television viewing habits are any indication, we have about seven minutes to catch your attention before you turn to another channel, fire up Netflix or turn to your phone. But I promise you, we won't need all seven of those minutes for you to be hooked to the action. Let me bring out our first two contestants, Sam and Tom."

The teleprompter told Mark to gesture to the left, and two men stepped out of the shadows. They were geared up in the best athletic wear: Nike shoes, compression pants and sweat-wicking tank tops. But they weren't exactly the athletes the audience may have been expecting. In fact, both men did not look particularly fit or even well. The contestants looked around nervously before their gaze landed down at their sneakers. They were under strict orders not to speak, so Mark continued for them.

"Sam is a 39-year-old investment banker from Naperville. He has a wife of fifteen years and three beautiful children. Tom is 37, divorced and lives with his girlfriend in Champaign. He and his ex-wife have joint custody of their daughter. Sam and Tom have at least one thing in common; they are both in need of a life-saving kidney transplant. According to both men, they are both far down on the transplant list and are unlikely to receive a donor kidney before it is too late. Out of respect for patient privacy, we won't be revealing any additional medical information, relevant or not. Sam and Tom are both here today to do whatever it takes to stay alive." Mark paused for some tentative audience applause.

At this time, Sam took his gaze off his sneakers and aimed it at the audience. There were so many bright stage lights on him that he had to squint against the glare. And all he could see of the audience were their silhouettes, stacked end to end and up rows of metal bleachers. His wife and children weren't in the audience at his request, despite production wanting them there for his storyline. And he wondered how the audience in front of him would react when they found out what they were here to witness. He guessed that they would be happy they only appeared as dark silhouettes at that point.

Sam thought back to how he came to be standing here. Things had gone perfectly growing up: popular in high school, captain of the football team, made it to the University of Michigan on a scholarship, met his future bride in college, injured himself out of being a professional football player, but he still had a finance degree to fall back on. From there, he and his wife bought a beautiful house and had beautiful children.

Sam worked and Diane stayed home with the kids. Sam's job was intense and challenging, and he had to work harder and harder to keep up with the new recruiting classes that entered his firm. Eventually, his old back injury began to flare up, and he was prescribed pain medication by his doctor. Sam quickly became addicted and was on a downward spiral which would eventually wreak havoc to most of his internal organs, but his kidneys took the brunt of it.

Sam was able to keep his addiction secret from everyone except his wife and his doctors. With his medical history, and the fact that he still couldn't seem to kick the pills, he had no chance of receiving a donor kidney through traditional means. Diane had tried sending him off to rehab, but the truth was that they still needed Sam working so they could pay the bills, so he always ended up slipping again.

Sam felt terrible to be in the position that he was in, but even though the pills were killing him, he was unable to stop taking them. He had signed up for this experience hoping it would be as life changing as the producers claimed. At this point, Sam looked over at Tom and their gaze met briefly.

Tom too was wondering how his life had taken this abrupt turn. Tom was born with polycystic kidney disease, but due to poor medical care in his youth, it wasn't diagnosed until it was in an extremely late stage. The stress of his divorce had been too much, and he hadn't been able to keep up with his dialysis treatments. Because he had already proven he was unlikely to follow proper medical care, his doctor was reluctant to help advocate to get him moved up on the transplant priority list.

Tom had finally begun to move on with his life, mostly due to Jill entering it and giving him hope for a better future. But at this point, things looked pretty bleak as far as his health was concerned, and he wasn't sure how much time they'd have left together if he didn't take drastic measures. And that's how he found himself here on a makeshift stage in the Chicago summer, about to embark on an obstacle course of pure terror.

Mark's words interrupted Tom's thoughts: "Both these men are here to compete against each other for a donor kidney. Whichever one of them makes it through our mile-long obstacle course through the streets of Chicago first will receive their life-saving kidney donation from a willing donor, John. Let's bring John out now."

The audience gasped loudly as a tall, lanky man in an orange jumpsuit and shackles was escorted onto the stage by two armed prison guards. Had John been wheeled in like a masked Hannibal Lector, there wouldn't have been any less surprise on the faces of the audience members. But Sam and Tom knew what was coming, having agreed. However, they both couldn't help but gulp perceptibly as the convicted serial killer was brought out.

Sam snuck another look at the audience, although he could still see nothing on their silhouetted faces, but he did catch a glimpse of some of the horrified faces of the production staff off to his left. After that, he resigned himself to looking back at his shoes until it was time to go.

"This is John," Mark continued, keeping a steady tone, "John is joining us from Thomson Correctional Center, a maximum security prison, where he is serving three consecutive life sentences for being convicted of murdering three women." The audience again gasped and began to look around nervously to see how their reactions compared to their neighbors, but Mark pressed on. "The three women were beaten, strangled and stabbed in 2007 and 2008. John was arrested in 2008 and convicted in 2010. If it weren't for this event tonight, he would be spending all his remaining time at Thomson."

At this point John tensed up and shot an angry gaze toward

Mark. They were at least fifty feet apart, with John surrounded by guards with guns, but Mark would be lying if he said the gaze didn't chill him to his core. John didn't appreciate that Mark made it sound like he was doing him a favor. John had agreed to be here, of course, but the show wouldn't exist without him. As far as he was concerned, he was the star. It meant nothing to him that he was more like the bearded lady at the circus, something they were there to gawk at; all he cared about was the attention.

John also couldn't make out the audience over the bright lights, but he was sure there were some women out there he would love to meet. In fact, he was in this position because of what he considered his love for women. After his drugged-out whore mother left him, he'd spent his teenage and young adult years chasing after women to replace what he had lost with her, but none of the women were ever right, so he got a little carried away sometimes. This is how three women had ended up dead by his hand.

But John wasn't the kind to wallow in the past. He was here for a very important reason today, and he was excited. Sure, he'd agreed to give a kidney to whichever of these pathetic excuses for men were able to finish the race first. But his reason for being there was much more tantalizing. Because as the men raced each other through the streets, John would be chasing them. John would get a four-minute handicap, and then he would be set loose to catch up with the sick men. What he did to them when he caught up with them was at John's discretion. He had been promised immunity for whatever happened between him and the men on that course. This would be so much better than any of the prison fights he'd been involved in since he'd lost his freedom.

While John was thinking of this, nearly salivating, Mark was explaining this twist to the audience. They had grown increasingly anxious and a few had walked off the bleachers. But the camera focused on those who seemed most intrigued, and there were plenty leaning forward in anticipation. After Mark finished his spiel, it was finally time to cut to break. He had sufficiently captured the audience's attention in less than seven minutes.

Mark walked off stage during the break, distancing himself even more from John. But he also needed to distance himself from

Sam and Tom. He felt ashamed for what could possibly happen to them, and his role in it. The Agents had convinced Mark that this show would help revolutionize the health care industry and even the prison system, shining a light on just how broken the two American systems had become. They knew Mark's daughter was dealing with some medical issues of her own, and Mark needed the money to help pay for her treatments. His last hosting gig had ended abruptly, and he hadn't been prepared with good insurance at the time.

Now he found himself in need of a significant influx of cash and perhaps the means to change the system; and this is precisely why The Agents chose him for this role. But now that he was here, going through with it, he felt sick with himself. Was this what little Maggie would want? She wasn't watching, of course, but how many wrongs were too many wrongs to make a right?

As Mark stood off to the side of the stage pondering all this, his make-up was touched up and he was given a bottle of water. He overheard production and the crew talking in his earpiece. "#RunforYourLife is trending first nationally," someone said proudly. It was easier for the crew to focus on things from a distance: make sure the course was set up, have cameras everywhere, get the contestants prepared, make sure the show was reaching the broadest audience possible, etc. Those were all such simple tangible things.

But the crew were also nameless, faceless blurs behind stage and behind camera lenses, whereas Mark would be known for being the face of what was about to happen for the rest of his life. This is what his daughter would see when she Googled his name, if she lived long enough to be able to do that. Mark sighed internally and put on his sparkling charm before getting back on stage and cutting to live.

Before cutting back to Mark, the show had aired the background pieces on Sam, Tom and John, making sure to sugarcoat Sam and Tom's situation and villainize John as appropriate. The audience never needed to know the full truth if they understood who they should be rooting for. They were supposed to be rooting for the men who had been harmed by the current health care industry and rooting against the man who was imprisoned but willing to donate an organ to save a life. The message was clear, and received as such, according to the focus groups The Agents had spent considerable time working with before production.

Once the audience was almost as invested as the three men who would be participating, they were ready to begin. "Welcome back. We don't want to prolong the suffering of these two men further, so we will be starting shortly," Mark opened with. At this time, Sam and Tom were stretching awkwardly and looking around nervously. Sam took a few sips of water to try and quench his dry throat, but mostly he wished he had packed more of his "special medicine." Tom was glad that his daughter was out of the country with his ex-wife, but he really hoped he'd be able to see her again. He bent his knees and retied his shoes for the fourth time. John was still on the other side of the stage, but the guards surrounding him were readying to remove his shackles. At this point, they were prepared for anything.

Mark started again "Now, just a reminder of the rules. Sam and Tom will begin at the same time, and they will race through the mile-long street obstacle course. We have cameras lining the course, along with several camera crewmembers who will be following behind and also strategically placed throughout the course, so we won't miss any of the action. There are three obstacles: a two-story wall with a rope to scale, a 50-yard water tank to swim through and 20 feet of monkey bars. Failing any obstacle requires contestants to stand in place for two minutes."

Mark paused and looked at the two men who nodded to confirm they were clear. "The men will have four minutes to get as far as they can before John is released from the starting point to complete the same obstacles. If John catches up to either man, their fate is in his hands. Whichever man finishes first will be the recipient of a kidney from John. Are we clear?" Mark finished. Sam and Tom gave verbal agreement, as necessitated by their contract. John smirked and looked like he was just itching to be set free . . . no matter how brief the moment would be. "Okay then. We'll begin . . . after this break."

Mark again hopped off stage as soon as the red live light was extinguished. John was still making him feel uncomfortable, and he was awfully close to being sick to his stomach. He thought of Maggie again, but that just made him even more guilty. While his make-up was touched up yet again, he focused on the never-ending voices from his earpiece. Apparently their Twitter mentions were skyrocketing by the second. "Oh goodie," he mumbled to himself.

It was inevitable that everyone he knew would see this unless they were smart enough not to watch. But how many people could resist looking at the carnage on the road that caused a traffic jam? Not many. And even a good 95% of the live audience remained, even though some of them looked frozen in shock.

The 10:00 PM time slot meant next-to nothing in this age of DVRs, On Demand, YouTube, social media and live streaming. The Agents had an "in" with the FCC, so they wouldn't be cut off from live air, unless someone swore, because that was still not okay. This was going to happen, and the vast majority of America, and probably the rest of the world, was going to see.

Things had become a little more tense on set now that everyone on the crew was aware of what was about to happen, but they were professionals receiving a large paycheck for their part in it, so they soldiered on. The cameraman in front of him counted down, and they were back. Sam and Tom lined up at the starting line, and John was still accompanied by the guards about fifteen feet behind them. Mark was safely on stage for the remainder of his part.

"It appears that all of our contestants are ready, and the course is set, so let's do this!" He actually had to yell the "let's do this" with excitement and enthusiasm, as specified in his contract. It was hard for him to muster up the right tone. "On your mark, get set, run for your life!" Another phrase he was contractually obligated to enjoy saying.

A gun fired to signal the start, or was it just a sound effect, he wasn't sure. And Sam and Tom began to move. Tom got the early lead, perhaps because of his two-year age advantage, but it was quickly apparent that neither man had likely ran a mile since Clinton was in office. The first obstacle was at the ¼ mile mark, giving their legs a break but requiring a large amount of arm strength.

Mark watched on the monitors. He was not required to do the play-by-play as The Agents had brought in a separate disembodied mystery voice to cover that part. His next task would be to interview the winner, hopefully, if it came to that. He glanced over at John, who was frenetically pacing at this point, two minutes in to his four-minute penalty. The camera captured this on split screen as well, while watching Sam and Tom attempt to scale the first obstacle. Both men were already winded from the two-minute sprint and were having a hard time convincing their bodies to pull them up a wall. They were even at this point, but Sam seemed panicked. It took about a minute for them to both get over the wall and then they were back to running. In a little under a minute, John would be joining them.

    John had been in prison for several years, but they didn't tend to do a lot of cardio in the rec yard. Most of his physical exertion came from lifting weights and fighting with fellow inmates. However, it was clear to him that he had a chance to catch up to both these men, since they both probably started with a pace they could not maintain in their condition. There was another quarter mile until the second obstacle, and it was likely John would be released before the men reached it.

    The production room was intense as the shots switched back and forth between static cameras on the course and the live camera operators, switching between Sam and Tom and John. The disembodied voice excitedly but seriously kept up with the play-by-play. Now the guards had moved John up to the start line, and the camera woman who would be following him got in position, at a comfortable distance.

    A separate timer counted down John's remaining penalty time as the guards released his shackles and stepped away quickly. A second gun shot, or sound effect, was heard, and John was on his way. The sound startled both Sam and Tom, and it was clear they were trying to pick up the pace, despite their exhaustion.

    Right out the gate, John was much faster than Sam or Tom had been. He took off, not in a full sprint but definitely close to top speed. The way John saw it, he had relatively nothing to lose from this. He was here for the notoriety and maybe a little extracurricular fun before heading back to his cell. Regardless of how this adventure would end for him, he would have quite the story to share with all the guys in the pen.

    The production room now stuck to their split screen view.

John was monitored by the camerawoman following him with a steady cam; she had deliberately been selected for this position as the fastest female camera operator on the crew. Sam had a dedicated cameraman and Tom another camerawoman. There were also separate camera crewmembers at each obstacle to allow the mobile camera operators to take a brief break while their subject worked the obstacle. Another camerawoman was stationed at the wall obstacle. John reached it at a little under two minutes and, with a running head start, tried to mostly jump up the wall without using the rope.

But his confidence was higher than it should have been, and he failed on the first try, awkwardly bouncing off the wall and getting tangled up in the rope as he fell back to the ground. John could feel the eyes of the faceless audience staring at him and judging his failure, and he snapped in an instant. His designated camerawoman was off to the side, a little distracted while trying to catch her breath. He swore she looked at him with a face of contempt, the one way his mother used to look at him when all he wanted was a basic childhood necessity, or one of the many women he'd tried to date but failed. Suddenly, he was on her.

He grabbed her by the shoulders and threw her hard up against the concrete wall, headfirst. He then quickly wrapped the rope around her throat and used his large arm muscles to pull it tight. She had been knocked unconscious by the blow against the wall and wasn't able to fight back as her body was being deprived of oxygen. The static camerawoman who was also at the scene was frozen in fear. This was an unexpected complication.

The disembodied voice kept reporting the play-by-play and the production crew cut away from the split screen to focus solely on John and the poor camerawoman who had been filming him. "We've got to stop this," Mark frantically whispered into his com, but production stayed focus on the task at hand. The audience gasped, but their eyes were riveted. Some stood up and called out, but no one in production stopped John.

Due to security, the course had been set up with no ins or outs other than the starting line and finish line. Sam and Tom had just completed the water obstacle and were moving forward, Sam taking on a bit of a lead as he seemed to have more swimming experience. Both of them, along with their dedicated camera operators were oblivious to what was happening elsewhere on the course.

After it was clear that the life had drained completely out of John's first victim, he focused his attention on the remaining camerawoman stationed at the obstacle. She was still frozen in fear and likely waiting for a rescue that never came. John's rage focused solely on her now that he realized not only had she also been witness to his failure, but she was also the spitting image of his first kill from 2007, Angie.

Seeing her flooded him with anger and also intense satisfaction as he relived that moment. He'd never had two potential victims served up to him like this, and he would take advantage of it. In that moment, she knew her was coming for her, and her fight or flight instinct finally kicked in. She threw the heavy camera at John and took off further down the course. It would have been better to turn around and head back toward the starting line, but she wasn't thinking clearly. John grinned and seemed to look forward to this chase even more.

She did not make it far before she let out a blood-curdling scream as he tackled her to the ground and repeatedly bashed her head against the asphalt until blood spurted everywhere and her eyes rolled back into her head. Even though both camerawomen's cameras had been incapacitated in their attacks, there were still many unmanned cameras on the course catching everything.

The scream had been registered by Sam and Tom and they hesitated in their jogging for a moment to look around nervously at each other and their camera crew. Production radioed to their camera crew to keep going, so they nodded to Sam and Tom who picked up the pace again.

Mark was stunned, his jaw dropped, and he stared at the closest monitor, feeling helpless. The remaining audience seemed secure in their positions but sat down with apprehension as to how this would end. John was still standing over the body, relishing in his kill as Sam and Tom reached the third obstacle. They moved across the monkey bars, oblivious to what had taken place elsewhere on the course and solely focused on which would make it to the end first and receive their life-saving gift.

As Tom regained the lead, Sam found himself looking back a few times to see if he could see John catching up to him, but all he saw was his cameraman following behind him. The production crew had now cut back to the split screen shot to see which one of the ailing men would reach the finish line first, while also keeping an eye on whatever John chose to do next. John finally left behind his dead bodies and started moving through the course again.

The dedicated cameraman at the second obstacle watched as he completely bypassed the water obstacle and continued running. John had never felt like the rules applied to him, and now he realized it was silly to try to play by the ones he had been given for today. Clearly, he'd broken a few already. He had no desire to catch up to the ailing men, because they weren't really his type. But he had no idea if the crew had any more women, so he wanted to see if he could find something more tempting to him.

What had started off as an inclusive, diverse crew had become a recipe for disaster. The unmanned cameras picked up John moving again. Mark and the audience let out an audible sigh of relief as John left the cameraman alone and moved on quickly. They were resigned to witnessing this play out fully but were happy to be spared from another death.

Meanwhile, the men out front were dredging up the last of their strength to make it through the last section of the obstacle course. Neither had enough energy to sprint, but they were going as fast as they possibly could. Tom remained in the lead and the audience could see the hope fading from Sam's eyes. Around the time that Tom crossed the finish line, John was skipping the third obstacle and also choosing to bypass the static cameraman at that position.

Tom was elated as he crossed the finish line and collapsed, with Sam slowing and unenthusiastically crossing it about twenty seconds later. They were both surprised that no one from production was there to greet them. After Sam finished, a drove of armed guards descended on the area and ushered them and their respective camera operators away from the finish line. In an adrenaline rush from what they had just accomplished, they did not seem to be overly concerned by this development.

The armed guards then drew their weapons and swarmed the finish line as John came into view. John could see what was up ahead of him, but he felt invincible at this point and carried on, beginning to sprint. It was at that moment that all four guards unloaded several rounds of gunfire into John, dropping him on the ground instantly in a bloody and unrecognizable wad.

Tom looked back and screamed and then collapsed in horror as he watched his kidney donor bleed out in the street. Sam just stood there, shocked. Mark and the audience, having known why John was gunned down, felt some vindication of justice; but they were still very uncomfortable about all the killing they had witnessed in the last few minutes. The disembodied voice was systematically wrapping up the play-by-play of this awful turn of events before production cut to commercial.

In his earpiece, Mark heard the voice of the leader of The Agents saying, "well, he only ended up getting two of the three women we put out there, so I guess we should have picked someone with a little more drive," and chuckling. It was at that time that Mark finally threw up.

Brandi Fruik is still a Certified Public Accountant, Master in Taxation and wannabe writer. Being published in this year's anthology is the highlight of her year . . . which would mean more if it wasn't 2020. Thanks for reading and wear a mask.

The Spirit of the Mountain
Scott Fowler

His family called him crazy. His wife threatened to divorce him. Perhaps she already had. He hadn't even spoken with her in months, since the day he went off on this expedition, one that was still to be determined if it was foolhardy or not. At that moment, sitting in his tent bundled in every piece of clothing he had with him to keep warm and shivering above a small stove brewing coffee in a tin kettle, he was almost certain this whole adventure of his was as foolhardy as foolhardy could get.

Still he was there and still alive, despite the conditions. He took a couple of puffs from his oxygen mask and then set it aside. He needed to preserve the tank for the final push to the summit. He breathed heavy without it but still had breath. He seemed to always be in a state of lightheadedness at this altitude but he could feel his fingers and toes and, well, down there, so frostbite hadn't gotten to him yet which was good.

He scratched his gruff beard, the one he started to let grow months ago when he left. His wife never let him grow a beard. It was full and dark now, with particles of ice sticking to it like icing on a cake. The ice didn't seem to want to melt, even in the relative warmth of the tent.

The mountain called to him like the thousands she had called out to before him. He dreamed of her. She spoke to him through the wind, coming alive in his dreams, just as alive as his wife and kids but touching a place deep within his soul, shining a light on an empty hole there he thought his family would have filled but didn't. Even in the comfort of his warm bed at home, he'd hear her voice whispering in his ear, begging him to come climb her; she needed him at her bosom.

It took him years and thousands of dollars to learn the right skills to climb such a mountain. One simply didn't go and climb her without knowing her intimately. He struggled to climb many different mountains of varying sizes like a teenager paws at his girlfriends, learning from each one how to become a better lover. All through it, his wife would fight with him, trying to squash his dreams, perhaps jealous of his intimacy with the mountain. She didn't like all the money he was spending to reach these idiotic goals. Didn't he know that he had a family to support? Didn't he know he had a wife he needed to keep in fashionable clothes and jewelry? Didn't he know they had a lifestyle they needed to maintain to keep the neighbors envious?

The day he left for Katmandu was the last straw. She came home to find him there with all his bags packed waiting for the taxi to take him to the airport. When she asked why he wasn't at work, he told her how he had quit his job that day. It was a boring office job. One where he wasn't appreciated and his talents were lost. He could see her pale face turn a deep red at that.

And then he told her he was leaving to finally climb his beloved mountain. She had collapsed on the sofa near the door, a tear falling down her left cheek. He was sure this wasn't a tear of sadness but suppressed anger. They sat in silence, waiting for the cab. When it arrived, she told him she was going to divorce him as he stepped out the door, arms filled with bags. She didn't help him carry anything to the car. There wasn't a "good luck," or a kiss goodbye. There wasn't a "come back safe," or an "I'll miss you." There was only a red, wet face with fire in her eyes.

As he rode off to the airport, he smiled. *Wait 'til she finds out how I financed this trip,* he thought to himself. He had refinanced the house to get the several hundred thousand dollars that was needed to get the permits and gear to climb the mountain.

Even as he sat, drinking his hot coffee, the wind whipped the tent canvas and the sounds of the others at the camp filled his ears. Most people his age were using one of several "adventure capitalists" companies to help them climb the mountain. He saw those climbers as weak. The need for sherpas and other experienced climbers to nursemaid one up the mountain was pitiful in his mind. The mountain wanted you to work for her. She wanted you to prove your love for her. There were no shortcuts. Shortcuts led to death.

And on this mountain there were a lot of deaths, over two

hundred at last count. There are corpses which are used by climbers as landmarks along the route to the summit. The mountain was so high that dragging bodies down only endangered the lives of those recovering them. So, bodies were just left where they fell to freeze and mummify in the frigid air. Their families justified it with words like "he died doing what he loved" or "he would have wanted to be left on the mountain." It was understood by everyone who attempted the climb that they could become one of those signposts for future climbers.

He had seen two already getting to the highest camp. This first was just after the ice flow. It was a laying on its side facing into a crevice in the rock. The body didn't have a hood on and its hair was sun-bleached almost translucent. He thought it once was a dark black color, similar to his own. He guessed the climber's hat had blown off during an earlier storm since no experienced climber would be at that altitude without his head covered. The skin on its cheek had a brown leathery look to it. He couldn't tell how long the corpse had been there, probably decades.

The second was a woman just below the highest camp sitting upright, cross legged like she died while meditating, perhaps contemplating the mountain as a harsh mistress. Her eyes, even years later, were open and a perfect blue. They seemed to regard him as he passed. Her long dark hair, just showing the beginnings of a sun-bleached blonde, blew in a frenzy around her head in the wind. It had the effect of looking like a dark halo around a frozen angelic face. A face perfectly preserved with icicles dangling from her nose and ears.

He found the bodies both fascinating and frightening. There were many more to come, he had been told. The higher you went, the more bodies accumulated. It wasn't called the Death Zone for nothing. Human beings simply weren't meant to live up there. But come morning, he was going into that zone.

He slept fitfully in his sleeping bag that night, shivering throughout from the cold. The stove in the center of his tent didn't seem to keep much of the cold away. But still he slept, dreaming, of course, of the mountain. She was all he dreamed about anymore. In his dreams, he always makes it to the summit, sometimes naked, sometimes not, but always aroused and always there. He would stretch his arms out and let the frigid wind pass through him, causing his entire body to turn black and hard from frostbite until he dropped off the ledge and fell, dropping through the clouds toward the Earth below, calling out the mountain's name all the way down. He'd always wake up just as he hit the ground.

It was still dark when he got up. After drinking more coffee off the stove to try to warm up his body and eating a protein bar as a bit of a breakfast, he tightened his outer layers and unzipped the tent flap. A cold wind blew in some of the snow but he ignored it and stepped into it, zipping up the tent behind him. He stood for a moment looking around himself, re-familiarizing himself with the camp and where he was. There was a rainbow of tents, all lit up from the inside looking like Chinese lanterns dotting the steep slope. To the north were jagged rock formations that pointed at the sky, many of those rocks were covered in snow. He couldn't see them because it was still dark but he knew they were there, seen them clearly in the daytime, marveled over them from afar and now it was time to see them up close.

In the darkness above, beams of yellow light bobbed and weaved, each some distance from each other. Others had already started their push for the summit, with their headlamps moving in thin triangles on the ground as they moved slowly among the cracks and spires. To his left, he saw a line of figures still in camp preparing to make their own assault on the summit. One of those adventure capitalist groups apparently from the number of people wearing similar clothing and a man in a red coat paced up and down the line checking everyone's equipment.

He checked his own equipment accordingly and then joined the tail end of their line as they began to move out of camp. Like everyone, he was having problems just getting air into his lungs. He inhaled and exhaled in heavy puffs. He had to concentrate hard to keep up the heavy breathing. He thought about going to his oxygen supply, a thin bottle of compressed air in a bag strung across his shoulder, but opted against it. It was too early. He imagined he would need it closer to the summit. For now, he just needed to keep going.

Before long, the line of about twenty people he had joined found themselves spread out about a hundred yards apart from each other. He took up their rear though there was another group starting a hundred yards behind him.

He passed one of the group sitting on the ground, the man in the red coat kneeling next to the man who was sucking on his oxygen mask with abandon. They would be going back to camp, he knew just by looking at the man.

A couple of hours later, as he was approaching what amounted to a cliff face with ropes held in place in the rock, the sun broke over the horizon. The clouds crossing over the peak turned from a dark black to a bright pink hue. He stood there for a moment watching it. It painted the rocks on the mountain in a rose color. The mountain was waking up and as beautiful as ever.

He stuck his boot into a crevice and began to climb the rocky face, following the ropes placed there earlier in the season by the sherpas. They reached a small ledge, only about three or four inches in width. He began to slowly shimmy himself along it, carefully gripping any small protrusions he could reach as he went. He stopped often to move his rigging hook along the rope.

At one point, he put on his facemask and breathed in cold oxygen. It felt good and his burning lungs thanked him. Quickly, his vision, which had been blurry since he left camp began to clear up. He held onto the rocky wall and just breathed.

He looked down (every climber tells you not to look down but ignores the advice themselves) and saw a good mile or two of shear drop. The area below him was a massive pile of gray stone debris at almost a ninety-degree angle. From his vantage point, he could see the gray field dotted with about fifty to sixty darker objects. It took him a second to realize the objects were the bodies of people who had fallen. Many of the bodies seemed rather recent with their brightly colored clothing, suggesting nylon coats. Others were obviously older with sun bleached skin, hair, and clothing. They dotted like leopard spots on the skin of the mountain.

He began moving again, feeling the tingling in his feet and hands, that tell-tale sign of oncoming frostbite. But he kept going, one foot in front of the other, hand over hand, sliding along the cliff face. No matter how much pain shot through his knees and shoulders, he had to keep going. Each step was an affirmation of life and a slap at his wife. That's all he thought now to keep him moving. *If only she could see me now.*

He reached the end of the tiny ledge he'd been trudging along on when the set ropes moved skyward with the rocks. About a hundred yards above was a small ridge, only about two feet wide and covered in snow, that led for a half of a mile to the summit. It looked tantalizingly close but still miles away. He had a lot of work to do before he could reach his goal.

Up until now, he'd been pretty much by himself. The group he'd tagged along with had been way ahead of him, some may have likely reached the summit already, and the group behind was over a football field behind him. But now, at this step, the distance between climbers was getting smaller and smaller. He was about ten feet now from the climber in front of him.

He had to wait to mount the cliff face and begin his climb to the ridge for the final push. He stood holding onto the rope while the climber in front of him began his own assault on the cliff. Someone else was coming down passing the man in front of him as he went up, having made it to the summit and making his way back down. He had to smash himself against the side of the mountain to let that summited person pass over him. It felt intimate being hugged to the mountain rock like that. He found himself smiling even though his face hurt. His cheeks felt sunburned.

It was a good twenty minutes before he got moving again. By then, his shoulders were crying out in pain and his knees creaked like rusty hinges. But still, he couldn't stop now despite that his body was demanding it. He wedged his boot into a crevice and began to lift himself up the rocky face. Another person who had reached the summit passed on their way down but he ignored them, hardly noticing anyone else there at all. He climbed in silence, his lungs huffing and puffing. Even with his oxygen mask on, his chest felt tight and burning.

When he reached the top of the step, he pulled himself onto

the small ledge and then groaned as he got to his feet, every muscle in his body protesting. The ledge was not much bigger than two feet wide with a shear drop on either side. It led along a not quite straight line in deep snow to the top of the world. He gazed for a moment along the ledge, following the trail broken in the snow by the other climbers and saw a blurred image of a group of people clustered at the summit, waving flags and arms in celebration. He thought he could hear their screams of joy but the wind took the sounds away with it.

He had to will his right leg to move and then his left. His wife now forgotten, he spent his entire mental capacity to will his legs to move one after another. He found he couldn't feel his feet or his hands and much of his face felt numb like some crazy dentist had shot too much Novocain into his mouth. He could hardly see anything now but blurry figures. But he trudged on.

The climbers who had reached the summit were now making their way down in a line. Each one that past him would almost push him off the side, getting his heart racing. Finally, after the last climber past him by, he found himself practically alone on the ledge. He glanced behind himself and saw no one there. The climbers behind him must have turned back to camp. He didn't know why they would do that when they were so close to the summit but he put it out of his mind. He had a job to do and he desperately needed to finish it.

It was quiet except for his heavy breathing and the wind that threatened to blow so hard he feared it would knock him over the side causing him to fall into eternity. *Just you and me now, babe*, he thought to himself.

His brain couldn't think at all anymore, except to will his legs to move. He found himself saying the words out loud into his oxygen mask.

"Left," he would say and his left leg would move forward and plant his boot onto the rock in front of him. Then he would say, "right," and his right leg would do the same. Then repeat. Left. Right.

Left. He just had to keep going no matter how much pain his body was in nor how blank his mind became. This was a test of endurance and the mountain expected your all and nothing less.

For the most part he looked only at his feet as he trudged along. At one point, he stopped to catch a breather and looked up at the summit. Small, ragged flags from practically every country were tied to the granite tip and not a little bit of trash was left behind on top of the snow. He figured the top of the world was about fifty yards away but it could have been fifty miles away, same difference to him at that moment.

The temptation was hard to resist to just sit down on that ledge right there and go to sleep, become one of those corpses other climbers use as landmarks on their way to the top. But he could hear her voice on the wind. The mountain spoke to him, begging him to join her at her summit. She promised paradise.

He began to move again, one step after another, in a deliberate and slow fashion. He stared at the faded colored fabrics at the top as they flapped in the wind, focused on it like a missile targeting its objective. He had been hunched over ever since he reached the ledge but now he stiffened straight, ignoring the sharp pain that went up his spine. He picked up his pace, almost to a run, every inch of his being crying out in pain. He realized he was screaming into his oxygen mask but the wind took the sound before it got to his ears.

And then he was there, at his objective, at the summit. He stopped next to the mound of collected flags and collapsed onto his knees, breathing heavy, his heart racing as fast as he had ever felt it. He reached and touched the pointed top of the rock, caressing it like it was a woman's breast. The wind seemed to blow even harder as he did that. He took that to mean the mountain felt his touch.

Holding onto the mountain summit, he looked around himself, seeing for the first time other mountains around him, seeing dark clouds in the distance with periodic flashes of lightening, seeing the sun to the west about to dip below the horizon. It had taken him all day to reach the summit and the view was both breathtaking and frightening. The sky was turning a deep purple and he realized that not only was night coming, a dangerous thing when on the mountain, but a storm was coming too.

His oxygen mask suddenly felt constricting and he unclipped it and let it fall against his cheek. He sucked in the cold air but there wasn't enough oxygen for his lungs. They screamed out to him and his head quickly became light and fuzzy. But that only made him feel giddy and he began to laugh, a deep hearty laugh, a laugh of triumph, a nervous laughter that came from him in short bursts before developing into a serious coughing fit. He bent over and watched blood drop from his mouth onto the white snow.

When he sat back up, his breath made a wheezing sound and his eyes had drops of blood in them from burst capillaries. His nose was running fiercely, snot freezing almost instantly in his beard. It was time to head back down, he supposed, before the night got too dark and the storm actually hit the mountain. He stood up, his spine again sending a spike of pain from neck to buttocks.

He put his oxygen mask back on and turned to make his way down the way he came up but stopped in his tracks. Some distance away, was a line of figures climbing up the pass. At first, he thought it was other climbers making a push for the summit after all but realized quickly that it would be suicide for anyone to come up with the light getting so low and a storm coming in. Those people who had been behind him would have abandoned their attempt and went back to camp, resolved to try again in the morning. Besides, these figures were standing full on two legs, not using their hands to help climb along.

With the final light of the setting sun hitting them, he could see that none of them had on masks and even some of them didn't seem to have coats on. There was something about these strange people that unnerved him. Then he realized what it was. They weren't actually walking on the rocky mountain. Their legs weren't moving. Instead, they seemed to be floating along the ridge.

The person closest to him, the one first in line, was about twenty yards away. That person was a woman. She looked familiar but he couldn't place where he'd seen her. Her hair blew backwards in the wind but seem to disappear into the darkness. Her blue eyes staring forward at him. Then he realized, he could see through her to the person behind her. Her body looked like a lace, wedding veil, there but see through enough to see something behind it.

He staggered backward in shock, bumping into the flag covered piece of rock that was the summit. He almost fell but hung on, his butt dropping so he sat on the top of the mountain. The wind was picking up, threatening to blow him over the side for sure. Snowflakes began to fall.

A dark cloud, the leading edge to the storm, covered the last sliver of sunlight and things were dark as night. The people gliding up the slope toward him seemed to fade away into the darkness like the ghosts they were. He reached up to switch on his headlamp and then hesitated. They had been almost on him. Did he really want to turn on the light to see something pale and dead in front of his face? But he knew he couldn't get back down without light. On the mountain, the darkness of night can be as penetrating as in a deep cave. One misstep and he could fall to his death.

So, he switched the light on.

He jumped to his feet and his heart raced. In the beam was the pale face of the woman who was leading these spectral beings. Her skin white as chalk. Her eyes frozen in place stared at him. He instantly realized who this person was. This was the woman whose corpse he passed on the way up the mountain. Other faces came into view in the light. All looking frozen and mummified with dark brown skin. Some only wore frayed cotton pants and nothing else. Others wore brightly colored nylon coats and snow gear. One had a rope wrapped around his neck as if he was hanged for being a criminal. Almost all had some black marks on their face or hands indicating frostbite. And all, every single one, he was able to see through to the snowy mountain behind.

He turned, panicking, and began to run, oblivious of where he was. He had not plan of where to go and knew better than to try to run at night on top of a small ledge on a mountain. But run he did. Or he tried to run. His boot slid on the snow as soon as he put it down and off the edge. He stumbled, clutching at the flags to catch himself but only got a glove full of fabric. He pinwheeled in mid-air and then fell over the side.

As he fell, he saw all the faces of those lost on the mountain looking down on him and he wondered if that was the last thing everyone saw before their soul left their bodies, sacrificed to her, the mountain. He wondered if he would be joining those figures soon. Just before he hit the gravelly rock pile beneath the summit, he smiled. He felt happy. He was going to be with his love forever.

Scott Fowler was born in Washington DC in 1969. He currently lives in Maryland with his wife and son. He has published two sets of his short works; Back Looks The Abyss and other Stories and Tales for the Blood Oath which can be purchased through Amazon and Scott's website (http://scottwfowler6.wixsite.com/fowlerfunnyfarm) where he publishes some of his other works.

Vox Odio
D. Paul Angel

     The Voices returned. The quiet whisperings in his sleep reminding him who he was. *Who he became* . . .
     Nico tried to will himself back to sleep, but the Voices were insistent, filling him with flashes of memories, overwhelming him with images of loss, of violence, of *Her* . . . Of her falling backwards from him in slowed time with the obsidian knife still in her heart. Of her landing in the fresh, pristine snow in a cloud of white flakes and bloody drops. Of him welcoming the sharp cold on his bare skin as he stared at her face, hoping its numbing pain would take him too. Of her slowly changing from an unrecognizable creature, shunned by even God Himself, to his beloved. And of her eyes, finally seeing him and returning his love, before widening in pain from the excruciating torment of her death throes. Her words were lost, her voice nearly forgotten, drowned out by the cruel laughter of the Voice's gleeful jeers at the memory of her loss—his One, his Love, his Katareina.
     Conceding the loss of further sleep, he awkwardly extracted himself from the hammock, shaming himself for once again trying to brush away tears from eyes ungraced by them in years. He struggled up the wooden ladder towards the deck, his bare feet slipping twice on rungs worn smooth from use as the Voice's cackling shouts distracted his balancing the ship's rolls. He breathed a tired sigh of relief as he came topside, happily trading the stale mugginess below for the warm Tropical breeze above.
     Alone in a starless sky, the low harvest moon's brightness left an angular mix of shadows and muted light across the deck under taught, glowing sails. He listened where he stood for the crew, straining to hear them past the Voices, the aged barque's creaks and groans, and the wind's swift rippling of her canvases. When he could finally distinguish their words from the Voice's harsh chitterings, he turned the other way, slowly walking to the bowsprit's

solitude across the rough, sand-grit deck. Looking out at the ocean's crinkled swells, he reveled in the spray's salty sting across his face, embracing the moment of tranquility as the Voices grew ever softer. He closed his eyes, willing his pulse to slow to the beat of waves and hull, until the Voices finally faded to a near silent susurrus.

He didn't know how long the moment lasted, or even if sleep had visited him where he stood, when his eyes opened of their own accord—pulling his attention to a light on the horizon.

He strained through groggy, unfocused eyes to make out its form, but could tell neither its distance nor veracity. He tried blinking and rubbing his eyes till spots overwhelmed his sight, but the light ahead remained stubbornly unchanged. He was still trying to see it out of the corner of his eyes, shifting both his head and focus when the image resolved in a blink to a woman. She turned his stomach in revulsion as he saw she was both solid and translucent, surrounded by a bright, pearlescent radiance. It lit the Ocean not just around her, but through her too, as she gracefully "walked" across the waves.

Anger and terror and dread and hate and duty vied for his heart and gut—again. She was but a mere cable's length away when they all gave way to panic as he clumsily fumbled for the obsidian knife dangling from his neck. Finally freed, he wrapped its leather cord around his wrist to secure it, before squeezing its handle with a trembling fist. The ancient blade's long, narrow profile absorbed the light around it, becoming a shadow within a shadow as he held it ready before him. The harder he held it, the more he could feel its knapped edges' familiar shape, the more his feelings resolved into hardened determination stronger than even the stone's, and the more his focus returned to the water—as she was close enough now that he had to look nearly straight down to see her.

He flinched when she looked up at him with sultry eyes and a wicked smile.

He sighed as he lost himself in her look, his sharp edge dulled in a moment. A heartbeat later she disappeared into the ship's bow-wake, only to immediately coalesce just behind him. He turned at the railing as she looked him up and down, judging him as a rancher would a steer. She walked back and forth in front of him while reaching out to his face and running her hand across his stubbled cheeks. Even the echo of her feigned caress felt colder than a deep winter's snow, as he reached his hand to where hers had just left.

    She twirled on a toe in front of him slower than even the most adroit ballerina ever could, as he stood mutely before her, his forgotten hand still holding his face. Without ever losing his eye she came to a stop with her back to him, her long, flowing curls cascading down her back whilst flitting between shades—redder than the hottest lava; blonder than summer straw; whiter than a lightning's arc; browner than the eldest bark; blacker than the pupils in a dead man's eyes.

    She spun again, lowering her head and looking up into his eyes. He felt a sudden peace in her gaze, a respite from the sufferings of his world, a tranquility he hadn't known since Katareina's arms. She smiled at him with lustful arrogance before sauntering to the foremast, leaving his mind adrift in an addled trance. Like a malevolent horror sloughing off the vestments of innocence, she rose through the rigging while otherwise still. The Voices awoke at her unnatural ascent, their shrieks of rage returning his will.

    Blinking away the last wisps of her fog, he found most of the crew still transfixed in muted stillness. Then Nico looked up to the crow's nest, where the lookout was either wholly oblivious to her, or fast asleep on his feet. She met Nico's gaze with an elaborate wink before bending over in front of the lookout, suggestively gyrating before him while slowly raising her dress.

    Nico shook his head in frustration, desperately trying to silence the Voices enough to think as we watched the lookout arch his back and look to the sky. Running out of time, he let the knife bounce on its cord while grabbing a musket. He continued swearing at himself for his sluggish response even while thanking God that its powder was near. With rote efficiency he primed and raised it, but the poor lookout's breeches were already down by the time he fired, its loud retort waking the crew with a violent start. They were soon pointing and shouting incoherently at the crow's nest scene, where the lookout was desperately shaking his head and trying to flee, despite the rest of him staying frozen in fear.

She turned and glared at Nico with seething hatred for interrupting her infernal desires ere they could be consummated. He dropped the spent musket with a clatter in answer, desperately trying to get the knife back in his hand under the crippling force of her furious stare. In a grain of time she was simultaneously at the crow's nest and mere inches from his face, her unearthly beauty replaced by an ugly grotesque of human features—eyes of embers and rows of jagged fangs lit by the last vestiges of moonlight. She shrieked at him in a soprano wail of icy rage, cursing him in the guttural terror of Shadowspeak.

The Voices answered—through him. Their inhuman words choking his mouth and throat in dull, rasped pain, as his will staggered under the combined assault of them fighting for power over his being. The more his spirit flagged, the more frenzied their attacks, until he could feel his soul shuddering against their desperate grasps. His whole body was shaking under the taught strain of their tableau when her visage blurred and slowly returned to her earlier beauty, graced by a kind, apologetic smile. He felt the rest of his strength begin to collapse, ebbing along with the softening of her features—until they resolved into *Her*.

"NOT HER!" he shouted in his own tongue, drowning out every other voice as his heart was wrought in horror at her wearing Katariens's face. "NEVER HER!"

He tried to stab her but she instantly grabbed his hand with hers as a cat would a mouse, its delicate softness turning to a vicious, chitinous claw. Her shrieking overwhelmed him as he fought until hers was the only "Voice" he heard. The searing anguish from the face she now wore, *Her* face, fueled the frenetic rage of his resistance. The closer he came to loosening her grip, the more solid she became, until all of her form and focus were upon him.

Yet despite it all, he still felt himself weakening and succumbing to her power. Then he met her eyes. How many times had he stared into the depths of Katareina's eyes? How many times had he studied within them the sparks of her joy and wit? Her love, kindness, and intelligence . . . Her lust for him. Only for them to now be little more than odious simulacrums of Katareina's effervescent vitality?

Swept by a mad, red surge of primal rage, he broke her grip with a croaky howl, thrusting the knife into her chest. He held it there, its blade buried to his knuckles, even as her body violently flickered twixt solid and spectral, before bursting into roaring, verdant flames. He was still recoiling from their unnatural heat when with a loud *WHUMPFF* they were just as abruptly extinguished, leaving naught but char marks and a smear of burnt, unidentifiable flesh on the deck.

As he stood there, knife in hand, stunned and overwrought, he watched the crew finally headed up towards the lookout. They approached him in fear, crossing themselves even though he'd already puked over the side and collapsed at the rail. With a raspy bark he shouted to them and their bewildering fear, "Oy! The succubus is gone. It's safe."

In the dubious silence that followed, the first light of dawn lit the sky. Over the far rail it crept, burning her sickened remains with an unearthly fire wherever it touched. Nico stood back watching until the last of her slag was removed by its rising rays, and the wind had claimed the last of her soot.

He stood there alone a long while, too tired to think, too drained to move, simply feeling the rising Sun on his body. As his senses and awareness returned, so too did the sound of distant voices. Blessedly though, it was only the crew as he slowly moved towards them and away from the vile, lingering stench of her stain.

The captain approached before Nico got far, his hands up in peace. "'Twas a succubus you say? Here, so far at sea?"

"Aye," Nico quietly answered through his throat's lingering pain. "A rarity of rares. Your lookout?"

"Gibbering, but alive. And you—you exorcised her then, Father?" The captain crossed himself in awe at Nico's nodded reply. "Thanks be Father, truly. And—that is—could you, perhaps, please to bless the ship and crew as well?"

"Of course," he said, nodding and forcing a smile to ease the captain's lingering discomfiture, "but, after I rest."

While the captain's departing thanks were more wary than grateful, at least the fortitude of command had returned to his bearing. Nico was soon enough below, back in his now comfortable hammock along with the fading memories of a meager breakfast and double ration of rum handed to him by the cook's own trembling hands. With his eyes closed in exhaustion, he let his mind drift with the lulled rocking of the ship. Memories of the succubus surfaced and the Voices returned, but only as if they were carried to him from afar by a particularly capricious breeze. Louder and softer, they drifted in sync with the disjointed reveries of his mind. The succubus. The sea. The fight. The lookout. The captain's fear. The succubus' hate. Katareina.

    Tired and numb, slow flashed memories of *Her* filled his being once more. Not just the nightmares, but their happiness too; her smile as she laid on his shoulder, her laugh as they danced. A laugh derisively echoed by a cacophony of Voices in the cruel mockery of a single, shrill Voice, railing at her sudden perdition. They soon faded too with the last scenes of Katareina's joy, as he fell asleep at last, as silent tears wetted his cheek.

Paul is a writer, photographer, and nerd. His fiction, when he actually finishes it, tends to smudge the lines separating SciFi, Fantasy, Horror, and Comedy. He's been a proud co-editor of the Fark Fiction Anthology since its inception, and has also edited textbook quality histories of the 727, 737, and 757. Paul's photography explores the everyday intersections between nature and architecture, where initial simplicity flows into unique complexities. His wanton nerdery speaks for itself.

A Skirmish Outside Beaufort
E. A. Black

Dawn approached the fields outside Beaufort, South Carolina this November night in 1861. In the Union camp, infantryman John Malcolm Reed pulled at his collar. Nervous energy ran through his veins. He watched Captain Stephen Ellison ride his filly as the regiment prepared for siege. The regiment would travel at dawn the ten miles to Beaufort, South Carolina and overtake the town in the morning. It would be an easy raid.

Warmth bored through Reed's wool shell jacket and he felt slightly sick. Queasiness wasn't going to prevent him from firing as many shots as he could at rebel heads. The nausea masked his anxiety, so he pretended it was caused by tainted stew.

His best friend and fellow infantryman Sam Rogers rustled on the ground next to him. They attended the same church in Gloucester, Massachusetts and signed up to defend their country. They wanted the United States to remain united, and they opposed slavery. Neither man had expected to end up so far south amid mosquitos, a bout of dysentery, Spanish moss and infected blisters from boots that either had worn down or were poorly fitted.

"Can't sleep?" Reed asked. He then shoveled stew in his mouth. Had to keep up his strength.

"No. Too excited. You ready for the raid?" Rogers asked.

"I suppose I am." Reed swallowed hard, doing his best to keep the stew down. He knew damned well his problem wasn't the chow. It was the realization that he could very well end up riddled with bullets at the hand of some Southerner who was likely as scared as he was. *Keep talking and you'll take your mind off your worries.* "We'll surprise those rebels so much when we show at their door they won't know how to react."

"I can't wait to see the look on their faces when we corner them. I'm ready to fight." Rogers said as he sat up and put on his jacket. "After all the trouble our fine soldiers went through during the War of American Independence to have established this country, it's hard to believe some people want to tear it apart because they refuse to give up their slaves."

"I know. My grandfather would be angry and disappointed at the position we find ourselves in today. He kicked a bit of English ass near these grounds in the 1780s and lost his life here."

"Hear, hear. I fully intend to kick some southern ass," Rogers said.

"How's the little one?" Reed asked to get his mind off his anxiety.

"Doing well. He's two years old and sharp as a rapier. The wife is five months along, too. We want a girl this time."

"I hope you get one. You have quite the life. My Sarah waits for me at home." Reed's pulled a small box from his jacket pocket. "I'm giving her this ring when I get home. My grandfather who died here gave it to my grandmother. I keep it in my pocket for good luck."

"Nothing to envy, my friend. I know Sarah's going to say 'yes'," Rogers said. "She's a good woman who will—"

"Man the barricades! Man the barricades!" A scout shouted as he raced towards the camp. "Rebels are coming through the woods!"

Startled, Reed jumped where he sat and dropped his cup of stew on the ground. He was in such a rush to put his boots back on he nearly put them on the wrong feet.

Reed grabbed his musket, balls, and powder horn and rushed for the meager battlement while Rogers stamped out the campfire. The hair crackled on his head. Static rose in the air, causing the hair on Reed's neck to stand on end. What was this about? No storm lurked on the horizon, something for which he was grateful. The last thing he needed was rain. It had rained when the regiment passed near Lynchburg, Virginia, wetting the gunpowder so that their muskets wouldn't fire.

As he fastened his bayonet to his musket, he listened to the call of the crickets and night peepers. Seagulls cried in the distance. The camp was near water; he could smell the ocean. It was a shame such a peaceful area had been swept up in war. Fireflies sparkled about them like fairies dancing in the night.

Once his bayonet was in place, a chill ran up and down his spine. Something seemed . . . off. He couldn't put his finger on what it was until he noticed the silence.

The cacophony of night critters had suddenly stopped. The crickets and night peepers had stopped their incessant call. The fireflies ceased their light show. Sparrows went quiet. Even the wind stopped blowing through the trees.

"Rogers, do you hear that?" He whispered.

"Hear what?" Rogers asked.

"Exactly," he whispered. "Nothing."

Rogers lifted his head and sniffed. "Air smells strange, too."

Reed took in a deep breath. It smelled like it did right before a lightning storm, but there wasn't a cloud in the sky. The sharp scent sailed up his nostrils and threatened to give him a headache. Damn this queasiness! Why had he been feeling so sick all night?

Billions of stars covered the heavens. The Milky Way split the night sky in half. A meteor sailed by, an omen of trouble to come. The pink of dawn blushed at the horizon.

Mist rolled through the trees and shrubbery. Most of the men had fallen into position and waited for the soldiers to come out of the tree line, but no one came. No breeze blew Reed's greasy hair away from his face. His heart thumped. Shaking off the eerie atmosphere, he blinked several times in quick succession as if such an act would take the creeps away.

"Do you hear anything?" Reed said.

"No. I only hear our men. Nothing else." Rogers said. "Everyone's almost in place. We'll make short work of those rebels. They won't know—"

"Wait," Reed pointed towards the woods." Look at that. What in God's name is going on?"

The mist glowed as several figures walked through. They did not make a sound. Reed recognized them immediately.

Soldiers.

Captain Ellison held up one hand to halt the regiment from firing. These soldiers were dressed in blue. What other Union regiment was all the way down here? Twelve men emerged silently from the woods followed by twenty more, all surrounded by an unearthly green glow tinged with white. Dozens more followed. Soldiers carrying flags appeared, and one was that of the state of Massachusetts.

Reed strained to get a better look at the other one. Were his eyes deceiving him?

That flag had 13 stripes and 13 stars in a circle. Why would confederates dress in blue and carry a Massachusetts flag and a flag for the thirteen colonies?

Captain Ellison's hand remained in the air, and everyone froze in place. The quiet fell upon the regiment like a cloud of heavy smoke. Sweat dripped in Reed's eyes, burning them. He wiped his sleeve across his face. Illness overwhelmed him, but he fought the urge to vomit. As the soldiers approached the regiment, their footsteps muffled and their expressions blank, he saw that they walked a foot above the ground.

"Lookit that," Rogers whispered. "Their legs aren't moving. They aren't walking. They're sliding towards us."

The regiment remained in place and prepared to fire, but Captain Ellison held them back. Reed kneeled in front of the fence and held out his musket, waiting for an order that seemed would never come.

One of the spectral soldiers pointed at Reed. Why was the man pointing at him? Then, the man jerked his arm downwards, aiming at the ground. Reed knitted his eyebrows, confused over why the man acted as he did. Once again, the soldier pointed at Reed and then jerked his arm downwards towards the earth.

When the soldier stood within thirty feet of him, Reed drew back with a gasp of surprise. The man who approached him wore a bedraggled beard, a tri-cornered hat, and a blue coat with red facing and large wooden buttons. His expression held no emotion, but Reed recognized the familiar face of his grandfather as the man once again pointed towards the ground.

Reed took the hint and bent low to inspect his bootlace as he fought an overwhelming urge to puke. At that moment, a cannonball sailed through the air past where his head had been. It smashed into Sam Rogers' face and tore his head off at the neck. Roger's body fell on Reed as blood sprayed from his wound, splashing him on the face and spurting as far as three feet. He screamed. His best friend's arms and legs convulsed in spasms as Reed shoved the man's body off him. His stomach could no longer take the constant assault and he vomited the still-warm stew onto the dirt. He turned to run away when he glanced to where the soldiers had been.

Once the phantom soldiers passed about twenty feet in the distance, they faded away like so much smoke. What the hell? Reed blinked his eyes a few times to make sure he wasn't seeing things. A moment later, the sound of footsteps racing through the woods rumbled into the clearing. Rebel soldiers appeared through the mist where the apparitions had walked, but thanks to the specters, Reed and the men were prepared for them.

The soldiers raced from the woods, screaming out a blood-curdling rebel yell that sent the chills down Reed's spine. That sound was unlike any other he had ever heard, and no matter how many times he heard it, he could never get used to it. It was as frightening as the howling of packs of coyotes near his home he often heard in the dead of night. Despite his fearful shivering, Reed knelt in his place in front of the fence. His trigger finger would react when the Captain gave the order. The rebel soldiers were still too far away for musket fire to accurately hit them. He waited without much patience for the moment the Captain lowered his arm. Reed held his musket so tight his hands threatened to cramp.

How much longer? They're almost on us! Captain Ellison was a fine commander who knew the exact moment to call his infantry into action. Reed trusted the man's judgment. All he could do was wait, but his legs wanted to flee the area. To do so meant certain death since he'd be an easy target for rebel gunfire.

He chose one soldier and aimed his musket at the glittering spot on his breast. Despite his many kills, he never grew accustomed to death. Killing a man wasn't like shooting dozens of squirrels. They didn't haunt you or leave you burdened with guilt and shame.

When the men were close enough to see the lead buttons on their gray coats, Captain Ellison yelled, "Fire!"

Reed pulled the trigger without thinking twice. His mind turned off when he killed; otherwise, he could not do it. These weren't men he killed. In his mind, they were not living, breathing beings with a wife, a two-year-old toddler and a baby on the way. No, these men were stinkin' rebels who killed his best friend so they deserved to die.

He tossed his musket aside and grabbed one from the man behind him. He aimed at a scowling soldier rushing towards him and blew his face off. Good, there's one for old Rogers, a grade school buddy who was felled just outside Lynchburg. Bullets zinged past him, and one grazed against his ear, cutting off much of the lobe. Blood flowed wet and warm down his neck. Reed winced at the pain but did not stop his assault. He tossed aside that musket, grabbed the next one handed him, and fired, striking a man in the chest. That one was for Allan King, his younger sister's fiancé killed by grapeshot in Virginia. Then one for his cousin Jacob Reed. He picked off men left and right, firing shot after shot as the bellowing horde closed in.

Gunshot and cannon fire exploded around him. A man to his left took a bullet to the chest and fell limp over the fence. Another infantryman used the body as a shield as he fired upon the crowd. Cannonballs sailed through the air, smashing into men and spreading their guts across the field. Blood sprayed in Reed's face, but he did not miss a beat. He kept firing. The boom from the muskets and cannons was so loud his ears buzzed and he was momentarily deaf. He felt as if his eardrums were enveloped in cotton. The lack of hearing unsettled him but provided him emotional and mental distance so he could keep firing. If he couldn't hear the screams of terror and pain from both Confederate and Union soldiers, he could continue to pull that trigger.

Eight rebels dropped to the ground in one fell swoop as dozens of metal shards pummeled them. The shot was fired from a cannon only twenty feet away from Reed. Metal balls and slugs filling a canvas bag fired into the crowd, spreading shrapnel in a wide arc to do maximum damage.

"Grapeshot! They're firing grapeshot!" A Confederate shouted. More cannons loaded with the deadly bags fired upon the screaming throng. Reed stopped firing momentarily to watch as a man turned his back in a feeble attempt to run away when a volley of slugs peppered his jacket. In seconds gray turned to crimson as he fell face-down in a heap amid the bluebonnets.

"Fall back! Fall back!" The Confederate commander yelled. As quickly as they had emerged from the woods, the men retreated into the shadows from whence they came, leaving a litter of bodies on the ground. The call of crickets and songbirds accompanied the gloom as the sun rose in the sky. Captain Ellison rode his filly amid the regiment with an intent look upon his face as he prepared for a second attack that never came. One by one, the Union soldiers stood in the safety of their solitude. Reed's heart trip-hammered in his chest. Pain on the side of his head brought him back to the present and out of his trance-like state while firing on rebels. He touched his hand to his head. It felt sticky with blood. Another inch to the right and he would have been lying dead on the ground next to Rogers.

Reed held his musket to his side as he assessed the carnage. The stink of gore filled his nostrils and he fought off another bout of nausea. Swallowing hard, he looked around the field as he swatted from his face flies and gnats attracted to the blood. Infantrymen pillaged the dead. Reed approached a rebel felled by grapeshot. The shot had thrown the man onto his back, eyes half open, his legs and arms splayed about him like a discarded doll. Reed held his musket in one hand while he rummaged through the dead man's pockets. He smiled as he snagged a few coins and a pewter flask. Oh, what he would do for a dram of whiskey right now. He shook the flask and determined there was enough liquid in it for one or two good swigs.

When the soldier opened his eyes, it startled Reed so he lost his balance and tipped over onto one knee. The man's face contorted in terror. He whimpered and whined in a high-pitched voice. Raising himself up on one elbow, he pushed his body backwards away from Reed. Reed pulled out his pistol to shoot him when he realized the man wasn't looking at him. He stared over Reed's shoulder. Reed glanced to his left.

A phantom wearing a tri-cornered hat and heavy blue overcoat stared down at the soldier. This revenant's face, devoid of features, was as smooth as river stone. The blank visage before Reed scared him so much he screamed. The man screamed in turn, which caused the creature to lean closer to him. Reed fell backwards onto his ass as the soldier grabbed a pistol from beneath him and aimed a shaking hand in the direction of the ghastly being. Reed aimed at the soldier and shot him point blank in the face. He collapsed, dead.

The phantom rose without acknowledging Reed and moved towards the woods. Dozens of blue-clad soldiers moved silently through the clearing to disappear into the trees amid a glowing mist. Union soldiers ran towards the camp in an effort to avoid the wraiths. Reed stood. A chill overcame him, and his teeth chattered.

He glanced up and froze when he saw that familiar bearded specter hovering in the trees ahead. The ghost of his grandfather pointed to a spot behind Reed, who turned in time to see a soldier brandishing a pistol. He screamed and jabbed his bayonet into the man's chest, but the sword caught on bone. He leaned into the musket with all his weight and drove the blade home, but not before the soldier got off a shot that struck Reed in the upper left arm. Bone snapped like a tree branch. He howled in agony, released his musket, and fell to the ground. He rolled away from the dead soldier and looked towards the woods where the phantoms had walked, but he saw no one. Writhing in pain, his vision blurred until he passed out.

Moments later, he awakened in the field. His shredded arm throbbed. The pain threatened to cause him to pass out again. Soldiers moved around him, but he heard no sound. No chattering of night peepers. No cannons. Nothing. A soldier knelt next to him. He turned his head to look the man in the face.

He stared into the solemn face of his grandfather, who seemed to guard over him until he felt two hands grasp his feet by the ankles and drag him across the field. He held his arm against his chest, but the pain only intensified. In moments, he was lifted onto a stretcher and moved through the field.

A man appeared next to him. "Soldier, you're injured. We're taking you to the field hospital."

He thought of his grandfather and turned to the medic. "Did we beat them?"

"The rebels? They fled like rats. I know you saw what I saw."

"Yes. Phantoms."

The medic's face took on a stony expression. "Let's not talk out loud about that. You're off to the hospital. Try to get some rest. You won this battle. It's off to Beaufort in a few hours, but I have a strong notion you're going home."

Reed smiled and fingered his ring box with his good hand. He imagined the face of his sweet Sarah before passing out. He's coming home to her at last. All thanks to his grandfather and the phantoms who he knew would be proud.

ms_lara_croft writes horror with the pen name E. A. Black. Her stories have appeared in numerous anthologies which may be found at http://amazon.com/author/eablack.

Meat. The Parents.
Mark Hooson

Hollywood told us a zombie outbreak would end in one of two ways. Either the humans would starve the zombies out over time, or the humans would be completely annihilated. End of days stuff.

But when it happened for real, the outcome was far more predictable. Boring, even. Science did its thing and developed medicines. Then Big Pharma and the health insurance industry did their thing and monetised the crap out of them.

They couldn't cure the Romero Virus, but the drugs they invented kept the symptoms in check for the most part. On Mortisol®, your levels of the virus are so low that it's no longer transmissible.

That's a fancy way of saying it stops you from wanting to chow down on the your friends' and loved ones' innards—which is great, as long as you remember to take your Mortisol® every 24 hours.

It's not so great when you're three hours into a six-hour drive to meet your boyfriend's parents for the first time and realise you forgot your meds back home.

I feel Aaron's eyes on me, watching with concern as I bite my nails. He wants to ask me if 'I'm sure that's a good idea', but he doesn't want to be insensitive. I internalise his non-warning and return my hands to 10 and 2.

By the time we reach Aaron's home town, I'm wound pretty tight. Two days off my meds shouldn't be too noticeable, I remember being told, but the thought fills me with dread. How much research could have possibly been done in the time between the virus' outbreak and the drug hitting the market?

I could visit a specialist clinic up here to see if I can get a prescription, but the outbreak was less widespread in the north and so the clinics are fewer and farther between—besides, I'd probably be back home again anyway before they processed me.

So I decide to cross my fingers, which is harder to do these days, and hope I can get through the weekend without any obvious decomposition, blood lust or social faux pas.

We follow a long dirt track from the highway until the trees clear to reveal a beautiful, modern log cabin. Mr and Mrs Anderssen's place appears to have been untouched by the recent unpleasantness with the undead. It would have been a great place to hide out.

I don't feel it anymore, but it must be cold because the Andersenns are stood by their front door, pink-faced in heavy coats, scarves and hats. They grin and wave as I pull the Prius into the parking spot they gesture towards.

"Before we go in,", I say, turning to Aaron, "I need to let you know that I've forgotten to bring my Mortisol® with me.". He fumbles around for a supportive response before assuring me it'll be in our bags.

It isn't.

His parents and I exchange awkward pleasantries in the doorway and head inside. His dad's hand brushes mine as he takes my luggage.

"Cold, ain't it, Emmy?" he asks. I am not sure if he means my skin or the night.

We're welcomed in with hot cocoa and photographs of Aaron as a child. "Aaron was so cute." Says his mother, Judith. "Couldn't you just eat him up?"

Judith compliments my hair. It's red like hers, although no quite so... ... big. I joke that we could be mistaken for sisters and she seems genuinely flattered, if a little oblivious to the obvious brown nosing.

As we sit to sip our drinks, the family cat, Rusty, jumps onto the coffee table between us -puffing up his ginger coat while hissing and 'mrowing' in my direction.

Everyone in the room except Rusty, whose narrowed eyes are trained on me, looks to Aaron. He's obviously told them about my condition, but he hasn't told me that he has told them. It's awkward.

Judith jumps to her feet and bundles the cat off into another room. I feel like I'm just as flushed with embarrassment as she is, but it doesn't show in my complexion. A small benefit of being a Romero Virus survivor.

Dinner won't be ready for a few hours, so Aaron and I head to a guest room to freshen up. I go through the motions of checking our bags for my missing meds and Aaron reassures me I'll be okay for a couple of days.

He's in and out of the room catching up with his parents, fetching home comforts and so forth as I unpack our cases. I don't know what we're having for dinner, but every time the door swings to and fro I can smell raw meat. Poultry of some kind. Fresh.

The evening goes off without a hitch and I feel like I've made a good first impression. After a few drinks I even start to relax a little, almost forgetting the weekend of withdrawal I'd been imagining earlier.

Rusty still isn't sure about me, and sticks to his basket in the corner of the
living room as he continues to give me the stink eye.

We get to bed around midnight and I ask Aaron if he told his parents about my health. I try not it make it sound like an accusation. He says he didn't, which I'd be inclined to believe if it weren't for that awkward moment earlier this evening. I don't have the energy for the fight it'll cause if I press him on it, so I prepare for bed and fall to sleep within minutes.

Despite the dark, heavy drapes, I'm woken by the sun's searing light the next morning. It leaks through the spaces between the fabric and pounds the back of my retinas. I feel the throb from behind my eyes to back of my skull. Is the sun brighter in this part of the country, or did I just drink too much last night?

It's late morning, which totally throws me since I'm an early riser. Back home I'd have already showered, eaten and taken my meds by now. It's important not to take Mortisol® on an empty stomach, and at the same time each day.

Embarrassed by my lateness, I lunge out of bed, scrape my hair up into a ponytail and quickly wash my face in the en-suite basin before applying a light layer of foundation to give me some colour.

Breakfast is finishing up, but Aaron's on his usual second or third bowl of children's cereal. I hop onto the stool next to him and

Judith is already coming at me with a cup of coffee that reads 'Rather a redhead than a dead head.'.

Cute.

She stops short of the counter with a quizzical look on her face. Then, she approaches and lifts her hand to my face while maintaining her expression and focus on the top of my head. She reaches over and pulls something from the top of my head. An entire fingernail. My entire fingernail.

It must have come loose when I fixed my hair. Crap.

"The way Aaron described you,", says Judith, "I wouldn't have expected you to wear false nails. Too fussy." I look down at the bare fingertip of my left index finger, hidden beneath the counter top. There is a mushy, oozing patch of flesh where the nail once lay.

Flustered, I reply: "I wanted to make a good first impression, I guess."

She starts telling me that she doesn't feel fully dressed leaving the house without wearing at least some make up, but I'm tuning her out as I fixate on my finger. It has been 27 hours and 18 minutes since my last dose of Mortisol®. It will be somewhere in the region of 36 more before my next.

The plan for today is take a walk along the beach to the next town over. Aaron says the howling wind and spray from the frigid sea is good for 'blowing off the cobwebs.'. I hate to admit it, but 15 minutes into the hike and I have to agree. It's hard to dwell on anxious feelings when your breath is being taken away by gusts of salty bluster.

We're headed toward a local cafe whose sandwiches you absolutely have to try, according to Aaron's dad.

A flock of seagulls gathers and begins to follow me—squawking aggressively and taking it in turns to dive bomb my hat. They pursue me all the way to our destination and line up on the window sill outside to monitor me as we eat.

Flea-ridden jerks.

I ignore them and enjoy a pretty decent sandwich. Not nearly as good as Tom said, but I don't want to seem snobby so I tell him he was right.

The crusty bread scratches the roof of my mouth and gums,

while the gaps between my molars capture the crumbs. I should floss more.

I try to fish out some of the detritus as discreetly as I can, sliding one of my remaining fingernails between the porcelain. Then, suddenly, I'm flushed with panic as I feel a wiggle, then a kind of click followed by a disconnect, then the unsettling sensation of a disembodied tooth sitting on the back of my tongue.

I'm sitting here, lips pursed, like a dog hiding something in its mouth that it knows it isn't allowed to have. First nails, now teeth. Fuck.

I excuse myself as best I can without opening my mouth, which results in a strange half-curtsy coupled with a squeak, and I rush to the bathroom. I spit the tooth into a hand basin and check my gum line where it once lived.

There's a dark red hole in its place, so I rinse my mouth with water from the faucet, swilling the bloody pink solution around my mouth before spitting it into the plughole.

My reflection shows me where once there was a tooth, there is now rot. It extends to the inside of my cheek and down the back of my throat. It's already happening—the decomposition.

Its putrid smell snaps me out of my panic and seems to physically strike my gag reflex, sending blood, bile and semi-digested sandwich rushing up past my oesophagus.

Chunks of bread and vegetables clog the plughole, leaving the basin filled with a greasy red fluid that shimmers under the bathroom's fluorescent lights.

Disorientated, I stumble out into the cafe. I need air. Need to be outside.

Tunnel vision prevents me from seeing Aaron's parents' reactions. The little bell attached to the cafe door emits a thunderous clang as I swing it open and lurch out onto the sidewalk.

With the bell still reverberating in my brain, I'm set upon by the flock of seagulls. They bat me with their wings and grab at my hair, cackling as it comes right out of my scalp in their talons.

I'm conscious that I'm on the ground. Someone covers me with a jacket. Then I am unconscious.

Wake up in hospital bed. Not feel good. Try to move arms

but not able to.

    Something restraining me. Aaron at bedside look worried.

    Judith and Aaron-father enter room. Long-time no Mortisol® now. Not feel word I forget. Not feel… . . . unbad.

    Aaron speak with parents but not hear words. Muffle. Judiss approach bed and sit beside. Close. Not hear Judiss' words. Loud muffle.

    Judiss reach for Emmy face.

    Attack?

    Emmy fight back. Bite hand. Clamp jaw down hard.

    Hand crunch. Chewy outside, hard inside. Stringy and tough. Wedding ring scrape mouth ceiling.

    Judiss scream. Muffle scream. Room fill with white coat. More muffle. More scream. Need out. Pull hard on restraint until break. Almost free. Hands all over. Try put Emmy down.

    Fight.

    Bite.

    Need Mortisol®.

    Aaron-father understand. I tell. Lunge at Aaron-father to tell. Speak in ear. Everyone try stop Emmy, but almost make it to ear. Neck too long. Make short. Bite. Wet red everywhere.

    Wet red muffle.

    Gurgle.

    Aaron-father understand. Think he like Emmy. Make impression good.

    Hope Aaron happy.

    So cute. Eat him up.

Mark Hooson is an aspiring fiction writer from Wales, UK. He can be found on Twitter as @hoostweets.

My Two Dads
Dwayne Josephson

    My mom has been acting strangely. She was always a bit strange, but my dad is the one who pointed it out. They are both getting up in years, and of course you worry about them.
    I decided to give her a call and check on her. She is chatting away like normal, when she asks me the oddest question.
    "Have you seen your other father?"
    Now, my Dad is technically my step-Dad, so for a moment I thought she was talking about my biological father, but I've never met him. The question didn't make sense. I ask her what she means.
    "You know, your other father. Dad goes to work and leaves me here, and then the other David (my father's name) comes and takes me out to do things, but I don't trust him. Sometimes he takes me places I don't want to go!"
    I ask her what kind of places?
    "All kinds of places, but the bad doctors, and dentists, and people who are mean to me."
    My mom doesn't like doctors.
    My father has retired recently. Obviously there is something wrong. My dad has worked hard enough for two people his entire life, but he doesn't have a clone to my knowledge.
    "Nobody believes me about the other David. Betty doesn't believe me, either."
    I tell my mother there is only one David. He's my dad, he doesn't have a twin brother. I want to comfort her, and make everything all right. I can see the "two Davids" problem is troubling her. It damn sure is bothering me.
    Later I text my dad about it.
    "Is she going on about that again? That's part of the reason we had to take her to the hospital. She had a urinary tract infection recently, and we had to take her in."
    I didn't know. This is very upsetting to me. My mom hasn't

always had the best mental health. She's always been full of anxiety, but this kind of delusion is an entirely new level. My dad doesn't seem too concerned about it, but I know him. He's the strong, silent type.

"Rub some dirt on in and carry on son!"

That's what he'd say, back in the day. I go back and visit with my mom for a while. My dad comes in two and she acts like she's fine. I hope she puts the "2 Dads" thing out of her mind. I tell my dad you have to tell her psychiatrist about this delusion, the next time you go. He agrees.

A few days later, another call from my mom.

"The other David was here again. He brought me chicken I didn't like!"

What?

"I asked for fried chicken, and he's brought back grilled instead! I think he might have done something with your father, because he's not here right now."

Put dad on the phone.

"He's not here! I told you it's the other David! I'm in the bedroom so he can't hear us. I think he's doing something to the kitchen."

He's probably doing the dishes I tell her. Leave the room and put whichever father is in the house on the damn phone, mom! Only family can get on your nerves, while you're deeply concerned for their mental health!

"No. I don't want him to know. It will make him suspicious of me. Why don't you believe me? I'm telling you he's not your father, he's some other man who looks exactly like him, but he's not the same person!"

We loved *Invasion of the Body Snatchers* growing up. This sounds just like that. I am heartsick, and quietly text my dad to let him know what's going on, while I'm still talking to her on the land line.

"Thanks for letting me know. I am doing dishes. She hardly touched her dinner. I think she's mad because she's on that medical diet for her diabetes."

We go on texting, while my mom switches gears and starts to reminisce. She could always switch topics quickly in the past, and for the moment she's rambling on about her sisters, and her great grand-daughters curly red hair. She switches to talking about all the people she loved who've passed away. I listen a while longer, hearing her struggle for names at times, but mostly recalling all sorts of family triumph and drama over the years. I tell her I love her, and we say "Night, night."

I'm off the phone on onto google. It's not long before I discover people with Alzheimer's or dementia can have these kind of delusions. God, that's terrifying, and I'm afraid for my mom. I pour myself a glass of my good whiskey to sit and ruminate on things.

I put on the classic *Star Trek* where Kirk is duplicated on the transporter pad. There is solace in its familiarity, and I follow it up with the *Twilight Zone* in the subway with the dopplegangers. That one was always frightening to my when I was younger. The lead actress with the jaunty hat reminds me of my mom. I'm remembering watching these with my mom and dad, and I'm tearing up now.

I shouldn't have drank at all. One jigger of whisky, and I'm expressing my feelings on the outside. That's not the way the men in my family do things, but I have always been a bit of a maverick. I go outside with my dog, and stare into the sky at the wonder of it all. It's still dark where I live in the sticks, so the sky is magnificent, and somehow seeing how small I am in the grand scheme of everything makes me feel better.

I doom scroll my phone for a while, and head to bed. My dog sneaking up and lying at my feet. I'm grateful for her support, and fall asleep hoping for another day tomorrow. Once you're pushing 50, every day is precious, and every night is just a little scary. There was some peaceful sleep, and then the nightmares came.

It was very odd. There was another version of my mom, not my mad, as a nurse. She was younger and thinner than reality, and wearing blue scrubs. That's a fashion choice mom would have never made! Impostor! And then she screamed that body snatchers scream!! The one that says "kill the other!"

I'm awake now. My loyal dog at my feet sleeping quietly. I get up and walk around for a while.

Evil mom is not an image you want in your head. I check the phone and it's 4:40AM. I wander to the bathroom, and then back to the bed. There's a fitful attempt to rub one out, so I can get back to fucking sleep, but it's no use. I'm fucking awake now.

I rise from my grave!

That's Sega. Altered Beast to be exact. A fine game I played a lot of when I was young. You should check it out. I don't know the backstory, it could be as rich as Star Wars, but I tell you it ate tons of quarters from me in the early 90's. Now it's a MAME emulator full of fun. But not now. It's cool for Florida and just before sunrise.

We go for a walk. Not too far from my house is a flying eagle preserve. Ok, an eagle preserve, but they do fly, and that's the name of the place, and it's early . . . so fuck off. We walk down in the gloaming to the park.

It's so early that deer are outside and playing! I love it when we get to see them. I let my dog off her leash and she off and running and having a blast! Fear me! I can see it in her eyes, and she bounds within 20 feet of deer twice her size. Fearless, she is! Like baby Yoda. We do our 3 miles for health, and start back to the house now that the sun is up, and the Florida heat begins to punish us for being outside.

My cell phone rings. It's my mom.

"I got rid of the other David."

Hi, mom! What's going on? I didn't hear you that well? Everything ok?

"I got rid of the other David. Have you seen your father?"

What do you mean? This is not ok for me.

"The other David is taken care of, but I can't find your father anywhere! Have you seen him?"

My dad isn't responding to my furious texts, and I resort to calling him on voice.

My mom answers his phone sweetly.

"Hello?"

Mom! Put David on the phone! I yell into the receiver! Put my dad on the fucking phone!

"I will when he gets here! This is the other David's phone. How did you know his number?"

I called dad's number mom! You're talking to me on his phone! What is going on! What did you do?

"I shot him! He's not your father! He's been entirely too mean to me! I knew the combination of the gun safe. It's our wedding date. We were married 52 years this July! David will be so happy I got rid of him! The imposter! Now help me find your dad, I don't know where he's gotten too?"

I put my mom on hold and call 911.

"He's going to be so proud of me for taking care of this myself. He always says he takes care of me. He didn't know about this imposter, and neither did you. None of you would believe me. But now you'll see, now you'll see the other David! Nothing is wrong with me! Fried chicken is so tasty! Can you and dad bring me some when you find him? The other David won't let me have it anymore!"

I put the phone down to cry.

I'd call my dad and ask what to do, but he's not going to answer me.

Dwayne Josephson is longtime Farker AtomPeepers, teacher, and writer. This story is dedicated to my Mom and Dad.

Nightrunner
Steve Ball

(With thanks to Bob Medeiros for a perfect thought.)

As day departs in red washed sky, I rise from where within I lie.
Safe now from sun's alluring light, to greet the cooling cloaks of Night,
Which always seem to brace my *soul*, and *sometimes* seem to make me whole . . .
At least until I've once more killed, for *emptiness* unfilled . . .

I thus meet Night with sour smile, and pause myself to think awhile,
Of what's been gained but also lost, from when my Rubicon was crossed:
Command by night, and hide by day, where *all* are foe, or tool, or prey,
With few to know and none to trust, and childhood dreams resemble dust.

I find it *hard*, at times, *to* dream, and often think that it *does* seem
That urgency of Human death . . . gives mortal mind its bated breath,
And though the quick uncoiling years can drive the Human soul to tears . . .
. . . Of all my long-lost mortal traits, this is the one whose loss most grates.

Of how to live and when to die: for some *these* rules do not apply;
I have my own which I must heed, wherein I hunt . . . and *you* must bleed.
The rules are very hard and clear: I *drink* the life that you hold dear,
And should I stop before your death, you'll be my thrall 'till final breath.

* * *

When Sun descends on blood red hills and Human flags are furled,
The cloak of darkness comes at last and Nightrun claim the world;
Until this Undead flesh feels fear at dawning's early light,
Of shining orb's keen killing rays, veiled always from the sight.

* * *

I now depart through well-worn door to greet again the nightly horror
Of who has luck and who is prey; a choice that I can *seldom* say
Is all a circumstance of dice, where I won't *have* to pay a price
In fresh remorse and rash desire to face that all-forgiving fire.

For how to pick who's time I take? The claim of *gods* is hard to make.
And which is worse, of choice or chance? Wherein my head the "*what-ifs*" dance;
For each has worth, or so we're taught, and wrong to kill without a thought.
... So if I take the task to choose, what, then, the gauge that I must use?

If judgment thusly outweighs fate, then I'll embrace what I most hate
Of Human brute, or beast, or fiend ... or of other hope demeaned.
I'll stalk the prey and make it mine, and quaff its life like common wine;
So *thus,* I'll take my measured grue, my nightly meal ... (perhaps it's *you*).

I therefore run like razored wind, and seek out those who have most sinned;
Then - finding mind of cherished prey, fling all the doubt and guilt away;
The Hunt becomes a lesser ill, when *lesser* Men become the Kill;
Uncertainties become absurd ... when Nightrun cull the Human herd.

* * *

When red-rinsed sea consumes the Sun the Nightrun claim their right,
The day's last judgment comes around when Vampires rule the night;
For each there is a purpose plain, for each there is a plan,
And Nightrun serve to mitigate the fatal flaws of Man.

* * *

I close to kill with practiced speed, but slow my strike, your fear to heed.
My kiss consumes your very soul, my self absorbs your every goal;
I feed on lives and loves and fears, I drain your smiles and drink your tears;
Unless I have your life to steal, I have no *form*, I am not *real*.

My vampirism, thus defined, is *kinder* than the Human kind,
Where self-serve words of sacrifice are claimed the keys to paradise;
And treachery and death and hate become the chosen tools of State;
And Bottom Line exceeds the scope of faithful worker's final hope.

... Or even, dare I say, the pain that makes your lover go insane,
From bloodied hand or harsher word ... or confessional unheard;
Of partnership where trust has died, where duty's pilfered all the pride;
... For Human mores and *loving* heart, of all *these* things, I have no part.

Yet - times there are that I recall ... and thirst *exceeds* the physical,
Then fancy soars on flimsy wings, for addict dreams of *mortal* things,
Where turned and tilled immortal clay will walk in bright green fields of day
And feel the warmth of *gentle* sun ... and in the Night no longer run

* * *

When sunrise sears the shrouds away and Nightrun go to nest,
The world returns to barter, war, and other Human quest;
But we always walk among you, well hidden by your pride,
Ignored, the Lord of Life and Death: the Vampire at your side.

* * *

As dawn ignites the night below, I drift to where within I go
To shun the sun's vast burning might, 'till next I greet the cloaks of Night,
Which always seem to brace my soul, and *sometimes* seem to make me whole . . .
At least until I've once more killed, for emptiness . . . never filled . . .

Steve Ball is a retired accountant living in Orange County, CA. His interests are science fiction and vampiric horror. He is currently writing a lighthearted science fiction novel about alien invasion, <u>The Voyage of the New Beginning</u>.

The Triumph of the Claw
Brian Bander

     This morning when I woke I found a severed human hand at the foot of my bed. I buried it in the back yard with the other parts. I keep a shovel at the ready, these days. The yard has become a field of horrors.

     The house is sealed as best I can. The windows are nailed shut and the doors are boarded over. Yet from where I sit, overlooking the town and listening to the wind rising, I still feel as if I know how this will end. Maybe everything has its ending contained within its beginning. If that's the case, then none of us has ever had a chance at all.

     The beginning, then. I will start there.

     The tragedy of justice is that even after you are found to be innocent of a crime, you are still judged by everyone who knows your past. Anyone who will ever search my name on the internet will find a horror story. Even worse, my name was front-page news for twelve violent days, eight years ago; other terrors have since pushed my story out of the spotlight, but the hostile glare of the court of public opinion will never set me free.

     I have always been a silent person. I have found that it's easier to say nothing and be thought a fool rather than open my mouth and prove it. I am solitary by nature, as well; most times I have no interest in companionship of any kind, preferring my books and my studies. It was for the latter reason that I could give no alibi for myself on the nights of the first three killings in the small town where I was born. It was because of the former that I had no better defense when accused than that of silence and confusion.

     When they found the fourth victim of the killer that the news media chose to name 'The Surgeon' I had the best alibi imaginable: I was in jail. Several hundred of the good citizens of the town were my witnesses, holding furious vigil outside while the nervous deputies tried to keep the peace. In dark moods, I sometimes wonder what they would have done, had they managed to storm the building and lynch me only hours before it was proven that I could not possibly be the killer that walked the streets after nightfall. I wonder what they would have said to themselves, if they would have even been able to admit they had murdered me as surely as The Surgeon was murdering them.

But then, it was not possible that I could have been guilty in the first place. No one in their right mind could have thought a skinny kid like me would have been strong enough to overpower Jessie Thibault, a forty-year-old construction foreman, and leave his dead body with broken limbs and excised flesh and an expression of such pure terror that the superintendent who found him claimed nightmares for weeks. Perhaps I had the strength to lift the second victim, a sixteen-year-old transient, to the spire of the church and harvest her internal organs; but no sane person would have believed I could have killed the third victim, a gun collector and survivalist. When the sounds of violence drew notice the police had found him torn and broken, and . . . reduced in the most terrible of ways.

No, it could not have been me. A loner, and a bookworm, and . . . someone with a past, does not a killer make.

Whatever they might have thought, I will never know. I moved out of the town of my birth, haunted by whispers and dark looks and threatening letters nailed to my door in the night.

My aunt, my last living relative, was broken by the scandal and passed on within the year. With what inheritance she left me, I bought the shunned Drake House in the mountains overlooking the small town. The house was said to be haunted. I didn't care; at the time, I feared the living more than the dead.

It was a ninety-day scandal, of course, but one that spread little beyond the small community in the mountains. *Of course a murderer would want to live in the old Drake House,* people said. The fact that I was never even charged with murder and was later exonerated by events never came into anyone's mind, save as a preface for *well, this just proves he got away with it then, doesn't it?*

The court of public opinion is not one in which you can file an appeal.

If the fear of a haunted house kept the simple away, so much the better. I wanted nothing more than solitude. At the time, less than two years had passed since the night of the potential lynch mob and my murderous salvation; you'll forgive me if I was still shy of the public eye.

I had managed to make a small income writing horror fiction under a pseudonym, and in full disclosure I had hoped the atmosphere of the place would lend electricity to my writing. This was a secondary thought, but one I had nonetheless. I almost hoped to find blood dripping down the walls and glass jars filled with . . . but never mind. I took possession of the house, real estate agent warnings be damned.

The first order of business upon moving in, then, was to research the Drake House itself.

The Drake House sits on a small spur of natural rock in the Cascades, sheltered on all sides by thick forests of evergreens, and commands a majestic view of the small community in the valley below. Even on cold and foggy nights—which are most nights here in this corner of the Pacific Northwest—you can see the lights from the post office and the small grocery store from my living room window. I suppose some in the town below might say it lurks in the hills. It's only called the Drake House by locals; on official documents it's simply a number on a street that has no other residents. It's shingled and roofed in cedar shake that blends in with the trees all around; when I first saw it, the building was nearly invisible until it coalesced out of the shadows like a malign illusion.

It's named after Edmund Drake, the original builder, who in the nineteen twenties had almost single-handedly created the town below by transforming a tiny logging camp into an artist's retreat. A writer and painter of the macabre, not to mention an occultist and hypnotist according to some sources, he held enough influence in the art world that for a dozen years creative minds followed him to this secluded place in the mountains. Several other houses were built at the same time by the rich and famous; reading the list of names of the people in Drake's orbit is like reading a who's who of the brightest lights of the Great Depression.

Those bright lights of course fled in the winter of nineteen thirty-four when Edmund Drake was found hanged dead in the front room of the second story of the house, in the closed office in which he worked and into which he allowed not even his closest confidants. Some of his paintings from this period right before his death are masterworks of shadow and light; his most famous, *The Triumph of the Claw* dates from this time and features little more than liquid black and gray in oil on canvas, in which a viewer might see shadows hiding a lurking fear that scuttles and chitters, just out of sight.

I have a print of this over my desk, in the room where he is said to have hanged himself. Looking at it now, knowing what we now know, it holds even more sinister connotations. Drake was found swinging from a rope in a studio that was splashed with paint and ringed with glass jars filled with preserved human body parts; hands, intestines, brains.

Where had they come from? There were no murders reported in the area at the time, but in the depression years a man with means and power would have been the equivalent of a medieval lord. From this perch over the town, Drake could have paid to cover up any number of his sins. Perhaps that's the ultimate significance of *The Triumph of the Claw*: the undulating grey and black and hints of a horror barely concealed were nothing more than a view into his own soul.

I am particularly interested in the contents of a soul—but more on that later.

The similarities between the evidence of crimes that may have been committed by Drake, and the actuality of the crimes committed by the unknown murderer who surgically removed Jessie Thibault's lungs from his shattered body, are superficial. In one case, a killer with no identifiable victim; in the other, victims missing body parts that were never found. For what it's worth, as a writer of the fantastic I immediately leapt to an assumption and was disappointed; there were no sets of lungs in the collection of horrors that Drake had amassed. It was kind of a shame. A time travelling organ collector would have made for a great story. I could have made a killing selling it.

Figuratively speaking, of course.

Even now, no one had conclusively identified the sixteen-year-old transient who was the second victim of my era, who had given her kidneys and stomach and the skin of her breasts to her attacker. The missing parts were never located, but the precision with which they had been taken from her dissected corpse gave her killer a name for the nightly news, at least; the terrified residents of the town found out that night that The Surgeon had struck again.

This was the killer's mark, as they say. In the years since, I have had time to study what details have made it into the public record. All four victims had been savagely attacked, brutally murdered and destroyed in ways which would have left no marks on the body parts The Surgeon collected. Medical examiners from the FBI could point to lack of bruises on the incision marks showing that these most intimate of all possible thefts had occurred bare minutes after death.

The third victim, Theodore Jorgenson, had been found—or at least, what was left of him—on several of the upper levels of an apartment building under construction. Details were maddeningly vague; all I could find was a transcript of an anonymous company agent, almost certainly site superintendent William Jenner, who described the scene of the crime in a post-traumatic stress disability hearing. The head of the deceased had been placed at the center of a spiderweb of intestines and internal organs, strung about the top three floors of the building site. One severed hand was found embedded in a particle board wall. The other was never found.

For what it's worth, Jenner's disability claim was approved, with few details making it into the public record.   Some sources suggest the judge had been bribed to silence; reading the text, I suspect he simply did not want to hear any more. What Jenner had to say was insane. Ultimately, it did him little good; a heart attack carried him off only two months later. By several accounts, he was already far gone by that point, twitchy and easily startled and flinching at shadows. The most that could be pieced together from his nurses was that he feared The Surgeon had come for him.

The Surgeon never did, however; Jenner went to his grave

with his body intact.

    The fourth victim of my era, the one whose death perhaps saved my life, was a prostitute and methamphetamine addict who had been harvested of the long bones of her arms and legs perhaps some minutes after her death. Like the other missing body parts, these were never found. Several internal organs had also been removed, but according to the police report these were located during a search of the abandoned house her screams had been last heard in. The report doesn't say much, but the fact that the organs—heart, liver, and a section of the large intestine—were not recovered until a day after the body had been removed by the coroner suggests that the scene was similar to what Jenner had stumbled into. According to what I could read of the public record, they had called in a specialist team who were skilled in cleaning up the worst imaginable crime or death scenes; from reading their website, they claim to do far more than simply mop up the blood and pick up the stray pieces.

    According to the human resources files, one of the crew members involved in the cleaning quit his job and was admitted to Lighthome Addiction Counselling, only a bare week later. Perhaps what he had seen had scared him straight. From reading the records, it's hard to guess what it might have been; no one involved in the cleanup was willing to make any comment. No records exist to tell the tale.

    When I moved into the Drake House the walls were bare. The previous occupants, if there had been any in the years before, had not decorated the paneled walls of the two upstairs floors. The basement was simply poured concrete; a heavy box built of stone.

    There were no doors down there. I know that for a fact. It was a sterile concrete chamber of shadows that held nothing but an echo of malice.

    There were no doors down there when I moved in. I know that for a fact.

    Edmund Drake's works are commonly described by art experts as having four distinct eras: his first, early works, are of limited skill and are reaching, but are of mundane topics: still life drawings, landscapes or portraits. His second era, which was capped by his masterwork *The Physical Man Reduced* is called his macabre period: it began as almost an anatomical study, with lifelike drawings of human beings or individual body parts, swiftly descending into mutated darkness and horror. His third era was his Portal Period: he was fascinated by doors. Gone were the body parts and slithering darkness; in their place were arched Corinthian doors, portcullises in stone walls, ominous and unsettling gates set into brick walls to keep out what creatures the mind refused to imagine. Almost photorealistic, they captured impossible shadows and structure and the sense that something might exist that should not.

    I did not recognize the poured concrete walls of the basement in his paintings of that era when I first saw them. They were of the basement of the Drake house, but they showed a door that I did not see when I first moved in.

    No, scratch that; the door in the basement did not exist when I first moved in, even though the Drake painting *The Bloody Summons* showed one there. It was not there at first. I think I understand that now.

    Experts disagree on the existence of Drake's fourth era: light and shadow, which produced *The Triumph of the Claw.* Some say it is a continuation of his Portal period, or a re-examining of his Macabre period. In all three, the same theme of truth being hidden by the physical world can be seen. *The Physical Man Reduced* showed the truth of a man without skin; *The Iron Ward*, an almost photorealistic rendering of a heavy steel door set into a rotting wood wall, showed the viewer a truth denied. His works of light and shadow in that sense might refer to the same theme: something just out of sight, but hidden by nothing other than the observer's inability to see it. Paintings from this period were his most lucrative, perhaps due to his growing notoriety; questions were asked even then how he could render the internal organs of a human body with such precise detail.

    Were there in fact models who posed for him, postmortem? My research shows no investigations of any kind that were launched while he was alive. No one appears to have tried to find out if he had acquired the bodies of the recently dead for his art. Perhaps he could have purchased cadavers from a school of medicine; or perhaps, like one of the Nineteenth century resurrection men, he . . . found them on his own. But what spoiled grave could have given him an anatomical reference like the scaled, half-human hybrid, run through with tumors, which he painted in *Cousin Elise?*

Notoriety was one thing, but success was another. No art collector would display *Cousin Elise* in their drawing room, and the shifting, bleeding organic mass of *Palm Sunday* was an affront that was never, according to art historians, purchased by any collector. It was found in the basement of the Drake House by the investigators and reportedly donated to the art school at Squolnamic University, where it probably sits in a dark storeroom somewhere. Works from his portal period, however, were fast sales; they captured the occult sense of wrongness that was his signature style without offending tastes. Perhaps his fourth era, the shadowed scapes, was a way to further capitalize on this; that's the position argued in William Forster's definitive history of Edmund Drake.

Or perhaps the door that Drake tried for so long to paint closed had opened, and perhaps he had looked through it.

When I first moved into the Drake house, I kept as low of a profile as I could. In the years since construction it had had electrical service and even internet service installed, and for two months I was able to avoid going out other than to the small grocery for supplies or to the post office next to it to collect my mail. Perhaps it's an oddity of the present; I could research Edmund Drake's history over the internet, but the mail service wouldn't deliver this far up the road. I don't know if that's official policy, locals shunning the building, or the fact that the mailman was a sixty-year-old veteran who walked with a cane. Either way, I chose not to draw attention to myself by asking.

Low profile or not, I am still watched; I'm the outsider with the terrible past. Of course people will whisper and talk. I can often feel eyes on me when I am in town. My mail is sometimes loose, as if someone has steamed opened the envelopes and resealed them. If so, I can't imagine what anyone would find interesting in my utility bills and research materials.

Not everything, sadly, can be found on the internet. Forster's history of Edmund Drake went out of print years ago, and was never converted to any downloadable format. I found a copy for sale on a rare books website and ordered it; that book turned out to contain references to other works, which I tracked down as well. It's like something I read somewhere: If you find a footnote, make sure to step on it before it can breed. I did no such thing and paid the price by ultimately amassing a small library of reference works on Drake and others in his artistic circle, all delivered by physical mail to the post office for me to pick up on the days I ventured down for my groceries.

I had seen the old man in the grocery and the post office before and paid him no mind, other than a cursory glance. For whatever reason, Robert Browning's words came to mind: *My first thought was, he lied in every word* and I felt ashamed. The fact that others may assume me to be a murderer does not mean I can think the worst of everyone I see without being as wrong as they are.

On the day I spoke to him, I was picking up a copy of an autobiography which I had ordered. As was often the case, the packing was nothing more than a thick brown envelope, which was only loosely sealed. As I picked it up, the envelope split and the book fell to the floor. On some level I assumed that everyone in the town knew everything I ordered, probably whispering it to each other, but the man—Tobias de Roethl as he introduced himself—seemed interested.

"*The Life and Portraits of Jonas Grengen?*" he said, looking at the title. "Grengen was a contemporary of Edmund Drake, was he not?"

I murmured something in the affirmative, partly hoping he would leave, but partly curious. "Are you an artist?"

"No," he said. He might have been laughing; he had a European accent of some kind I couldn't identify, and mannerisms that seemed out of place. "I am a student of history, perhaps. And unless I'm mistaken, you are the new owner of the Drake House? The one everyone is speaking of? And you are studying Drake himself?"

I assented again, nervously. I dislike the idea that everyone knows everything there is to know about me, even though I should have been used to it by now. I made some small talk to change the conversation—I don't remember now what it was exactly that I said—but it did not distract him.

"You may find in that autobiography that Grengen spoke of him as a person to be feared," he said, with his unreadable expression that might have been a smile or a smirk. "Many thought Drake to be in league with diabolical forces. He was said to speak with beings not of this place. Some thought he was a wizard, a Luciferian, a student of Blavatsky or Steiner."

There was a line of thought I wanted to shut down at once. I did not want the good people of the town to get the idea that I needed to be burned as a witch. "I don't believe that hocus-pocus bullshit, he was an artist. He painted *The Triumph of the Claw*. And that's it."

"Ah! His best known work. It is a masterpiece, truly a result of great skill. Have you uncovered the secret of its message?"

"There is no message. It's just a painting. It's just a thing."

"No? All art is message. Else what is the point? What are we, other than animals, scratching and biting and dying? What is the purpose of art, if not to rise above the base nature of what we are?"

"Okay," I said, almost getting angry at the strange old man. Why would he put me at risk, drawing attention to me, and throwing around these preposterous ideas in front of everyone? "What is the message of *The Triumph of the Claw*, then?"

"Perhaps that is it: our base nature will always rule us. Our animal selves will always prevent us from being what we could be. Perhaps it is an indictment on being human. As hard as we try, maybe he is saying, the mind will always be a victim to the claw."

"You're reading an awful lot into something that's just a bunch of light and dark paints," I said.

"What else is it to be human other than to be a mix of light and dark?" He challenged me, obviously smirking now.

I heard a noise from behind the counter; one of the mail clerks, listening to us, had dropped something. I had no wish to be a victim of anyone's claws; I made an abrupt excuse and fled.

When I made it home to the Drake House I found evidence of a disturbance outside: one of the shutters had been broken off of a window, and the ground beneath it had been turned over. I am no Sherlock Holmes but I guessed that someone had been inexpertly looking in the window while I was gone, and fell, breaking the shutter. So long as they sated their curiosity by simply looking, I didn't care: I had nothing to hide. Even so, the invasion of the privacy I so badly wanted was deeply upsetting. The old man must have spooked me more than I thought; I half imagined faces hiding in the woods, staring at me.

I had a ladder and tools in the storeroom behind the house and managed to the put the shutter back in place before it grew dark for the evening. The whole time I worked, I saw no other human beings, lurking or not.

In those days after meeting de Roethl at the post office I found myself often drawn to the basement of the Drake House. I cannot say how. It is now as it was then simply a stone box dug into the earth, walled with concrete. There are no doors down here. There is nothing here, other than a damp and oily smell.

At least, in my waking mind. In my dreams I found a wooden door, oaken and bound with bands of iron, waiting for me. In my dreams there is a handprint in blood, in perfect detail on the wall; and just as the Drake painting *The Bloody Summons* shows a heavy wooden door, barred with iron, I dreamed I saw it set into the wall. In daylight I could place the exact spot where, in the painting, the door exists; I could see the rafters and plumbing and even a spidery crack in the wall, exactly as it appears in his painting, but no door was set into the wall. I could place my hand on the smooth cement and feel nothing. There was no door to be felt.

At least, that was true in those days. I am no longer sure.

I do not quite know how to say what happened next. I find this troubling, as I had thought myself a writer, able to put word to page with skill. Maybe when actual horror happens to us, we retreat into ourselves and become less than we were. I will simply say what happened as I believe I saw it, as all we can do is believe our senses.

Without that we are nothing, not even animals.

On a night not long after meeting Tobias de Roethl I was woken by a loud banging sound nearby. The wind had begun to blow with terrific gusts, and my first thought or lingering dream was that it had blown somehow into the room. The power had gone out, which was not unusual when the wind gusted; I keep a flashlight on the nightstand for such times.

When I clicked the flashlight on I must have still been asleep because I thought I saw something at the door of the bedroom. It must have only been shadows, twisting in the uncertain light of the flashlight, but it looked at the time to be smoke.

I halfway feared fire, and some deep still partly-asleep bit of me might have feared that some of the locals had come to burn me out of my house, but as I struggled out of bed I realized I didn't smell anything burning. I did smell something I could not at first place; hot and coppery.

There was something on the floor at the foot of the bed. It was red and lying in a pool of blood. Even now I am not sure what it was—an internal organ of some kind, some part of a body, large enough that it must have come from a large animal. An animal of course. It had to be from an animal. What else could it—?

I am not really sure what I did next. I was . . . confused is a kind word. My hands and feet were clean, and I had no marks on me. I had not put that . . . thing there. Wherever this had come from, it manifestly refused to turn out to be a figment of a dream and go away. I was less frightened than simply turned to stone by the sheer oddness of what I was seeing.

I had not placed that mess at the food of the bed. Was it a message? Had someone broken into my house, to leave a horrifying and incomprehensible threat? What is even the point of a message if it can't be understood? I skirted around the horrifying thing and checked the entire house, but no windows were open and no doors were open that I saw. I even checked the basement and for a moment I thought I saw the outline of a—no, not a door. There was no door down there, Drake's *The Bloody Summons* be damned. No one had gotten in, or if they had, they had found a way to leave and lock the doors behind them.

Had someone gotten a key to a door? I had changed the locks when I moved in, but—and now I remembered, with ice suddenly stabbing me in my stomach—I had had the new locks delivered through the mail and picked them up at the post office. Someone could have opened the package and made a copy.

Put yourself in my place: alone, terrified, stalked or threatened. What would you do, knowing you have nowhere else to go, and no one to turn to?

I don't know what you would have done, but I know what I did: I buried the goddamn thing in the back yard and tried to forget about it.

And then I started nailing the fucking windows shut and barring the doors.

I was hammering nails into two-by-fours across the back door of the Drake House when I was interrupted by a sound I had never heard before. It took a moment for to identify it: the doorbell was ringing. Someone was at the door and wanted my attention.

By rushing upstairs and craning my head from the top office window I was able to get a line of sight on the car in the driveway, parked directly behind mine. It was a white sedan of some kind with a star on the door and the words "Sheriff's Office" above it. A cop, then. My stomach felt hollow: I didn't exactly have fond memories of my dealings with police.

The doorbell rang again and I went downstairs. Wary, I removed the wooden bar I had placed on the front door in place of a trustworthy lock and cracked it open.

The man on my doorstep was wearing a uniform and had a gun on his belt. He had on mirrored sunglasses that hid what he was looking at, as cops always seem to. A badge was in his hand, but while I have had more experience seeing those than the average person I still had no idea how to tell if it were real or a fake.

"Mr. -------?" he asked, using my last name.

"That's me," I said. I probably sounded nervous.

The cop turned his head slightly as if trying to look around me. "Mr. -------, I'm Sheriff Dan Stillman, and I'd like to just take a few minutes of your time, if I could. Would you mind if I came inside?"

"I'd prefer not."

"Well, would you mind steppin' outside, so we can talk?"

"We can talk like this. What do you want?"

He looked down at my hand, still holding the hammer. "Doing some work around the house?"

I dropped the hammer on the end table next to the inside of the door. "What is it I can do for you, Sherriff?"

"There's been a killing," he said. He was probably watching my reaction closely, but not as closely as I was watching myself. I think I was putting so much effort into not reacting at all that I didn't even fully understand what he had said at first.

"What do you mean?" I asked.

"I mean a man has been killed, Mr. -------," he said patiently. "We're conducting an investigation into his death. Now, I don't have any reason to think that you might have anything to do with this, but considering your particular history, it makes sense for me to talk to you. I'll be glad to tell you that I've already asked around, and your car was seen right here at your house around the time of death. And I'll be willin' to bet that if you'd gone walking around at two in the morning, you'd have been seen, too. So I'm not thinking that you're exactly suspect number one, if you get my meaning."

"What the fuck?" The words were jerked out of me. I immediately thought about the . . . thing I had buried just hours before. I tried to turn my mind away as fast as I could before my face gave anything away. "How . . . how did, how was he killed?"

"Not sure, exactly," the sheriff said. "The coroner hasn't filled out a report yet. If I had to guess, I'd say someone went at him with a chainsaw." I couldn't see his eyes, but I could feel them drilling holes into me. "Funny thing, though. Part of him was cut open, just as neat as you could please. Almost like someone cleanin' a jacked deer."

Grasping at straws: "Look, sheriff, I don't know anything about any of this, I don't know what you want from me."

"All I want is peace and quiet. I'm just here to check off a checkbox, you know. People gotta know that I'm talking to anyone I might need to talk to, and considering . . . history and all, people are gonna want to know that I'm talking to you. Even if I got no reason to think you know anything about any of this."

His damnable eyes were still dissecting me behind his glasses. "Well, you've talked to me, then," I said. I later found I had been gripping the doorframe tightly enough to drive splinters into my fingers.

He nodded. "Well, I won't take up any more of your time. You can go back to your house work. I'd just suggest, to be on the safe side, you might want to lay low for a bit, keep outta people's sight while they're still worried about this. You understand me?"

"What are you saying?" I demanded.

"Oh, I ain't saying nothing. People talk, that's all." He nodded at me. "You have a good day now, sir."

I could not stop shaking after I closed the door and put the heavy wooden bar across it again. I felt weak and scared. So some asshole had gotten himself killed. What was it to me? Was I going to be blamed for this, as well?

And then I remembered the bloody organ, whatever it was, at the foot of my bed. Had it been put there by the actual killer, whoever it was? Was someone trying to pin blame on me? Should I have said something to the sheriff? No, I thought immediately, reflexively. If he was anything like any other cop I'd ever seen, he'd be happy to lock me in a cage just so he could check off his checkbox: *killer found*. Fuck him. If someone wanted to blame me for murder, they wouldn't do it with my help.

I finished nailing the windows shut and checked my supplies. I had enough non-perishable groceries that I could have lasted for weeks without leaving the house, if I had to, even under normal times; now, with my stomach clenched, I had no real desire for food or drink of any kind. With the Drake House locked up, bars on the doors, it was a fortress ready to hold off any—

But were all the doors barred? *All* of them? Was there a door I had missed?

I could think of one.

I could not help myself. I do not think I was completely

rational then. The basement was lit by a single naked incandescent bulb; the cement walls, faintly noxious and damp, still had no coverings. I had not put anything down in there at all. It was empty except for the furnace, ticking away by itself, and the door that could not have been there but was there nonetheless.

The oaken door shown in Drake's *The Bloody Summons* was a solid, tangible, undeniable thing set into the wall. Just as in the painting, it was bound with iron bands and had an old-fashioned knob with a huge keyhole directly below it. Seeing it made it impossible to believe that it had ever not been there. It was as real as my shadow and my hand reaching for the knob. It felt cold to the touch.

It'll be unlocked, I thought. *Why wouldn't it be unlocked?*

The knob twisted easily and I heard the latch slide open. It would open if I pulled on it. It would open, yawning into the shifting oily black and gray and then I was on the far side of the room, backing away, getting the hell away from that *thing* that couldn't possibly be there, shaking and trembling and terrified—

Between blinks, the door ceased to exist. It could not have ever have been there.

Unable to breathe at all, I stared at the smooth, unbroken wall. I ran my fingers through my hair. My hand still felt cold from touching the doorknob of the door that had never existed and did not, could not, possibly exist or have ever existed at all.

Upstairs in the kitchen I made a pot of strong coffee that I did not want. I must have imagined it, I thought. It was obvious in retrospect: the stress of the sheriff showing up and reminding me of the past, combined with my lack of sleep since waking in the middle of the night to find the bloody—

No. Maybe that hadn't existed, either. Maybe I was going insane. Either that, or in a particularly stupid inversion of trope I'd managed to lock myself inside a haunted house that was opening doors instead of locking them.

Evidence was what I needed. I checked the foot of the bed. The floor was clean, as I'd mopped up the blood, but the mop itself in the upstairs bathroom was wet and in the sink where I'd washed it off. It still had traces of washed-out pink on it; I'd been too distracted to clean it thoroughly. The shovel, in the back hallway next to the barred door, was dirty with fresh soil. Looking out the back window I could see the enclosed yard, ringed with a tall fence, and the plot of turned earth where something had been buried.

I checked the online news; Channel 7 had a brief blurb about a murder investigation that was ongoing. The victim had not yet been identified and the cause of death had not yet been determined. Sheriff Stillman was quoted; he had at least not been a total figment of my imagination.

I poured the coffee out without even tasting it. All of a sudden, fatigue struck me like a wall, and it was all I could do to drag myself upstairs to bed.

But even exhausted, I made sure to check the windows and doors.

Sleep during the day always leaves me confused, as if somehow my brain doesn't want to start up when my body does. I woke up as the sun was going down. Just as well, I tried to think; I could stand vigil at night. If anything was likely to happen it might be under the cover of darkness.

I tried to bury myself in my work; I finished reading *The Life and Portraits of Jonas Grengen* and found that de Roethl had been correct; Grengen was reported to have fled the Drake House in the early morning hours some weeks before Drake was found hanged dead. There had been a falling out over the possession of a book, some occult tome I had never heard of. Grengen afterwards would only refer to Drake as 'That devil' and would have nothing further to do with him or his works. There was no reference to murder or post mortem reference models.

Grengen himself was a skilled portrait painter, and an insert of full color plates in the biography showed his best work. He seemed to have a natural eye for capturing the essence of a person; his work was less photorealistic than almost a realistic caricature, if such a thing could be said.

A portrait of Edmund Drake was naturally included, as he was the most famous of Grengen's subjects. In it, Drake is seated in front of an easel covered with a cloth, hiding his work; his eyes are dark and penetrating, as if trying to pierce your soul and find your weakness. He has aristocratic features, as if too refined to possibly be the artist responsible for some of his more disturbing works, but it's dangerous to make assumptions about people based solely on how they look.

I searched the internet for the occult book mentioned in the text and found no copies available. One was available for study on request at Squolnamic University, but that helped me not at all. I chose to table that line of inquiry instead.

Around I think three in the morning, I had started to nod off again. The body does not naturally wish to be up at that time. I was still at my desk in Drake's study with his portrait judging me when I heard the wind gusting. It was forceful enough to sway the trees in the back yard to where branches scraped against the house.

I looked out the windows to make sure that nothing was likely to break and then checked and rechecked all of the doors and windows on the ground floor.

I was dreaming. I had to be. I was still in bed, staring at an oily, inky smoke or cloud as the wind smashed against the house. The thing could not have been smoke; smoke rises and fills the room, and this thing simply floated at the foot of the bed as if it wanted my attention.

From somewhere within the shifting haze a squelching, rasping noise echoed, and something thudded wetly and meatily to the floor. Still in a dream, I felt as if a door in my mind closed—it is impossible to describe—and then the thing was gone with the gusting wind that seemed to die down instantly.

I knew then that if it was a dream it was more real than most of my waking life. I did not wait until morning to find out what had been left for me; still in a haze, I found the shovel and flashlight.

This time it was a scalp with hair and one ear still attached. There was an earring in the ear. I buried it next to the other horror.

Morning light brought no new sanity. A cursory check of the news showed that a new murder had taken place; in some way I was unsurprised. No details were available. I supposed I could have told the news site that the victim had been blonde, but that would not have accomplished anything. The police no doubt already knew.

What was this thing? I could not deny its existence any longer. Perhaps it was what Drake had painted in *The Triumph of the Claw*. The painting showed an oily, shifting haze, but marked no other details; if it was a creature, then it was a thing of vile intent and little else.

Where had it come from? Had Drake summoned it, from one of his occult tomes? Was that the secret of *The Bloody Summons*, showing a door that only existed when it chose to exist? Or had the thing chosen him, and then chosen me in turn? The symmetry of history offered hints but no facts.

I scrubbed the floor clean again as I went over what I knew: It seemed to be connected to the door in the basement. The gusting wind seemed to be part of its passage or presence. It left me . . . gifts, perhaps. Like a cat, adopting an owner, leaving dead mice at the door as presents.

I felt faint and nearly vomited. Had I had anything in my stomach I would have brought it up, but I had not eaten for some time. The very idea of eating was nauseating; my stomach rebelled.

All at once, the entirety of it all hit me, like the weight of the house itself settling on my shoulders: *leave*, I thought, *get out. Run. Just go anywhere. It's the house, the thing is part of the house, it's coming through the door so it's stuck here, get away and—*

I made it so far as finding my keys on the table next to the door before I looked out the window and saw the two cars parked at the end of the driveway.

They were not hiding. Far from it; they had been parked nose-to-nose, blocking me from the road. Two men stood on the far side of them from me, apparently not looking towards the house. Neither was wearing a uniform. They wanted to be seen, I thought; they wanted me to know that I wasn't allowed to leave.

What had I done to them? What right did they have to fear me? Had they simply decided without any evidence at all that I was the cause of the murders, the person responsible for all evil? Was this going to be the lynch mob all over again?

For a moment I could put myself in their position: the murders in the town I had left had started up here almost as soon as I had moved in. The fact that I could not possibly have had anything to do with them would have been an argument of reason that they would not wish to hear.

I let the curtains fall over the window again and backed away. My mind was churning; my stomach boiled with acid. I wanted to go out to them, calmly explain to them that they were wrong, that I was innocent, I was not who or what they thought I was—

And then I heard the wind starting to gust.

I stayed inside the house all day. I watched the men at the end of my driveway be replaced by others; there was some organization among them. Like an immune system attacking a cancerous cell, the town itself seemed willing to lay siege to me.

Time and time again I wanted to open the door. Possibly to flee; possibly to try to make my case. I was not the killer they feared. And time and time again I found I had no way to say anything that I thought they would hear; my arms would rebel and refuse to reach for the bars at the door. If it was fear, it was not fear of them; it was fear that perhaps the thing had chosen me for some reason I could not see when I looked in the mirror. Perhaps they were not as wrong as I wanted to believe.

The wind gusted throughout the day. As dusk came on, I kept the lights low, the better to deny watchers any view of inside the house, and hid as best I could, nervously pacing from room to room. The shadows which should have sprung up at evening had been there all day, flickering with the beat of the wind.

In dim lights I could almost see the thing, waiting in the shadows of the darkened house. It had no readily visible form; it was a being of oily smoke, of guesses. It must have had claws enough to do its work. Perhaps I simply could not allow myself to see it, no more than I could see anything out of place when I looked in the mirror.

What was the thing doing? What was it looking for?

At some point I broke down and begged it. I called out to the house, and whatever lurked behind the door in the basement, to leave me alone; to leave, and never come back. For an answer I could only hear the wind. At first I feared it chose not to respond, and then I realized the greater fear; that it simply could not, that it lacked the ability or the mind to speak—

I understand it now. It has no more intelligence than the average cat. And like a cat, it has chosen me. It brings me gifts: organs, scalps.

This morning when I woke I found a severed human hand at the foot of my bed. I buried it in the back yard with the other parts. I do not need to check the news to know that someone else has been killed, incomprehensibly taken apart and left with pieces missing. Is it any wonder that the prey the thing hunts are desperate for a Jonah to throw to the whale?

The townspeople at the end of my driveway have grown to a small crowd. I can see several of them carrying rifles. I am tempted to check the basement, but I know with the core of my being that the door from Drake's *The Bloody Summons* stands ready to be opened. It may be closed for now, but it is never locked. Doors like this one are never locked.

Here in my office in the attic of the Drake house, where he hanged himself, I look through the Grengen biography for Drake's portrait. In the light of morning, it seems no different; but perhaps, knowing what I know now, I can read his expression more clearly. It is not much different than my own, seen in the mirror.

Sheriff Stillman is walking his way up my driveway, followed by the mob of armed townspeople, as I type this. Soon, if history repeats, he will ring the doorbell. I have made up my mind: this time, I will open the door.

I can sense the thing, but I cannot see it. I suspect it cannot be truly seen; at most it is a thing of oily smoke, a creature of evil will and nothing else. It hunts. Like a cat adopting a master and leaving bloody gifts, the thing seems to try to teach me to hunt in its terrible way.

I am human, though, and I choose to die as one, if I that is what it comes to. From my vantage point in the attic study of the Drake House, I can see the mob approaching. They have no idea what they are walking into. I can see the furious wind, the only shadow the thing seems to leave behind it, waiting.

In the back of my mind, I can sense the thing. It waits, uncomprehending, knowing only the bone hard law of claw and fang. The door is closed, and it waits in fury, and the great lie of it all is that I believe I have any control over what is to happen next. The beast will come, whatever I choose, whether I plead with the mob approaching my doorstep or I release it myself. The base nature of the claw will always win over the mind.

The mob is almost at the house. I know that the door will swing open without effort, and the thing will rend and slay and delight in slaughter again and again. It is such a simple thing, such a mindless thing of violence, and yet, it is no threat to me.

I wait as long as I can as the mob approaches, knowing that in the end, the claw will always triumph.

I open the door.

Brian Bander claims to be a writer, an editor, and a game developer in the Pacific Northwest.

Acknowledgments

Fark in the Time of the Covid

Editors and Readers

D. Paul Angel
Dan McKay
Daniel J. Arnott
Fred Blonder
James R. Fox
James Rosinus
Genevieve Shapiro

Editor-in-Chief

Brian Bander

Art

Genevieve Shapiro

Special Thanks

Drew Curtis
Heather Curtis

Copyright Acknowledgments

"Spring-Heeled Jacqueline" copyright © 2020 by Jason Allard

"The Golden Oscillator" copyright © 2020 by Russell Secord

"The Prey" copyright © 2020 by Trevor Carlson

"Diogenes the Talking Dog" copyright © 2020 by Erik Jorgensen

"This Town" copyright © 2020 by Tom Pappalardo

"The Resurrections of Amy Yakimora" copyright © 2020 by James Rosinus

"First Contact at the Second Hole" copyright © 2020 by Fred Blonder

"The Ultimate Monster" copyright © 2020 by Brian Hawley

"The Numbers Man" copyright © 2011 by Colleen McLaughlin & Terry Skaggs

"Janissars" copyright © 2020 by Willin D. Fenster

"Warped Drive" copyright © 2020 by Anthony Fabbri

"The Machine" copyright © 2020 by Tyson Prenter

"Tag 'Em" copyright © 2020 by Brad Earle

"It's Only Vampire" copyright © 2020 by Rebecca Gomez Farrell

"Florida Vacation" copyright © 2020 by Ralph Crown

"Basement Apartment" copyright © 2020 by Charles C. Montgomery

"White Line Fever" copyright © 2020 by Dan McKay

"The Terrible Burden of Love" copyright © 2020 by Brandon Stichka

"Hargis" copyright © 2020 by Eric Weir

"Murder, and a Multitude of Other Sins" copyright © 2020 by J. F. Benedetto

"Run for Your Life" copyright © 2020 by Brandi Fruik

"The Spirit of the Mountain" copyright © 2020 by Scott Fowler

"Vox Odio" copyright © 2020 by D. Paul Angel

"A Skirmish Outside Beaufort" copyright © 2020 by E. A. Black

"Meat. The Parents. " copyright © 2020 by Mark Hooson

"My Two Dads" copyright © 2020 by Dwayne Josephson

"Nightrunner" copyright © 2020 by Steve Ball

"The Triumph of the Claw" copyright © 2020 by Brian Bander

Made in United States
Orlando, FL
23 December 2023